IN THE FACE OF THE SUN

In the Face of the Sun

Denny S. Bryce

THORNDIKE PRESS
A part of Gale, a Cengage Company

Copyright © 2022 by Denny S. Bryce, LLC.
Thorndike Press, a part of Gale, a Cengage Company.

**LIBRARY OF CONGRESS CIP DATA ON FILE.
CATALOGUING IN PUBLICATION FOR THIS BOOK
IS AVAILABLE FROM THE LIBRARY OF CONGRESS.**

ISBN-13: 978-1-4328-9857-1 (hardcover alk. paper)

Published in 2022 by arrangement with Kensington Books, an imprint of Kensington Publishing Corp.

Printed in Mexico
Print Number: 01   Print Year: 2022

For my maternal grandmother,
Ella Elizabeth Green Joseph

PROLOGUE

The night Veronica Fontaine died, there was a blackbird in the sky with a red-and-yellow triangle on its breast. It squawked like a crow. No song in its throat, just a curse, a string of damnations, blasting my eardrums.

A blackbird interrupts the stillness of the sunset. Slowly flapping its wings, flying across the blue-and-crimson sky, the lone bird seeks its flock, but their numbers have dwindled, and the once-abundant bird no longer blankets the heavens.

I sit in the peacock wicker chair in the sunroom of the house on Naomi Avenue, holding a small cedar chest on my lap. The katydids' song and the high-pitched chirping of crickets fill my heart with memories as the savory sweetness of night-blooming jasmine soothes my lonely soul.

Lifting my gaze, I look out the tall mullion windows as the sun slips beneath the horizon. How many hours have I spent in this chair staring through the glass, thinking through the years? Most of a lifetime? Perhaps.

If only I'd learned to love more deeply and less selfishly, I could've staved off the loss and the loneliness. But, like the bird, I never knew my great love story wasn't a thing that would always be. Even at this stage of life, I sometimes believe I can fix the past with patience. As my mother used to say, a woman can accomplish many things — even in a world where she is outnumbered — if she knows when to leave and in what direction to fly.

Moving my fingers over the polished surface of the cedar box, I linger on the metal latch.

I am alone except for the young girl, Maxine, who glares at me with a cross expression on her brow. She is a constant of late, dropping by day in day out to ask about the past for an article she's writing for the *Los Angeles Times*.

"What's in the box?" Maxine says; she can be demanding.

"Letters, journals," I answer. "And a newspaper article."

"Can I read them?"

"Of course. It is why I searched every corner of this house to find them. They are my gift to you."

"For my article about an old hotel?"

"The story is important to you, right?"

"Why wouldn't it be?" Maxine replies sharply. "I told you, I need the family angle. The personal tragedies will give the article a human face. Otherwise, it's all about bricks and mortar. What's the appeal in that?"

"I knew a man once who would say there was little more to life than bricks and mortar." I study the girl's eyes, wondering if she knows more than she lets on. "Be careful how you write about them, the building, the design, the heart of it. They are important things to some of us."

"Things?" Maxine sighs loudly, showing her frustration. "My article also needs to be about people, family. Race and politics. Prejudice and hate."

"Don't get impatient with me. I'm your elder."

"You're not that old."

"Eighty-two is not that old?" I chuckle. "If you insist, I will happily agree with you there." I pass the box to Maxine. "I've given you everything I have that will help you flesh out your story on the early days of the Hotel Somerville."

9

"Do you mind if I read these here? I read fast, and we can talk about them this evening. Then, I can stay and help you finish packing."

I look at Maxine suspiciously. "I don't need any help. I have movers. You just want to keep an eye on me. Dig for more information, which is insane since I've given you everything you need."

"Don't get angry. I know you're helping me. And I will read through everything carefully. Trust me."

I pause, knowing I should believe her. She doesn't lie or deceive. Her curiosity is a strength. "Okay, then. You can help me pack the bedroom. The rest of the house the movers will handle."

"Outstanding." The young girl glances around and points to the piano bench. "I'll sit here."

"Before you get comfortable, pour me a whiskey, darling." I point at the small table in the corner with the silver tray and crystal brandy snifter.

"Yes, ma'am." Maxine places the box on the piano bench, walks over, and pours my drink. She raises the glass to her nose and takes a deep sniff. "I love the smell of a good whiskey. I wish I liked the taste." She passes me my drink.

I take a long sip, and the pungent liquid stings my nose and throat. "Do you want one? You're old enough."

"No, thanks. I can't do liquor." Maxine sits on the bench and removes the newspaper clippings. "What is this?" She holds up a piece from the *California Eagle.*

"I can't see what it says from here." But I already know what is printed on the page. I could never forget the headlines, even if they are more than sixty years old.

"Who's the Black man they arrested? For what? Going to a beach?"

"Keep reading," I say.

A few minutes pass, and she looks up; her face is as ashen as a brown-skinned girl's face can be.

"So, Maxine, I think you understand now."

She looks at me, teary-eyed. "She was murdered. Who killed her?"

Questions I have heard and left unanswered a million times. But the truth was the murder wasn't the deed of one person, and whether it happened in the hotel or on the corner of Hollywood and Vine didn't matter.

"Finish reading," I instruct Maxine. "Then we can talk."

CHAPTER 1
FRANKIE

Friday, May 31, 1968
Chicago

No one is to blame for my decision. Not the husband missing from my bed. Not my unborn baby. Not even my grief. Lying on my back, with a pillow behind my head, I catch a glimpse of my slightly rounded belly. And I know. I am leaving Jackson.

The thing about marriage is you can't count on it. It has this fairy-tale reputation. The outta-sight wedding dress, the bridesmaids, the lavish ceremony, the in-laws, the birthing of babies, and the dirty diapers. But what messed me up were those promises.

Thou shall not do this. Thou shall not do that. Then one thing goes wrong, like burning the rice, forgetting to pay the electric bill, lying about your time of the month, and someone (like me) ends up with their emotional clock unhinged, cowering in a corner, screaming like a banshee. It makes you think.

How did I get here, and why do I stay?

Sunshine slashes through the slats in the Venetian blinds, and the bedroom is light and shadows. I rise, feeling a soreness in my bones as I swing my legs to the floor and stand with a tremble in my knees.

Why am I so afraid?

Jackson is not home. He's working a double. So I can walk out of our second-floor apartment, luggage in hand, no fear, no fuss, no muss.

But I've always been afraid.

Squinting against the sunlight, I go to the window to close the blinds, but there's a noise, a revved-up car engine modified for speed and sound. I lift a slat, peer into the street, and can't believe my eyes.

A candy-apple-red Ford Mustang is parked at the curb outside my building. I recognize the vehicle. Everyone in the neighborhood knows this 1968 Fastback. How could anyone forget that color, that fancy model, or the fancy woman behind the wheel?

I imagine the entire block is sneaking a peek, and at least one of them will tell Jackson about this woman's visit as soon as he returns home.

14

"Your wife's fast-talking, fast-driving friend drove up and then drove off — heading that way — with your woman and her Lady Baltimore luggage in tow."

However, they'd be wrong. The driver is not a friend. She is my aunt, who, according to my mother, is an audacious woman that no one in our family speaks to. We only speak *about* her and never glowingly.

I met her in person for the first time two weeks ago, and now, she is part of my escape plan, my ride to the Greyhound bus terminal.

But she wasn't supposed to show up until nine.

I glance at the clock on the nightstand — it's seven o'clock in the morning. Damn! Why is she so early?

I mumble a quick prayer. But, dear God, please don't let her lose patience and blow the car horn. Just chill for two hours — but I can tell she's not the type to sit still. Pretty soon, she'll strut up to the apartment building's front door and ring the bell, and if no one answers, she'll start yelling, drawing more attention than her candy-appled-red automobile roaring into a parking spot.

I hear a car door slam. Has she lost her patience already? Does she have any patience? I don't look outside again. No time for a soak in the tub, I hurry into the bathroom, grab a washcloth, and scrub my face, armpits, and private parts. Next, I put on my traveling outfit. A beige high-waisted skirt. A bandanna-print blouse. A freshly polished pair of penny loafers. Then I remove the pink rollers and plastic clips from my hair and comb my coarse curls into a Jackie O. flip.

Staring at my reflection in the mirror, I think about my cousin Tamika. I wish I could've called her and told her I was leaving and asked her to help me, but I don't wear an Afro.

You see, she gets bent out of shape when it comes to the movement. I'm a kindergarten teacher at the elementary school in a conservative Hyde Park neighborhood. I'm not a civil rights worker or a feminist and don't plan to be. The last thing a Negro child on the South Side of Chicago needs from a kindergarten teacher like me, I tried to explain, was a lesson on hairstyles. She, of course, disagreed, but instead of a civilized conversation, she and I had a silly argument.

"You hate me and my permed hair because I've never joined you at a sit-in or marched in a protest. Don't lie. I know I'm not Black enough for you."

After my little speech, she came back at me hard, speaking on another subject altogether because that's her way.

"Don't get high-and-mighty with me. Jackson is the problem. Why don't you leave him?"

"I will. I am," I said.

She'd twisted her lips into an ugly frown. "Sure, you say that now, but then you crawl right back to him."

Well, today, I'll show her. The next time we speak, I'll have left Jackson and be on my way back to the city where she and I grew up — Los Angeles, California.

I pull my bangs into place and smooth my hair at my temples. A moment later, my fingers are wrapped around the handles of my luggage. I lift them, lengthen my back, and head toward the living room and the front door with determination in every step.

My aunt is in her Mustang, waiting at the curb, and it's time, long overdue, for me to give freedom a try.

Lord, help me. I think I'm having a heart attack.

I step into the living room, and there is Jackson, lying on the sofa, snoring like a bullfrog. He's supposed to be working a double shift at the paper company. Although

Tamika saw him the other day with the Miller girl, the hussy who lives on Stony Island near Sixty-Ninth Street.

Not the first time I've heard rumors about him with another woman. Frankly, I wouldn't be surprised if she was the reason behind some of his double shifts. For a man who works so many doubles, he rarely brings home double the money.

On the sofa, he clutches a bottle of beer in one hand and stirs cigarette ashes into the cushions with the other — in his sleep.

A sudden loud snore bursts from his open mouth, and my heart cuts a hole in my chest. Oh, shoot. He's going to wake up. Don't wake up. Please, don't —

He jerks into a sitting position, but as soon as he's up, he's down, eyes still shut and snoring louder than before.

My armpits are leaking sweat, and I blink a few droplets — sweat or tears — from my lashes. If Jackson sees me in my traveling clothes and carrying my bags, I'm not sure what he'll do, but I can imagine.

I am standing in the archway, shaking, but I can't remain here forever. I inch across the shag carpet toward the front door and open it carefully, quietly. Then I place my luggage in the hallway and start to close the door behind me.

18

"Where the hell are you going this early, Francine?"

I do not jump or squeal. I do squeeze my thighs together, hoping not to wet myself. "I'm heading to Piggly Wiggly." I hope I'm not showing the panic that's searing through me.

"I brought some groceries home yesterday." His voice is tired. "What in the hell you need to buy today? Already some ham and lettuce in the fridge. Why don't you make me a sandwich? I have to head back to the plant in a few, and I'm hungry. What did you say you had to get at the store?"

I step into the apartment and shut the door. "You're out of beer." I hope I'm right, but I can't be too wrong judging from the number of empty bottles on the living room floor. "I thought I'd buy some more beer and chips and ginger ale. Aren't you working a double?"

"Yeah, yeah. Got off early, but heading right back," he mutters. "Buy some ice cream, too. I'll have it with the apple pie that's in the fridge." Sitting upright, he rubs the sleep from his eyes. "When you're at the liquor store, pick up a pint of whiskey, too. Canadian Mist." He stretches his bulky arms forward, bowing his back until his elbows land on his knees. "I'll need you to

19

fix me a fresh lunch bucket, too."

"Another double?" I am repeating myself, but with the right amount of concern in my voice, I hope.

"Yeah." He pauses mid-yawn as his gaze travels from my penny loafers up to the edges of my Jackie O. flip. "If you're just running to Piggly Wiggly, why are you dressed up? You have on makeup and your good blouse. What the hell are you up to, Francine?"

My lip is quivering, and I bite down hard to make it stop. Then I'm able to speak. "I'm not up to anything but going to the store."

"Come here."

"Why?"

"Bring your ass on over here, girl. I wanna look at you. You're my wife. Can't I look at you?"

I hesitate, but I don't say no. I always obey.

I stop in front of him; he grabs my wrist and pulls me down onto the sofa next to him. "You ain't lying to me, are you?"

He isn't hurting me, but I know well enough how rapidly that can change. "I'm buying some beer and chips and ginger ale."

"That doesn't sound like my little Ms. Betty Crocker's usual list of groceries." He kisses me on the mouth in that rough, demanding way he has. He stops, wipes the corners of his mouth, and releases my wrist.

He tasted like warm beer and stale potato chips.

"Don't take all morning," he says with a warning in his tone. "That means no flipping through magazines at the checkout line or chatting with one of the girls you're always running into." He shoves me in the side, pushing me to my feet. "I need some food in my stomach before I have to get back to the job."

"No problem, Jackson. You rest." I wipe the sweat from my brow. "I'll be back before you know it."

"All right, baby girl. I'll be right here."

I'm out the door, down one flight of stairs, and on my way, but the weight of the luggage slows me down. I want to hurry. I want to run before Chicken Little (that's me) comes to roost and I change my mind about leaving Jackson.

The motor is running as I approach Daisy's car. Smoke clouds the windows, and I can't see inside. I place my suitcases on the sidewalk, take a deep breath, and tap the passenger-side window.

"Daisy. Open up." My voice is a stern whisper. I can't risk Jackson hearing a commotion outside the apartment building, forcing him to come to the window and see me, my luggage, and my aunt's car.

"Daisy!" I lean in, my nose pressed against the window, but there's so much smoke, and Otis Redding's "(Sittin' on) the Dock of the Bay" is blasting from the car's eight-track.

No wonder she can't hear me.

"Daisy!" I raise my voice, which I didn't want to do. But I feel a sudden urge to launch my suitcase through the windshield, but I don't. Instead, I walk around to the driver's side and bang on the window so hard I think the glass will break and slice the skin off my knuckles.

I realize my pounding fists will make as much noise as Daisy's music. It's a toss-up which one could wake up Jackson. Although I suddenly don't care. I want Daisy to open the car door more than anything and keep beating on the window.

It finally lowers, and smoke rises into the morning air, covering my face with a thin white sheet of marijuana.

I am annoyed with Daisy for arriving early, annoyed with her for blasting her music, annoyed with her smoking funny-smelling cigarettes and having red-rimmed eyes. A woman nearing sixty shouldn't smoke grass, at least not in public, but Daisy doesn't care about good manners or

22

lawful behavior.

"What are you doing?"

"Hello, Frankie." Her gaze passes over my face and skims my outfit. "You are dressed like a schoolteacher, not a woman planning an adventure on a cross-country bus ride."

The way she voices her dislike for my ensemble makes me want to smack her, but her face is too pretty for an old broad.

"Why can't you do what I asked you to do?"

"What are you talking about? You needed a ride to the bus station. When I woke up, I decided to arrive early. I'm doing you a favor. So why am I getting so much lip?"

"I'm leaving my husband, and I thought he wouldn't be home, and he's in the house."

She takes a long drag from her marijuana cigarette, extends it toward me, but I shake my head.

"Every woman leaves a man at least once in her life. It's not such a big deal. Not in 1968. We've got civil rights, feminism, and white boys killing Martin Luther King. The world is a fucking mess. So a woman finally leaving a no-count man doesn't mean as much as it used to."

"He wasn't always a no-count man."

"He's one now. Isn't that why you're leav-

23

ing him?"

"I don't want to discuss it." And I don't. Not with her.

Daisy rolls her eyes. How dare she?

I fight an intense desire to grab the cigarette from her slender fingers and, heaven help me, jam it down her throat, but I can't. Because goddamn.

I still need a ride.

She is just so damn high. Eyelids drooping, body swaying, as if she were wading in water up to her neck instead of trying to remain upright in the driver's seat of a car.

I don't want to die in a crash before I've had a chance to live, but dear God, as desperate as I am to leave, I can't allow Daisy to drive an automobile.

Suddenly, a hellish yawn consumes her body. A head-to-toe shudder while she sits in a bucket seat. Can you pass out from smoking too much weed?

Okay, then, if she can't drive, I can. She just needs to move into the passenger seat.

"Daisy, why don't you get out of the car and let me drive?"

She doesn't look at me before she pitches forward. Forehead resting on the steering wheel, arms limp at her sides — I swear to Jesus, she did pass out.

I try to nudge her. She is long-legged with

24

a compact figure, but I can't budge dead-weight.

I give up and glance around the block, seeking the house of a neighbor I can tolerate. But who can I ask for a ride? Who hasn't left for work?

I may not like them, but I know they are home.

With my luggage in hand, I hike across the street to the Averys' house. Not the best choice, but Mr. Avery does occasionally smile when I say good morning. Maybe he'll give me a ride.

I climb the steps onto the Avery porch and place my luggage behind a large potted palm. I imagine my aunt has opened her eyes and is watching me. But I don't glance over my shoulder. Instead, I ring Mr. Avery's bell. It takes only a second for him to open the door.

"Morning, Francine. Where you headed, all dressed up on a Friday morning?"

I wish everyone would stop commenting about my clothes. "Morning to you, too, sir." I'm shaking and can't help thinking that at any minute, Jackson will barrel out of the building, charge across the street, and drag me back into the apartment. I also worry that if he does, I won't have the strength to leave him again no matter how many times I'm hit or how loudly he yells.

"I need a ride to the Greyhound bus terminal. Jackson is working double shifts all weekend, and with Memorial Day yesterday, a lot of the men at the factory took off for a holiday." My nervous laugh is bordering on hysteria. "You know how much Jackson loves overtime. So, he picked up as much as he could."

"Take a breath, Francine."

"I'm going to visit my cousin Tamika. She's not well."

"Doesn't she live twenty blocks from here?"

The way he stares past me, I realize my mistake. Jackson's car is in the driveway and the potted palm isn't hiding my Lady Baltimore luggage.

"Does Jackson know you're leaving him?"

Sweet Jesus. Jackson must've told him we were having trouble. Why else would he say such a thing? "I'll be back in a couple of days."

Mr. Avery leans forward and lowers his head. "You sure about that?" He glares at me like I'm a checklist on shopping day. "I can't help you. Talk to your husband. Ask him to give you a ride."

"What's going on, Joseph?" His wife steps

26

into view, pushing her glasses up on her nose.

"Francine, dear, what are you doing here this early?"

Mr. Avery answers the question meant for me. "She needs a ride to the Greyhound station, but I'm not doing it, and neither are you. Jackson told me she might try and run off. And we're not getting in the middle of a husband and wife's spat." Mr. Avery turns and retreats into his home.

Who said men don't gossip?

Alone in the doorway, Mrs. Avery grins. She's always smiling, which makes it difficult to trust her. "I'm sorry, but you heard my husband," she says.

"Frankie doesn't need you to give her a ride."

I spin around. It's Daisy, standing at the bottom of the steps, waving a set of car keys, and behind her, I see Jackson on the other side of the street. He's not running, but he's not moving slow, either.

"You can drive, but we'd better leave now." Daisy points across the street. "Because your husband looks like he's about to lose his natural mind."

"I thought you were heading to Piggly Wiggly," Jackson calls from the curb. "Mr.

Avery's porch doesn't look like a grocery store to me." He moves his hand to his chin, rubbing at the short, stiff hairs of his morning beard. It's a simple gesture, a nothing gesture, but I'm too accustomed to what comes next, and my body goes catatonic.

"Come on, girl," Daisy yells. "I have places to be, people to see. I can't hang out here all morning."

The sun blazes in the sky, and sweat runs from my temple, knotting my roots and ruining my Jackie O. hairstyle. I dab my brow with my fingertips. I swear my skin is melting, but the heat has loosened the joints in my arms and legs. I can move.

"Give me a second," I say to Daisy.

I hike across the Averys' porch, remove my luggage from behind the potted palm, and walk right by Mrs. Avery, who is still standing in her doorway with that obnoxious grin on her face. I do not wave goodbye or utter a thanks-for-nothing or mention how much I hate her husband. I know the old bastard telephoned Jackson and told him to come fetch his wife.

I maneuver carefully down the porch steps to Daisy's car, giving Jackson a wide berth. When I reach her, she takes my Lady Baltimore train case, the smaller of the two bags, flips down the front seat, and tosses the small case in the back of the car. The suitcase she carries to the trunk.

I risk a glance in Jackson's direction. His arms cross over his stomach, making his muscle-bound veins double in size, and the speed at which his jaw clenches and unclenches must sound like a hammer pounding a nail into his skull. Or at least I hope so.

"Listen up, Francine." His deep voice trembles with rage and puts an ice pick in my chest. "I'm not gonna have this conversation with you and your dingbat aunt in the middle of the street with the entire neighborhood watching. Get back in the house."

Daisy slams the trunk shut. "That's not true, Jackson." Her voice drops an octave. "I'm not a dingbat. I'll be sixty years old on my next birthday. First in the family to graduate from college, wrote for magazines and newspapers about Black people doing great things. I'm researching my first book."

Her fist is on her hip as she steps toward him and pauses, letting her gaze travel from one side of the street to the other until she shifts back to Jackson. "I think you're loud-mouthing this girl because your neighbors are watching, and you don't like them seeing you for what you are."

29

"And what is that?"

"A piece of shit and a bully. Or a bully and a piece of shit. It's like the chicken and the egg; with men like you, no one knows which comes first."

Jackson's showy muscles wither as if the truth of her words is a needle bursting his balloon. But then he pulls Daisy to him, so roughly, for an instant, her feet leave the ground.

Panic builds in my chest. I've been on the receiving end of his temper more times than I will ever admit. I don't want to see her get hit. I want to help her, but I am unable to move or speak. I close my eyes, not wanting to see what happens next because I am friggin' useless.

"Take your goddamned hands off me." Daisy's voice has a fierceness I can't help but envy.

I open my eyes.

She is looking at me. Then she winks. "Your old man doesn't scare me."

My heart pounds.

Jackson damn sure scares me.

Then the strangest thing happens. He lets Daisy go, and for an instant, he looks petrified. He steps back, putting some distance between them, and with a shocked expression, he stares at her as if she is the snake in

30

the grass and not him.

I gulp air through my mouth as if it's parceled out in small boxes I must swallow whole. I'm dizzy. My knees are made of sticky wads of bubble gum, melting in the heat.

Daisy squeezes my hand, sensing how close I am to flipping out, I imagine. And she's right because, Lord help me, I don't remember moving next to her, but I hang on to her hand tightly, as if her touch can free me from the swirling sea.

"He's not going to bother you anymore today, Frankie. So stop worrying."

How can Daisy be so sure of such a thing?

I turn from her, and Jackson is shouting at me. "Your ass had best be in this apartment when I get home from work." He raises a middle finger, giving me a vulgar message.

He retreats to his side of the curb, continuously stepping farther back with each word. "Don't forget," Jackson shouts. "I'm the love of your life."

With that, he disappears into the apartment building and makes a big deal about slamming the door behind him.

Daisy still holds my hand, and I let her because, just like that, he's gone, which frightens me more than it should.

31

"I thought for sure he'd hit you." I release Daisy's hand. "I'd better go back inside. He never walks away. He likes to fight. Something's not right."

"Are you out of your mind?" Daisy snatches my hand back and holds it so fiercely I wince. "You asked me to give you a ride to the bus station, and that's why I'm here, isn't it?"

"I can't," I say this with confidence. After having the strength to leave, I am afraid Jackson's words are true: he is the love of my life; how will I survive without him when I'm having his baby? It belongs to him. Doesn't that mean I do, too?

"This is too much. I don't know what he'll do. Jackson might —"

"Might what?"

"He was going to hurt you. Don't you understand? When he gets angry, he doesn't think. He just does. And I should go back upstairs. I can't —"

She squints at me but has a smile on her lips. "Look here. I was ready to fight him, had my trusty switchblade ready." She removes a knife from her dress pocket and flips it open with one hand.

I'm gulping down boxes again. "Jesus Christ. You have a switchblade?" My eyes feel like they are popping out of my head.

"Did you show it to Jackson? Is that why he walked away?"

She shrugs. "I did more than show it to him, I held it to his rib cage, and he backed right up." She pauses, eyes half-closed and thoughtful. "He's not the type to own a pistol, is he?"

I shake my head.

"Good. That's the only thing that would scare me." Daisy sweeps a strand of hair from her forehead, but she isn't sweaty like me.

"You drive the car. I need to finish coming down from my high." She taps my closed hand. "You already have the keys, darling. So let's go."

I think I'm in shock. I should go upstairs. Take the licking Jackson will give me and forget this morning ever happened. But Daisy is a force. I can't turn my back on her or tell her the truth about how I talk a big game but then fold in half like a broken lawn chair.

I know what I'll do. What I usually do. Believe in my heart; I'm leaving Jackson for good. Have Daisy drop me off at the bus terminal, find a locker for my luggage, and get some breakfast before taking the Clark Street bus back home.

In the driver's seat of the Mustang, I put

the key in the ignition and rev the engine. Then, shifting gears, I pull the sports car away from the curb and head toward downtown Chicago and the Greyhound bus terminal.

Daisy immediately lifts a box of eight-track cassettes from the floor and riffles through them. "What are you in the mood for? Jerry Butler? The Temptations? Oh, hold on. I've got one for you. 'Heat Wave' by Martha and the Vandellas."

As Martha wails the chorus, Daisy joins in. " 'Burning in my heart.' "

She can't sing, so I don't mind when she turns the music up loud, but I keep glancing at her. She's interesting to look at. Not a young woman, but you can't tell how old she is. She's just so beautiful. How do you stay that pretty after that many years of living? My mother's fifty-five, so Daisy must be close to sixty. But my mom looks much older.

Daisy slips on a pair of cat-eyed black sunglasses with extra-large frames. They match her black-and-white-gingham boat-collared dress. It's a great ensemble.

The makeup is impeccable: arched eyebrows, mascara-thickened eyelashes, and the bright red lipstick, most of which covers the filter of her cigarette. She looks like a

1950s movie star. The Negro Ava Gardner, including the dimple in her chin, or, better yet, Dorothy Dandridge, if she'd lived to be sixty. That's the life Daisy Washington is living, that of a 1950s movie star.

I love old movies. The glamour. The snug, fit-like-skin dresses, and thick-heeled pumps.

Daisy has the curves for the clothes people wore back then. Shoot. She has the figure for any decade. I could never pull off that look. Nor could I learn how to use a switchblade. I'd hurt myself before doing damage to anyone else.

Some of her other traits, however, are the ones I wouldn't mind having. Her courage, for example. I could use some of that. Risking her skin for me, someone she met only two weeks ago, sure, a relative, but going out on a limb for essentially a stranger — well, that's something.

Or perhaps, that's just what she does — one of those people who brings home stray cats.

My mom would never do that. She struggles to take care of her own. When I caught the poliovirus, Mom had to quit her job, and we moved into the house on Naomi near the corner of Twenty-Ninth Street and Central Avenue with Grandpa Marvin.

My goodness, how she hated waiting on me when I was sick. Complained to Grandpa every day most of the day, loud talking, too, as if I couldn't hear or she didn't care if I heard.

Grandpa ended up taking care of me mostly. Then after I got well, we just didn't leave, and since my real dad, a soldier in the US Navy, had died in Korea, Grandpa raised me. He was the only person I could count on.

He also never spoke ill of Daisy. He just never mentioned her.

After what she did for me today, I wish I knew more about her. Something other than the things I heard my mother say.

CHAPTER 2
DAISY

Summer 1928
Los Angeles

The California sun was a devil of a child, blazing through her bedroom window, waking Daisy much earlier than she would've liked.

She'd closed her eyes only an hour or so ago — after the candle on the small table next to the bed had burned out. She'd been in the middle of rereading a poem in *The Crisis,* the monthly publication of the NAACP, edited by her hero, W. E. B. Du Bois.

"The Bird in the Cage" by Effie Lee Newsome had received an honorable mention for the 1926 Crisis Prize writing contest (an award Daisy hoped to win one day). The poem was about a bird imprisoned in a cage (evident from the title, of course) and a neighbor who didn't own a bird but envied the other neighbor's possession of one. The prose had a bluesy sound like a Bessie Smith song on the radio.

And oh, that bird. It kept flapping its wings and banging its small head into the cage's bars, trying to break free, despite having no way of escaping and no place to go if it did.

Late at night when the house was quiet, Daisy and her mother would spend hours discussing poetry and novels, and news articles in the *Eagle*. Stories about the struggle against racism, making it impossible for Negroes to own homes except for in the neighborhoods they decide. All the injustices that hog-tied colored people's civil rights.

But that was before.

Now, when the candle went out, the only parent on Daisy's mind was her father.

Every day, twice a day, he fussed at her and her sister about a dozen different things, but most recently, using up all the electricity was on the top of his list of complaints. Daisy was unsure how anyone used up electricity, but if she so much as touched the lamp's cord, he'd know. Papa could smell it. And Daisy didn't want any part of a disagreement with him.

She wanted to leave her home on Naomi Avenue without any trouble, no confronta-

38

tions, no problems. Just have one of those perfect days, but she hadn't had one of them since March.

March 13, to be exact.

Papa gathered them in the living room at a dreadful hour. Still pitch-black, and only one lamp lit in the dining room.

Daisy knew something serious had happened. The expression on her father's face told her so. He didn't have many expressions, but that morning a deep sadness lined the corners of his eyes and mouth and cut ridges deep into his brow.

He stood in front of the fireplace, holding a cigarette between trembling fingers, and his dark eyelashes glistened with drops of sweat or perhaps even tears.

But then he fixed his gaze on her mother, coughed into his fist, and began.

Faulty construction had caused the St. Francis Dam to crumble, and the structure fell apart as if dynamite had exploded at the base of the mountain. The floodwaters killed hundreds and hundreds of people. They'd be counting the bodies for months, Papa said. But two of the dead had already been found — her uncles Jedediah and Marion, her mother's brothers.

Daisy had loved them more than anything on earth other than her parents, her sister, and Clifford, her oldest brother, though he'd been dead a long time.

But Daisy didn't love Jedediah and Marion the way her mama had.

The three of them waited for Mama to do something, say something, scream or cry. But she was quiet, her silence frightening, and her body shockingly still.

When her mother's mouth opened finally, Daisy had thought she'd sob or break down in a heap of tears. But what happened next was unexpected.

She clutched at the buttons of her blouse and, like a stone tossed into a muddy river, sank to the floor, slow and loose.

Fear cut across Daisy's chest. Had her mama died, too?

Papa lifted Mama into his arms and pointed his daughters in the direction of the limousine parked in the gravel driveway.

Daisy and her sister hurried into the back seat as Papa placed Mama in the front seat. Seconds later, he was driving them to Good Samaritan Hospital.

It had never taken so long to get anywhere in her life as it had taken to reach that hospital.

That was March.

Now it was after.

Daisy climbed out of bed, put on a robe,

grabbed her basket of toiletries, and headed for the bathroom. But when she stepped into the hallway, she heard a voice from her parents' bedroom — the room next to hers. The voice had called her name, and it wasn't her father. He no longer slept in the bedroom, choosing the cot on the screened porch rather than lie in bed next to his sickly wife.

On the other side of the door, Daisy's beautiful, smart, loving mother, Sophie Washington, lay in bed, curled up like a baby, knees pulled into her chest, unwilling to move, dress, or feed herself.

When Daisy made enough money, she'd hire her mother the best doctors and get her into one of those private, live-in hospitals where wealthy white folks recovered from consumption. A sanitarium. Although her mother's problem wasn't consumption. She'd had a heart attack and apoplexy, which also had soured her mind.

Daisy leaned against the door, listening carefully. It had to be her mother. She might not have spoken in weeks, but it could be the first day, the first sign that she was coming back to them.

Please, God, let it be her.

Daisy reached for the doorknob, her chest tight, her heart full, but then a voice cried out from down the hall. Her sister's voice. The one Daisy had heard all along.

Why did she keep hoping for something that might never be?

"Daisy? Daisy?" The words are spoken in a hard whisper. "Come here."

Her sister, Henrietta, was in the bathroom.

The girl had best have a good reason for making such a ruckus so early in the morning.

It wasn't even six o'clock. Daisy marched down the hall and stopped in the bathroom doorway, shocked into silence.

Her sixteen-year-old sister, bold as brass and twice as hardheaded, swaying from side to side, stood in front of the vanity with a pair of sewing scissors in her hand and a mountain of black, coarse curls in the bathroom sink.

Daisy's hopes for a perfect day were fading.

"Papa will never forgive you." She shook her head in disbelief. "Why would you do such a thing?"

"It looks awful, doesn't it?" Henrietta groaned. "You should've cut it like I'd asked you to do."

"So this is my fault?"

Fat tears clung to her sister's cheeks.

"You're always too busy, writing, reading, working, and doing anything rather than help me."

"That's not true, and stop being dramatic, and don't blame me," Daisy ordered. "You're forever acting out." It was what their mother would've said about her. "How are you going to explain this?"

"Not exactly sure," she mumbled, swiping tears from her cheeks.

"Is that how you're going to explain your hair to Papa — with a *not exactly sure?*"

"I don't know. Maybe." Henrietta frowned at her reflection in the mirror. "It doesn't look anything like the hairstyles in the magazine, does it?"

"No, it doesn't, but those girls didn't chop off their hair with sewing scissors," she said harshly, hoping to put the fear of God in her sister's bones. "He's going to take the belt to you. You wait and see."

"It's unfair." Henrietta pouted. "He shouldn't be using a belt on us. We're grown."

"No, I'm grown. You're still a girl."

Covering her face with her hands, Henrietta sobbed into her palms. Tears slipping through the spaces between her fingers pooled on the bathroom floor.

Daisy touched the thickly coiled hair bun at the nape of her neck. A conservative style, unlikely to create the wraith her sister's would, but Daisy was old-fashioned. Out of style.

"Are you paying attention to me, Daisy?" Henrietta sputtered between sobs. "What am I going to do?"

Daisy crossed her arms over her chest. She could continue to chastise her sister for vanity and willfulness. There were rules at the house on Naomi. Daisy kept a list in her journal and made every effort to keep them once she stepped inside the house. These same rules Henrietta broke every other day. She deserved to see the rough side of their father's temper.

But Daisy also hated seeing her sister in tears. "Give me those scissors."

She snipped here and there, turning her sister's head this way and that. A few moments later, Henrietta's sniffles dried up. "Now, look in the mirror."

Henrietta let loose a yelp. "Oh, thank you. That's so much better."

"You're welcome."

Still preening, Henrietta asked, "What are you going to say to Papa about my hair?"

"So you want me to come up with an explanation for why you did it?"

Henrietta grinned. "He believes anything you tell him."

That was not true. "Okay. I'll think of

something. Meanwhile, you clean up this mess so I can use the bathroom."

"Yes, ma'am," Henrietta chirped.

"By the way, where is Papa?"

They had made enough noise for him to come roaring into the hallway long ago. And if he'd come home the night before, which sometimes didn't happen with his job as a chauffeur, it was too early for him to have left for work.

"He's in the dining room with the Butlers."

The widowed Mrs. Butler (an old friend of her mother's) had traveled from Chicago to Los Angeles with her teenage son on her way to Seattle for a new job. She was leaving her son, Isaiah, in our home until she was settled. But how could a mother move to a new town without her son?

"Oh, I forgot about them."

Henrietta jabbed her in the arm. "Papa's been so busy with Mama, work, and the Bible, he may not notice my hair."

"He'll notice. He notices everything."

With Henrietta slinking in behind her, Daisy entered the dining room determined to stand up to her father. Of course, she would've preferred a better reason than a haircut to do so. But she was a twenty-year-

45

old woman who lived at home and had never had a date or ventured into downtown Los Angeles with or without friends. A girl like that couldn't predict when she'd have another opportunity to show courage and defy someone like her father, a man she loved dearly, but he confused her.

Her mother had been the one who made sense of him, and everything and everybody. After her mother's collapse, fear flapped its wings around Daisy's heart. If her mother never got better Daisy would never understand life, let alone her father. Blowing out a breath, she pushed the thought from her mind and set her gaze on her father.

Papa sat at the far end of the walnut table, his fingers wrapped around a coffee tin and his wire-rimmed glasses slipping toward the tip of his nose. Almost bald and smooth-shaven, he was dressed in his chauffeur's uniform, ready for work. But the woman seated to his left, whom Daisy assumed was Mrs. Butler, held his attention at the moment.

Around her mother's age, late forties, Mrs. Butler had a light, feminine laugh, and her gloved fingers had found a resting place on Daisy's father's forearm.

Mrs. Butler had spent four days and nights on a train, but her hair was not a quick updo. Instead, it was piled delicately on her head, spit curls framing her face. Her pale blue tea dress with its white pinafore collar appeared freshly ironed, too. However, Daisy detected a hint of mothballs beneath her lilac perfume.

"It's good to meet you, Mrs. Butler." Daisy greeted her with a short bow and a nod to the young man standing between the dining room and living room in the archway.

It was her son, Isaiah, Daisy presumed. Tall and solidly built, he was seventeen, she believed, but looked younger with his delicate features, freckles, and thickly lashed round eyes.

Then she found her gaze lingering on his face, his shy smile, and the guitar case he held upright with a careful hand.

Daisy squeezed her eyes shut for an instant as the old pain, sudden and sharp, burrowed into her skull.

What was it about him that brought her dead brother to mind?

"So, you're Sophie's eldest," Mrs. Butler was saying.

Daisy blinked to attention. "Yes, ma'am. I am."

Mrs. Butler eyeballed Daisy from the top of her coronet cap down to her practical one-strap, low-heeled shoes. "You resemble your father," Mrs. Butler said. "A handsome young woman with such a healthy, big-boned figure."

With a cheery smile plastered on her face, she seemed unaware that her words might sting.

Daisy was taller than most girls and proud of her well-defined features, the long straight nose, full lips, and pronounced cheekbones, combined to make an attractive-enough girl, she believed. Although, she didn't draw the quick compliments Henrietta's saucy prettiness hoarded.

But Daisy didn't let these differences rile her. According to her mother, beauty came in different shapes and sizes. One day, Daisy would be loved by someone who appreciated her beauty and her flaws.

So there, Mrs. Butler.

"I like your uniform," the woman said suddenly, or had she been talking all along? "You're a housemaid."

"A chambermaid, at the Hotel Somerville. My sister is a laundress."

Holding on to Daisy's apron strings, Henrietta mumbled a short hello while striving to remain hidden from their father's view, Daisy imagined.

"I read about the Hotel Somerville in *The Defender,*" Mrs. Butler said. "You bet it'll make a difference for the Race in Los Angeles. Like with Chicago's State Street, Central Avenue will fill up with colored businesses — and they will thrive. You'll see."

So, Mrs. Butler didn't know that Central Avenue or Brown Broadway (as some called it) had been a thriving center of Negro businesses for a decade or more. But Daisy wouldn't embarrass her by giving her an education on the financial state of Negroes in Los Angeles versus those in Chicago.

Mrs. Butler leaned back in her chair, glancing down the hall. "How's your mother doing? I wish I could visit her before my train departs for Seattle, but your father says she doesn't rise before noon."

Her mother didn't rise at all, Daisy almost blurted. Instead, she glanced at her father, wondering why he hadn't told Mrs. Butler about her mother's condition.

"Isaiah," her father said. "I hope you slept on the train. Mrs. Keyes, the Somerville's housekeeping manager, will put you to work as soon as Daisy introduces you, which will happen this morning, by the way."

"Slept just fine, sir," Isaiah replied with a deep baritone.

"I know I've said it before" — Mrs. Butler gripped Daisy's father's arm with both hands — "thank you for taking him in. You and Sophie are so kind to help me this way."

"It helps us, too," Daisy's father said solemnly. "Isaiah will be paying his way here, and his contribution will help this household, too."

"We do have relatives in town," Mrs. Butler said to Daisy. "My late husband's cousin Helen already has a house full of people, though. You might know one of her girls, Yvonne? She went to the Jefferson school."

"I know her," Henrietta said from behind Daisy. "She was in my class."

"If you run in to her or her mother, do tell them I said hello." She looked at Papa. "I just wanted to be here when you met my son and to thank Sophie, but I understand she's still recovering." She reached out her hand, and her son came to her side. She gripped his outreached arm and used it as leverage, helping her rise to her feet.

"Henrietta. I couldn't get a good look at you, hiding behind your sister. How are you?" Mrs. Butler gestured for Daisy to move aside. "I can't see her."

Henrietta inched into full view.

"I love your hair," Mrs. Butler exclaimed. "Oh my. These new styles are so adorable on young people. That's a nice bob, too, I can tell, even beneath that maid's cap. I especially like the bangs. Very Clara Bow."

Daisy muttered a quick prayer: *Please shut up, Mrs. Butler!*

"Jesus Christ, Henrietta! What did you do?"

And there it was: Papa had noticed.

"Yes. I cut my hair," Henrietta said, with only the slightest quiver in her voice. Then she added with a sudden burst, "I'm sixteen. I should be allowed."

Daisy waited for her to stomp her foot. The words had come out with such defiance. But her attention was riveted to her father.

His face darkened into shades of black and red, the color of the sticky monkey flowers in the backyard.

Daisy wasn't sure what to do, what to say, or where to look. Henrietta's words had stunned her, too.

"Decent, well-mannered girls don't disobey their parents," her father said sharply.

"I am decent!" Henrietta shouted.

Daisy gestured for Henrietta to hush, but her sister was possessed.

"And why do you care about my hair?" she asked her father acidly. "Mama was the one who didn't want me to cut it, not you. She cared. Before she got sick, she watched over me. She combed my hair in the morning, washed my hair on weekends. Fed me, mended my clothes, talked to me about my day every night. But she can't do those things anymore. Not since the accident, since the heart attack, since apoplexy. Now she can't do a damn thing but lie in that goddamned bed and stare at the walls!"

"Don't you dare use that language in this house." Papa practically growled out the words, but he hadn't left his seat.

Oh, Jesus, Daisy thought, her chest hurting. She wished her sister would stop. Stop hurting. Stop taking out her pain on everyone around her. And in front of strangers, too.

Daisy stepped toward Henrietta, reaching for her, wanting to wrap her arms around her, but Henrietta jerked away.

She glared at their father. "Aren't you going to say anything?" she yelled. "Aren't you going to grab your belt?"

Papa still sat in the chair at the end of the walnut table. Palms flat, fingers spread, veins bulging, his knuckles protruded like the ridges of a small mountain range.

Daisy didn't want to look at his face. She glanced at the Butlers instead. Mother and son together in the archway, eyes wide with shock and a touch of fear.

52

"Why aren't you moving, Papa?" Henrietta was taunting him.

Dear Lord, what has gotten into her?

"I don't have to listen to you, Papa. You're never here, and Daisy is too busy, working every shift, scribbling in her diaries. With Mama as good as dead, I am on my own and should be able to do what I want."

"Don't speak of your mother that way!" Her father's voice grew loud. "Do you hear me?"

"Henrietta, please." Daisy could hold her tongue no longer. "Stop this, please —"

"I just hate that she'll never get better."

"That's not true, Henrietta," Daisy said vehemently. "She will get better. She needs better doctors."

"Shut up, both of you!"

The grating sound of splintered wood made everyone jump, including the stiff-backed Mrs. Butler. Daisy's father had pushed his chair back from the table so hard the legs had dug into the floor, ripping into the wood panels.

"No, Papa. You need to listen," Henrietta said, the pitch of her voice suddenly calm. "I'd rather she died than rot in that bedroom. And I think you would, too. I do. I just do!"

Papa moved across the room so fast it

53

didn't register that he was standing in front of Henrietta until Daisy heard the slap.

Her sister stumbled backward, her eyes full of tears as she rubbed her cheek. But what alarmed Daisy was the look of vindication that crept into her wet gaze.

Had Henrietta deliberately taunted their father into doing something he had never done before? Touch his daughter with his bare hand in frustration? Sure, a lashing with a leather belt or a small tree branch, but the way her father struck Henrietta had frightened Daisy.

"Papa." Daisy's voice shook as she moved between her father and her sister's hunched form. "Please, we have guests." If was the only thing she could think of to say.

Abruptly, her father turned from Henrietta and looked at the Butlers. "Say your good-byes. We'd better get going."

Mrs. Butler blinked, adjusted her dress, kissed Isaiah on the cheek, and said, "That's right. I can't miss my train."

Papa snatched his uniform jacket from the back of the dining room chair and marched toward the front.

He gestured to Mrs. Butler. "And I can't be late for my job. So we'd better go."

Then they were out the door, heading for her father's boss's limo. A wealthy white man with several automobiles, he allowed her father to keep the limo a couple of nights a week for cleaning and repairs.

Daisy watched them from the doorway, and once they reached the sidewalk, she said to calm a still weepy Henrietta, "Pull yourself together. We can't be late for work, either."

Her sister wiped her face with both hands.

"I don't have the time or the energy to discuss this now," Daisy said quietly. She was worried about her sister, but what was important now was arriving at the Somerville before her shift started. "Are you going to be okay?

Henrietta nodded.

"Are you sure? Speak up."

Through sniffles, she said, "Yes. I am ready."

"Good."

"I'm ready, too." Isaiah picked up his guitar.

Daisy had forgotten about him. "What do you need that for?" she asked. "You can't play the guitar and wash dishes or shine shoes or do whatever job Mrs. Keyes gives you."

He started to say something, but stopping to listen to his explanation would only delay their departure. "Forget about it. Let's just go."

"Morning, Daisy." Mrs. Weaver, their next-door neighbor, swung open the front screen door and strolled into the house. She kept an eye on Daisy's mother while the family worked. "It's a big day, the grand opening of the Hotel Somerville. I wish I could be there to witness it myself." She kept walking toward the rear of the house. "I'll check in on your mother. See if I can get her to eat some scrambled eggs. She likes eggs."

Whatever more Mrs. Weaver had to say, Daisy didn't hear. She was shooing Henrietta and Isaiah through the front door, down the porch steps, and onto the paved sidewalk toward Central Avenue.

"We'll have to run all the way to get to work by seven." Even if it wasn't the job she dreamed of, the Somerville was important to her. There was just so much for her to see and write about. It almost made up for scrubbing floors, dusting banisters, and making beds.

She reached into her apron pocket, touching the small notepad and pencil she'd slipped inside. At work, she wore two caps — and the one she liked best had little to do with changing sheets or delivering tea.

56

Once she arrived at the Hotel Somerville, she had something other than home problems to think about. Something more interesting than her job. A secret she kept from everyone, except her ally, the one person she could count on to have her back.

CHAPTER 3
FRANKIE

Friday, May 31, 1968
Chicago

I suddenly jam on the brakes. I'd come this close to rear-ending the car in front of me. I shoot an apologetic glance at Daisy, but she's in another world, grooving to Jerry Butler's "Never Give You Up."

I tighten my grip on the steering wheel. I think my driving skills are rusty.

Jackson never allowed me behind the wheel if he was in the car. And since I never went anywhere without him, other than to Tamika's (and I can walk to Hyde Park), I didn't drive.

The thing is, I love to drive. The most adult thing I've ever done (other than get pregnant) is drive a car — and Daisy's Mustang is a friggin' beautiful machine, and despite being buried beneath marijuana smoke, the new-car smell slips through and is outta sight.

Now, the vehicle isn't perfect.

The best way to describe the interior of a 1968 Ford Mustang is to discuss the seats. I'm about eight weeks pregnant, I think, but I swear my hips are in the third trimester. And let me say, the devil who came up with bucket seats should be horsewhipped.

I try to relax and focus on driving, but I keep having this image of Jackson falling from the sky and punching me in the face. Strangely, another part of me wants to chat with Daisy about her relationship with my mother. They haven't seen each other, as far as I know, in forty years. Something happened back in the day they can't get over. But the ride to the bus terminal isn't long enough for me to question her about that and avoid a collision when the rest of my brain is worrying about Jackson.

He scared me. Not for the first time, of course, but it felt new. I've never seen him so angry at a woman other than me.

I wonder if that is what makes me so curious about Daisy. Is there something in me that's like her? Did Jackson see it?

I'm not cool enough or pretty enough to be like Daisy. So I doubt it.

I clutch the wheel with both hands (I'm a two-handed driver) and merge onto Lake Shore Drive. It's not the way to go, but I want a last look at Lake Michigan.

Traffic is already bumper to bumper, and I'm driving as slow as a snail. The lake smells slightly fishy and the beaches look sweaty. I wish I could hear the waves moving over the sand.

It is a watery blue canvas of nostalgia, and I feel a ball of heat in my chest. I will miss the lakefront, those amazing — but too few — mornings spent in Grant Park. Summer evenings on my apartment building's front stoop, the smell of outdoor grilled meat, the taste of buttered corn, and Mrs. Avery's chocolate cake. The only thing I could tolerate about her, or her husband, was her cake.

Will I miss Jackson?

I won't miss his open-handed slap or the loneliness or being made to feel useless. Without him around, I can change and stop feeling sorry for myself.

Daisy lights a cigarette and suddenly, I'm thinking about my mother again. The way Daisy's wrist dangles at a delicate angle as she holds the butt loosely between two fingers and how it appears to be part of her hand — my mom smokes cigarettes the same way.

I remember two times my mother telephoned Daisy. Once was when I was sick with the poliovirus.

60

Smoke billowed around Mom's head as she held the phone, and when she said hello, her voice cracked, "Daisy, is that you?"

I didn't listen, didn't care too much what my mother did or said back then. I rarely saw her. My grandfather applied the moist heat packs to ease the disease's painful muscle spasms. A neighbor taught him how to make the Kenny heat packs he used on me every two hours for twelve hours a day or as frequently as every fifteen minutes if my spasms were really bad.

The second time, I was sixteen and Grandpa had died sitting in the wicker chair in the sunroom. I overheard my mom on the phone, talking to Daisy about his funeral. Don't know what they decided, but Daisy never showed.

The light at the intersection suddenly turns red. Surprised, I brake hard — again.

Daisy braces her hand on the dashboard. "You, okay?" She peers at me over the bridge of her sunglasses.

"I'm okay." I'd better keep my eyes on the road, or is it head in the game? No, that's what Jackson used to say when we were in high school. "We're almost there."

I turn onto Clark Street. "Thank you for helping me today."

"You're welcome, but frankly, I enjoyed

61

myself. Hadn't had to pull my knife on someone in a while."

"I wish we had more time to talk."

"We should've done that two weeks ago."

"I didn't want to introduce myself one minute and then drill you with questions about you and my mother's relationship."

"Or lack thereof. But too late. Look at where we are now." She jerks her hand toward the street. "Minutes away from the bus terminal. Not enough time to tell the tale and give it justice." She jams her butt in the ashtray and cigarette ash flies, landing on her hand and the car seat.

"Think about it," she continues, her voice calmer than I expected. "What if I asked you why you remained married to a man who beat you? And don't tell me he didn't, or it happened only once, or it was an accident. Plain as day, he strikes first and cries wolf later. So, I bet you would need more than two blocks to answer that question. Am I right?" She leans forward and side-eyes me. "You damn straight."

I feel a blast of heat on my cheek that has nothing to do with the weather. She thinks she can read me like the front page of the sports section: all headlines but none of the small print. She's wrong. But as she points out, there's not enough time to answer questions.

We don't speak as Daisy digs in her purse and lights another cigarette. I check the rearview mirror and pull into a parking spot in front of the bus terminal.

That's when I notice a medium-size piece of luggage in the back seat next to my Lady Baltimore train case.

"What are your plans for today? Going someplace?" I nod toward the back seat.

"Los Angeles," she replies.

I almost say that's where I'm going, too, but for some reason I don't. "I bet you're flying. I can't afford to fly. The bus works for my pocketbook."

"I'm not fond of trains, buses, or airplanes." Daisy blows a smoke ring (the speed at which she lights up a fresh cig is dazzling). "I'm driving to Los Angeles."

"That's a two-thousand-mile trip."

"I have some stops to make along the way, and I have my Negro Travelers' Green Book. So I'll be fine."

I don't mention they stopped printing the book in 1964. We're just sitting in the car parked in front of the terminal. Neither one of us is moving to leave.

"Where are you headed?" she asks.

"Los Angeles, too," I say, realizing I have

no reason not to tell her.

"Going to be with your mother."

I'm not, but I don't want to get into reasons why in case she asks. "Yeah, I guess."

She smacks her lips. "Oh, did you want to ride with me? I'm not sure that will work. I have several stops to make. It could take me a week or more to reach LA."

"I didn't mean for it to sound like I was begging for a ride. It happens to be where I'm headed. That's all."

"Well, good, because I can't alter my plans, and it's going to be — a complicated drive." She lights a cigarette. "Does your mother know you're coming?"

"No, she doesn't."

Daisy opens the car door but still doesn't move to get out of the Mustang. "You'd better call her before you show up on her doorstep. Over the years, things may have changed, but she never liked surprises."

The truth of that sentence makes me smile. "She still doesn't."

My hand is on the door handle, but I'm waiting for her to get out first.

She extends her right leg and props the heel of her shoe on the curb, positioned to make her exit. For a moment, I think we will part company with nothing more said between us but a quick goodbye.

She's hesitating, though, perhaps contemplating her words carefully. She drops her cigarette in the gutter.

"Make me a promise," she says in a different voice, one that sounds lived-in like the old house on Naomi Avenue. "Don't turn tail and go back to that man. You've made it this far. Keep going."

With that, she's out of the car and shuts the passenger-side door in my face. I remove the keys from the ignition and scramble out of the driver's seat.

"Why would I go back? You saw how he was. He's dangerous and mean and hurtful." I push forward the driver's seat and reach into the back of the car and grab my train case. "Why would you say such a thing?"

Daisy shrugs. "You're my sister's daughter, and I know the type."

"What type is that?"

"The type that makes excuses for going back to a man who treats her bad. You tell your friends you've left him and how you'll never go back, and then you remember something you forgot that you didn't mean to leave behind" — Daisy rests a fist on her hip — "*I left my sandals, my favorite jewelry, my favorite keepsake. I have no choice but to go back."*

Tears clog the back of my throat. "You're wrong."

Another shrug and a snarl of a smile before Daisy finishes with me. "I doubt it," she says. "I can just hear your excuses."

"And what are those?" I reply hotly.

"You know — I can't leave him; I still love him."

I am angry but also crushed. "You think I'm a fool."

It's not a question, and she doesn't answer.

"Goodbye." I pick up my luggage and, as fast as I can walk, hurry across the street.

Despite the noisy traffic, I can hear Daisy calling after me, "Have a nice trip, Frankie — and please, don't go back to Jackson."

The Greyhound bus terminal is a neon blue sea, the size of a city block with bright steel beams, white tile floors, and sculptures of long-necked dogs.

I stand at the top of the lengthy escalator, juggling my suitcases and squeezing my purse under my armpit.

Daisy is out of my mind, and now, my escape plan truly begins.

As soon as I make it down this escalator in one piece, I will buy my ticket to Los

66

Angeles, California.

The mile-long contraption is a cavernous beast with moving teeth. A possible exaggeration, but it doesn't feel like it. Hopefully, I won't take a tumble and land on my backside in the middle of the lobby, a broken mess.

"Excuse me." A woman shoves by me.

"Sorry." A teenager knocks into me.

"Are you going down?" An elderly gentleman stops next to me, holding his wife's elbow (I'm assuming she's his wife).

Two sets of old eyes crinkle with fondness, giving me that grandparent gaze elderly people bestow on the young.

"Sorry, I don't mean to be in the way." I move aside and smile at the wrinkled, dark-skinned couple and watch them step onto the escalator and disappear.

"Excuse me, ma'am." A dashiki-wearing white man, no older than me, with longish blond hair and eyes, an uncomfortable shade of blue, is speaking to me. "Do you need help?" He glances at my bags, and for a moment, I feel as if I know him, but from where? The only place I'd run into a white man is the Hall Branch of the Chicago Public Library — where I work as a librarian's assistant in the summer.

"Thank you. I'm fine."

I catch his wince. He can see I'm not okay but likely guessed why I refused his help.

These days, you can't trust white people, especially white men. Long-haired and young or not. Even if he's a hippie, and this man looks like one of them, it doesn't mean he was a freedom rider in '64 (Tamika told me about them). Or hadn't wished Dr. King dead.

A Black man, an older man, around Mr. Avery's age, steps between the white man and me. "I'll carry your bags, young miss."

"Thank you, sir. Much appreciated."

The white man backs away, nodding in apparent understanding but also disappointment.

I couldn't care less about his feelings and turn away.

The Black man picks up my bags, and I step onto the escalator with a lioness's grip on the railing as I descend into the main lobby below.

I thank the man for his help and move through the crowd until I reach the blessedly short ticket line.

"Where you headed?" the agent asks gruffly, pushing strands of brown hair from his eyes.

"Los Angeles," I reply.

"Roundtrip ticket is thirty-six dollars."

68

"A one-way ticket, please." I fumble in my purse. I can't find the place where I hide my money.

"Lady, if you can't find your money, why don't you move out of the line," the agent says needlessly loud. "People are waiting."

"Give me a minute, please."

He sighs. "Hey, just step aside."

"I have it. Give me a second."

"That's well and fine, but I've got to do my job. And I can't if you are in the way."

How rude is he, talking to me like I am a child? Or a simpleton. Or just another Negro he doesn't have time for, but I keep digging, and I swear, a week could pass before I'd step out of line. Then, finally, I find my money and hand it to the agent.

"A one-way ticket to Los Angeles." I say that with some vinegar in my tone (my grandfather would like that).

The agent places my ticket and change on the counter with a withering expression on his face.

"Oh, by the way," he says. "The bus is running late, something wrong under the hood. Will take at least three hours to fix."

"Is there another bus I can take?"

"It's today's bus to Los Angeles, so no."

I stare into his mousy eyes, trying to force him to acknowledge me, but it doesn't work.

"Why didn't you tell me before I purchased my ticket? I might've decided to go partway. Or make other plans. I need to leave Chicago now."

He leans forward, elbows on the counter, and I smell coffee and cigarettes and dislike. "I told you the bus is gonna be late. It's not my job to know if you're in a hurry to get out of town. But if you want a refund, no problem. Then you can take tomorrow's bus. Otherwise . . ."

His stupid grin makes me want to cry.

"Next in line."

CHAPTER 4
DAISY

Summer 1928
Los Angeles

The morning had gone as badly as a morning could go, but Daisy refused to dwell. The day could get better. She, Henrietta, and Isaiah would be busy working with no time to worry about the morning's happening on Naomi Avenue.

They arrived at the hotel and went straight to the basement, stopping by the room where the housekeeping staff kept their personal items. They dropped off Isaiah's guitar, to his chagrin, but Daisy cared little and rushed him and Henrietta along.

They then continued through the hallways of the basement with Daisy, assuming the role of guide, introducing Isaiah to the Somerville.

"It's the first establishment of its kind in America," she explained, leading them swiftly through the hallway. "A luxury hotel for Negroes only. Owned by, built by, managed by, and staffed by colored people, with Negroes in charge from day one."

Henrietta poked Isaiah. "You'll have to get used to Daisy. She talks like she's in the middle of filing a news article, but she's never had a job as a reporter. Just dreams."

"That's not true, Henrietta. I speak like anyone with a college education, and you have no idea what I'll be able to do from what I won't."

Henrietta rolled her eyes. "You didn't finish."

"Don't worry. I will."

"So, you're one of the talented tenth?" Isaiah added.

Daisy perked up, "You know of Du Bois's philosophy?"

"My mother taught me."

Daisy wasn't a college graduate (yet), a newspaper reporter, or writer for *The Crisis* or *Opportunity* magazines, but she would fill her journals with stories about the hotel's grand opening, W. E. B. Du Bois's NAACP meeting, and every big and little thing that happened in her life. Then one day, she'd write a book, and it would be amazing.

"This hotel has it all," Daisy said, hurrying Henrietta and Isaiah through the maze of hallways in the hotel's basement. "Several large storage rooms, laundry rooms, linen closets, maids' quarters, and walk-in iceboxes for vegetables, fruits, meats, and cheeses. And a padlocked room for the beer, wine, whiskey, and champagne.

"Wait until you see the first floor and the main lobby — and the crystal chandelier," Daisy continued. "Or the pool on the roof, or the grand hall, large enough for the NAACP's annual meeting. It begins next week."

They stopped outside the laundry room where Henrietta worked.

"Here you go," Daisy said before stepping back into the corridor, but Henrietta grabbed her hand and wouldn't let go.

"Can we meet in the staff dining room after our shift? I don't want to go home without you," she said. "Papa's been awful since Mama got sick, but never like this, especially not over such a small thing."

"You cutting your hair was not a small thing to him. You knew he didn't want you to do it. But you did it anyway."

"Isaiah, you agree with me. It's the 1920s. I just want to be modern."

"I do not wish to discuss this with him," Daisy said. "We don't need to bring him into our family's troubles."

Isaiah stared sheepishly at the ground.

"Why not?" Henrietta asked. "He lives in our house now."

"He's not family," Daisy blurted. "I'm sure you understand, Isaiah. We don't know you. We only met you this morning."

"I understand," he said quietly.

"See, Henrietta. He understands. Now, we have work to do. I'll see you later."

Henrietta opened her mouth as if to say something more, but Daisy raised her hand. "I mean it. We're at work. Home concerns remain at home." She gestured for Isaiah to follow. "Mrs. Keyes is this way."

Four doors down from the laundry, Mrs. Keyes stood outside the flower room, looking flustered. Daisy was accustomed to seeing her perfectly calm, perfectly organized, perfectly coiffed. Still dressing in styles more fashionable at the turn of the century, Mrs. Keyes looked overheated and distressed. It made Daisy feel uncomfortable, like she'd walked in on Mrs. Keyes as she'd awoken from a nap.

"Good morning, ma'am," Daisy said. "This is Isaiah Butler, the young man my father told you about."

"You're late, Daisy."

"I'm sorry. I'll get right upstairs, but my father asked me to bring him to you."

"He wasn't supposed to be here for another week, damn it." Mrs. Keyes had abandoned her normally pleasant manner. She seemed deeply troubled and angry. "Can't you see we were vandalized? Look at this mess!"

Flowers were strewn throughout the room. Vases tipped over, some broken water buckets leaked onto the floor.

"I'll spend half the morning dealing with this." Mrs. Keyes squinted at Isaiah. "I don't have time to train a new employee. The grand opening is today, and the Somerville's moved their daily tour up an hour from nine o'clock to eight, and two of the maids didn't show." She took a deep breath and turned to Daisy. "You and Yvette will work the lobby this morning. Make sure it's polished and dusted. I want everything perfect. No mistakes. Yvette is already upstairs."

"Yes, ma'am," said Daisy, raring to get away. "What about Isaiah?"

Mrs. Keyes glared at him. "Go to the laundry room. Always some work to do there. I'll have something permanent for you tomorrow."

"Thank you, Mrs. Keyes." Isaiah retraced his steps, heading to join Henrietta.

"I appreciate you doing this for my father," Daisy said, and then added politely, "Can I help you with anything here?"

"No, child. I'll take care of my flowers, but you tell your father that I'm done doing him favors after this. I do more for that man than I'd do for a husband — if I had one."

"Yes, ma'am. I will tell him," she said slowly, wondering how many favors Papa had asked of her.

Letting go of that thought, Daisy grabbed the supplies she needed from one of the storage rooms, a bucket of water, linseed oil, and washrags. Then she rushed up the stairway into the lobby to find Yvette.

The lobby suddenly teemed with workers, giving a final inspection to their various areas of responsibility.

The chandeliers, arched windows, flagstone floors, and murals on the walls were adjusted, dusted, and polished. Men hung the last of the flags and banners in the balcony as the orchestra set up in the gallery.

"Sorry I'm late," Daisy said, arriving at the front desk. Yvette was finishing a flower arrangement in one of the two green enamel carnival vases sitting on the long counter.

"Can you believe we are opening in a few hours?" Yvette said. "The florist will have to make an emergency delivery after what happened this morning. Poor Mrs. Keyes. She loves those flowers, and for someone to

76

sneak inside just to tear things up — it's crazy."

Yvette added a rose to the arrangement. "Why are you so late?"

Daisy sighed. "My father."

"Oh."

Daisy had known Yvette since they were kids: grown up on the same block, attended the same schools, including college — she knew better than to pry into Daisy's life at home. Just like Daisy didn't question Yvette's marriage the summer after high school or the baby girl born nine months later.

Her husband, Sid, had worked in the valley with Daisy's uncles, but hadn't made the forty-mile trip the night the dam collapsed. Their baby had been sick and he'd stayed home to help his wife. But since March, he'd only worked a few weeks as a pea picker. Jobs for colored men who were seasonal farmworkers were scarce. Yvette, the best stenographer in Daisy's college class, couldn't get an office job either. Negro girls were last in line if ever considered.

"I'm not that late," Daisy said.

"We were supposed to be here at six o'clock. It's after seven. Did you forget?"

She had. "It's a long story I don't want to

discuss, but what do we do next?"

Yvette moved toward the staircase. "We'll have a bird's-eye view of the Somervilles when they arrive."

In Daisy's heart, she shared Yvette's excitement, although the Somervilles weren't as incredible as W. E. B. Du Bois. However, Dr. John Somerville and his wife, Vada, were legends in the Los Angeles colored community.

Graduates of the University of Southern California, the same university Daisy had dropped out of in March, the Somervilles were the most illustrious Negro couple in LA. Champions of the Race and cofounders of the Los Angeles chapter of the NAACP, the Somervilles convinced W. E. B. Du Bois to hold his organization's annual meeting in Los Angeles.

Yvette removed a wet cloth from the bucket and wrung it out. "I have decided today is the day."

"And what day is that?"

"I'm going to introduce myself to Vada Somerville."

"You want to lose your job?"

"What's wrong with me saying, 'Hello, my name is Yvette Gibson'?"

"You ever hear of time and place? And not doing something jingle-brained?"

"I can't make beds and polish staircases forever. I went to college. Just like you, and I was the best stenographer in the class. So it's not in me to pretend the Hotel Somerville is the Taj Mahal."

"I have no intention of making beds for the rest of my life, either," Daisy replied with agitation. But she wanted Yvette to understand why she had to do what she was doing. It wasn't easy, telling her about things that happened on Naomi Avenue. It had never been. "My mother needs to have better doctors, and perhaps, even, round-the-clock care. It costs money to place her in a sanatorium or arrange for a room at a hospital like Dunbar that doesn't mind Negro patients. I mean, their staff is all Negro. To get well, she needs the best. And if that means I work extra shifts, or whatever, I'll do what I must to help her get well."

Yvette inhaled and exhaled slowly. It took a moment, but when she spoke, Daisy could hear the anger. "You act like you're the only breadwinner in your house. What about your father?"

"Yvette, please don't." It was a disagreement they'd had before. Part of the reason why Daisy didn't mention him or the problems that happened in her home.

"I shouldn't have told you," Daisy said sadly.

Yvette shook her head. "Okay. Okay. We'll stop, but your father is primitive. I swear." She picked up a rag and a bottle of linseed oil. "Let's stop arguing and finish up. Dr. John and Dr. Vada will be here at any minute."

The Somervilles led the tour group into the lobby, all of whom were smartly attired in summer suits and flowing tea dresses and stylish hats, a bouquet of pastel, silk, and feathers.

Dr. John strode across the flagstone floor in a wheat-colored single-breasted suit, casually twirling a Panama boater with a striped hatband. His wife, Dr. Vada, a dentist like her husband, modeled a wide-brimmed cloche trimmed in orange lace, the same color as her silk charmeuse. At her side, in a plain dark suit with a stern profile was Betty Hill, renowned civil rights advocate currently in a battle with the Los Angeles parks over the segregation of swimming pools and beaches. Entering solo was Charlotta Bass, owner and editor of the *California Eagle.* The prestige of her newspaper bestowed her with the opportunity to cover the news most important to Negroes throughout the state of California and the country.

Daisy's dreams had never included polishing banisters, emptying spittoons, or changing bed linens. She never saw herself as someone who stood aside as the newsworthy people paraded by. If her life hadn't twisted sideways in March, she'd be in this group, interviewing Mrs. Hill, Dr. Vada, even Dr. John, for an article in the *Eagle*.

Most of these guests had joined the Somervilles previously on their morning stroll through the hotel. Boxing champion Jack Johnson, for example, still an impressive figure in his fifties. The very light-skinned woman with him might be the actress Fredi Washington. But she kept turning around to speak with someone behind her and not showing that much interest in the champ. But what would the actress be doing in LA? Daisy thought she worked mostly in New York's Harlem.

Perhaps she could find out.

She removed her pencil and paper from her apron pocket as two more men came into view, or at least their shoes and the cuffs of their pants. The faces were blocked by the large leaves of a potted palm. Both men, however, were snappy dressers judging from their white pants and black-and-white oxfords.

Daisy scooted closer to her water bucket for a better view, only to be disappointed when she recognized Lincoln Perry — or Stepin Fetchit, his stage name. The fumbling, mumbling, half-wit he'd portrayed in the motion picture *In Old Kentucky* had made him Hollywood's Negro darling. But Daisy believed his on-screen antics embarrassed the Race. No way would she gather gossip on him. He garnered enough attention without her help.

She was gawking at the Somervilles and their friends, as if they were jars of candy in a general store. Then that thought faded. The man who had been standing slightly behind Fetchit came into full view.

Daisy brought her hand swiftly to her throat to ease down the gulp. Handsome had found a new face to adorn. His features weren't exactly perfect, but so close, his face stunned: angular but not thin, strong-jawed, high cheekbones, smooth brown skin, and penetrating dark eyes. So intense was his gaze, she could feel it even from a distance. But what was he doing looking at her? The light-skinned woman was hanging on his arm now.

Daisy quickly turned away, busying herself with brass banisters. Only to risk another glimpse and be rewarded with a smile that beamed like a thousand electric bulbs.

Her father would hate him for that alone.

Lord. She needed to stop. This was how Henrietta behaved around boys. Not Daisy.

Tearing her gaze away, she moved herself and the bucket of water to a corner of the step and tried to appear small as she dug in her apron pocket for her notepad and pencil. When she was sure she couldn't be seen, she scribbled a few notes and strained her ears, hoping to catch the names of the handsome young man she'd never seen before.

It took a minute, but she learned his name was Barnes — she didn't catch his occupation or confirm whether it was his first or last name. The woman she thought was Fredi Washington was an actress named Veronica Fontaine, and she wasn't just light-skinned. She was white. Jack Johnson was known for his attraction to such women (all his wives were white), but this one wasn't his wife. That would be according to Daisy's recollection of the last photo she'd seen in the *Eagle* featuring him and Mrs. Johnson.

"Young lady," Dr. Vada called. "Chambermaid."

Daisy glanced around, expecting to find Yvette nearby, tripping over herself, attempting to respond to Dr. Vada. But unless Daisy had gone partially blind, Yvette had disappeared.

"Chambermaid?" Dr. Vada had climbed a few steps and was close.

"Yes, ma'am," Daisy replied, beginning to rise.

"Our group has decided to have coffee on the roof by the pool instead of the dining room." She gestured to her guests with a delicately gloved hand. "Could you please inform Mrs. Keyes?"

"I will, Dr. Somerville."

Just then, Yvette appeared on the staircase, smiling brightly, her lips rosy and her cheeks flushed. Daisy's jaw dropped. Unbelievably, her friend had slipped away to put on rouge and lipstick. Now, trying to make a grand entrance, she was descending the stairs and an inch away from ending up with her foot in the bucket. Quickly, Daisy grabbed the handle of the bucket, trying to get it out of Yvette's path. But instead, the bucket tipped over.

Water spilled down the steps, covering the front of Daisy's uniform, but more agonizing were the huge drops of soapy water that splashed Vada Somerville's dress and her pale blue pumps and shiny silk stockings.

Daisy froze. What had she done? "I'm so

84

sorry." She picked up a rag and, scampering down the few steps that separated them, dropped to her knees in front of Dr. Vada, sopping up the mess on the landing. She started to wipe off the woman's dress, stockings, and shoes but stopped before she humiliated herself further.

The lobby was silent, a body could've dropped from the ceiling, and no one would've moved or spoken. The numbing quiet didn't last long, though. A man's deep laugh tore through the room. Daisy glanced up to see who was making fun of her, and sure enough, the handsome young man was the one grinning and whispering into Dr. Somerville's ear. If he turned to the white woman, Daisy would've screamed, but he didn't. He moved on to say something to Jack Johnson and Mrs. Bass. And, again, the group smiled, except for Dr. Vada in the lace dress, and when he finished his joke at Daisy's expense, the Somervilles and Betty Hill, and Charlotta Bass, a humorless woman from all accounts, burst into boisterous laughter. Even the white woman giggled into her gloved palm.

"My shoes are fine," Dr. Vada said, smiling down at Daisy, waving her lace-gloved hand. "Not to worry, dear. Only a pair of old shoes and old stockings."

Nothing Vada Somerville wore looked old. And once Mrs. Keyes heard about the watery mishap, Daisy could lose her job. And if that happened, well, she refused to think about it.

A pair of white leather lace-up oxfords stepped within her view, and a deep male voice said, "Next time you save a friend from a tumble, make sure you move the bucket the other way."

The young man's deep-set eyes twinkled with humor. Who did he think he was? Why embarrass her further? She was already mortified, couldn't he tell?

"Malcolm, come along now," said Dr. Vada to the young man who was making fun of Daisy. "John, where should we go next?"

"The grand hall. The NAACP meeting will take place there next week. It's a brilliant room."

After a few glances of sympathy directed at Daisy, the group departed. But as they walked away, she overheard Dr. Vada call the man who had made fun of Daisy *Mr. Barnes.* Joe Johnson called him *Malcolm,* and Dr. John added *the architect.* However, learning his name and occupation didn't ease her pain.

"Damn." Yvette's voice startled her. "I

can't believe I blew it, or you blew it for me."

"I could strangle you."

"I'm the one who lost out," Yvette said. "Mrs. Somerville will remember you."

"As a clumsy ox."

"It wasn't that bad."

"We'll see about that," said Mrs. Keyes, swooping onto the landing from God knows where. Had she been watching all along? Waiting for Mrs. Somerville's departure before pouncing?

"It was an accident," Daisy explained.

"We'll see what Mrs. Somerville has to say when I meet with her this afternoon. Now, I must arrange coffee on the roof." She strutted off.

Daisy spun toward Yvette. "I'd better not get fired."

Chapter 5
Frankie

Friday, May 31, 1968
Chicago

I reach the street level outside the Greyhound bus terminal and exit onto Randolph Street, but I am not crying. I'd thought about it, but that jerk of a ticket agent doesn't deserve my tears. The baby in my belly, on the other hand, deserves to be fed, and I'm hungry. I also need to sit down and rest my brain, or my chicken-hearted soul might board the next Clark Street bus back home.

A few doors from the terminal, a neon sign blinks above the entrance to Toffenetti Restaurant. I walk right by the place. It's too pricey for me, but there's a diner farther down the block.

I step inside and nearly choke on cigarette smoke, but the underlining smell of eggs and sausage on a grill cuts through the cloud.

As much as I want to hurry to the nearest open seat, however, I take inventory of the customers' faces. Hungry or not, I will stay only if some of those faces belong to Negroes. The last thing I need is a run-in with another ticket agent with an attitude or a waitress who, through action or words, needs to express how much they don't like waiting on colored girls.

April 4 was just last month. Some neighborhood storefronts set on fire during the riots after Dr. King's assassination still smolder. The pain is fresh, like a shot deer with a gaping wound. There's too much blood on the ground to ignore.

My survey brings me peace of mind, though. We occupy half the seats, and I hightail it to an empty stool at the counter.

I arrange my luggage next to me and sit. A waitress emerges from the kitchen's swinging doors — dressed in a cinched-waist full skirt, a frilly blouse, collar and sleeves, short ankle socks, and penny loafers. Her skin is so pale, she must use white powder on her face like a circus clown.

She asks what I want. I order black coffee and the cheapest plate of food on the menu — scrambled eggs and toast. The grill cook wears his Chicago Cubs baseball cap backward, trapping his sweat in the cap's elastic band.

I started making up stories when I was bedridden with the poliovirus. And after, when I am upset, they help distract me from whatever fear and pain is beating down on my head.

I am good at it, too. I wrote an entire book in the journals my grandfather brought me. But my mother found them and threw them out without an apology or an explanation. By then, I had recovered from the poliovirus but went back to bed for two days, heartbroken.

After that, I kept my stories locked away in my mind. My story now is about the burly cook in need of a shave.

He is madly in love with the waitress in the fluffy-collared black blouse and alabaster skin.

What else?

A young woman enters the restaurant cradling an infant in one arm and dragging a toddler by the armpit with the other.

Just in time.

I immediately add her to my story — she's the cook's wife.

Their love has died. He isn't ready to be a father. She is unhappy at twenty-two and believes her life is over. Her son, the toddler, is holding a steel spinning top shaped like a funnel. The infant is pulling her hair. I see the pain in her glance — she didn't want the first child, let alone the second.

My stomach tightens. The baby inside me doesn't like this story, and I swallow the rush of nausea in my throat.

I wonder if my baby can tell I don't intend to keep him. Hoping he understands that not wanting to raise a child doesn't mean I won't treat it right while it lives inside me.

The woman with the infant orders her toddler to sit on the stool next to mine. She sits on the one on the other side of him.

"Mama. Mama. Cherry soda. Mama. Cherry soda."

"Not for breakfast," the mother says.

"I want pancakes!" he counters with a squeal.

Then the child spins on the stool and comes scarily close to a tumble. The mother looks at me with a smile and a cry for help in her eyes.

I recognize the expression. When I moved to Chicago four years ago, I became friends with two women who both have small children.

"Mickey, you're gonna crack your head open." The mother says calmly. "He is quite the handful." She looks at me and nods at my Lady Baltimore luggage. "Is that yours? Where are you heading?"

I don't answer, but she doesn't need me to respond. She's one of those birds that sing to herself.

"I'm heading west," she says. "St. Louis first. Maybe farther if things don't go well there." She adjusts the baby in her arms. "I'm tired of this town. Too many dark days, cold nights, and riots. It'll screw with you if you don't watch out."

She moistens her lips and tilts her head. "You didn't tell me where you were going."

Honestly, I don't believe she's noticed that I haven't said a word let alone answered any of her questions.

"Who knows, I may end up in Arizona," she says. "My dad lives there, and he's never seen my boys."

My God, she is persistent — and has guilted me into coming clean: "I don't want to talk."

Without missing a beat, she responds, "That's okay. My friends accuse me of talking enough for everybody." She laughs and scoops up her toddler, making her hip a barrier between him and the floor.

"My oldest boy has been particularly rambunctious since my husband passed. He was killed in February in Vietnam during

92

the Tet Offensive." She licks her upper lip. "He joined the army right after high school graduation. We grew up in the same neighborhood. Most of the boys on our block enlisted around the same time and went overseas together. But my husband, Mickey, he's the only one dead so far." She smiles sadly. "His luck was never that good, anyway. We should've known —"

The waitress interrupts, delivering my plate and a fresh coffee (I hadn't noticed the old cup). She also gives me a look like I've been caught with my hand in the cookie jar. She must've overheard me tell this woman I didn't want to talk, and again, guilt stirs me into action.

"Sorry," I say to the mother. "I'm having a bad day."

"I've had a bad day every day since February fourteenth," she declares. "I got the news about my Mickey on Valentine's Day. Can you believe that? I swear, there've been times when the only thing I could do was run my mouth or lose my mind."

She laughs, and I decide to contribute to the conversation.

"My husband isn't dead, but he was in some part of the South China Sea back in 'sixty-four." I take a sip of my coffee. "He didn't enlist. He was drafted a month before

93

our wedding — and hurt almost as soon as he stepped in the jungle. When he returned home, he was angry, but he'd been mad long before Vietnam. I probably should've left him then."

The mother gestures toward my bags. "What's making you leave him now?"

"What makes you say that?"

"You said he wasn't dead, but I can tell, you wouldn't mind if he were dead. It would solve some problems for you."

"I guess."

"You're about my age — early to mid-twenties." Then, without looking, she grabs her scampering toddler by the wrist, pulling him to her side.

"Twenty-two," I say.

"How long have you been married?"

"Four years."

"If you don't mind me asking, what was the last straw? What finally caused you to make up your mind to split?"

I glance at the baby in her arms and the toddler she holds by the wrist.

"I'm pregnant," I say.

Her eyes soften, and the care in them surprises me. "I'm sorry," she says.

She reminds me of Tamika, juggling problems in the palm of her hands without breaking a sweat. "Oh, God. I didn't tell her I was leaving town."

"Tell who?"

"My cousin Tamika." I pick up my purse. "Is there a pay phone here?"

The waitress points.

"Will you watch my bags?" I say this to the mother of two. "I have to call her."

"No worries. Go on."

The pay phone is near the front door. I pick up the receiver, drop in two dimes, and dial. Tamika should be in her apartment on a Friday morning. In law school at U of C, she volunteers Friday afternoons and didn't schedule any classes Friday mornings.

"Hello?" My cousin picks up the phone.

"Tamika, I need to talk to you. Are you alone?"

"Francine?"

I can barely hear her. "It's me. I need to tell you something."

Her voice drops so low I am struggling to understand, but I think she just said: "Jackson is here, and he's pissed."

"He's in your apartment?"

"I think he got fired today. You should get over here. He's a mess."

"I can't. Just tell him to go home. Don't tell him I'm on the phone."

"He came here looking for you," she says, her voice almost inaudible. "He thinks I'm

95

lying about not knowing where you are. He's drunk and crying, and I can't deal with him, or you, or any of this. Just come on over and take him home. I can't have him in my apartment, behaving like an animal."

She never liked Jackson, and she's not kidding about wanting him gone, but Lord Jesus, I've made it this far, and I can't just go back. Not even for my cousin. Besides, I can still hear Daisy's words in my head, more of a taunt than a plea: *Don't go back to Jackson.*

There's a nasty noise on the other end of the line — angry voices. Jackson is cursing. Tamika is saying something, but mostly I notice her tone. She sounds afraid, and she doesn't scare. That I learned when we were kids at the Inkwell beach, she'll fight a boy. No matter how tall or how many muscles. She'll stand as tall as she can and go toe-to-toe. But she's never been on the bad side of Jackson.

I'm holding the receiver tight against my cheek. I probably will have a bruise, but I am listening to a struggle.

"Is that you, Francine. Baby girl." Jackson has the phone. "Shit went wrong at the job. I don't know what happened. But it's bad. Real bad. I can't handle losing another job. You know that? I ain't had nothing but hard times since high school, honey. I need you, babe. This shit is messing with my mind. I think I'm losing it."

Is he breathing? I can't tell, he talked so fast, but the hurt in his voice touches my heart. I feel sad for him, sorry for him. "Jackson, calm down. Tell me what happened."

"Come home, and I'll tell you everything. It was just that knowing you were so mad at me, again, that you up and left. I lost it." He was hoarse, choking on fear, tears, and frustration. "Where are you, Francine? You at the bus station?"

"I bought a ticket for Los Angeles. I'm leaving today, but I, um, well, I will only be gone for a little while. So you go home, Jackson. Leave Tamika be, and I'll call you tonight. I promise. Then we can talk."

"What do you mean, call me tonight?" The teary, weepy man-voice had vanished. "I want your ass home right now. You understand?"

I find an ounce of courage in the valley of my soul. "No. I'm leaving today. Already purchased my ticket. We can talk on the phone this evening. I'll call you."

There's a loud bang; something struck something hard. I imagine Jackson has slammed his fist into the wall above the telephone.

I hear Tamika's tight voice in the back-ground. "You need to get the hell out of my apartment."

Then he's back on the line. "I'm coming for you." There are no more tears or yelling, only his quiet baritone in a rage. "Right now. And you'd better be at the Greyhound bus terminal. I know that's where your crazy bitch of an aunt dropped you off. Keep your ass there, you hear me? I'm coming for you. Francine. Right the fuck now, and you'd better be there, too."

Click. The line is dead.

I'm shaking so badly I can't put the receiver in the cradle. Blood burns through my veins from my heart to my stomach and into my ankles. I want to run. "Damn it. Damn it. Goddamned it."

"Are you okay?" The waitress in the frilly black blouse appears next to me, but I can't answer. She takes the receiver from my hand, puts it back where it belongs, and passes me a napkin. "Wipe your face, honey. I'll get you a fresh order of eggs and toast."

I stare at her then touch my cheek — my face is soaked with tears.

"I'm sorry. I've got to go." I move to the counter, put two dollars next to my plate of cold, untouched eggs.

98

"Are you okay?" says the mother of two.

"No. No. I'm not." I grab my luggage and hurry out of the diner.

Now, a flood of tears stream from my eyes, blinding me, but I can't stop my feet. I've got to keep moving, running, getting away from him, but I'm stumbling. The damn Lady Baltimore bags are too heavy.

I'm at the crosswalk waiting on the light to turn, but I need to be on the other side. My feet don't want to believe that he is still twenty minutes away. Did the light change? Everything is blurry — too many tears in my eyes. I step off the curb.

I am not watching where I'm going, and the next thing, I hit something, or something hits me and knocks me down. Or did I trip over my luggage?

However it happened, I'm on the ground; half of me is in the gutter, the other half on the curb. Bright white spots flash like electric bugs dancing in front of my eyes.

Then the world blinks — and everything turns black.

CHAPTER 6
DAISY

Summer 1928
Los Angeles

Three hours after the disaster on the stairwell with Dr. Vada, the last thing on Daisy's mind was whether she was employed. She was too busy doing her job.

Two thousand people showed up for the grand opening of the Hotel Somerville, lining the streets, crowding into the courtyard, and pushing into the lobby, whooping and hollering.

Workers had constructed a large square platform in the middle of Central Avenue decorated with banners, flags, and signs, as part of the grand opening celebration. Hollywood motion picture stars and government dignitaries sat in special sections near the stage, sipping from silver flasks and laughing at whatever caught their fancy.

It was a surprising sight, coloreds and whites sitting side by side like it wasn't a

100

once-in-a-blue-moon kind of day.

The speeches began at noon, and Daisy slipped outside for a few minutes to listen. The mayor, city council members, and Los Angeles's Negro elite offered a steady flow of praise for the hotel and the couple who had made it happen. When Dr. John gave his speech, humbly accepting the praise, he also reminded the audience that Somerville Finance and Investment was offering stock to the public for ten dollars a share to help finance the $250,000 project. Somerville stated emphatically that the goal was to always keep ownership, financing, and management within the Race.

Daisy hadn't felt such joy in so long; it frightened her. Feeling good was like a mountain moving toward her faster than a locomotive, and she couldn't get out of its way. There would be no sadness or hurt holding onto the pencil in her hand or the words in her mind.

Daisy didn't want to leave the celebration, but once the doors opened, so many people checked in to the hotel, every one of the eighty rooms was full before afternoon tea. By early evening, her feet were numb, and her back ached.

But when Mrs. Keyes caught up with her and Yvette on the fourth floor and asked if the two girls could work an extra shift, they both agreed.

"I still need to have a word with you, Daisy, about the incident with Dr. Somerville, but first, I must drop these off," Mrs. Keyes said, holding a bouquet of white roses. She loved sprucing up a room with fresh flowers and scented candles and was on her way to deliver them to one of the suites. "I'll catch up with you later."

As Mrs. Keyes departed, Daisy groaned. "She might still fire me."

"No, she won't. She asked us to work *another* shift. Would she do that and then fire you?"

"You tell me." Daisy glanced at the wall clock. She'd nearly forgotten her appointment. "I need a break. I'll be back in a few minutes. If Mrs. Keyes returns, make up some excuse for my absence, please."

Yvette's eyes widened. "Are you serious? You can't disappear and leave me to do your work and mine."

Daisy twisted her mouth into a frown. Since Yvette seemed disagreeable, she'd have to resort to what often worked with her friend — begging. "Pretty please. Sugar on top? It's been a long day, and now we've got another shift. I need a short break for a breath of fresh air. I'll be right back."

Yvette rolled her eyes but added a last-second smile. "Okay. Okay. But hurry up. My turn next. I could use a break, too."

Daisy dashed down the hall and toward the staircase. Before she hit the top flight, she slipped her hand into her tea apron's pocket, touching her notepad and pencil. She had wanted to tell Yvette what she was up to weeks ago, when they worked long hours, day in and day out, preparing the hotel for the opening. But, as close as they were, this was something Daisy couldn't share with her. Could never share with her. Could never share with anyone, especially someone who worked at the Hotel Somerville.

The quickest path to the courtyard was through the lobby. Although the hotel staff usually went through the alley, Daisy was late and willing to risk the lobby.

It was packed. Hotel guests, celebrities, other important people — she had never seen so much silk, rhinestone-encrusted cloches, and dangling pearl necklaces.

Still, she had to be careful and avoid being stopped by people asking her to fetch something, fix something, or "take these items up to my room."

Fingers crossed, she stayed away from the

merriment best she could, hugging the wall and slipping behind the grand piano and the potted palms. Her plan was working, too, until a trio of slang-talking men, likely jazz musicians, in loose-fitting suits forced her to halt.

Guzzling bootleg hooch from shiny flasks and smoking fat cigars, they flashed red-rimmed eyes and toothy smiles between demanding Daisy bring them another round of drinks. With no other choice, she started for the bar, but three flappers in low-cut (front and back) jade chemises and glittery jewelry grabbed the men's attention. Quickly, the musicians waved for another maid and ordered drinks for six, having forgotten about Daisy.

On the move again, she only had a few more feet to travel to reach outdoors where the young man she was meeting would be waiting. But someone grabbed her hand.

"Slow down, Daisy. It's just me, wanting to say I've missed you."

She recognized the voice of the man she was supposed to meet but kept moving. Harry Belmont should know better than to stop her while she was still inside the hotel. Someone might see them.

"Come on, Daisy. There's no need to run. I'm not a guest at the hotel. Too pricey for a hardworking Joe like me."

Daisy faced him, but her gaze moved around the room. "Of course, a Joe like you wouldn't spend a buck fifty a night for a hotel room. That's too cheap," she said in a low voice. "You like the ritz and the glamour of the Beverly Hills Hotel or the Biltmore. If coloreds were allowed to sleep there, you'd check in with bells on."

He released her hand and, gesturing for her to walk ahead of him, said softly, "I don't wear bells, babe, but you could. You look swell in anything, even a paper bag, sugar."

He stayed close and kept talking as Daisy maneuvered by him.

"I like the way that maid's uniform fits a girl with your . . ." He paused and, blocking her path, gave her a head-to-toe leer.

Daisy didn't squirm until he breathed the word *talents*.

"Ugh," she exclaimed with a shudder, but her smile wasn't far behind. They'd known each other since high school, but he was three grades ahead of her and Yvette. A reporter first, last, and always, Harry was ambitious, tenacious, clever, and one of the best writers in the city as far as Daisy was concerned. When he asked her to be his "eyes and ears" inside the Hotel Somerville,

105

she didn't think to refuse him. It might not be something she bragged about, spying on hotel guests, but she needed the money to help her mother, and she liked it.

"Don't kid a kidder, Harry. You are the one who wanted to meet. And I have no clue why."

"Should we bet on that, darling?"

"A bet? I shouldn't be surprised." They had made it to the middle of the courtyard, near the fountain, but Daisy gestured for them to move behind two large potted palms. "You always bring gambling into a conversation. Why is that?"

"Because I'm a betting man," he said.

She chuckled. Harry had never made a truer statement. "Yes, you are a betting man, but I know the real you, too."

"This is the real me, doll." He spread his arms wide, palms up, very dramatic.

Daisy waved her hand. "You're blocking my view."

Harry bowed his long frame and dropped his arms to his sides.

Daisy removed her notes from her apron pocket. "There's not much here. But I expect a lot more now that we're open." She looked around the courtyard, the smell of roses and lilies calming her. "But this can't be the reason you insisted upon meeting.

On a day like today, after all."

"You were never one to dillydally." He stuffed the note into his vest pocket. "I have news." He grinned. "I am the first colored reporter with permission to work on a Hollywood studio lot."

"Well, isn't that the bee's knees," she said tightly, fearing her side job might be in danger.

Harry continued excitedly. "I'll have access to all of the Negro actors, extras — and now with talkies, they'll be making shorts with colored musicians, dancers, and singers."

"Will you still need me?" She sounded desperate but couldn't help herself. "I need the money, Harry. You know that."

He took a step back, shock lining his brow. "I absolutely still need you. You're my gal, and I want this column to shine, which means it must have the latest, greatest gossip and facts on Black actors, actresses, musicians, even the country's Negro elite, all of whom will be staying at the Somerville. And you will keep me in the know."

She exhaled with relief, but Harry's eyes twinkled with something devilish. "That's great, but what else? What more is on your mind?"

"Nothing much, except this will mean

more business for you, dear." He smiled and winked, suddenly staring past her, checking the courtyard for what? Or was it who? "You're a chambermaid on the fourth floor, too, right?"

"How do you know that?"

"I just do." His wide grin annoyed her.

"Come on, Harry. No games, please. I am supposed to be working. My short break isn't so short."

"But you work on the fourth floor, and that's where the tenants will reside. Those wealthy indulgent Negro few who will move in and call the hotel home."

"Yeah." Some of them had moved in that day, but most were expected over the weekend. Daisy hadn't bothered to check reservations for the names. But judging by the smirk on his face, Harry had.

"There's one Hollywood star moving in. I need you to keep both eyes and all ears on." He tucked his chin down. "I'll pay you twice as much for any information you get on him."

Her stomach clenched. "What's the name?"

"Lincoln Perry."

Now, the back of her neck was suddenly hot. "The comedian Stepin Fetchit? He's moving in here?"

"Yes, he is. Check with your front desk, Daisy." This grin was so wide it showed his gums.

"I'm betting he'll be the biggest Black Hollywood movie actor of the decade," he said. "The rumors are spreading already. Stepin Fetchit will be the first colored actor to sign an extended contract with a major studio. No one-time deals for him. I heard Fox Hills Studios is floating the contract."

"I hadn't heard." Why would she? Motion pictures weren't her cup of tea. That was Henrietta's dream, Lord knows. And Stepin Fetchit wasn't someone Daisy spent time thinking about.

"You want the assignment or not, babe? You're my first choice." Harry lifted an eyebrow. "But if you aren't interested, there are others I can work with."

"I didn't say I wasn't interested." Daisy had socked away some money, but not enough. With the cash she'd get from Harry, she'd have enough money for her mother in a couple of months — unless Sophie got better. Then, Daisy would have money to return to school.

"How much more cabbage to spy on Mr. Perry?"

"You bring me as much as you can on Stepin Fetchit that I can use — how about two dollars?"

Daisy bit her lip. It was more money than she expected. Now, she made a dollar or two a week, according to what Harry used in the society column. The *Eagle* paid him about eight bucks a column but he wrote a sports column, news column, the society column and now Hollywood. "For Perry alone?"

He nodded.

She and Harry had almost worked together a while back. Still, she'd learned something new about him. Something she hadn't known in high school — he wasn't always a scrupulous man. But he was one man she wouldn't judge. Not when she had goals, too.

"Let's be clear," she said. "I'll still be paid for my regular notes on the latest goings on at the hotel for the society columns. Correct?"

"Same deal. A dollar for any scoop that appears in the *Eagle*."

She nodded. "Okay, Belmont. It all sounds jake to me."

After meeting with Harry, Daisy chatted with Mrs. Keyes and miraculously, still had a job.

An hour later, she found Yvette and apologized, making feverish promises to watch her baby and cook Sunday dinner (Yvette rolled her eyes). But she didn't yell at her when Daisy had to let her sister and the family's new boarder, Isaiah, know she wouldn't be walking home with them.

"Another eight-hour shift?" Isaiah sat on the bench at the long table in the basement staff room.

"More like ten more hours. I'm on call overnight," Daisy explained.

Isaiah frowned. "Sorry, I don't mean to pry, but why would they ask you to work that many hours?"

A laughing Henrietta hit the table with the side of her hand. "You didn't hear? Daisy spilled half a bucket of water on Mrs. Somerville."

"It wasn't half a bucket." Heat rushed to her face chased by annoyance. "Why don't you just clam up, Henrietta."

Isaiah folded his hands on the table. "You spilled water on Mrs. Somerville, the wife of Dr. Somerville, the hotel's namesake and builder?"

"It's not Mrs. Somerville, it's Dr. Somerville. They are both doctors," Daisy corrected him.

"Everyone was talking about it. They thought she'd lose her job," Henrietta said,

111

without a hint of concern for her sister's misfortune.

"Well, let's see how you fare facing off with Papa without me there after what happened this morning." Daisy raised an eyebrow, reminding Henrietta that her day hadn't started so well, either.

"Are you sure you don't want us to stay and help you?" Isaiah asked.

Daisy stared at him. "Well, aren't you thoughtful." She glared at Henrietta. "But you don't know anything about housekeeping."

Henrietta shrugged. "She's right, Isaiah. You don't, but I do. I'll stay and help."

"No. I can handle it. Besides, Henrietta, you need to make sure Isaiah gets home."

"I know my way back to your house. Fifteen blocks that way on Central Avenue." He pointed. "And a block and a half that way to Naomi Avenue."

Henrietta grinned. "You paid attention."

"I always pay attention."

Daisy mimicked one of her father's stern expressions. "And now, I'm putting my foot down. Go home, both of you." She placed her hands on her hips. "I'll see you tomorrow."

CHAPTER 7
FRANKIE

Friday, May 31, 1968
Chicago

I wake up in a hospital emergency room. I can tell where I am by the sounds — metal wheels on linoleum and hurried footfalls, loud voices, male and female, at different heights of agitation, urgency, and fear — a cough, a groan, a scream.

I go to roll onto my side, but a sharp pain stops me. Panic runs through me.

The pregnancy.

Did something happen to the baby? I am trembling and panting and can't catch my breath. Something sizable sits on my chest. Did I hurt my unborn child?

Oh, Lord. This motherly fear is suffocating. I can't stand the crippling guilt; what did I do wrong? I can't even blame Jackson. This is on me, and the twisting pain squeezing my heart is my fault.

Each breath feels like I'm pumping air

113

into a flat tire.

Then I notice it's not my stomach that hurts but my arm.

What in the hell did I do to myself?

Loud voices on the other side of the drawn curtain grab my attention. A woman is cursing up a storm, demanding immediate treatment of her daughter and her injuries.

If I were that doctor or nurse or whoever she is yelling at, I might do what the woman asked me to do — to keep her quiet. She sounds fierce, formidable, relentless — a bunch of words that mean the same thing — but I can barely keep my thoughts inside my head. My arm hurts.

The curtain suddenly opens. Daisy waltzes into the room and sits in the folding chair between the scale and the medicine cart.

How did she get here? How did I get here? I have no idea. "What happened, Aunt Daisy?"

"You fell."

"I fell?" I don't understand what she means. I was at the diner, talking to a girl with two kids, and then I called Tamika on the pay phone, and I remember Jackson was with her, yelling at me, threatening me, making me cry.

"I didn't fall. I hit the ground but not because I fell." I rub my brow when the realization hits. "You hit me — with your car."

"That's not exactly true, dear." The corner of her red-lipped mouth twitches. "And you should hush, anyway. You want everyone in the hospital to hear you?"

Daisy crosses her leg. "One of these busybody nurses might misunderstand and call the police or some such nonsense. And cops ask too many damn questions." She removes a lace handkerchief from her pocket and dabs her brow. "I can't afford another run-in with the police."

"Did you break my arm?"

"I didn't hit you. You ran into my car like you were a bull in a china shop. You hit us — I mean me." She uncrosses her leg and stands, hands on her hips, jaw as rigid as knotted rope. "Calm yourself, and I'll tell you what happened."

She glances around the empty, curtained room. "I didn't hit you with my car. You stepped into the street and stumbled into the passenger-side door. The car was barely moving. If at all."

"But it hurts."

"Doctor said you have a few strained muscles and tendons and something with your shoulder. Nothing too serious. You'll have to keep it still for a few days."

My nerves are jumping. Daisy isn't telling

me the whole story, and I don't like looking up at her from my prone position. I go to push myself upright, but I can't. "Help me."

In one step, she is at my side. As soon as I'm upright, I raise my good arm (my left arm and shoulder hurt too badly to budge). "Okay, I'm up. Now, let me go."

Daisy steps back.

"What time is it?"

"A little after twelve," she says. "The nurse will return soon to put a sling on your arm. It'll keep your shoulder in place for a few days."

I'm still worried about my pregnancy, but I don't want to mention the baby to Daisy. "You sure I only hurt my arm?"

"That's what the doctor told me."

We wait in silence for a few minutes, but eventually, the curtain opens, and a nurse enters with a cart, cloth, and some clips. She puts my arm in a sling. My fingers can barely form a fist. I won't be able to manage my luggage. Or run if I need to.

After the nurse leaves, Daisy removes a pack of cigarettes from her purse. "Jackson may be on his way here."

"What?" My body stiffens, and something sucks the air from my lungs. "How? Why?"

"Calm down. I said *may be* on his way."

"Why would you say that? Did you

116

call him?"

"I didn't call him." Daisy wets her lips. "He's on your ID and medical card. Jackson is your emergency contact. I thought I'd convinced that bug-eyed nurse I was your mother, and your husband didn't need to be contacted, but she didn't buy it."

"Did they reach him? Is he on his way?"

"Do you want to stick around to find out?" She flicks cigarette ashes into a paper cup and rubs the corner of her mouth with a fingernail.

"What is it?" I ask, sensing there's something more on her mind.

"The nurse says you're pregnant. Is that true?"

I don't see any point in lying. "Yes. I am. Did someone tell Jackson? Does he know?"

Daisy snorts. "Probably. That's what doctors and nurses do. Tell your damn business to every soul on the planet. Have no respect for a woman's privacy. No respect whatsoever." The last part she says loud enough for half the hospital to hear.

"God. If he knows I'm pregnant —" I pause and try to swallow. "He'll come after me for sure."

"I thought he was coming after you no matter what." Daisy hooks her purse over her arm and grits her teeth before letting

117

out a chest full of air. "You could come with me to Los Angeles. It won't be a direct trip. I have stops to make. But I feel slightly — and let me emphasize — only slightly, responsible for your condition although, we — I mean I — didn't hit you with the car. You fell. You understand?"

I stare at her. "I don't believe you."

"About what? My invitation for you to come with me to LA, or that you fell?" She starts for the door as the nurse walks in. "Either way, I need to split."

The nurse pulls back the curtain and walks in. "Here's your prescription for Percodan. I have a pill for you to take now — it will stave off the pain until you get this filled. Careful with this medication. It will make you drowsy." She drops the pill from a paper cup into my palm and passes me another paper cup full of water. I take the medicine.

Having been pushed to the corner, Daisy speaks up. "Is she done?" She asks the nurse.

"She has to sign some paperwork, release forms. So, when you are ready, stop by the front desk."

"Then we can go?" Daisy asks.

The nurse nods and retreats the way she came.

As the curtain closes behind her, I glare at Daisy. "I don't believe you and I thought you had to split?"

"I decided to give you a moment to consider my offer."

Her expression is blank as if to have me believe she could care less either way. How does she manage that cool, aloof exterior? It's the opposite of the hard-talking, chain-smoking, marijuana-smoking woman who has been with me all morning.

Can I handle two thousand miles of taking orders from Daisy? She's the kind of woman who says what's on her mind without a filter: first thought, first words out of her mouth, she runs with them.

Then add that she looks like a model, thin-waisted, delicately curvy hips, and a perfect curly flip that is more Dorothy Dandridge in *Carmen Jones* than my Jackie O. hairstyle.

Everything is a good look on her. Nothing will ever look that good on me.

A weeklong drive? It will throw off Jackson — me traveling west in a car instead of on a bus. During the long ride, Daisy and I could become chatty, and maybe I'll learn what happened between her and my mother.

Maybe, by the time we arrive in Los Angeles, I'll know what I want to do about the baby.

Meanwhile, Jackson won't have a clue about where to find me. He might even give up. It could happen.

I take a deep breath. Eyes wide open. Chest lifted. Chin up. I must not think like a fool — Jackson will be looking for me, especially if he finds out I'm pregnant. Riding with Daisy might be my best bet on avoiding Jackson with my hurt left arm — until I reach Los Angeles.

"Okay, Daisy. It's a deal. I'm coming with you."

After filling my prescription at a drugstore a block from the hospital, I'm in the Mustang with Daisy driving. Pulling away from the curb, she presses down on the accelerator and speeds down the street, making the tires scream. She doesn't slow down until she reaches the corner and makes a sharp turn toward Jackson Boulevard and Lake Shore Drive, and Route 66.

I know this is the way to Joliet. I got that far the last time I ran from Jackson.

"Are you going to slow down?" I ask, eyeballing the speedometer.

"We start fast. We stay fast."

I clutch the armrest. I feel dizzy and faint. "Could you slow down, please?"

Daisy laughs. "Don't worry. I'm a good driver. We keep moving. We won't get caught."

"Who's chasing us?" The dizziness is borderline hallucinogenic, not that I have ever tripped, but the Percodan is messing with me. "Are you talking about Jackson?" I turn as much as I can to look out the rear window. "He drives a LeSabre. I don't see a LeSabre."

"You are high as a kite. Close your eyes and sleep. Let that medicine do its job."

"You didn't answer me. Is it Jackson? Who's going to catch us?"

"Pigs. Illinois State Police. Every other state police from here to LA. We see any pigs. We outrun 'em."

Did I hear her right? My ears are stuffed with cotton. "What did you say about the police?"

"I don't like coppers. And if one of 'em tries to stop me, they'll be in for a surprise."

I open and close my eyes, wanting to make sure she's there and not my imagination. "I don't have a great love for the police myself," I say. "But I am extremely, singularly, afraid you are serious."

"I said close your eyes and rest, Frankie. I'll wake you up when necessary. Relax. You've had a tough morning."

121

She's right. It's difficult to keep my eyes open, but I had a story to tell her about when I called the cops on Jackson. "They don't care too much about a woman getting beaten to death."

"Who does these days, honey?"

"Cops," I say aggressively, feeling as if my blood is on fire. I'm stunned by how Daisy looks at me as if I don't make sense. "Yes, I said cops. They want to calm everyone down. It's a domestic dispute — which means none of their business. The police captains' rule–it's a beef between husband and wife, not a patrolman's job to interfere, other than to make sure they are mellow." I wipe my mouth. "Daisy, I need to use the bathroom."

She pushes her sunglasses up on her nose and glares at me with an abundance of judgment. "How about you hold it until we're farther out of the city."

I chew on the inside of my cheek. "I'll try, but I can't make any promises."

"Look in the glove compartment," Daisy asks while reaching over and popping open the compartment. Impatient woman. She is sorting through the papers and packs of cigarettes with only one hand on the steering wheel. That makes me nervous.

"What are you searching for?" My life

could be in jeopardy, I realize, as some of the drug haze settles. "You tell me what it is, and I'll find it."

"My *Green Book,*" she replies, agitated. "Do you see it?"

I move her hand out of the way. "You drive. I'll look."

She slaps my hand. "Do you know what you're looking for?"

"I know what a *Green Book* is — the Negro motorist guide that they stopped printing four years ago. Remember the Civil Rights Act of 1964?" My sarcasm surprises me, but I go with it, blaming the Percodan. "Afro Americans can travel anywhere we want these days. We don't have to patronize only the Black-friendly services listed in that old guide."

"And I bet you believe everything you read in a newspaper. I thought you were smarter than that," Daisy gripes. "The world has shown us its colors. Most people who matter to the Negro, who can make a difference to Black lives, are murdered. I don't trust one damn thing promised to me by the United States of America. Nor any damn thing written in a newspaper, unless it's a Black-owned newspaper."

Daisy huffs. "That's why I trust my *Green Book* and, on occasion, the good Lord,

123

when I'm on the road."

"Here it is." I remove the pamphlet. "Now what?"

"Search for a roadside store with a restroom and a gas pump."

An hour or so later, we stop at a place in Daisy's book. I run from the car like snakes are chasing me, but I don't wet myself, although it's a close call.

When I finish and return to the car, I peek inside the gas station. They sell Ruffles potato chips, candy bars, and Tab. Daisy offers to pay, and I load up.

"Why are you heading to Los Angeles?" I ask for no reason I can think of, which means it must be the drug. "I mean, you haven't been to LA since when? The 1920s?"

"I'm not going back to Los Angeles. It's just where I'll end up after I finish my business." Daisy rests her elbow on the rolled-down car window. "Are you going home to have your baby? How's your mother? Is she doing all right? You know sickness runs in the family, the women in the family."

That is quite a string of questions and I'm unsure if I'll answer any of them. Mainly, I won't answer the one about my mother's health and skip any discussion on my return to her house. "You should go see her. Black sheep of the family or not."

Daisy flicks her cigarette butt out the window. "I am not the black sheep — a black sheep is invited to family funerals, weddings, and baptisms. I never receive invitations. I'm the relative you hide from the children and the in-laws." She lights a fresh cigarette. "I'm the family secret."

"That's a lie."

"I have many faults, Frankie, but I do not lie."

"You were invited to Grandpa's funeral, and you didn't come."

"I received a phone call. Not an invitation, and how is that a lie?" she asks, her voice gravel. "Now, go to sleep. That painkiller got your brain in a fog and your mouth running overtime. I'll wake you when we get to where we're going."

"Some place in St. Louis is where we're headed, right?"

"Yes, I found a place for us to stay." Daisy points to the *Green Book.* "We just need to make a stop first. That's all."

CHAPTER 8
DAISY

Summer 1928
Los Angeles

In the kitchen on Naomi Avenue, Daisy stood over the stovetop, watching a pot of water boil. She had waited hours for her father to pull into the gravel driveway. Now, it was almost dawn, and still, he wasn't home. Determined to keep her eyes open until he showed, she made a fresh pot of Maxwell House. She'd stay up as long as necessary.

The morning disagreement that included her father slapping her sister's face had frightened Daisy, but her father had a quick temper. More so since her mother took ill.

Hot embers burned close to the ground until the wind stirred, shooting flames toward the sky. That was her father's temper: fire.

Daisy had asked her mother why he got so mad. Sophie explained a man like him had to wear a false face when he left home for work. He was only his true self with his family.

"So, he's an actor," Daisy had said, thinking she was clever.

Her mother replied, "Every Negro in America is an actor."

Her father chauffeured Alfred Lunt, a wealthy, white motion picture producer, who paid him a wage, of course, but Lunt didn't treat him with respect. That bothered him mightily. There was always so much sadness in her mother's eyes when she spoke of her husband's disappointments and pain.

Daisy couldn't understand what her mother had meant on those Saturday afternoons. As they cleaned the house, she talked of Negro hardships and what white men did to make colored men feel less.

Then she heard the car pull into the driveway. She poured herself a cup of coffee, grabbed a biscuit from the cookie jar, and sat in the chair at the kitchen table to wait.

It would take her father a few minutes. He always washed and cleaned the limo before coming inside.

"Hi, Daisy."

Her hand jerked, knocking her cup and

spilling coffee on the table. The voice had come from a dark corner of the porch. "You startled me, Isaiah."

"Sorry." Standing in between the hall and the kitchen, he held his guitar.

"What are you doing up this early? It's not even four o'clock."

Dressed in overalls and an undershirt, he stepped forward, hugging his guitar. "Practicing my music."

"I didn't hear any music."

"I wasn't playing. Just practicing."

"How do you — ?"

"I hear the music in my head." He tapped his temple with his finger. "I've always done that since I was a kid. That way, I don't disturb the household."

She'd only known him a day, but he did have a kind way about him. "When did you start playing?"

"When I was five or six." He laughed softly. "As soon as I could hold a guitar."

She grabbed a dish towel and wiped up the spilled coffee. "You want a cup?" she asked.

He hovered at the edge of the table, gangly and shy, but nodded.

"Then get rid of that guitar and grab some joe but be quick about it. My father will be in the house in a few, and he and I — have some things to discuss."

"I'll hurry," he said quietly.

He placed his guitar carefully in a corner and, a few minutes later, gulped down a cup of black coffee.

"No cream or sugar?"

He shook his head.

"My brother, Clifford, drank black coffee," Daisy said, taking a seat at the table. "The way you do. And he played guitar, too. Played it all day and night."

"You have a brother?"

"I *had* a brother — but he died a long time ago, when we used to live in Texas."

"I'm sorry." Isaiah sat at the table opposite her. "I've never been to Texas. Where did you live?"

"Waco. But if you've never been, don't bother going. They have Jim Crow real bad, and most all the white folks are in the Klan. Things are a hundred times worse there than here."

Her coffee was cold. She rose and poured a fresh cup of Maxwell House while peering out the kitchen window, checking on her father and how much longer he might be.

In the predawn light, she could see that he'd removed his chauffeur's jacket and rolled up his shirtsleeves. He'd be outside for a while longer.

129

Daisy stirred cream and sugar into her coffee. "You chew tobacco, Isaiah?"

"No, ma'am."

"Chew tobacco is what got Clifford killed." She returned to her seat at the table. "He wanted to be like the older boys who chewed tobacco, but he wasn't allowed — he was only eleven."

Daisy stared at the tabletop. There were plenty of scratches on the old table. Years of dropped plates, sharp knives, and hot pots had left their mark. "I keep forgetting you just got here. There are biscuits in the cookie jar."

He was up and back to his seat quickly after grabbing two biscuits from the jar. "Thank you."

He grimaced a smile. "I don't say much no matter where I am or for how long. I usually play my guitar." He glanced at the instrument with love in his eyes.

Her stomach twisted as she remembered. Clifford would've done that, too.

Daisy covered her face with her hands, not to hide tears but to help guide her memory. She wanted to see his smile, his eyes laughing, his dimpled chin. She always remembered her brother more clearly in the dark.

"You okay?" Isaiah asked.

130

"Clifford loved his guitar and his chew," she muttered into her palms. "He even had me help him steal a package once."

She lifted her head and dropped her hands into her lap. "We were at the drugstore near our home in Waco, but not the one in the colored neighborhood. The Tolbert family owned this one."

Daisy wasn't sure why she was telling Isaiah this story, but he was attentive, leaning forward, holding his coffee tin with both hands.

"They were white," he said.

"Oh yeah," she said, nodding. "Clifford had shoved some chew in my pocket, rather obviously, too. Mrs. Tolbert stormed over to us and took hold of my arm and Clifford's ear. She said, 'Show me what you have in your pockets. Right now, you little Black thieves.'

"Clifford jerked free of her grasp. But she held on to my arm, and my brother tried to get her to let go. I felt like a piece of rope in a tug-of-war.

"My arm hurt bad, but Mrs. Tolbert was strong, and I cried out when I heard it snap."

Daisy shut her eyes. "I was screaming, and my brother was yelling, begging her to stop hurting me. But she'd hear none of it."

131

Daisy rubbed a hand over her mouth. "I was crying bloody murder. But then Clifford did the silliest thing. He kicked her in the shin. Hard, too. Then he called her a witch. A white witch and punched her in the gut. She let go of me then."

"My goodness," Isaiah said. "He did what he had to do to protect his sister. He was a hero."

"Right. An eleven-year-old colored hero. A whole bunch of them in Texas." She pressed her lips together to keep them from trembling. "We ran home, told our parents what had happened. Papa gave Clifford what for, but he didn't get a whipping. They had to take me to the doctor. The white witch had broken my arm."

Daisy took a deep breath. The rest of the tale was the tricky part. "A day later, Clifford never came home from school. A week after that, his body was found floating in White Rock Creek." She massaged the bridge of her nose. "Everyone knew what had happened, and everyone knew the men who had killed him. They owned the grocery store, worked at the mill, the usual white men who killed an eleven-year-old boy for punching a white woman who broke his sister's arm."

Isaiah's lips twisted.

"We moved away from Waco, Texas, the day after Clifford was buried."

"I'm so sorry," Isaiah said.

"Don't be sorry. Just don't play your guitar when I'm home. I hate the sound of guitar music in the house."

"That's a sad story my daughter just told you, boy."

"Papa," Daisy said with a gasp, surprised to see him in the doorway, despite expecting him.

He walked across the kitchen to the sink, turned on the faucet, rinsed his hands, and splashed water on his face. He then picked up a dish towel and dried off. All the while, he talked.

"She left out the part where it was her idea to steal the chew because she wanted a candy bar. Clifford never would've gone in that drugstore unless his baby sister hadn't begged him to do so. He knew better than to mess around in the Tolberts' store. He knew what kind of woman Mrs. Tolbert was. Isn't that right, Daisy?"

His eyes fastened in on her, and the deep creases surrounding them cinched his narrow gaze and swallowed her whole. She hated her father's eyes, eyes that judged, sentenced, and punished her. That part of the story he'd just told was the part she tried not to remember. But it was true. Clifford had adored his baby sister and would do whatever she asked him to do. That Daisy could never forget, and her father would never let her, no matter how much she hurt.

Anguish filled her chest and emptied her lungs, but he wasn't wrong. "Yes, Papa. You're right, Papa."

And the truth was a worm with teeth.

Isaiah left the kitchen so fast, Daisy could still see the trail of him in the air. But she applauded his common sense.

"What are you doing up?" Her father said, standing at the counter, pouring a cup of coffee. "Go back to bed. I don't want to talk about what happened yesterday morning. If you are here to apologize for Henrietta, I do not wish to hear it. A child of mine will not disrespect their mother."

"I don't want to talk about Henrietta," she said, almost adding *not exactly* under her breath.

"You don't? Good." He gulped down his coffee and immediately poured another. "I've had a long hard day and no interest in anything but rest."

Exhaustion wrapped around him like a blanket too thick to fold. The lines around

134

his mouth were caverns, and his pupils floated in a reddish-brown lake instead of white clouds.

It was how colored men showed tired, her mother had said, bone-deep and decades-old. They dragged themselves home, barely conscious, more like death than a man.

Still, Daisy's sympathy was shaded by her unhappiness. His words about her brother had cracked her heart apart, leaving her broken and bloody. She felt ill.

But then it came to her. Maybe, he hadn't meant her harm. He'd spoken to her kindly just now, hadn't he? Maybe there was something else on his mind?

"What happened today, Papa? You can tell me. I can listen."

He walked from the counter, coffee in hand, and sat opposite her. "White people can do or say anything they please." He gritted his teeth and exhaled loudly. "I hate them for that. But now, I must also put up with the colored boys who just started making money and think hanging around with whites makes them better than the rest of us — those are the ones I can't stand. Those are the ones who canonize men like Mulholland, who build things, only for them to fall. Still, they are treated like gods.

"I never want to see what I saw tonight

again." He pointed his cup at Daisy. "You know who had the loudest mouth? Lincoln Perry. They say he's moving into the Somerville. Did you know? He and his bunch of yahoos are the worst of the lot. They had the nerve to harass the colored chauffeurs and maids, and any colored working man or woman who wasn't them."

He shook his head. His lips curled in disgust. "Young rich Black boys, prancing around like dandies, with girls so light-skinned, I think some of them are white. Hanging on to colored boys like they are prize ponies. With that fancy hotel's doors open, you're going to see a lot of things, Daisy. But I don't ever want to see you or Henrietta associating with that lot, especially that damn comedian — Stepin Fetchit. He's a show-off with his women, cars, and clothes, him and his running-about-town crowd.

"I'm telling you — if I ever see either one of my girls near any of them, I'll put you out on the street. You hear me?"

"Yes, sir."

"I mean it, Daisy." His voice rose sharply. "They are evil, and I swear to God — I won't let you in this house."

"Don't worry, Papa. I don't socialize with anyone."

It wasn't a lie. She'd never be in the same social circles as Lincoln Perry or his apparent friend, Malcolm Barnes. Her brief introduction to him hadn't been pleasant. So, what she'd said was positively, absolutely, nothing but the truth.

She'd swear to the Father, the Son, and the Holy Ghost.

She sat stiffly across from her father, watching him sip his coffee and thinking about what to say next. What should she do? Her plan had crumpled, but then he spoke.

"Why do you leave out the part about the candy? It's always only the chew. You'd tell your mother the story the same way — she never corrected it or you." He stood and went for the counter, more coffee, except the pot was empty. He started another. "Isaiah is new to our home but has already seen us at our worst. No point in hiding anything from him."

"Yes, sir." Why was it so hard speaking with him? He had shattered her feelings with his accusations about Clifford. Perhaps she should tell him. But where to begin? "I was six years old, Papa. Six. How can you blame me for Clifford's death? I was a child."

She searched his face, wanting to see he

137

understood — she was a good girl and would be a fine woman like her mother one day. She watched and waited, but so many things were misleading. His steady speech and calm tone, the flinch in his cheek when he'd said Clifford's name, the nostrils that flared too wide when he looked at her. And something more she couldn't pin down. Lately, the rage was always there, painted on his skin, covering him like tar.

"Why are you so mad, Papa?" She leaned forward. "You never hit one of us like that before. Is it because of Mama? Is that why?"

He didn't look at her — just stared at his coffee cup. She lowered her head and went on.

"I can help with Mama, Papa. You take care of the house, and we all pitch in, but I've been working extra shifts and have an idea. Now that the hotel is officially open, I'll be able to work even more hours." Daisy paused to catch her breath but wished she didn't need to breathe. It might give her father a chance to interrupt, but he didn't. "We could have Mama admitted to one of those sanitariums, where she can be cared for around the clock."

Her father was silent, and Daisy panicked. Had he left the room without making a sound? Was the chair across from her empty?

Why was she too afraid to raise her head? Then a noise; he'd shifted in his seat. She looked at him.

"Your mother is not getting better," he said.

Daisy swallowed. "But she will. With the right care and the right doctors, she'll be fine."

"She'll never be the same. You should accept that. As disrespectful as your sister was yesterday morning, she knows. I just didn't like hearing her say it."

Every part of Daisy's body was shaking. "It's not true, Papa. Mrs. Weaver said she ate just fine today. If we put her in a sanatorium, she'll regain most of her strength in a few months. They'll take care of her around the clock, and she'll get better. I know it."

It was as if he hadn't heard her. He leaned back in his chair and rubbed a hand over his mouth. "You know Mrs. Weaver has helped us for months. She's been a godsend, but she's leaving town in December. Heading to Chicago to be with her family."

"That's okay. I'll have enough money by then, Papa. Trust me."

"Daisy. Daisy." His voice was sad, and then, again, he wiped his mouth as if the taste of the words lingered. "Your mother's heart is weak, but she also is sick in her mind."

Daisy shook her head. "She's just sad, Papa. Sad about her brothers and having to stay in bed so much."

He covered his face with hands, then placed them palms down on the table. "Listen to me. Your mother had these bouts of sadness before. After Clifford died, after I came back from the war. You were a child and didn't take heed of when she'd go to her bed for weeks. But I've never seen her this bad before. And if she's not better in her head" — her father jabbed himself in the temple — "I will have her admitted to the state hospital for the mentally ill."

"Papa, no." Daisy's eyes widened. "You can't do that to Mama. Do you know what those places are like? She'll die there." She rose swiftly and, leaning forward, fired her words at her father. "All she needs is the right doctor, the best care, and she'll get better!" She pounded the table with her fist. "Please, Papa. Don't do this. I can raise the money. She can go to a hospital where she'll get better, not worse."

Her father looked away, but she swore his eyes were damp, though his voice didn't waver when he spoke. "Everyone in this house can work twenty-four hours a day, and I'd still have to admit her." He rubbed his eyes with the heel of his hand. "A sanitarium won't help her, Daisy. She's never coming back to us."

Daisy circled the table and held her father's arm. "Don't give up on her, and don't give up on me. Give me until December. I swear I'll have the money and find a place for her by then. December. Please, Papa."

He touched her hand on his arm. "December, then."

CHAPTER 9
FRANKIE

Friday, May 31, 1968
Highway 66, East St. Louis

The sky is a canvas of stars and moonlight. The darkness makes the sports car feel smaller and less connected to the road. We zoom over concrete, and the bumps vanish as the moonlight sweeps across the night sky. On this stretch of road, the scenery moves with the speed of a storm, propelling us forward on an endless dark highway as the eight-track plays Daisy's Laura Nyro cassette.

I close my eyes, hypnotized by the soft wail of the lyrical singer's vocals. I call her style soulful folk, the cut "Billy's Blues."

I must've fallen asleep because I don't remember anything before this moment. But we must've made a pit stop at a gas station. I don't have to go to the bathroom.

The car's headlights shine on a road sign, and Daisy turns the steering wheel. We're getting off the highway.

Daisy is smoking a cigarette. Her lips tremble as she inhales and exhales too quickly. It looks like she thinks the cigarette will disappear between puffs. The butt burns down fast, and she lights up another. The ashes fall, gathering on the skirt of her black-and-white gingham dress.

"What's wrong?" I ask. "Where are we?"

"You fell asleep — we're almost there."

"To the hotel where we're staying to-night?"

"No. I told you I had to make a stop first. Need to pick up some —"

She abruptly pulls onto a side street in a part of town I can't figure out — residential, Black, white, I'm not sure.

I adjust my position, sitting taller in the seat, wincing as I look around — I keep forgetting about my arm.

"Just another few blocks, and we'll be there." Daisy tosses the cigarette out the window and digs in her purse for Lord knows what. Doesn't find whatever it is and starts searching through her box of eight-track tapes that somehow ended up in my lap.

We pull into the parking lot of a Mc-Donald's. Inside, the golden-arches restaurant is deserted. However, we aren't the only ones in the lot. A young blond-haired man, lugging a sizable duffel bag and wearing a bomber jacket over what looks like a dashiki, is truckin' toward Daisy's car.

"Roll up your window," I say nervously to Daisy. "That white man is coming this way." The fear in my voice is not accidental. I'm genuinely frightened. We're in a strange place, a poorly lit parking lot somewhere on the east side of St. Louis, I'm guessing. Not that it matters. Wherever we are, I don't know this white man, and he looks like some hippie freak. Or the return of the Boston Strangler except in East St. Louis.

Daisy wraps her fingers around the steering wheel and hunches forward, eyes narrowing.

The lighting in the parking lot is dim. But why does she need a closer look at the guy before she rolls up a window?

"What are you waiting for, Daisy? Let's get out of here."

Suddenly, she opens the car door, glides right out of the car, and runs — runs across the lot into the white man's outstretched arms.

A strong breeze vacuums the air from my lungs — I am that surprised — and I feel a tightness in my chest as my anger is a medley of what-the-hells, which I then say out loud. "What the hell is going on?"

The odd couple is standing on my side of the car, with a few dozen yards between them and the entrance to the restaurant. So, no one is in the car to answer me, and clearly, neither one of them is thinking about me. Aunt Daisy is hanging on to this man like he's her long-lost puppy, petting his head, squeezing his cheeks, and hugging him hard enough to smash him in two if he wasn't so tall and broad-shouldered.

I am outdone. Someone, namely Daisy, needs to explain what is going on.

Eventually, she unwraps herself from his embrace (he hugged her back with as much enthusiasm as she hugged him) and guides him toward the car. I can't roll up the windows fast enough, not with one arm in a sling. So, here I am, sitting in the car in openmouthed shock.

The car door is still open on the driver's side, and when Daisy reaches the vehicle, it begins.

"Frankie, Frankie, I want you to meet my best friend, Tobias Garfunkel. His last name makes me laugh, too. But call him Tobey. That's what I've called him all his life."

"Hi," he says with a voice deeper than expected — and an oddly familiar one. "Frankie and I have met before, not for-

145

mally; we stood at the top of an escalator side by side."

Darn. I knew I'd seen him before.

Daisy nods vigorously. "Yes, that's right — at the Greyhound bus station. I felt guilty, letting you walk off the way you did. So I sent him inside to give you a hand with your luggage."

"She didn't need my help."

She'd sent him inside?

My forehead suddenly feels like I walked into a furnace. "You did what? Why? Where was he? In the street, waiting for us to park?" My head is exploding. I'm full of questions, which these two ignore, smiling at each other as if everything is normal. "Come on, Daisy. What's happening here? Who the hell is he?"

A pickup truck rumbles into the parking lot, full of plaid-shirt-wearing, drunken, loudmouthed hillbillies, as Jackson would call them, and I quickly shut my mouth. Of course, there is no real way to know if these men are hillbillies, but they are white no matter where they were born, and Jackson warned me they can't be trusted. Not that I needed a warning.

The truck slows, and the window rolls down, revealing a red-haired man in the driver's seat. I might be imagining the sour smell — the vehicle is fifty feet away, but the stench of spilled beer surrounds me like a cage.

"Hey, boy, what you got there?" Comes a voice from the truck's open window.

Tobey's body stiffens and grows an inch taller, too. Daisy doesn't budge. She's still hugging him around the waist, her cheek resting on his chest.

The driver sticks his head out the car window, his bright face and snarled lips visible even in the dim light — the others in the truck jeer or laugh or curse, mutually satisfied with their stupidity. "Hey, man, I like to do colored girls, too. You need some help, or can you handle her on your own?"

Their laughter hurts my ears, but my attention is on the young man with Daisy.

Tobey jerks away from her and steps toward the pickup. She grabs his sleeve, stopping him.

"Watch yourself, now, darling," she says. "Let's leave these boys be. It's not why we're here."

I expect trouble. Can taste it, frankly. The truck crawls by, and the occupants leer at us. Then the lights go out in the McDonald's, and the hillbillies wail in unison. No burgers or fries for them tonight. Then they drive away.

Relief fills me but it's short-lived. There's still the young man next to Daisy.

"No Mickey D's for anyone tonight," she says, tugging his sleeve and guiding him toward the Mustang.

I have no clue how to deal with the problem walking next to Daisy. How did he get here? Why is he here? There isn't another vehicle in the parking lot, and the good ole boys didn't drop him off.

Lord knows, he didn't fall from the sky.

When they reach the car, Daisy slips into the back of the Mustang. "Get that ridiculous look off your face," she says to me. "He won't bite."

Glassy-eyed confusion is the best I've got for now. "Are you going to let him in the car, just like that? I don't know him. And he's —"

"He's a good guy, Frankie. You don't have to worry."

Yeah, right. I swear every wrinkle in my brow is taking a deep dive off a short cliff and turning into the biggest frown on earth. "But he's white."

"That's obvious," says Daisy in dizzying brevity.

"You saw what just happened." I point at the spot occupied only minutes ago by a pickup truck full of white men.

148

The trunk slams shut, and I cover my mouth with the hand not attached to the arm in a sling. Daisy has shoved aside the suitcases and settled into the back seat. Tobey returns to the car without his duffel bag, which means he put it in the trunk. So a discussion about whether he's coming with us isn't about to happen. My objections won't make a difference.

He slides into the driver's seat, car keys in hand. "Where to, Daisy?"

"Found a place in my *Green Book* nearby, where we could spend the night."

I am not looking in the direction of the man now sitting next to me. I glare at Daisy and shout, "Did you hear me? He can't come with us. Look at what almost happened here. We can't drive cross-country, even with your precious *Green Book,* with a white man in the car! Two Negro girls — and him? We're asking for trouble."

"You seem agitated, showing off your temper, Francine." Daisy chuckles. "Oh, dear. Does anyone even call you Francine?"

"Everyone calls me Francine. You're the only person I know who calls me Frankie."

"Well, now, me and Tobey," she adds with a giggle.

"Come on, Daisy." Tobey adjusts the seat, giving himself more legroom. "Don't tease her. You should've told her about me."

"I didn't have a chance," Daisy says, which is a ridiculous claim. "Her newly found temper must be a side effect of her pain pills."

"Pain pills?" He looks at my arm in the sling. "Are you okay? I'm sorry about what happened. You fell right next to the car."

"Which was coincidental as hell," Daisy adds firmly.

"You were in the car, driving when I was hit?"

"I didn't hit you. I swear to God." He taps two fingers over his heart like that's enough for me to believe him. "It was a freak accident. You were running. Daisy called for you to stop. You didn't hear us. We pulled up next to you, and you slipped. I think you fainted. I grabbed you, and we drove straight to the hospital emergency."

"So you were driving when the car hit me."

"We didn't hit you, Frankie," Daisy exclaims.

Tobey blows out a loud breath. "We should get going before another pickup with a new batch of fools drives into the lot, looking to give us grief. I'm wide awake. I got a nice nap on my way here. I'll be fine driving for a few hours, at least until we make it to

150

Oklahoma City. You two can catch some shut-eye."

"Wait a minute. Wait one damn minute." The meaning behind his words stings like a slap across my forehead. "Is he coming with us to Los Angeles? We may not need a *Green Book,* but we certainly don't need him. That's begging for trouble. Wherever we go, Black or white. And why wasn't he in your car in Chicago? He's in the bus station and then disappears while I'm in the hospital emergency room. Then reappears in a Mc-Donald's parking lot."

"He's not a stranger to me, Frankie," Daisy says from the back seat. "And I can tell you how he got here. He took a bus. Now, if you want to learn more about him, which I suggest you do, ask him — by morning, you'll know him better than you know me."

"I'm not a bad man, Frankie." He puts the key in the ignition. "Daisy and I go way back — I've known her since I was a kid." He smiles at her in the rearview mirror.

"That's right — since he was a child." Daisy taps me on my shoulder. "Besides, this is his car, and I can't boot him out of his own automobile, now can I?"

151

CHAPTER 10
DAISY

Summer 1928
Los Angeles

Around one o'clock in the morning, Daisy had finished cleaning the suites belonging to guests who had checked out or, like Mr. Perry's chauffeur and his secretary, had used their rooms but weren't spending the night at the hotel. One more tenant suite required her attention, and then she could disappear for a few hours and take a nap in the staff room in the basement.

Stepin Fetchit had left word with the front desk that he wouldn't return before dawn. She should've cleaned his suite first, but she blamed Harry Belmont for her hesitancy. Whatever he was called, Lincoln Perry or Stepin Fetchit, he was someone she now had to pay attention to. There might be a morsel of gossip in his room she could write up for Harry.

Gathering her supplies, she traipsed

glumly to room 416 and, after a few moments of fumbling with her master key, realized the door was ajar.

Stepin Fetchit had left it unlocked, just like a man of wealth and privilege, thought Daisy, expecting things to be where he left them.

She stepped into the parlor and darkness but wasn't too concerned. All the suites had the same shape, the same furnishings and decorations. Even in the dark, she could find a lamp. But something was amiss; something felt out of place.

She put down the bucket and the cleaning supplies and walked toward the master bedroom. Near the archway, a Tiffany glass table lamp was within arm's reach. She pulled the chain.

Daisy couldn't see every detail in the room, but she saw him.

A man sat in the shadows in the chaise armchair at the end of the bed, elbow bent, foot propped on a stool, and ice clinking in the glass he held.

Her heart pounded.

No one was supposed to be in the room. Of course, Lincoln Perry could have returned early, but this man was not him.

The man in the chair was long-limbed, and his profile, even in silhouette, was more

153

striking than Mr. Perry could hope for.

"Excuse me, sir, I didn't know anyone was here." She politely waited for a reply, but the man didn't respond, and she cleared her throat.

Still, he did not move.

Daisy's eyes adjusted to the dim light. Now, she could make out the outline of his jaw, the dark jacket, perhaps navy, white trousers, and lace-up white oxfords —

She gasped.

It was him. The man from her grand opening morning fiasco with Vada Somerville — the man who cracked a joke, cementing Daisy's humiliation. The man, the architect, or whatever he was — Malcolm Barnes.

"What are you doing in Lincoln Perry's suite?"

"Excuse me?" he whispered. "What did you say?" He wiped his brow with the glass. "I'm sorry, dear. I'm having some trouble. A b-bad h-headache." He had slurred his words. The drink in his hand wasn't his first of the night. "I'm not at m-my best. Sorry, d-doll."

Daisy bristled at the name doll. Harry called her doll, sugar, a litany of other inappropriate endearments she didn't like, but she and Harry had known each other for years, and he hadn't embarrassed her in front of Black Los Angeles luminaries like Mr. Barnes had.

"If you don't leave Mr. Perry's suite immediately, I will report you to the night guard." Her voice surged with sufficient authority, and she fully expected him to rise and depart. But he simply relaxed his long torso more deeply into the chair's curves. Then he made a sound. A groan? Was he hurt?

"If you check the register," he said, his voice steadier, "you'll find that I'm a guest at the Somerville with full access to Step's room."

"How do I know if you're telling me the truth, Mr. Barnes?" she said. "I can't leave you in a tenant's suite to investigate."

He sat forward, removing his foot from the stool with a grimace, and placed his glass on the table nearby. "You know my name?"

"Yes. I know who you are and that you could be some kind of famous architect — since you were with the Somervilles."

"There are only a handful of Black architects in Los Angeles, and I'm not one of them — not yet. So that means also not the least bit famous."

From the way he sat, she could see only half his face. "You're the maid from that morning."

"I am."

He picked up his drink but raising the glass to his lips seemed difficult. Was that a tremor in his hand? And the way his head tilted to the side, exposing the length of his throat, made him look vulnerable and oddly sad. Or was she putting too much stock in the way a man sat in a chair?

Daisy pursed her lips. That was not a game she should play. She was already familiar with his type.

Young Hollywood. Even if he wasn't an actor, he possessed all the traits. He was brash, arrogant, rude. The type they called a man's man, which gave him license to be mean, disloyal, untidy, and cruel. And yes, she knew these things instinctively, although she'd had only one brief, embarrassing encounter with him.

But she couldn't let go of first impressions.

In his fashionable suit and the part in the middle of his wavy black hair, smoothed with brilliantine, he was trendy and sought-after and drank much of his own medicine.

His fingernails were manicured, too, and his clean-shaven face only enhanced his flaws. The other morning, in the lobby, she had noticed his slightly crooked nose, the scar in the corner of his full lips, and his deep-set eyes, so black they almost vanished beneath his thick eyebrows. Although a brighter shade of brown than what usually drew her attention, his skin wasn't light enough to pass for white. A choice in Hollywood and elsewhere she found disgraceful.

She had judged him sharply on the stairwell, but her mother's manners suddenly came to her. "Is everything okay?"

He didn't answer.

"Mr. Barnes?" She stepped forward into the light and gasped. He had bruises on his chin, a strawberry-shaped knot, swelling under his left eye, a bump on his forehead, and blood on his cheek.

"Do you need some cold water for your face? I think so. I should get you a glass of water." Shaking, she grabbed the ice bucket and a crystal water pitcher from the small table next to the chaise without waiting for a reply. "I'll be right back."

As she hurried to the pantry at the end of the hall, she prayed there was still ice in the bin and fresh water in the barrel. The maids kept a supply on every floor to avoid too many exhausting trips up and down the stairs. When she found what she needed, she picked up a towel, too, and then sped back to the suite.

He still sat on the chaise. "Did you know that this building took twelve weeks to erect?"

Daisy placed the pitcher on the table, filled a glass, and offered it to him. "A glass of water?"

He blinked as if noticing the proximity of her body to his. Perhaps she was too near and abruptly eased toward the door. Then he took the glass of water she offered, his fingers touching hers lightly as he did so.

Daisy ignored the awkward pause, watching him as he touched the rim of the glass to his lips and released a faint moan.

"Thank you," he said. "What do you have there?" He nodded at the washcloth draped over her forearm.

"You have some dirt and blood, I believe, on your cheek."

He raised an eyebrow and smiled weakly. "Aren't I a total mess?"

"Oh, no. It's just a drop, but I thought you might wish to —"

She went to wipe his face, but he met her midway, taking the cloth from her hand and touching her fingers again.

Their eyes locked for an instant, and her stomach quivered. Lowering her gaze, she stared at the floor, hopeful the nervousness she felt hadn't shown on her face. But now, at least, Mr. Barnes held the cloth.

"The hotel had to be built quickly for Mr. Du Bois's annual meeting of the NAACP," she exclaimed in a nervous ramble. "But you already knew that. Did you assist Dr. Somerville in designing the building?"

An unsettling pain clouded his eyes. "I'm a draftsman until I earn my California license. So, no. I didn't design this building, but Dr. Somerville honored me by allowing me to work on the plans. But, I'll be able to create my own ideas, build the kind of buildings that will —" He cradled his forehead in his palm. "Sorry, but I'm at my worst."

The passion in his voice when he'd spoken the word *building* had caught Daisy's attention — almost as much as the pain she heard now.

"I should go," Daisy said. "I'm sorry for disturbing you."

"Oh, you no longer think of me as an interloper. You believe I am a friend of Step's, and it's okay for me to be here?"

She shrugged. "I did see you with Mr. Fetchit and the Drs. Somerville on the tour the other morning. I can't imagine the Somervilles associating with — an interloper. It would be indecent."

"Are you angry with me?" He smiled and winced in the same motion.

She had been very angry with him but didn't want to ask him why he'd made fun of her. What she wanted to know was more about his relationship with Stepin Fetchit, Jack Johnson, and who was the white woman with them? But none of that was her business.

She sidled toward the door. "If there's anything you need, please let the front desk know, and we'll be right here."

"You don't have to leave." He reached for the brandy decanter on the table. "You could join me."

He removed a fresh glass from the silver tray and poured two drinks, one for her and a refill for himself.

Mesmerized by the invitation and his agility — he had poured the drink so fast, she hadn't moved. She did think of how insane it would be to accept his offer. Joining a guest for a drink in their suite sounded like a sin. A chambermaid and a soon-to-be-licensed architect. It would be an outrage.

"Mr. Barnes, I am employed here as a chambermaid. I am not a guest at the hotel."

"You have me at a disadvantage."

"A disadvantage?"

"You know my name, but what is yours?"

160

"Daisy Washington — and we didn't meet. I spilled water on Dr. Vada Somerville's shoes, and —"

"Yes. Yes. You were so serious and down-hearted. It was such a small thing. I only wanted to lighten the mood."

Daisy gasped. "I was mortified and didn't appreciate being the brunt of a joke between you and Dr. Vada Somerville."

"Sincerely, I apologize if my desire to smooth the waters appeared to be insincere. Not my intent."

He rose, and Daisy flinched at his bruises. They had darkened and swelled in minutes. "Sir, I believe you should see a physician. I will let the front desk know."

"No. I don't need a doctor. But let me explain." He touched the cloth to his bruised cheek. "I had a run-in with some men who didn't care for my looks and tried to make some changes."

"Are you sure about not seeing a doctor?"

"Can you keep a secret, Daisy Washington?" He placed his glass on the table.

"Don't worry," she replied quickly. "I won't mention that you were in Mr. Perry's suite tonight. There is no need. A chamber-maid working at a hotel like this must be discreet."

He folded his arms over his chest. "My

being here is not the secret I wish you to keep."

"Then what secret am I to keep?" A reasonable question, Daisy decided. She had asked it boldly, too.

"Don't mention the condition you found me in. I was supposed to attend a party at the Biltmore, but on my way, some white thugs accosted me. As I said, they took issue with my appearance."

She tilted her head, assessing him further, but he didn't look any less handsome than when she'd seen him the first time.

"To be precise," he began, "they hated the color of my skin — among other things."

His voice had dropped into his belly, and she could touch the rage inside him; it boiled out of him like a pot of thick stew over a firepit.

"Did you talk to the city's police?"

He laughed. "Where were you raised, Daisy Washington?"

She stiffened her spine. Was he implying that she knew nothing of prejudice and hate? "Waco, Texas, until we moved to Los Angeles when I was six."

"Well, Daisy Washington, originally from Waco, Texas, I'm not the man you think I am."

"I have not said a word to indicate what I

think of you."

He sat on the arm of the chaise, whiskey glass in his hand, smiling at her. "Perhaps not, but your eyes are quite expressive, and I think you believe I may have deserved some of these bruises."

"I would never think such a thing." Daisy's skin felt warm and cold at once. "I don't know you well enough to judge."

"You have an astute awareness of character, I can tell. You had me pegged five minutes after you walked into the room — and you were right, I am a sporting man."

She didn't believe Malcolm Barnes, but to say that out loud might prolong the conversation. That was something she didn't want.

He folded his arms over his chest. Smugness wrinkled his brow, and the shock of his bruises lessened. "For some reason, Miss Washington — it is 'miss'?" He glanced at her left hand, which she moved behind her back.

"Yes," she managed.

"I'd like you to have a better opinion of me."

"Again, you make assumptions. My opinion of you shouldn't be made hastily or based on one or two incidents."

Humor settled in his eyes. "I guess you're

right. We should spend more time together."

Lord. "That was not what I meant." What was she doing? What was she saying to him? "I'll keep your secret," she blurted.

His face brightened. "You will?"

She smiled self-consciously. "Yes."

"Why?"

"I don't know." He moved toward her, not stopping until he was close, very close, too close.

"I should leave now."

"Of course." He walked by her, his hand brushing against hers. He held the door open. "Thank you for your discretion — and until we meet again."

Compulsively, she contradicted him. "I doubt we'll ever speak this way again, Mr. Barnes."

She backed out of the suite, holding her bucket and cleaning supplies as his dark eyes studied her. And for a moment, she thought he was about to ask her back inside. But then his lips parted into a wry smile. "Have a nice evening, Miss Washington."

He closed the door, leaving her in the hallway, staring at the lion door knocker and suite number — 416.

How could she have these thoughts in her mind? She cocked her head, still looking at the door and admitting that she had enjoyed talking with him.

Perhaps her brain was addled after a long day at work. A handsome man shouldn't cause a sensible girl to lose her senses.

If that was true, then why could she still smell the soap on his skin and the whiskey on his breath? That didn't sound reasonable.

After a long exhale, she retreated, putting some necessary distance between her and the door. Then she spun on her heels and marched down the hall toward the staircase, all the while chastising herself.

She'd wasted enough time splashing about in Malcolm Barnes's pond.

There were too many things, too many important things Daisy had to accomplish, to allow a brief encounter with an unspeakably handsome man to divide her focus. She must remember his less intriguing traits: arrogant, rude, and inappropriate. And no matter what fantasy he might provoke, Malcolm Barnes would never be more than a footnote in one of her journals.

CHAPTER 11
FRANKIE

Saturday, June 1, 1968
Route 66

It is past midnight.

Dark clouds heavy with rain loom so low in the sky, I can touch them.

Not a drop of water has fallen, and my window is down. The wind whips across my face as the scenery races by, except it is too dark to make out details, just a blur of shapes and shadows on the side of the road.

However, staring out the window gives me a chance to think through my anger, fears, and frustrations. It also helps me make up my mind.

I will split in Oklahoma City and take a bus to Los Angeles. I'm almost sad about my decision. I was close to looking forward to the drive. Ready to believe Jackson would never find us on the road. I could relax for the first time in years. Listen to Daisy's cassettes and ask her why she and my mom don't get along and haven't spoken in forty years.

But with Tobey in the car, what else can I do but strike out on my own?

There is a Greyhound bus station in Oklahoma City. I'll return my old ticket and buy a new one for Los Angeles. I'll leave my bags in the car. Daisy can drop them off at my mother's house, or if she refuses to do that, I'll try and handle my train case. She can toss the large suitcase in the garbage if she insists upon avoiding my mother.

Sitting in the passenger seat of a candy-apple-red Mustang with my right shoulder, my uninjured shoulder, pressed against the front door, I am as far from the car's driver as possible. I am unbelievably uncomfortable.

Daisy is curled up in the back seat, pretending to be asleep, I wager. She looks too perfect curled up neatly, her head resting lightly against the rear seat's cushion, her hair unmussed.

Meanwhile, I'm attempting to size up the white boy next to me, who is Daisy's "best friend" in the whole wide world.

And yes, my brain is about to explode.

Tobey Garfunkel has been behind the wheel of his car — let me repeat that: *his* friggin' car — since East St. Louis. Now, he's heading to LA with us.

God, I'm so mad at Daisy, I can't swallow.

"I demand an explanation," I blurt in his direction.

"Excuse me?" Tobey squints. "What did you say?"

"Don't act as if you've lost your hearing."

I sit upright in my seat and take a slow, deep breath. "How did you know where to find us?"

"You don't have to answer her," Daisy interjects, confirming my suspicion she was faking sleep.

"Come on, Daisy," Tobey pleads, as if I need him on my side. "You told her to talk to me. She's just doing what you asked."

"You did say that," I point out. "Besides, I want to hear him talk."

Tobey glances in the rearview at Daisy, like he needs her permission to continue.

What's up with them?

Feigning disinterest, Daisy squeezes her eyes shut, resuming her "I'm asleep" charade.

Tobey glances at me. "Daisy and I decided to hook up at that McDonald's because we've been there before, and both of us remembered where it was."

"Why didn't you stay with her in Chicago?

I think you left because the cops might arrest you for hitting a pedestrian with your car."

His right hand tightens on the steering wheel, stretching the skin on his knuckles. He has very pale skin in the moonlight.

"Cut us some slack." Tobey's voice rises. "We didn't hit you."

"Yeah, right."

A glance at the left-hand mirror, and he veers into the opposite lane, accelerating by the car in front of us.

"That was a needless thing to do," I say. "Taking that kind of risk — I hope it made you feel better."

"Look." He sighs. "I wanted to stay, but . . ."

Daisy sticks her head between the bucket seats, awake again. "You two are missing the point."

I dive in. "Oh, you mean the point where someone stops lying about why he is even here? Or one of the other points, like why you didn't mention him before, or why he hit me with his car?"

"Would you stop harping on that?" Daisy snaps. "You were the one who ran into us. We weren't moving. The light was red, and you were running like a madwoman. I saw your face — tears flying every which way.

What were you running from?" She jerks backward, striking the rear seat cushion with a thud.

I have no answer. I look out my window, watching scenery I can't see, thinking about Jackson, thinking about trusting myself enough to get out of this car and take a bus to Los Angeles.

"Daisy, don't get worked up. Relax," Tobey urged. "You are supposed to be resting. She gets it. Don't you, Frankie?"

"She was resting or pretending to rest," I say sharply. "And don't tell me what I'm thinking or feeling. I don't know you. Christ, I don't know either one of you."

"Don't yell at him," Daisy scolds. "He's the one who convinced me to help you. If he hadn't been so insistent that I help my sister's daughter, I'd be halfway to Albuquerque by now."

"So I should be thanking him because he's the Great White Hope?"

Daisy shoves the back of my seat.

A pain shoots through my arm. "Ouch."

Daisy groans. "You're right. You don't know anything about him or me, so mind your mouth."

I twist to look at her face. I can't believe she shoved my seat. "That's right. I don't know anything." My chest is tight. "How

170

dare you try to make me the problem. You two are the guilty ones and are just trying to convince me otherwise."

Daisy leans forward again and gives Tobey the side-eye. He nods, encouraging her to go ahead with whatever she has to say. "Okay. Truth is, Tobey is on the run, dear. That's why we played this cloak-and-dagger game. After you fell and we got to the emergency room, we didn't want anyone asking him questions."

"Why? He's on the run from what?"

"The police, of course," Daisy states flatly.

I turn to him, astonished. "What are you, the Fugitive? Running away from some petty crime you didn't commit, or murder you did?"

"Good Lord, Frankie, how much television do you watch?" Daisy's laughter is damn annoying.

Tobey clears his throat. "Killing people is what I'm trying to avoid." His voice sounds hoarse and raw. From his tone, he has something to confess. I wonder if he's honest enough to tell the truth.

Daisy's lingering laughter stops abruptly. I turn to him, watching him closely. Is he upset? Emotional? About what?

"Come on, Tobey," Daisy begins. "You don't have to —"

"I'm a deserter, Frankie." Tobey's voice is stark, emotionless. "I was reported, and I had to pack my bags in a hurry."

He stares straight ahead, watching the road, but the curtain has fallen, separating him from me, and I sense at this moment, even from Daisy.

"What did you do?" I ask.

"Not past tense, but present. I am currently dodging the draft."

"Are you sick?" I ask too quickly, and from his closed expression, he thinks I am judging him — and he is a smart boy.

Tobey shakes his head. "No medical conditions. No religious considerations. No wife, no college, no kids. It's a war of independence, and we shouldn't be there. It is not our fight."

I cringe. Too many soldiers in my family to embrace this line of thought. "So, you're a conscientious objector."

"Nope. I'm a coward. Afraid I'll die, or if I live, of what I'll become if I fight in a war."

Someone else might not blame him for being a coward or fearing death. Since I was ten, after spending weeks and weeks in bed, hoping to survive the poliovirus, death and fear are my friends, and they stay close. "But isn't fighting in a war a man's duty? My grandfather fought in World War One, and he was the best man I knew. And my dad was a good man, too. He died serving his country in Korea." I stop and take a breath. "Even Jackson was drafted to go to Vietnam.

"His number came up the summer after we graduated from high school in 'sixty-four, and he was off to camp a week after we were married."

"Now, a few years later," Daisy begins, "you're running away from him because he beats you." She says this casually as if the news is posted on a billboard.

What the hell? I smack the dashboard. "Damn it, Daisy! Why do you say things like that? You have no business . . ."

"I'd say you have a leg up on why I won't be going to war," Tobey says.

And I am ready to jump out of my skin. I'm that mad. "Who asked for your two cents? We don't even friggin' know each other. What gives you license to make assumptions about me?"

"Calm down, Frankie," Daisy calls from the back seat.

Tobey looks away from the road for a second. "Sorry, Frankie."

"Shut up!"

His blue-eyed apology does nothing for me. I stare out the windshield, unwilling to open my mouth until I calm down.

The moonlight dances across the concrete highway, and with no other cars on the road, the Mustang's headlights illuminate the path ahead. It's almost like I can visualize the end of time.

"I don't have a leg up," I say after a few minutes of meditating on self-hate. "The first time my husband hit me, we weren't married, and he hadn't enlisted in the army, let alone gone to Vietnam. So I can't blame the war for the man he is."

"Then who do you blame for Jackson?" Daisy's question puzzles me for a second, almost as much as what I'm about to admit.

"Part of the reason Jackson is Jackson — is me. If that's what you want to hear."

"You think?" Daisy practically sings the words like the chorus to a song I don't want to hear.

My eyes are suddenly wet around the edges, and I can't stop blinking.

"Hey, all of us need to chill," Tobey says as if he can save us from this pit we've fallen into.

Now, he's in charge of our moods. I see — just like a white man to seize control. I'll show him. I'll show them both. "It doesn't matter what either one of you says. When we arrive in Oklahoma City, drop me off at the bus station. I'll make it to Los Angeles on my own."

My last words stun my fellow passengers into silence. Conversation inside the car abruptly halts, which is fine with me. I had twisted and turned to keep an eye on Daisy in the back seat and Tobey behind the wheel, and now, my shoulder is aching again. I had to pop another pill and swallow it dry.

The medicine calms me, and without the constant flow of idiotic speech, I drift into a fitful slumber. Waking up at every bump in the road and every other shift in gear.

Daisy is right, though, I don't recall the last time I spoke up for myself without regard for the consequences. I blame the Mustang for my bold mouth. Inside the car, I am in a different world — a world where only the two of us exist. Well, what had been only the two of us.

The third wheel is Tobey, the deserter.

My father and my grandfather both served their country in the military. On the other hand, Tamika marches against the war in Vietnam. She also marches for civil rights, women's rights, all rights.

Jackson didn't go to war because he loved everything about America. I mean, seriously, I may not wear an Afro, but life isn't fair to a Black man in America. Shit. There isn't much in this country that's fair to the Negro, male or female. Back in 1964, when Jackson went to war, Jim Crow was still legal in the South until President Lyndon Johnson signed the Civil Rights Act on July 2 of that year. The Voting Rights Act was signed in August of 1965.

A Black man had to tune out a lot about America to enlist and fight for his country.

At Jefferson High, the school Jackson, Tamika, and I attended, she was the first person I knew to mention Vietnam.

I kept a diary when I was in school, and I remember I wrote about Vietnam for the first time because of her. I recall the words as if they were printed in my palm. It was the winter of 1963.

Tamika should've told me right away. But I had to wait to learn the truth.

Two weeks had passed since Jerry's parents had given her the news. Her boyfriend, a soldier in the US Army, had died on an island in the South China Sea days before he was set to return home.

She hadn't hesitated to keep the news from me, knowing I wouldn't learn about his death from any of our friends — he had gone to a different high school and lived in Baldwin Hills — and no one in our neighborhood knew him other than me. After she told me, she claimed my sensitive nature stopped her from telling me right away.

She had met Jerry at a basketball game in the fall during our junior year. He was a senior, and after his graduation, he enlisted, the summer of 1963.

Six months later, he was gone.

Tamika said she didn't even cry when Jerry's parents gave her the news. She told them how sorry she was for their loss and how much she loved him and would miss him, and then she hung up the phone.

The next thing she knew, she was in her bedroom on her knees, pulling a shoebox from beneath the bed. It was full of his letters, most of which she hadn't read in weeks. She didn't understand them. All the stories about boys getting hurt, crying for their mamas, and smoking weed, and making love to their sheets, she was seventeen, like me, and barely had a thought in her head other than the next episodes of our favorite television shows.

What did we know of love, let alone a conflict in the middle of the Pacific and the pain young men suffered through and died from? All Tamika knew was that she'd never see Jerry again.

Every day for weeks, she'd read each letter and organize each piece of mail by postage date before putting the box away.

Tamika had found out about Jerry's death the same day I told her Jackson had proposed marriage and I'd said yes.

I recall she hadn't seemed as happy as I would've liked. She kept saying I was too young and unprepared for what might happen, how things could change without warning. But I didn't want to hear any of it. I was happy for the first time in weeks.

Just before high school graduation, my beloved grandfather died, sitting in the wicker chair in the sunroom in the house on Naomi Avenue. He had loved me, treated me with more care and affection than any human I'd ever known.

"Frankie. Frankie, wake up."

"I'm awake."

"Frankie." Daisy's voice comes at me from the end of a tunnel. "You'd sleep through an earthquake. It's pouring cats, dogs, and a few farm animals I never want to see again, and Tobey can't drive well in bad weather."

178

"I can drive in this weather," Tobey counters, however, his voice is shaky. "But I sure as hell don't like to."

I sit upright and can't see anything out the windshield but rain. It drops from the sky in thick sheets and pounds the highway so hard it bounces back up from the road, looking like fingers trying to grab the car's hood and spin us into a ditch.

Tobey is hunched over the wheel, his eyes peeled, searching for an escape from the downpour.

"Look out your window, Frankie." Daisy points. "Are there any road signs? An exit coming up?"

I narrow my eyes and concentrate, but my brain is in a Percodan fog.

The car skids. Both Daisy and I gasp, although, I might've let out a small scream.

"My God," I look at Tobey. "Daisy's right. You can't drive in bad weather." I stare through the windshield as if I can help him drive with the power of my eyeballs.

"That's why we need to pull off somewhere," Daisy hisses. "So I can be behind the wheel."

"And you're that much better at driving his car than he is." My voice is the queen of sarcasm.

"I don't want you to go off half-cocked

179

when I tell you this, Frankie," Daisy says.

"Oh, okay. Should I prepare myself?" I place my right hand on the dashboard.

"I lie on occasion," Daisy shouts above the rain and thunder.

"Oh, really." I am suspicious of Daisy's joking tone, but perhaps she's trying to calm Tobey. "Okay. Go on. Spill."

"This beauty is my car, bought and paid for with my money. Tobey doesn't have the taste buds for a vehicle as wondrous as this." She taps him on the shoulder. "Isn't that right, young man?" She smiles at me. "Now, would one of you darlings please hurry up and find an exit so that I can drive my damn car."

"Why in the hell did you lie about the car?" I ask, confused. "What difference did it make?"

"I had to shut you up about Tobey getting into the car in East St. Louis, and it was the first thing that came to my mind." She sits back and pulls out another cigarette. "Now, see if you can find an exit."

I stare straight ahead, wondering how much longer I'll last before I crack.

CHAPTER 12
DAISY

Summer 1928
Los Angeles

The nineteenth-annual meeting of the NAACP had come to the West Coast (for the first time) — and Brown Broadway would never be the same. Neither would Daisy if she made it through the day.

Who cared that she was scheduled to work from 6:00 a.m. to midnight? No matter what she had to do, who she had to lie to, or bribe, she would be outdoors, on the sidewalk, perhaps in the middle of the street when W. E. B. Du Bois arrived.

She'd proudly be among the first to welcome her hero to the Somerville (or at least see his automobile drive up).

Everyone was talking about how the motorcade carrying W. E. B. Du Bois and the NAACP dignitaries, had left the East Los Angeles train station for the Hotel Somerville thirty minutes before. In a few miles the motorcade had grown into a full-fledged parade, heading for Central Avenue and Forty-First Street and the Hotel Somerville.

As soon as she stepped outside, Daisy held her breath as the excitement pulsed through her veins. Flags and banners hung from lamppost to lamppost, crisscrossing the streets and flapping above the caravan of automobiles, roadsters, Mercedes-Benz sport-tourers, and Rolls-Royce limos.

She quickly maneuvered to the curb, angling through the crowds waiting for W. E. B. Du Bois's automobile to drive up.

Then Henrietta and Yvette surprised her.

"What are you doing here?" she asked. "What if someone catches you? All three of us can't sneak out of the hotel to see him."

"Half the hotel staff is here somewhere," Yvette said, smiling. "And you don't own him. This might be the only chance we'll ever have to see him in person."

Henrietta nodded enthusiastically. "Mrs. Keyes said she'd fire any staff that bothered him or the other NAACP dignitaries, once they stepped inside. We are professional maids, butlers, waiters, cooks — we take care of hotel guests. Period."

"Oh, so you memorized Mrs. Keyes's speech, I see." Daisy had heard the same, but she couldn't be in the same building, on the same block, or in the same city as W. E. B. Du Bois and not see him. "Okay. But as soon as he pulls up, we get back inside."

The line of automobiles approached, and Daisy was bouncing on her tiptoes. The same wild expectation poured from the crowd.

Then she spotted Harry Belmont moving toward her with decisive strides.

She stepped from the curb, putting some distance between her, Yvette, and Henrietta and hoping they wouldn't notice.

"How has the first week gone?" Harry stopped behind her, a few feet away.

She turned her head to hear him better but didn't face him. "I thought you'd be at the hotel this past week, every day, every hour. Where have you been?"

"Went on a cruise. Took a water taxi out to sea."

Daisy had heard of these gambling ships. "That's illegal, Harry."

"Not if I'm three miles off the shoreline."

She sighed. "Lucky for you, I've been working, jotting notes, and listening in, and I'll have my report this weekend. So, don't worry, you'll have plenty for your columns."

"I never worry when it comes to you,

Daisy. I just stopped by to say hello." He spoke in a low voice, close to her ear, uncomfortably close.

She leaned forward.

"We don't have to be all business all the time," he said.

She tilted her head. "Yes, we do. And we talk plenty."

"Funny, to me, we don't talk about anything that doesn't have to do with my columns."

"That's the way it should be, Harry." She touched the small notebook she kept in her apron pocket. "With the hotel open and things at home — my family needs me. You know about my mother."

"Yes, I do, and I'm sorry she's not doing well. I didn't mean to push." He wiped his brow. "Maybe I can help you with your mother."

She turned and looked at him. "My mother. What could you possibly have . . ."

"On the cruise, I met a nurse from St. Helena Sanitarium in the Bay. I asked her about rates and if they had beds for Negroes. It might be segregated, but I'll let you know when she gets back to me."

Daisy's heart pounded. St. Helena was one of the oldest health resorts in California. "Are you sure? Please just don't forget."

"I won't. But it could cost more than you think, especially if they have to treat your mother off the books." He made a gesture with his hands she didn't understand.

"What do you mean?"

"If they allow Negro patients, they are likely kept far from the white population, and to give coloreds care could cost extra. I'm just guessing. But when she returns, she'll get back to me, and I'll get back to you."

"Thank you, Harry, and sorry if I was snippy. It's been a rough week."

"Hey, doll. Just wanted you to know, I'm thinking about you, even on my days off." He touched the brim of his fedora and started to turn. "Oh, by the way. You have anything on Step Fetchit? I'm hearing some rumors."

A flutter in her chest threatened to climb into her throat. "No. Nothing." Not that she hadn't thought about Malcolm Barnes in the week since they talked in Step's apartment, but it never crossed her mind to write about him and that night in her notes for Harry. It would be such a betrayal. "Nothing at all."

"Don't worry about it. We've got plenty of time." He nodded, took a step to her right, and disappeared into the crowd.

With a sharp pivot, she returned to her sister and Yvette, stepping in close and draping her arms around the two girls' shoulders.

"You just wait," Daisy said to them. "W. E. B. Du Bois will be here any minute."

She rose onto her tiptoes and lifted her chin to see above the bodies huddled on Central Avenue.

A woman squealed, "Clara Bow. Clara Bow!" Daisy pivoted, and sure enough, there was the motion picture starlet in the back seat of a yellow roadster holding on to Douglas Fairbanks Jr.

Most Hollywood actors Daisy ignored, but Fairbanks was almost as handsome as Malcolm Barnes.

Another clamor of excitement rose from the crowd. "Chaplin. Chaplin." More shouting. "Robeson. Armstrong. Jelly Roll."

She wondered why so many Hollywood stars and famous musicians had shown up for the parade. But Hollywood was a booming city with a small-town attitude. The mayor and most of his office were in attendance. It was a huge city-wide celebration almost as large as the hotel's grand opening the week before.

Daisy nudged Yvette. "I think people imagine folks they wish were here but aren't."

Henrietta waved her hands. "No, I saw Chaplin, too. Over there, I swear."

It was a sprawling crowd. Daisy got caught up in the energy like everyone else around her. Mutterings in the crowd claimed the NAACP dignitaries were only a few blocks away. Daisy looked around, suddenly dissatisfied with her location.

That's when she saw him. Malcolm Barnes reclined on the rumble seat of a red and black Rolls-Royce, his arms stretched behind him, leaning on his hands, and wearing a dazzling red suit.

She blinked at him, lips parted and eyes wide. What was he doing in the parade? Not watching but in it.

Sitting on the rumble seat between Lincoln Perry and Jack Johnson, he waved at bystanders and shouted and cheered. He acted as if he was the star attraction instead of the two men on either side of him.

Daisy's chest knotted. Was her father, right? Did Negro men like Lincoln Perry and his crew, including Jack Johnson and Malcolm Barnes, cause trouble for the Race? Did they behave like they were better than the average hard-working Black man?

Why had that thought come to her? During their conversation, she hadn't thought of him as a dandy.

The next moment, Daisy was out of minutes to spare worrying about Malcolm Barnes. *He* had arrived.

"Yvette! Henrietta! Look. W. E. B. Du Bois!" Daisy shouted and pointed, her excitement, a form of electricity, sparking and jolting.

Du Bois stood in the sleek black automobile, next to the mayor of Los Angeles, both men waving their hats at the crowd. Dressed in summer tweed, he was impeccably groomed, but he didn't smile. His lack of merriment bothered Daisy at first. She hoped he wasn't worried about holding the annual NAACP meeting at such a new hotel. Dr. Somerville had built the hotel for him. The serious matters for the Race were on his agenda. His serious expression was necessary, not some crowd-pleasing antics. There were plenty of actors in Hollywood to do that. Coloreds needed to focus on change and improving the lives and opportunities in America for all the Race. That was what Du Bois intended.

Her heart swelled. "Yvette. Henrietta. There he is, the most important Negro in America," she said, her cheeks aching from the broad smile on her face.

Daisy's body trembled with joy. She had seen him with her own eyes. How amazing was that?

Well, not as amazing as the possibility one day she'd be a reporter for a major newspaper, like the *Eagle,* and interview him. Or better yet, she would write articles for W. E. B. Du Bois, the editor of the weekly column in *The Crisis.*

Unforgettable.

Daisy exhaled a long sigh. The parade had ended, and reality was calling. She tugged at Yvette and Henrietta. "We'd better get back inside."

The hotel lobby was as crowded as Central Avenue and twice as loud. An orchestra played in the balcony, bellhops shouted, and hotel guests were checking in and out. The noise was deafening.

Groups of colored businessmen and Negro society's elite and members of prominent women's auxiliary clubs descended upon the lobby, the dining hall, the restaurants, the bars. They were everywhere. Sipping tea, emptying flasks into china cups, and talking unabashedly about the NAACP program, the dinner meetings, the parties, and more.

As soon as Yvette and Henrietta reentered the hotel, they scattered. Daisy was about to race up the staircase when Delilah Jenkins, one of the maids from the third floor (who kept trying to inch her way to the fourth floor), stopped her.

"One of the girls had taken off to watch the parade and isn't coming back," began Delilah. "Mrs. Keyes needs you to work the lobby as a parlormaid for a few hours." She then winked and skipped away.

Delilah was a mystery. On the outside she was like rainbows and poppies. But inside, Daisy suspected barbs and broken glass.

The chores of a parlormaid consisted of dusting, picking up trash, emptying containers, and generally keeping the lobby and lounges on the first floor tidy. It did pay better, which Daisy had a hard time understanding. The work was less taxing. But the parlormaids also had to be sociable and among the prettiest on the housekeeping staff.

As a parlormaid, Daisy could wander from one side of the hotel to the other, pausing to listen in on any number of conversations or happenings. It was a perfect fit for a snoop like her.

However, holding a pencil and paper and a duster would draw attention. She'd have to remember until she could write everything down.

One group caught her eye, and she

wormed in close enough to hear their chatter.

These women were higher-ups in the NAACP and throwing out names, places, and things that sounded very important. One appeared to be the leader, a Mrs. Louis Davis from Cleveland. She would preside over a meeting on the value of women's clubs in helping to elevate the Race. The other women were from New York City, Dayton, New Orleans, St. Louis, and Chicago.

Then a young woman, a lawyer from Oregon, strolled up to the group. Daisy recognized her from a photo in the *Eagle.* Beatrice Morrow Cannady was on the NAACP dais to give a big speech during the NAACP's annual meeting.

A civil rights leader with the same fire and dedication to the Race as Charlotta Bass, Cannady also owned and edited a well-known, highly regarded newspaper, the *Advocate,* the largest Negro newspaper in Oregon.

Daisy walked slowly toward the group with Cannady. She tried to overhear what was being said, but Cannady's voice was hoarse and whispery.

Daisy stopped to dust a tall vase. Then the oddest thing, she felt the walls pushing in on her, except it wasn't the people in the room, but the person standing next to her.

"Miss Washington," he said.

Her first thought was why people, well, honestly, men, kept sneaking up behind her. She glanced over her shoulder, but her gaze didn't linger. The floor was safer. "Mr. Barnes. So you've returned."

"Returned? I hadn't gone anywhere."

It was at that moment she realized she'd made a mistake. Why had she let him know she'd missed seeing him the past few days? A good thing she wasn't looking at him. It gave her time to quietly ask heaven or hell to place a hand over her mouth.

"How are you?" Malcolm Barnes asked.

She waved her duster. "Working," she replied, hoping no one like Mrs. Keyes saw them talking.

"You shouldn't speak to me here," she said quietly.

"Why not?"

Slowly, she lifted her chin, cocked her head, and looked him directly in the eye. "I'm a chambermaid working at the hotel. Not a guest here."

He bowed slightly. "I know that. My apologies. I only meant to say hello." He had been more confident, intoxicated and bruised, that night in Stepin Fetchit's suite.

Now, his voice was shy and his gaze imperfect.

"If you'll excuse me, I'm late for an appointment," he said but then didn't move. "Hopefully," he continued, "we'll run into each other again. Do you agree?"

Her palms itched and she squeezed the handle of the duster. "Yes, that would be very . . ." She stopped.

What was she about to say? *Heaven help her* — words never intended to be spoken aloud, especially not to him.

A voice called his name, and he was gone.

Daisy stood staring after him, trying to recall what she'd been doing before he interrupted.

Oh, yes. Beatrice Morrow Cannady.

Without moving a muscle, Daisy searched. But Cannady was nowhere in sight.

Damn that Malcolm Barnes. She blamed him for missing her chance to listen in on whatever Mrs. Cannady had to say.

The behavior of a schoolgirl — she scolded herself. Daisy and her bleary-eyed infatuation would end with pain, disappointment, and embarrassment. All rolled up in one bucket of dirty water.

Her choice, the only one she had, was to erase him from her mind — beginning now.

■ ■ ■ ■

For the first time in a while, Daisy was home before midnight. She entered the bedroom she shared with Henrietta and quietly changed from her gray muslin into a pair of pajamas and a robe. Then in the kitchen, she made a cup of tea, placed it on a tray, and walked down the hall to her mother's room.

Before her mother had taken ill, she was the last one in the house to go to bed. Sophie would wait up for her husband, no matter how late or early he returned, kiss him on the cheek, and make him a plate of food if he was hungry. Then she'd listen to him talk about his day.

When Daisy was in college, her mother helped her finish her assignments. They'd study over a pot of tea and freshly baked sugar biscuits and sit on the back porch, sipping, eating, and talking until Daisy's father arrived.

She stepped into her mother's bedroom, holding the tray and cringing at the smell of rubbing alcohol and medicine.

A white porcelain pitcher and a cup sat on the nightstand, along with a washcloth and a jar of cotton balls. A thin sheet was pulled to her mother's throat. Her eyes were open but unseeing.

"I have news, Mama." Daisy rested the tray on a stool next to the bed. "Harry Belmont — you remember him from school — now he's an influential newsman, writing for the *California Eagle.* He has a friend who is a nurse at St. Helena's Sanitarium. She is looking into what might be available for Negroes there and at what price. It's pretty far from here, near San Francisco, but if they take you in, you could be well by spring."

Her mother hadn't moved since Daisy entered the bedroom. No sounds had come from the bed except her breathing. A faint, faraway noise, but she was breathing.

Daisy kissed her mother's cheek. "I'll make sure you get better, Mama. I promise I will."

After a long while, Daisy picked up the tray and returned it to the kitchen and stepped outside onto the back porch for some fresh air. The night-blooming jasmine was strong enough to distract her from the alcohol and other medicines.

She sat on the top step, rocking back and forth, arms hugging around her shoulders. Her mother's condition was worse. The sightless stare and the clammy skin. The breathing that was barely a breath. *Oh, Christ.*

Something hard crashed inside her, ripping her into pieces: her mother was dying. Her mother might not live until December.

A thud in the corner of the porch made her look. "Who's there?"

"It's just me, Daisy."

"What are you doing out here, Isaiah?" She hadn't seen him hiding where the moonlight couldn't reach.

His shadowy silhouette stepped into the light. He smiled shyly.

"What are you doing?" Daisy repeated her question, but then she knew, catching sight of the guitar he held at his side.

"Practicing my music."

"Oh, that's right. You don't play, just practice."

He stepped closer. "You remembered."

"It's been a week. I can remember things. Believe it or not," she teased. Since telling him about Clifford, Daisy felt more comfortable around Isaiah. "So playing the guitar is your passion, isn't it?"

"Yes, ma'am," he answered quickly. "I started playing banjo when I was three and jazz guitar after that. I've listened to every jazz recording I could find and visited every nightspot I could sneak into. Chicago is a great town for music. When I wasn't in school, I was on the Stroll, that's State Street in Bronzeville, where all the jazz joints are. I'd get into the clubs through the kitchen and just watched, listened, and learned."

"I understand that kind of passion," Daisy said, staring at the sky, thinking of her journals. "I had planned to finish college. My mother wanted that for me. Though I don't need a degree to be a reporter, I want to write for the *California Eagle* or move to New York City and work with W. E. B. Du Bois at the *Crisis* magazine. You know, write stories like Ida B. Wells, Alice Dunbar Nelson, or Lillian Thomas Fox — stories that make a difference for the Race. Or maybe just poems."

"So you will be a civil rights advocate one day." He said it as if he believed she would be.

She felt encouraged. "Or I'll write about the Race's accomplishments and help make sure everyone knows the world is changing."

"You think about such things a lot, don't you?"

The earnestness in his tone put a lump in her throat. She smiled at him.

"I guess I do, Isaiah. But imagine how different America will be for the Negro in forty, fifty, a hundred years," she said. "It will be an amazing world."

Caught up in her own thoughts, Daisy had to shake herself. These were the dreams that broke hearts.

She pointed at Isaiah's guitar. "What about you? You have big plans, too."

"I do. I do," he said with a touch of melancholy. "I appreciate your family taking me in, but I didn't want to leave Chicago, and I intend to return as soon as I can. Right after my mother gets settled."

Daisy didn't mention that his mother's version of getting settled made no sense to her. "Mrs. Butler will be all right," she said. "She strikes me as a woman who is accustomed to doing what it takes for what she wants."

He nodded solemnly, but then his face brightened. "Tomorrow is a big day with the kickoff of the NAACP's meeting. I met one of the speakers when I was in Chicago. I wonder if she'll remember me."

"Which one?" Daisy asked, thinking about her notepad.

"Beatrice Morrow Cannady."

A breeze swept through the yard, and Daisy shivered but not from a chill. "You know her? How?"

"She used to sing at some of the speakeasies. I'd see her onstage when I was there to watch the musicians."

"How old were you?"

"Nine or ten."

Daisy's thoughts tumbled over themselves, but a somewhat desperate idea had flown into her head. She'd missed her chance to spy on Mrs. Cannady in the lobby because of Malcolm Barnes. But Isaiah might be able to help her. "Do you think she might remember you, and if she did, could you do me a favor?"

"She promised never to forget my guitar playing, but I'm not so sure about me."

"Just ask and see what happens. Then you could arrange for me to meet her, and I'll —" She paused as her harebrained idea became a plan. "Let's say I don't make a fuss about you practicing your guitar out loud — for short periods, very short periods, even while I'm home. All you have to do is ask her to meet with me." She smiled encouragingly, hoping he'd agree.

He shrugged. "Sure. I guess. What can it hurt? Right?"

"Absolutely nothing."

The back door swung open. "What are you two doing out here?"

199

It was Henrietta, rubbing sleep from her eyes.

"We're talking," Daisy replied. "What are you doing?"

"It is hot as Hades in the house. I need some air."

Daisy tilted back, eyeballing her sister. She didn't look as if she'd been asleep or hot. There was a tremor in Henrietta's voice. Daisy glanced at Isaiah. His entire body had stiffened, and even in the moonlight, she could see the flush in his cheeks. Was this a planned late-night meeting, Daisy wondered?

She shook her head. Their awkwardness, the long gazes, caused her to think of Malcolm. Had she looked at him the way her sister was staring at Isaiah?

"I'm going to sleep," Daisy said. "Are you coming, Henrietta?"

"I think I'll stay here for a few minutes to cool off before heading back into that oven."

"Don't stay too long. You don't want to catch a chill." Daisy narrowed her eyes at Isaiah. "And you don't want to be outside when Papa drives up."

"Sure thing, Daisy," Isaiah said. "And also, I won't forget. I'll find her tomorrow and let you know what she says."

"What who says?" Henrietta combed her

fingers through her bangs.

"None of your beeswax," Daisy said, waving her finger at her sister. "And don't you two stay down here too long. Papa could show up at any moment."

CHAPTER 13
FRANKIE

Saturday, June 1, 1968
Route 66 near Tulsa

The clap of thunder startles me. I blink back to consciousness, momentarily confused by where I'm not. This is not my apartment. The man next to me, driving the automobile, is not Jackson. The giant billboards speeding by put me in a trance. For a few seconds, I think I am somewhere I'm not. But my senses return, and I remember what I'm supposed to do.

See if I can find an exit — that's what Daisy said.

"There." I point. "The next exit is a mile ahead."

"Thank God." Tobey's exclamation is a reverent whisper. I give him a cautionary glance. I want to make sure he doesn't raise his hands from the steering wheel in supplication.

He leans forward, shoulders hunched, eyes

peeled on the sheet of water falling from the sky that hides the road. I can't see ten inches in front of us. I don't think Tobey is breathing from the lack of a visible rise and fall of his chest.

It takes ten minutes to make it to the exit. As the car veers off the highway, the rain slows, and from the acres of flat land, tall grass, and the smell of manure rising like cattails in a swamp, I can tell we aren't very close to a city, any city.

"Where are we?" Daisy places her elbows on the edges of our seats as she leans forward.

"The sign said we're coming up on Tulsa in another twenty miles."

"Not far from Oklahoma City." Tobey's voice aims for mellow, but he sounds exhausted. The rainstorm must've interfered with his joy of driving.

We pull into a gas station with two pumps. "This is a safe stop for us," Daisy announces. "The Thistle Filling Station is the last — or is it the only? — Negro-owned service station on Route 66 near Tulsa."

I stretch my neck to the side and give her a look. "Well, I'm impressed. How do you know this stuff?"

"I read," she says without hiding her annoyance. "Mostly Afro American newspapers, like the *Oklahoma Eagle,* which took over for the *Tulsa Star,* after 1921." An expression, equally of sorrow and hatred, reaches her eyes and turns down the corners of her mouth. "Yeah, the *Oklahoma Eagle* — not the *California Eagle,* mind you — is one of the oldest in this part of the country."

A sign reads RESTROOM on a small building with a pointed roof next to the station. Suddenly, it is all I care about.

"I need to go there." I nod toward the sign. "Are either one of you going into the store? Could you bring me something to eat?" I direct this request to Daisy, but Tobey, halfway out of the car, bends forward and holds his door open. "What would you like?"

I start to refuse him, but my belly growls loud enough for the crows in the cornfield to hear. "Pop-Tarts, Ruffles potato chips, a hot dog or sandwich of any kind, and a Tab."

"You sure?" Daisy chirps. "None of those foods, except for the sandwich, sound healthy enough for a pregnant girl or her baby."

What the hell?

"Are you pregnant?" Tobey lowers himself down to eye level, so he can see me and Daisy, who is still in the car.

He wipes drops of water from his eyes and

pulls wet strands of hair from his face, and, with a worried smile, says, "Congratulations?"

The question mark in his voice is as loud as a firecracker, and I could kill Daisy for sharing my private business.

"Why would you announce that to the world?" I scowl at my aunt.

Daisy shrugs and rolls her eyes. "I thought it was a secret you kept only from your husband."

"I could go to hell right now for what I'd love to do to you and your big mouth."

"My. My." Daisy chuckles as if I'm some adolescent having a tantrum. "You are speaking up for yourself. I'm glad to see it. Hope it lasts."

"Ladies, please." Tobey groans. "Let's pretend I didn't hear you, Daisy. Or better yet, I promise I won't remember a thing." He closes the car door, leaving Daisy and me to fight.

"Telling him about my pregnancy without my permission is uncool."

"Getting pregnant by a man who hits you is uncool."

"Jesus Christ. Talk about harping. I'm not going back to Jackson, but I'm not staying with you two, either. I'll do better on my own." Because I will be on my own in Los

Angeles, no one in that city who will help me, including my mother.

We are out of the car and Tobey shoves his hands into his pockets, looking pensively from me to Daisy.

"Frankie shouldn't go in a public restroom alone at this hour," he declares. "I'll go inside, pay for the gas, and pick up the items you ladies would like."

"I've been out of cigarettes for nearly fifty miles," Daisy exclaims. "I'll buy my own smokes, and she can scream if someone bothers her, and we'll come running."

"Daisy, please," Tobey pleads.

He is blessed with another classic Daisy shrug and a sigh. "Fine. Fine," she says. "But you wait for us before you go inside — hear me? Come on, Frankie."

Tobey crosses his arms over his chest and frowns. "I won't move an inch."

Daisy struts toward the restroom, and I follow.

When we enter, my senses already know what we will face. I wager every stall in every bathroom on Route 66 reeks of urine and other odors I don't want to think about, and this one doesn't disappoint. I rush into the first stall and immediately throw up.

"Are you okay?" Daisy asks from the stall next to me.

I can't answer and vomit at the same time. I hold up a finger, asking her to give me a moment, but she can't see through the stall.

"You'd better answer, or I'm coming in, Frankie."

I wipe my mouth with the back of my hand. "I'm fine. I drank too much Tab."

"And ate too much of whatever I brought you at the stop before this one."

Daisy is still in her stall, and I'm in mine, waiting for the nausea to pass. "Hard to use the bathroom when someone is talking to you."

She laughs. "You're too self-conscious." She is quiet for a few seconds. "I don't care about you taking off for Los Angeles alone. But if you can't handle your luggage, you won't be able to handle Jackson if he comes for you. He could know about the baby. Remember that nurse at the hospital?"

"I remember," I say solemnly.

The toilet flushes, and I follow suit. But when Daisy's stall door slams shut, I stay put. My stomach is queasy. I'm not done yet.

"My mother says you're a communist."

"Because I smoke weed?"

"She doesn't know whether you smoke weed or cigarettes. She doesn't know anything about you, except who you were forty years ago."

"Tell her I smoke both."

Something in her voice makes me want to see her face. My stomach is hanging in there, and I exit the stall, dying to wash my hands.

Daisy stands in front of a small sink, smiling at her reflection in the cloudy mirror, showing off perfect white teeth and deep, soulful dimples. She is unsettlingly attractive. A woman of her age should be less — less good-looking, less loud, less of everything she seems to be.

"If you're not a communist, why does my mother hate you?"

"You think she hates me because of politics?" Daisy giggles.

"I don't know. I'm just searching for answers. Forty years is a long time. Something happened that made being in the same room, house, city, or state unbearable."

"Let me ask you this —"

"Go ahead."

She is holding a lipstick and covering her mouth with a deep red color. "Do you hate your husband?"

The sudden tightness in my chest feels like something cold has a hand on my heart. "What?"

"Can you imagine never speaking to him again for the rest of your life?"

The question chews on the parts of me that care about Jackson. "I hadn't thought of never seeing him again. I just thought about leaving him."

"There you have it." Daisy finishes freshening her makeup. "The last time I saw your mother — the only thing I cared about was leaving. And what happened after I left was — well, life, with all its twists and turns. Forty years happens fast. Like sunlight bursting through black clouds on a stormy day. The years happen in a flash like a bad storm or the first day of spring."

"What does that mean? Sounds like a poem, but it doesn't tell me what happened forty years ago."

"Does that matter now, the distance between your mom and me, when your husband could be coming after you?" she asks. "Does he know you're going to Los Angeles? Did you tell him?" she snaps. "Frankie, stop staring at yourself in the mirror and answer me."

"I spoke to him on the pay phone in the diner, but he doesn't know you're with me." I glance away from her dark glare. "I talked to him before I got hit — Sorry, sorry. Before I fainted and fell."

She shakes her head. "You shouldn't travel on your own." She turns on the faucet and rinses her hands.

I grab a bar of soap, but she slaps my knuckles. "Don't use that. Where has that soap been?"

I drop it and just rinse, like her, but I also cup water in my palm and swoosh the vomit from my mouth.

I face Daisy. "I can't travel with Tobey, Aunt Daisy. Driving around with a white man through small towns and stretches of highway where Blacks are few and far between — and with just two months since Martin Luther King's assassination — is begging for trouble from Negroes and white people."

Daisy stares at her reflection in the mirror. Her eyeliner and lipstick are perfect. Her hair is flat on one side, but she looks pretty, just slightly mangled.

She removes a compact from her purse and begins to fix what's wrong. "If you feel that strongly, I can't force you to stay with us. So you are on your own as soon as we make it to Oklahoma City."

"Thank you." I wipe my damp hands on my skirt. "Can I ask you something about my mother and you?"

Daisy shakes her hands, flinging drops of

water. "Why is it that you like to ask questions when there's too little time for a proper answer?"

"One question, out of curiosity. Did you and my mother argue the way you and I argue?" I'm smiling, but she wrinkles her brow at me.

"You want me to say you remind me of your mother?"

"Oh, no. I wonder if I remind you of you."

She laughs. "Not yet. But give it time. If some of me is inside you —" She taps me on the chest with two fingers. "It will come out sooner or later."

She leads us from the restroom, and Tobey is where we left him, standing in the same position, next to the Mustang, arms crossed, head tilted to the side, but now he's smiling.

"You two look pretty refreshed."

Daisy marches by him and makes a sound that is more purr than growl. "Let's hurry. I want to cover a few hundred more miles before we call it a night."

Tobey and I trot into the store behind her. The place is small and empty except for the cashier, who nods in our direction. Absently, I wonder if he's a Thistle. There are three short aisles. Daisy grabs a carton of Kent cigarettes from the rack.

211

"He'll pay for these," she shouts at the Black man behind the cash register and points at Tobey.

I ramble off toward a rack of chips and candy while promising to eat something more substantial than snack food as soon as we arrive in Oklahoma City.

Daisy follows me, but she's tearing into the carton of Kents as we walk. "You want a smoke?"

I rub my hand over my mouth. "I don't smoke, but I might as well with all the smoke I've swallowed since we left Chicago." I shrug the shoulder with the sling. "You'll have to light it for me."

Loud voices enter the store, and we both look in the direction of the front door. A group of Black men thunders through the door, single file, heading for the cashier. I make out a few voices. They are shouting for "Larry's secret stash."

I frown at Daisy. "Stash of what?"

"Liquor, most likely from the way half of them are staggering." She inches forward. The aisle we are in aligns with the checkout counter, and we can see what's happening, like watching it on a movie screen.

Daisy has stopped ripping into her cartoon and is watching the men like it's the shower scene in the Hitchcock movie *Psycho,*

212

which I've never seen. But I heard it made grown men scream.

Her face twists into something I've never seen before on her. She looks worried, but more than that, she looks scared.

"What's wrong?" I ask her.

"Where's Tobey?"

A half-dozen men are hanging out in front of the checkout counter. Afros; thick, long sideburns; dashikis; and bell-bottom jeans. Silver-gray temples, bald heads, button-down plaid shirts, and pressed slacks. A mix of generations.

The smells of beer, cigarettes, and marijuana stick to the walls as thick as the stench of gasoline. But just like back home on my block in Chicago, by two o'clock in the morning, a group of men out this late, full of drink and smoke, should be left alone. A band of brothers can turn into an explosion in the beat of a heart.

I wonder if that's what has Daisy panicked. What might happen if they run into Tobey in their frame of mind? We might not know what these men are thinking or what might happen to Black men when a white boy trespasses on their terrain? Neither one of us knows for sure.

"They aren't going to bother him," I say,

going for optimism. "Unless he bothers them. Besides, they are having a heated debate about Muhammad Ali versus Cassius Clay."

Those are the names they are yelling at one another. Of course, Ali and Clay are the same man.

"Stop worrying, Daisy. Those men have no interest in a lone white man buying Tab, chips, and cigarettes."

"Where is that boy?"

She is not listening. She's also not searching. We're standing in the aisle. So I grab a candy bar and some other snacks and move toward the cashier, but she grabs my wrist, holding me still.

I shake loose. "I'm going to pay for my chips and my drink and will wait for you in the car."

"You aren't going anywhere." She grabs me again. "I just want him out of here before he opens his mouth and says the wrong thing. A white boy with long hair in a dashiki is begging for trouble in a town like Tulsa." She bites down on her lip. "Let's just find him."

The conversation among the men grows louder. Daisy and I do an about-face and head toward the back of the store. Still no sign of Tobey.

"He's not in the store, Daisy," I whisper.

"He was right behind you when we walked in."

One of the men at the counter is loud. "I ain't got no goddamned time for a Black man changing his name to join somebody's Nation of Islam."

"Clay ain't no boxer." The cashier is sixty or so, with a shiny bald dome, but a ring of nappy gray hair circles the lower portion of his head. He looks like a monk (and it is not a good look), but he isn't going to miss his chance to make a point. "Clay is a showboat and was lucky to beat Liston."

A chorus of *hell no*s and *you're damn straight*s follow.

"Sonny Liston was a boxer," the cashier adds emphatically.

"Liston was a drunk." One of the men staggers forward and pounds his fist on the counter.

He gets a playful round of shoves in the back and punches in the arm for his trouble.

"You're a drunk, Terrence." The cashier announces with a shake of his head. "And what the hell are you talking about?

"Clay was a fighter who didn't want to fight for his country," the cashier continues. "All you young bucks want to make him a hero. He ain't no hero."

215

Terrence and his muttonchop sideburns and floppy Afro lunge for the cashier, but the man is too far away, and one of Terrence's friends has hold of his shirttail.

A chorus of loud sighs turns into frustrated mutterings. I wager these men have had similar if not the same disagreement for as long as they can remember.

"You ain't calling me an Uncle Tom, are you, boy?"

"You ain't calling me a boy, are you, fool?"

"Not in front of a white man. You better not."

I look at Daisy, "That must be Tobey."

"He's at the register." Daisy marches toward the front of the store.

"Whaddaya bet, man? Cassius Clay, or Muhammad Ali, or whatever you want to call him, I think he could take George Foreman."

"You lost your fuckin' mind." The cashier waves his hand, dismissing the question as insanity. "Foreman would annihilate Ali, or whatever the hell his name is."

"Hey, white boy, what do you think?" says Terrence. "Or do you hippies care about boxing?"

"Leave him be, Terrence."

"Who was the last white heavyweight champion?"

216

Tobey adjusts the merchandise in his hands. "I'm not a fan of boxing."

"Everyone's a goddamn fan of boxing." Terrence turns to the others. "I bet he liked the sport when Rocky Marciano was the champ. Am I right?"

One of the men laughs. "Damn. Rocky was the champ in the fifties, son. This boy ain't no older than you."

"Yeah, Terrence, calm down," says another man. "This boy ain't done nothing to you. Why are you trying to pick a fight with him?"

"I'm just wondering how come he doesn't know shit about boxing."

"I'm not a fan."

"Why's that?"

"I don't condone violence," says Tobey. "I don't believe a man should fight for something he doesn't believe in. I guess I see Mr. Ali as examining both sides of the equation —"

"So, you're some kind of expert in what a Black man thinks or why the hell we do what we do?" Terrence steps in on Tobey, practically bumping him in the chest. "Is that why you wearing a goddamned dashiki because you are down with the Black man?"

Terrence raises his fist in the Black power sign, but he's still too close to Tobey, and my nerves are shattering. I swear Tobey's conscientious backside is about to get kicked.

"Can we pay for these and go?" Daisy swings her hips to the front of the line, waving for Tobey and me, I think, to join her in a group exit.

"What you mean by —" Terrence begins but abruptly stops and looks from Daisy to me and then at Tobey. "You with them?"

Tobey doesn't answer that question. He keeps going on about Ali versus Cassius Clay. "He fought for a living, and he refuses to fight for a country that denies his people a fair chance at life."

The cashier harrumphs. "Well, listen to you."

Another man's voice is tinged with sarcasm. "Yeah, he's one of those hippie white boys who understands the problems of Black people."

Daisy places her items on the counter. "Can you ring these up, so we can get out of here?"

"You are with these two ladies, then?" It's Terrence again.

Tobey moves by Terrence and stands next to Daisy. Then the energy in the room shifts, as do the gazes of every Black man in the store — all eyes move from Terrence to Tobey.

"I asked you a question, boy. Are you with these two ladies?"

"Terrence. Cool it," advises the cashier. "You ain't got no beef with him."

"I'm just asking." Terrence leans against the counter, staring at Tobey but talking to the cashier. "Don't you think it strange? Here he is with his long hair, in a dashiki, traveling with two Black chicks — you don't see that every day. Shit. You don't see that around here at all. Do you know where you are at, boy? Tulsa. Oklahoma. Or what day it is? June first. Do you know what happened here on June first in 1921?"

His rage strikes the room like a bullwhip.

Daisy reaches into her purse and steps toward Terrence.

I place my bag of chips and bottle of Tab on the counter and head for the door. I am halfway to the exit when the memory takes hold. The last time Daisy reached into her purse with such purpose was outside my apartment building. I hadn't seen the blade then, but my gut is flipping inside out. I just know the pearl-plated switchblade is about to make an appearance.

I spin on my heels. "Tobey, get Mama and let's go. I'm not feeling well."

All eyes are now on me, which I imagine is my intention, but I'm unsure what to do next. Even Daisy looks bewildered, but her hand hasn't stopped digging in her purse.

My mouth goes dry.

Tobey turns to me, blinking at me with a crazed plea in his eyes. He must know about Daisy's switchblade, too. "We can't have you getting sick in the man's store, darling." Then, smiling, he walks around the men and rests a hand on my shoulder.

I place a hand over my mouth, another on my stomach, and heave.

"Oh my God." The words sound like a chorus of a song sung in unison by the men at the counter.

"Don't just stand there," the cashier says. "Get her out of here before she throws up."

CHAPTER 14
DAISY

Summer 1928
Los Angeles

On her way to the Hotel Somerville, there were three things on Daisy's mind: Beatrice Morrow Cannady, Harry Belmont, and a nagging *what if* someone spotted her with Harry. Talk, rumors, gossip, and lies spread at a hotel like a bad cold. Most of it fueled by the staff. Daisy could lose both jobs if someone found out she was the Mata Hari of the Hotel Somerville.

It was Friday morning, and the NAACP annual meeting had a full day of speeches and meetings scheduled. As soon as Daisy arrived at the hotel, she telephoned Harry and asked him to join her during her break at one of his favorite spots, Roy's Diner.

"Hey, doll, funny running into you here." Harry strolled into the restaurant with his familiar crooked grin.

"How are you?" Daisy said with a brief,

anxious smile on her face as he slid into the bench opposite her. "Thank you for coming. I'm just a little worried and want to be careful. I can't have anyone suspecting that I'm your gal inside the Somerville."

They sat in a booth in the rear of the restaurant that Roy set aside for his special customers, which Daisy knew meant Harry.

"I'm fine," he said. "But you are acting mighty mysterious. What's the story?"

When she lifted her gaze, she sat up straighter, squared her shoulders, and cleared her throat in a final move of confidence. "I have a chance to interview Beatrice Morrow Cannady. If I pull it off, I want to strike a new deal."

"I'm listening."

"She's a major speaker during the NAACP meeting, traveled from Oregon, and is editor of the *Advocate*."

Roy interrupted then with two cups and a pot of coffee, cream and sugar and a menu. Daisy squeezed the blood from her hands as he and Harry made small talk for several unbelievable minutes. Roy finally departed, but Harry was the one who spoke first.

"I know who Beatrice Morrow Cannady is, Daisy," he said. "What's your new deal?"

She took a deep breath. "I want you to pay me five dollars for my notes from the interview."

"Five dollars for notes? And what makes you think that if I wanted an article on Mrs. Cannady, I wouldn't interview her myself?"

Daisy suddenly felt she hadn't thought her idea through. Harry was right. He was covering the NAACP annual meeting for the *Eagle*. She searched her brain for an answer. "I didn't think you'd have time or perhaps wouldn't be interested in her speech. She's an advocate of the rights of colored women and will speak on the subject in her remarks. W. E. B. Du Bois himself approved her as a speaker." Daisy held Harry's gaze. "She's the Charlotta Bass of Oregon, a true zealot of the cause and a godsend for the Negro woman." She paused. "I also would do a better job of interviewing her than you."

Daisy looked away, focusing on her cup of coffee. It had been quite the declaration; one she hadn't expected to make. But since she had, she had no doubt she'd spoken the truth.

Harry leaned back in the booth, palms flat on the table, and frowned. "I love Negro women and their rights, Daisy. I'm hurt you think otherwise, but if I wanted to interview Mrs. Cannady, I'd find a way because I'm a good reporter. I know how to get the story."

He was scolding her but also hadn't answered her question. "Yes or no, Harry?"

"Give me a moment. I'm trying to recover from your low opinion of me." He grinned and arched a dramatic eyebrow — ever as much an actor as a newsman.

Exasperated, Daisy exclaimed, "You can't be everywhere at once. There's too much happening this week, Harry. My notes will be the bee's knees. Please. You need me to do this."

Upsettingly, still unconvinced, he said, "You know, there are other reporters at the *Eagle*."

"Have you assigned one of them to the story? I'd wager no. You are paid by the article. You want your byline on as many stories as possible."

He scratched the tip of his nose. "Okay. I'll pay you five bucks, but only if you write it up."

Daisy's heart somersaulted in her chest. "I don't write articles." Harry knew this. "You've never asked me to write an article before. Why now?"

"I'm no fool, Daisy. I notice things, and you've wanted to be a reporter since high school."

"And I will be one day. Just not today."

He looked at her with genuine concern. "I

can't believe you're still thinking about Mulholland."

Oh, my, she thought. Harry could see into her soul some days. "Not a lot, but enough," she said.

The city's civil engineer, William Mulholland, built Los Angeles. He also wrecked it. He was responsible for the St. Francis Dam. The man whose negligence had caused the disaster that had killed her uncles — and hundreds of others. A jury convened within days of the disaster but concluded he wasn't at fault. Others disagreed. Daisy was among the latter.

"It would've been my first stab at being a newswoman, but —"

"You were grieving, Daisy." He reached across the table in a gesture of kindness, she assumed, but her hands were in her lap.

"Death and sickness had destroyed your family," Harry said. "What were you supposed to do, ignore your feelings?"

"No, but if I'd been stronger, I could've used them."

She'd had the opportunity to write a story about the dam's collapse. She'd heard from one of her friends, who worked as a maid of a city official, that there was proof Mulholland was at fault. She'd help Daisy get ahold of it, too, if she wrote an article for the

Eagle. But Daisy refused.

"Darling, you were the wrong skin color to get any mileage on that story."

Even if Harry was right, she couldn't blame Race for her failure. "Not if I'd done as you told me and gone for it. With proof, the *Eagle* would've run the story."

"Maybe, and maybe not. Mulholland is a white king in this town."

"You don't understand." How could she explain that it wasn't only Mulholland's white skin or her grief that had kept her from writing the story? She was afraid. The attention, the judgment. It was one thing to write in journals she hid under her pillow or notes scribbled hastily about hotel guests — an altogether different circumstance to write an article with her name on it.

"Daisy, now it's your turn, will you or won't you — yes, or no?"

She chewed her lower lip. "Okay, okay. It's a deal. But no byline, promise." She blew out a chest full of air.

Harry thinned his lips and sighed. "Okay. You've got a deal. And, do you feel better?"

She nodded.

"Good, now, what else do you have?"

She smiled. "I overheard some guy from Central Casting at the bar the other night. His name was Charlie, I think. He's the head of all-Negro employment for Central Casting and claims that King Vidor is making a movie with an all-Negro cast. It says it will keep him a busy man for months."

Harry was in the middle of a sip of coffee. "Yes. Yes." He gulped. "His name is Charlie Butler. I heard the same rumors about the Vidor moving picture. It's a talkie."

Oh, Daisy wondered if he was related to Isaiah. She'd have to remember to ask. "I think Stepin Fetchit is vying for the lead," Daisy added hastily. It was a tidbit she'd overheard but wouldn't have normally included since it came from only one person. But Harry was desperate for gossip on Fetchit . . . so why not?

"Step? In a lead role." He laughed. "And it's not a comedy?"

She shrugged a shoulder. "It's possible."

"Okay. Okay. Good job, Daisy."

"One thing, though, I'll need the article and your notes today. No later than a quarter to five. And you'll need to drop it off at the *Eagle*."

He said it as if the request was perfectly reasonable. Daisy groaned. "I start my second shift at five and Mrs. Keyes has been keeping her eyes on me." Another reason for her concern about meeting Harry at the hotel.

"Sorry, babe, but I've got to set the presses early. Heading out on a cruise tonight." He smiled slyly. "Which I won't miss, so if I don't have your article before I leave, I can't use it, and you don't get paid."

Daisy felt a moment of panic but had an idea. "Isaiah, our boarder, will run it over."

"He'd better or no money for you."

"You'll have it."

Harry waved for Roy, who brought them fresh coffee. Daisy waved off the refill. "No, thanks." She stood next to the booth. "Sorry, Harry, I've got to dash, but thank you."

"Hey." He took her hand. "We're partners, doll. You can always count on me."

Later that day, outside the main meeting hall, Daisy caught up with Isaiah.

"You're all set," he said. "She'll meet you in her suite at four o'clock."

"Thank you, Isaiah. Thank you," Daisy said. "I'll need another favor from you, though. You'll have to run the article over to the *Eagle* before five o'clock."

"Consider it done."

Beatrice Morrow Cannady swept into the suite's parlor where Daisy was waiting, trying to stop her nerves from exploding.

A handsome woman, she wore a gorgeous

silk shawl draped over her shoulder with embroidered flowers, roses mostly, with long rainbow-colored fringe.

"Good afternoon," she said, tugging off her gloves and tossing her hat onto the chaise.

"Thank you for doing this." Daisy's voice squeaked slightly to her dismay. "I am humbled that you agreed."

"Of course I would agree. Isaiah and I met in Chicago when I planned on becoming a singer. I spent years in the city, learning and listening to jazz and the blues, but from such a young age, Isaiah's talent was apparent. Did he tell you how he'd sneak into the back of the clubs to listen to the Creole Jazz Band?"

"Yes, ma'am. He did," Daisy replied. Isaiah had shared the story more than once. "And you remembered him."

"Have you heard him play? If you had, you wouldn't ask if I remembered him — he's unforgettable. Even as a boy playing his guitar, he was amazing."

Daisy still felt like a stranger to Isaiah's musical talents, but that might change. She had agreed to allow him to practice in the house — even out loud.

Mrs. Cannady cocked her head. "You seem nervous, young lady."

Daisy swallowed a giggle. "This is unusual, ma'am. I mean, I'm a chambermaid, and you know Isaiah, but still, to do him — us — such a favor is very generous."

She waved her hand elegantly. "You're a young Negro woman with a mind. If I can help you better understand a woman's role in the struggle, I can sacrifice a few minutes of my day to talk about the mission." She wrinkled her nose delicately. "Where will this story appear?"

"I have high hopes of it running in the *California Eagle,* but I will definitely post it for the women who work at the Somerville."

She nodded, pleased, and some of the tension left Daisy's body.

"Excellent. Okay, then, let's get started." Mrs. Cannady sat on the desk chair.

Still standing, Daisy removed a notepad and pencil from her apron pocket. "I heard you had a tough time getting a spot on the dais."

Mrs. Cannady lifted a finger to her temple, tapping gently. "The important thing to remember is that I delivered a speech. Any supposed difficulties I might have had on the way to the podium were resolved. So, let's not discuss them."

Properly rebuked, Daisy continued. "You mentioned the role of the Negro woman in

230

your remarks, but did you mean for it to sound as if our sole job is to take care of our home, husband, and children?"

"Is that what you understood I meant?" She smiled, but not with her eyes. "You don't have to answer that. Let me start again." She paused. "Negro women in positions of leadership are too often lukewarm about the Race and end up responsible for much of the indignities handed out to our people."

Now, Daisy frowned. "How so?"

"These times demand women who must first believe in the Race before we can persuade others."

Daisy stopped scribbling. "Aren't there plenty of colored women who are doing that, especially now. Women like Zora Neale Hurston and Helene Johnson?"

"They are artists, and their jobs are to stir the emotions of the Race. They seek to inspire through a creative challenge. When a wife sees her husband, father, or sons forgetting that the most precious thing in life is freedom, it is her mission to keep that man on course."

Daisy had to think on that for a moment. Was Cannady implying a Negro woman contributed best as a wife and mother? Daisy wasn't sure she agreed but wasn't

231

sure why. "You mentioned Wendell Phillips's wife in your remarks."

"When faced with temptation, she told Wendell don't 'shilly-shally.' "

"That sounds out of place."

"How so?" Mrs. Cannady asked sternly. "Was she making fun?"

"It carries a whiff of humor, yes. But the point is no different from the words of Sojourner Truth, who helped Frederick Douglass when he had all but lost hope of freedom."

"I believe she asked him if God was dead?"

"She did. And W. E. B. Du Bois reinforced these ideas when he also spoke about what Negro women can do for the Race and nation." Mrs. Cannady took a deep breath.

"I paraphrase, but he said something like the Negro woman's duty is to keep the histories of the Race by . . . they are the historians in the home. They maintain the books of fiction, poetry, and pictures, paintings, et cetera. In addition to supporting their men."

Daisy pictured a woman like her mother in some ways but also a woman who had ambition for her daughters. And to do best for them, she read newspapers, periodicals, magazines, books, fiction, and nonfiction.

She loved to learn and had plans for her future, not only for her husband and children. In a way, she was the woman Mrs. Cannady described.

"The Negro mother should also spend less money on furniture and more on books and music about the Race. It will help our youth grow up with pride."

"I agree knowledge about our history is critical."

"I'm glad we agree on something."

Daisy gasped. Had she been so obvious? "I didn't mean to imply I disagreed with you, Mrs. Cannady."

"Then you need to develop a better poker face." The smile returned. "You may not have said so, but your expression gives away your thoughts whether you want them known or not." She placed a hand on the arm of the chair. "Do you have enough to write your story?"

Daisy nodded. "Yes, I have more than enough."

"Excellent, thank you — what was your name again?"

"Daisy Washington."

"I enjoyed our chat," said Mrs. Cannady, and Daisy was dismissed.

She thanked her profusely and left the fourth-floor suite, closing the door quietly behind her. Standing in the hall, she quickly jotted down a few more thoughts in her notes, and then she went straight to the pantry and slammed the door shut.

She glanced at the wall clock and tried not to panic. Her article had to be ready in thirty minutes if Isaiah were to get it to Harry and the *Eagle*'s office in time.

She wrote furiously, first the headline and the opening paragraph, which needed the most work. It was the one that grabbed the reader. But she was writing at a furious pace, and to her surprise, it took her only fifteen minutes to transform her notes into something readable. After that, she just had to censor her opinion of Mrs. Cannady's thoughts on Negro women and the fight for freedom and come up with a strong lead.

The knock on the door came as she scribbled the last sentence of the article. "Isaiah? It's done."

"No, it's Yvette. What are you doing? Hiding?" She glanced at the notepad and pencil in Daisy's hands. "You came in here to write?"

"I did, but I have a good reason, but I can't explain anything now." Daisy looked over Yvette's shoulder. "Have you seen Isaiah?"

She shook her head.

Daisy moved past her into the hall. "He's supposed to meet me here."

"Who?"

"Isaiah," Daisy repeated. She checked the time again. She was seconds from dashing down the stairs when Delilah appeared in the hallway outside the pantry.

"Are you looking for that new boy, the guitar player? He's a handsome young man. I know where he is — he's with your sister," she said with a sing-song voice. "One of the shoeshine boys stopped by the Apex on his way to work. Said that boy and Henrietta are tearing up the joint at some afternoon party, with his strumming and her singing and dancing."

Daisy placed a hand over her heart to keep it from bursting through her ribcage. "Are you sure?" Her voice was as high as a startled ten-year-old. "My sister and Isaiah Butler are at a nightclub?"

Yvette took her by the elbow. "Why are you yelling?"

She jerked free. "You did hear what she said. Lord. He was supposed to do something very important for me."

Yvette folded her arms. "The way you're acting, what was he supposed to do, build you a castle or something?"

"A castle? No." Daisy glared at her friend.

Why did Yvette make jokes, as if they calmed Daisy when she was upset? Well, they didn't.

A bad feeling and a flash of heat attached themselves to Daisy's skin and squeezed. "Isaiah was supposed to meet me here."

"What's going on, Daisy? You seem so upset."

"Can you cover for me?" She started to untie her tea apron.

Yvette's shoulders sagged. "I told you I'm getting off, and Sid is waiting for me with the baby."

"Yvette, please. I swear I won't take long."

Delilah interrupted. "I can stay. I'd love to get in some time working on the tenant's floor."

Daisy put her hands on her hips and gave Yvette a pleading look. Delilah wasn't someone they wanted working with them. She was too much of a busybody, even for Daisy.

Yvette closed her eyes briefly. "Fine. I'll cover for you. But if Sid leaves me, it will be your fault."

Daisy blinked at her, tears in her eyes. "You are the cat's meow."

"Yeah. Yeah. Just get back quick. Go on, go over to the Apex and try not to kill your younger sister."

236

Daisy hugged Yvette. "I'll be back as soon as I can. This won't take too long."

She ran down the flights of stairs, across the street, and down a block to the *California Eagle* offices on Central Avenue. She said a quick hello, here you go, and dropped the article on Harry's desk. Then she apologized. "Sorry, I've got to go."

Now she was headed for the Apex Club. Five o'clock in the afternoon, and she was going into a nightclub. What in the hell had gotten into Isaiah's head, and why had Henrietta lost her mind with him?

"I'll drag them both out of there by their damn roots." Running, she glanced around. Thank goodness, no one was near enough to have heard her curse.

CHAPTER 15
FRANKIE

Saturday, June 1, 1968
Route 66 near Tulsa

Tobey peels away from the Thistle Filling Station, burning rubber like we're being chased.

I check out the back window. "They won't come after us," I remark without a lick of confidence. "They probably think we're civil rights activists, heading south to help get out the vote for the primary on Tuesday."

"You are out of your mind, Frankie," Daisy huffs a chuckle. "That idea won't make it past the gas pump outside the store — not after you and Tobey's little show."

"We did have them fooled, didn't we?" I say proudly. Then I add with a giggle, "I swear Terrence was a drunken inch away from punching Tobey in the jaw."

He glances at me, irritation blazing from his gaze like Superman's X-ray vision. But I don't believe his unveiled anger is meant just for me.

"What were you digging for in your purse, Daisy?" Tobey's tone hides nothing. He is pissed.

"Did we pay?" Daisy ignores him and lights a cigarette. "I don't think we did."

"Daisy, answer me!" Tobey isn't letting up, and I think I understand why. "Were you about to stab someone over a dispute about boxing?"

So, it's exactly what I thought. "Yes, she was reaching into her purse for her knife. Unbelievable. Here I am worried about Jackson when the real danger is the woman in the back seat. Good Lord. I'm so glad I'm out of here when we reach Oklahoma City."

Leisurely, Daisy stretches out as much as one can in the back seat of a Mustang. "The only thing I was hunting for was a pack of matches, children."

"Don't lie, Daisy." I turn in my seat to glare at her.

Tobey slams the steering wheel with the heel of his hand, making a loud whacking sound. It sends a shudder through my body.

"It is two o'clock in the morning," he exclaims through clenched teeth. "I'm tired and need to sleep."

"First, drop me off at the bus station."

"The bus station is closed." Daisy exhales, filling the car with a lung of cigarette smoke.

"So, I guess that means our adventure hasn't changed your mind about leaving us?" Tobey leans over the steering wheel, blinking against the brightness of oncoming headlights. "You should stay."

I look at him confused because he sounds like he's begging.

"We're heading to the same place," Tobey says. "Just makes sense for you to stay."

He can't disrupt my resolve, and I go for honest. "My aunt smokes like a chimney, and I may die of smoke inhalation before we get to Albuquerque if she doesn't slow down. Both of you drive too fast. And you're white. And Daisy keeps flashing her switchblade. That's plenty of reason for me to be on my way."

"I thought it was your husband you were running from, not Daisy. Not just me?" Tobey adds bluntly, gripping the steering wheel with both hands. "Your arm is in a sling, and you're pregnant, and it is late, and I'm tired, and Daisy is tired. And we were almost in a brawl, or maybe we weren't, but it felt that way, and I don't fight, remember. I'm a deserter so, it's best to let the coward among us get his rest before he collapses into a ball of nerves and anxiety." He pauses, closing his eyes, which scares the crap out of me because he is *driving*. But his eyes open. "Anyway, we should find a hotel and rest. We can discuss the bus station and Los Angeles in the morning. Agreed?"

It might be the longest speech Tobey has made since he got in the car. Though he was talking about more than needing to get off the highway and sleep, I think. But I'm not interested in what plagues his world.

Still, somewhere in the frayed bell-bottom jeans and dashiki, I am witnessing a man in pain.

Daisy rolls down her window, and the wind zips through the car, hitting my cheek with the cold night air.

The strike of a match and the smell of sulfur fills my nose. I am worried about being on a road trip with these two, but I'm also worried about being alone if Jackson catches up to me on the bus. I'd better find out if he's after me or not. I'll call Tamika in the morning.

"Fine," I say. "Tomorrow is just fine."

A few miles down the road, I remember a question I wanted to ask. "What is June first? Terrence acted like he wanted to kill us because it was June first."

"Not us. Just Tobey," Daisy answers. "He was talking about the massacre. Though it happened long before his time."

"What massacre?" I ask.

She takes a long tug on her cigarette that sucks in both her cheeks. "The June massacre that happened in 1921. Hundreds of Negroes were killed by angry whites, who didn't like successful Black people. That's the short description for that bloody travesty. I was a girl when my mother read me the news story. A few years ago, I wrote an article commemorating the senseless tragedy, forty years after the slaughter. You want more details — you can find a copy of what I wrote for the Associated Negro Press. Though the ANP doesn't exist anymore, closed its doors in 'sixty-four."

I look at Tobey, who has his eyes on the road. So, I figure he already knew Daisy had worked for ANP, probably knew about the Tulsa massacre, too. "So, how long did you write for them?"

"On and off for twenty years." She lights another Kent. I can't keep up with how many cigarettes she smokes. She put the chain in the chain-smoker.

"Let's listen to some music," she says. "We need to dance in our seats for a bit, work off some of these bad vibes."

242

"Daisy, I want to talk about the knife," Tobey says flatly. "Next time don't jump to 'I need to stab someone' as the solution for every situation we may or may not run into, if you don't mind. We can walk away without a fight or putting on a show."

"I told you. I was looking for matches."

Tobey huffed. "In the middle of all that, you were going to open a carton of cigarettes we hadn't paid for, pull out a pack, rip it open, and light a smoke?"

"So, I was right. We didn't pay."

I can see the veins in Tobey's throat, and I swear he's about to blow his stack. "I didn't see a knife."

"You were too busy throwing up," snaps Tobey.

"To be clear, I was pretending to throw up, which may have saved us, or you, from a butt-whipping."

"I didn't know you were pretending. You're pregnant, aren't you? I thought you were sick."

"She was sick in the bathroom," Daisy chimes in.

"Lord Jesus." I clap my hands like I am herding a group of kindergartners. "Stop, please. Can we have one conversation?"

"Adrenaline," Daisy says calmly. "I think we all just had a shot of it." She puffs on

243

her cigarette.

"I said it before — we should listen to some music and dance in our seats."

I pick up the box of eight-tracks and pop in "Dancing in the Street" by Martha Reeves and the Vandellas.

In minutes, we are singing along with Martha, and except for the fact that Daisy is tone-deaf, we don't sound too bad as a group. We listen to the entire cassette before I change tempo and put in some Otis Redding.

His deep soulful voice is soothing.

"What time is it?" I ask.

"Close to three a.m.," Daisy responds.

"Our hasty departure from the Thistle Filling Station tuckered me out," Tobey says. "We just passed a sign about an inn five miles down the road."

"You hold your horses. Let me check the book." Daisy taps me on the shoulder, and I remove the *Green Book* from the glove compartment. "What's the name?"

"The Peacock Inn."

Daisy spends five minutes flipping through the book's pages. I'm feeling as tired as Tobey looks.

"The Peacock Inn isn't listed in the *Green Book.*"

But she's too late with this news since

Tobey has pulled into a parking spot outside the so-named inn.

"I'm not sure the Peacock Inn is listed anywhere, including the yellow pages." My judgment is based on the exterior of the broken-down building.

"We aren't going to make it to Oklahoma City. Hell, we aren't going to make it halfway. We haven't even made it to Davenport." Tobey makes no effort to stifle a yawn. "I'll drive us into a ditch unless I get some sleep, which I can't do in a Mustang. My legs will cramp."

I only half listen. The inn is a scene straight out of Hitchcock's *Psycho* — which I've never seen, but Tamika told me about it and that was enough.

Finally, Daisy gives in, softened up by Tobey's mention of wrecking her automobile, I imagine. Her only demand as we park and exit the car: we enter the lobby separately and don't speak to Tobey.

Pretending not to know him is a knuckle-headed plan, I'm thinking since he's carrying my powder-blue Lady Baltimore suitcase when we walk inside.

But I don't argue. Between leaving my husband, the bad weather earlier, the anger of Terrence at the service station, and our sing-along, I've had enough excitement.

"Whatever you say, Aunt Daisy. I'm just as beat as you. All I want is to lie down."

We stagger into the inn, following Daisy's instructions. She hands the teenaged night clerk a handful of cash. He passes her a room key (she and I are sharing), and we exit the lobby and walk along a dark pathway and up a flight of stairs until we reach our room. I unlock the door, and Daisy jets into the bathroom ahead of me.

Seedy, old linens, furnishings from the 1940s, and a lingering odor I can't place other than to acknowledge its unpleasantness have me motionless in front of the hotel room door, which I quietly close while contemplating sleeping in the Mustang.

I jump. There's a knock on the door, and I open it to find Tobey delivering our luggage.

"My room is a few doors down," he says. "If you need anything."

"What could we need?" I am too sleepy to be polite. "It's after three o'clock in the morning. The only thing I want is to sleep. I'm just not sure sleeping here is the best choice." I wrinkle my nose, searching for signs of a lazy maid's lack of interest in cleaning.

Tobey's eyes are wide and watery with exhaustion. "If you can't sleep, give me a few hours, and I'll be ready to get back on the road."

"I'll hold you to that."

Just then, Daisy exits the bathroom in her nightgown and climbs into the bed without checking for dirty sheets, bedbugs, or some other calamity.

"We'll find a restaurant in the morning." She lies on her back, pulls the faded yellow sheet taut over her chest, and tucks the edges beneath her armpits, resembling a mummy. "Someplace where we can have a decent breakfast before we get back on the road."

"Well, I hope there's a restaurant near the bus station because that's where I want to be first thing in the morning."

Daisy huffs. "We'll talk about that at breakfast." She closes her eyes.

I spin toward Tobey. "I'm not kidding. I want you to take me to the bus station tomorrow morning."

A small smile creases the corner of his lips as if I'm pulling his leg for the joy of pulling it.

"What's so funny?"

He rubs a hand over his mouth. "Nothing, but I can tell you two are family. I'll see you in the morning." He walks down the hall, and I close the door.

I am taken aback by his comment. I'd suggested the same thing to Daisy in the bathroom at the Thistle Filling Station. I'm not sure how I feel about Tobey and me sharing the same thought, but I guess it's okay, as long as we share them about Daisy. Other topics are off limits — you know what I mean?

I lay on the bed fully clothed. But as soon as my head hits the pillow, I'm back on my feet. My bladder is a fickle thing. Once in the bathroom, I can't help but take a few minutes to clean before using the accommodations. I am fastidious about cleanliness. It's a compulsion I discouraged around Jackson. It makes him nervous, he'd say, watching me flit about, picking up after him, sweeping up after him, wiping up after him.

One of the things he doesn't like about me — once I start cleaning, I can't stop.

After my session in the bathroom, I change into my nightshirt. Then I examine the sheets, frayed off-white sheets that have seen plenty of use and plenty of bleach — I pray. I check the corners, smooth out any folds, but nothing grimy is visible and I lay down.

As I curl onto my side, I can't imagine falling asleep. Not in a place like this. Not after a day like this one. But I do sleep and dream about Jackson, of all things. The one where he's chasing me and my heart beats so hard and loud, it scares me. So, I pray it will stop beating in case Jackson can hear it and find me.

Still deep in the dream, I stop running to listen. Has he given up? Has he stopped chasing me? No. He's right there, not even breathing hard. Why in the hell did I stop running in the first place? But I guess I always do. Too afraid to save myself.

Goddamn it. I hate this dream.

CHAPTER 16
DAISY

Summer 1928
Los Angeles

By the time Daisy reached the Apex, she was riled up enough to grab a handful of Henrietta's bobbed hair and snatch it out by the roots.

How dare her sister sneak off to a nightclub of all places when she should've been working? They could all be fired. And Isaiah? Daisy could barely think his name without wanting to spit.

For the two of them to pull something like this — she was tempted to tell their father. What if one of his chauffeur friends spotted Henrietta at a nightclub — mixing it up with flappers, hooch, and jazz — and told him about it? Papa would slap Henrietta into next week. And Daisy wouldn't be able to say a word other than turn the other cheek.

Daisy marched into the nightclub full of

vinegar, but once inside, her anger faltered, replaced by a flood of self-caution.

The room was full of color — gold, orange, green, and silver — and brightly painted canvases covered the walls. Palm trees and Mexican lanterns hung from the ceiling. On the tables, tiny electric lights had silk shades shaped like small umbrellas — and a spattering of candlelight danced with the tiny fires floating from the ends of cigarettes.

It was a large glamorous space, but Daisy felt like one of those fumbling, mumbling lady's maids in the cinema, chasing after her mistress. Her maid's uniform — the gray shift, the tea apron, and coronet cap — was ten miles beyond a sore thumb in a room teeming with silk, jewels, and pin-striped suits.

A hundred pairs of eyes judged her as she elbowed through the crowd, searching for her freckle-faced sister and the lanky Isaiah. Although, after a moment, she realized no one was paying attention to her. The standing-room-only crowd was captivated by the guitar player and the music coming from the stage. The lack of chatter or clinking glasses emphasized how the audience was keyed in on the stage.

Daisy paused to listen. The playing was as

perfect a musical sound as she'd heard in a long while. Now that the standup piano and musical instruments in the sunroom on Naomi Avenue were no longer in use.

The guitarist strummed his strings fast and precise, slow, and loose, with those jazz rhythms that stirred the soul. It reached inside her bones and made her toes tap.

Daisy squeezed by a few people, seeking a better view of the stage. But flappers in pumps and gents in fedoras didn't yield as much as an inch.

It came to her that she wasn't listening to just anybody playing the guitar. Delilah had said Isaiah was tearing up the joint. So, the guitar player had to be him. Daisy maneuvered another few feet forward until the crowd parted like the Red Sea.

A shoehorn-shaped stage jutted into the nightclub. Daisy pushed forward, but somehow, she was wedged between a sidewall and a group of flappers.

Straining her neck and rising on her tiptoes, she could finally see.

Isaiah stood in the middle of the stage. His fingers moved up and down the neck of the guitar, racing against himself but making a beautiful sound. Heads bobbed; feet tapped, and the ache in Daisy's throat threatened to undo her.

Clifford never played this well, but he might've if he'd lived longer. He might've been better than Isaiah if they hadn't killed him.

There were other musicians in the orchestra, but they weren't playing. They were enjoying Isaiah's strumming as much as the audience, throwing back their heads and nodding with each note he played.

Her awe turned to shock, disbelief, and fear as Henrietta strutted to the tall microphone at the lip of the stage. Wrapping her fingers around the head, she closed her eyes. Then, Isaiah played a chord, and Henrietta opened her mouth, and God, her little sister could sing.

It was a tune by Alberta Hunter. One of the songs her mother played on the stand-up piano in the sunroom. Then she'd sing the same song on Saturday mornings while her daughters helped her clean the house. Dusting, mopping, washing clothes, and singing — that's what they'd do on weekends while Papa and the uncles were away.

Henrietta had always been able to carry a tune, but Daisy never imagined she had a voice for the blues. A voice full of pain and passion, joy and laughter, disappointment, and a heart that knew love, all poured into her singing.

Henrietta and Isaiah must've spent the past week practicing to perform at the Apex. The first day in the laundry room had to be when it started.

Somehow, for a few minutes, while she listened, it didn't matter to Daisy so much how they'd begun. Henrietta and Isaiah had the crowd in the palms of their hands. The swell of her sister's voice flowed into every corner of the room while Isaiah's guitar took command of everything left. When they finished, the joint erupted. Yelps and screeches swept through the room. Henrietta and Isaiah hugged, and their smiles beamed from the stage.

Across the sparsely lit nightclub, despite the cigarette smoke, the applause, and the clanking glasses of whiskey and champagne, Daisy's and Isaiah's eyes met.

She had thought she couldn't be seen in a dimly lit room full of patrons. Perhaps it was the maid's uniform and cornet cap that made her stand out, but whatever, Isaiah gave Henrietta an insistent nudge. The sisters locked eyes, and for a moment, panic distorted Henrietta's features. But Daisy couldn't stop smiling. She also didn't want to steal any of her sister's joy by playing the unhappy parent. Henrietta and Isaiah were too talented to scold.

An explosion, a series of loud bangs burst into the room as the club's doors broke open. Men in black hats and suits surged into the space. Screams and shouts echoed from floor to ceiling.

In unison, the crowd veered back a sudden step, chairs tilted and tumbled, crashing to the floor. Women shrieked. Men grabbed the arm of a companion or pushed them aside in a race toward the nearest door: panic and chaos, voices unintelligible, except for the word *run.*

Daisy crouched against the wall, too frightened to move.

The attacking white men in black jackets with brass buttons stomped farther into the nightclub. Now, Daisy knew what they were: *coppers!*

Everywhere. Billy clubs raised; pistols pointed. People dumped their illegal hooch on the floor. The yelling suddenly made sense. "It's a raid! It's a raid!"

Someone pushed Daisy away from the safety of the wall, shoving her in the chest. The back of her head striking a hard surface. She couldn't see what. Dizzy, vision blurred, her neck and shoulders aching, she winced as a needle-sharp pain traveled down her leg.

"Run!" someone shouted.

Run where? There was no place to go.

Another wave of bodies pressed against her, but a hand grabbed her shoulders, a hand with strong fingers and a strong arm. She was pulled to her feet.

"Miss Washington, come with me. We've got to get you out of here."

She blinked in confusion. Who had her? She went to raise her head, but her neck hurt, her back throbbed, and her leg tingled with that strange pointy pain.

But she didn't let go of his hand.

The man guided her to the rear of the club, shielding her from the crush of the panicking patrons. Within seconds, they had moved into a dark hallway. A few minutes later, she was across Central Avenue opposite the Apex.

Breathless, they stopped to watch coppers dragging musicians and colored customers into police wagons. The white clientele walked to their chauffeured limousines or strolled away, free as birds.

"Are you okay?"

His dark eyes and strong brow were full of concern and reminded her of the night they'd talked in Perry's suite. Except this time, his attention wasn't divided. He was wholly focused on her and her only.

"Thank you, Mr. Barnes. Thank you for

helping me." She had thought it was him, knew it, frankly, as soon as they stepped outside beneath a streetlamp.

"You are welcome, but are you sure you're okay? Is your leg okay?"

Daisy patted her thigh. It ached, and she'd likely have a bruise the following day, but nothing felt broken. "I lost my cap."

The hair bun at the nape of her neck was undone. She grabbed a handful of loose thick hair and, using the bobby pins she had left, tucked the heavy strands into place. "God, I must look a sight."

"You look fine," Mr. Barnes said quickly, but she hoped he didn't think she'd been fishing for a compliment.

"Thank you," she said quietly. "I had no idea what was happening. I don't know what I would've done if you hadn't helped me."

"How could I leave you to be crushed by a mob of fleeing flappers and dandies?" The touch of sadness in his voice was the same as that night, too.

"I appreciate that." She laughed nervously. "I've never seen a police raid."

"Curtis runs a legit business." He took a deep breath. "But the Apex is Negro-owned, and he serves bootleg whiskey, like most establishments on Brown Broadway.

But the coppers tend to visit these clubs more regularly than the ones in Culver City."

"You mean the colored-owned businesses?" Her stomach tightened. "You know we serve liquor at the Somerville. Will the coppers raid us, too?"

"Dr. Somerville is an important man for a Negro, even to the white men in Los Angeles. The mayor and police chief Two-Guns Davis were guests of honor at the hotel's grand opening. Ate dinner with W. E. B. Du Bois and Lincoln Perry. I wager they also had a brandy after dinner."

He removed a pack of cigarettes from his pocket. "Would you like a smoke? It could help calm you."

"No, thank you. I don't smoke."

Malcolm Barnes lit his cigarette. "We should move. We're too close. Don't want the coppers to come for us, too."

"What are they doing?" Daisy asked. "The coppers — why are they only putting the band and barkeeps into the police wagons?"

"It was a raid, which is to be expected now and then. Prohibition after all," he said between puffs. "And serving liquor is illegal."

Malcolm likely thought he didn't need to respond — and she wasn't surprised when he didn't.

He started to walk away, but Daisy didn't follow. She searched the line of musicians, barkeeps, and chorus girls who were waiting to be shoved into a police wagon. But she didn't see Henrietta or Isaiah — they must've gotten out okay. "God, I hope they weren't arrested."

"Who?"

"My sister, Henrietta, and Isaiah, our boarder."

He stopped. "We can see everyone being hauled into the police wagons from here," he said. "If you don't see them, maybe they ran? Let's watch for a minute." Then he asked, "Is that why you were here tonight?"

She nodded sheepishly. "My sister was singing on the stage with our boarder who plays guitar." She looked at him. "Why were you here?"

"I love jazz." He took a puff of his cigarette, which was nearly ashes. "And when I saw your head rise above the crowd, I came looking for you, but then the raid happened."

"Why would you do that?"

"What?"

"Come looking for me."

"To apologize again. I can't remember every moment of the night we had our chat, but that day, I believe I hurt your feelings, and it stayed on my mind. I wanted to make certain I'd apologized." His eyes were soft and his voice low.

"You did that already," she said, looking away from him, focusing on the line of people being shoved into police wagons.

He smiled. "Then it must be that you deserve more than one apology."

She folded her arms over her stomach. "Well, if you can help me find my sister and our boarder, I will gladly accept your second apology, Mr. Barnes."

There was a pleased look in his eyes and a warm quirk on his lips. "After sharing such a harrowing experience and accepting my apology again. I'd appreciate it, Miss Washington, if you'd please call me Malcolm."

Chapter 17
Frankie

Saturday, June 1, 1968
Route 66

Later that morning Daisy is still asleep when I rise at ten. Silent as a mouse, I dress in a shapeless shift, a navy-blue cotton number with contrasting white cuffs and collar, and then I slip out of the room. When I reach the lobby, I ask the desk clerk where I can find a phone booth.

"There's one on the sidewalk, right outside. You can see it from here." He gives me a strange look like I'm stupid, but I don't want to make this telephone call too close to the motel. Too much of a risk I might be seen by Daisy or Tobey. Well, mostly Tobey, since Daisy was out cold when I left the room. None of which I intend to explain to this old man.

"I misspoke," I say to the withered desk clerk, a different man from the one working in the middle of the night, when we arrived.

Judging from the wrinkles on his skin, he's checked in a million guests over a thousand years. "The next nearest phone booth is what I'm looking for."

"Outside the Piggly Wiggly, half a block down the street."

As I exit the Peacock Inn, I feel like the grocery store chain is following me. One little lie to Jackson about Piggly Wiggly, and another Piggly Wiggly appears just before I learn if Jackson is coming after me or not.

I step into the booth, all glass, and I feel like I'm standing in the picture window of a department store on Michigan Avenue. I close the door behind me and scrounge in my purse for some change. There's no reason for Jackson to be at Tamika's apartment this early, so I think my call isn't too risky, but my fingers tremble, nonetheless. I dial the operator to make a collect call.

"Will you accept the charges from Francine Saunders?" the operator says when Tamika picks up the phone.

"Yes. Yes." No time passes before she drills me with a flurry of questions. "What in the world is going on? Jackson scared the shit out of me. Twice. Robbie had to spend the night with a club in his hand because of that fool husband of yours. What in the hell is wrong with him?"

This is a question I have asked the universe on several occasions.

"Tamika, slow down. I only have a few minutes."

"Then I'll talk fast because I need to tell you some things." She takes a deep, slow breath. "Your husband came here last night around eight o'clock. Drunk on his ass, raging about a phone call from a hospital claiming his insurance card was used by his wife. You were in an accident. Not hurt badly, but you and your mother left before you signed some paperwork. They called him at his job to tell him, which sounds like some shit to me. A woman has no privacy."

"Christ."

"I'm not done." She sounded angry. "Now he knows you got hurt. Knew you were with Aunt Daisy, and he went to the hospital to sign those papers. That's when he runs into some nurse, and guess what she told him?"

Tamika stops to breathe and my lungs constrict.

"Oh, God," I mutter. "That damn nurse."

"You damn straight." Tamika groans. "You're pregnant, Francine?"

"Yes. About eight weeks, I think, maybe ten, but I can't be sure." The pay phone suddenly is an oven, and I'm burning alive. "Jackson knows then."

"Hell, yes, he knows." Tamika's laugh cuts. "And lost whatever mind he had left. Are you keeping it? The baby? 'Cause he said some crazy stuff when he was here. Damn."

A white man walks by the phone booth with a lip-curled glare. He couldn't have heard Tamika's question. So, he must be judging me because of what? My clothes. My skin. Or he's having a bad morning and blaming me. I boldly snarl back.

"Francine?" Tamika blasts my eardrums. "What are you going to do?"

"About the baby? I don't know, but I can't be tied to Jackson any longer."

"You ask me, what does your baby have to do with him? I know he's the father, but a baby won't change him. You need to decide if you can raise a child on your own. That's the question to be concerned with."

"I guess."

"He knows you're going to Los Angeles."

"Yes, but he doesn't know how I'm getting there."

"What do you mean?"

"Daisy is driving me to Los Angeles."

"Oh, is that okay?"

Tamika hasn't met Daisy, but she knows of her. I can stretch the truth. "Yes, it's good. Seriously, we're fine.

"Do me a favor, Tamika. Go by my apartment and see if he's left. If he doesn't answer, you have a set of keys. Check for his duffel bag, or if the LeSabre is parked out front."

"Girl, I'm not risking my ass."

"Take Robbie with you. I need to know if he's left. Ask the Averys. They are always watching the goings-on in the neighborhood."

"Where are you now?"

"Somewhere in Oklahoma. Davenport, I think."

"Check in with me tomorrow?"

"Of course, as soon as I can. Maybe tomorrow night."

"So Daisy is driving you. Excellent. I wouldn't go anywhere near a bus station. Jackson will check every last one between Chicago and Los Angeles looking for you."

"I hope so. That will slow him down because I won't go anywhere near a bus station."

"This is so crazy, Francine. Please stay safe."

"I will, and don't worry. I'll call you tomorrow night."

"You should call your mother, too."

"I'll do that, and thank you, Tamika. I love you."

"Love you, too, sugar."

After my telephone conversation with Tamika, I return to the Peacock Inn, trying my damnedest to stop worrying — or at least stop shaking.

Perhaps I will skip calling Tamika for a few days. Every time I talk with her, I end up feeling too much. Too much worry, too much fear, and too much Jackson sloshing around inside me.

When I enter our room, Daisy is wearing a pair of tan pedal pushers and a peach-colored, short-sleeved, Peter Pan–collared blouse — a cute outfit she calls pajamas. I call it something I wish I could afford.

She is not only smartly dressed, but she's also demanding we eat lunch before heading to the bus terminal in Oklahoma City. I don't mention I am no longer interested in the bus station. I'll wait a bit before I come up with a reasonable excuse for changing my mind. I'm not in the mood to handle Daisy taking me to task about my inability to stick with my decisions.

She won't listen if I try to explain how Jackson hasn't always been mean, violent, and cruel. A passenger on a long train of bad news since high school, he never had

266

the strength of character to handle life's circumstances — big or small. It turned him into a whimpering child, who strikes out, sulks, has tantrums and hurts those he doesn't remember how to love.

"I'm starving," Daisy says. "Let's find some food."

"You want to tell Tobey we're leaving?"

"He'll find us. This isn't downtown Chicago."

A diner is next door to the inn, and on our way, Daisy decides to give me a lecture.

"Your arm is in a sling," she says, stating the obvious. "And you won't be able to manage your luggage. Why would you want to go off on your own? Why take a bus to Los Angeles when you can travel in style in a shiny candy-apple-red Mustang?" She holds a lit cigarette, waving smoke at me. "Doesn't make any sense whatsoever for you to go it on your own."

"Can't we discuss this after we get some food in our bellies?"

"Where'd you go this morning? Why didn't you eat then?"

"Wanted some fresh air and went for a walk."

"The baby bothering you?"

I touch my belly. "He's fine, Daisy. Don't worry about him."

267

"He or she. You don't know which."

"Okay, then, she, he, or it, does not need to be worried about."

We reach the diner and slide into the booth opposite each other. "I want a big breakfast," Daisy confesses. "Pancakes, a stack with sausage links and scrambled eggs in butter, and coffee with cream and plenty of sugar —"

The booth is near the front door. "Are you sure Tobey will find us?"

"He'll be here soon enough. What's wrong? You miss him?"

"It was only a question."

"Don't get testy, but I warn you — he's not the boy for a girl like you."

"I have no interest in him. All I asked was whether or not he'd find us."

"Considering the kind of man you left in Chicago, you could do far worse than a To-bey Garfunkel, be he Black or white."

"You were married. Right? What kind of man did you marry? Was he perfect? Is that what gives you the right to remind me end-lessly about the mistake I made marrying Jackson?"

"The man I married is none of your busi-ness."

"So my mother did get that story right, you were married, and from what she recalled, you married a wealthy man. Was he white? Is that why you have such a thing for Tobey?"

She laughs a humorless laugh. "My husband was not white, nor does he have anything to do with Tobey, and now, let's move on."

In a contrary mood, I keep at her because I am sick of her controlling every conversation (and I don't care if that's true or not. It's the way I feel). "Did you and my mother fall for the same man? Is that why you don't speak to each other?"

"We never had the same taste in men."

I take quiet delight in hearing their breakup wasn't over a man, but I don't show it.

A gum-smacking waitress walks up to our table.

"What would y'all girls like?" A hand on her hip, she takes our order, her southwestern twang grating against my ears.

Also, a young lady should keep her mouth shut when she chews gum, just like she should never spit in the street. And if she's a smoker — never smoke in public. My grandfather's rules for ladylike behavior make an appearance in my head on occasion. I think Daisy never paid much attention to her father.

"That's what my mother would say."

"Excuse me?" The waitress's brow is lined with confusion. I imagine she had asked me for my order, but I'd been lost in thought.

"I didn't mean to say that out loud." I laugh nervously, attempting to diffuse the awkward moment. "I'll take waffles and an order of bacon and a glass of milk."

As the waitress leaves, Tobey enters the diner and, after a quick sweep, slips into the booth next to me. I scoot close to the wall, keeping my distance. I don't want to encourage Daisy's speculation about my interest in him.

"Did you order?" he asks.

"Remember, Frankie is in a hurry to leave us for Oklahoma City and the bus station, but I explained I was hungry."

"What did you get?" His tone is oddly pushy, demanding rather than a polite inquiry.

"I told you last night I wanted a big breakfast," she replies.

"You take your medicine?"

"Don't talk about my medicine in front of her."

Medicine?

Tobey pulls his fingers through his blond hair. "I wish you would stay with us. I think Daisy needs a woman's company on this trip." He pauses to glare at Daisy. "She should know what's going on with you, Daisy. Period."

Her lip pokes out. "Frankie either wants to stay, or she doesn't. I can't force her."

Tobey scrubs a hand over his face. "If we tell her what's going on, it could make a difference. I can't do this on my own. What if." He squeezes his eyes shut but then looks at her, his eyes a flaming blue. "Damn it, Daisy, what if?"

"I can take care of myself. Let her go if she doesn't want to travel with us."

I raise my hand to get their attention. "Stop talking in code and tell me what's going on."

Daisy removes a pack of cigarettes from her purse. "Nothing's going on."

"Daisy." Tobey's voice is low. "Tell her, or I will."

She plants her elbows on the table, arms folded, and leans in. "If you tell her my business, I will tell her yours."

"I don't care, Daisy, I swear to God. I don't give a damn." Tobey pushes back into the booth, the gesture of a man who has decided he's had enough.

Daisy places her unlit cigarette in the ashtray. "Okay. Okay. Sorry I didn't mention this before, Frankie, but I have a fussy heart. Which means I should watch what I eat and remember to take my goddamn pills." She gives Tobey an evil eye. "There. Are you happy?"

I swear — my mother all over again. "Why does Tobey have to push you to give me this information? Is he your doctor?"

Daisy laughs. "Hell no. He's a pain in my ass."

The waitress interrupts with a tray of food. "Would you like more coffee?" She places plates in front of Daisy and me. Then she stares at Tobey, trying to figure how he fits into the picture. "You want something to eat?"

"Bring me what she's having," he points at Daisy's plate. "Except leave out everything and make it a bowl of cereal, a cup of OJ, and toast with jam."

I swallow a chuckle. The give-and-take between these two has its moments.

"Is that what you want to order?" The waitress addresses this question to Tobey.

"Coffee, an egg sandwich, cereal, and a glass of OJ," he says.

We are silent as the waitress fills coffee cups.

"Your blood pressure will be sky-high," Tobey remarks as soon as the waitress walks away.

272

"Don't tell me what to eat, Tobey."

"It was a suggestion."

I glance at Daisy. "Your heart is pretty bad, then?"

She picks up her smoke from the ashtray. "Don't start counting your inheritance money. I don't have that much left — and my heart isn't nearly as bad as Tobey makes out." She lights another cigarette.

I sigh. "My mother has a heart condition, too."

"I didn't realize she had a heart." Daisy rolls her eyes and grins at her weak joke. "Yeah. Yeah. I told you the women in our family are sickly."

Daisy puts down her cigarette, picks up her fork, and shoves a mouthful of pancakes into her gullet. "Tobey is right. I don't want to drop you off at a bus station. I lied before. I like your company. Surprise."

I grip the edge of the table. "Seriously?" Unexpected tears cloud my eyes. "Why would you say something like that. That's not fair."

"Finally, you make sense, Daisy," Tobey says. "I'll drive straight through for the next twenty-four hours. We will stay in the car and only stop for gas and snacks —"

"You can't guarantee anything," Daisy laments. "Coppers could stop us for bookin' down the highway, and the very next thing, you're in San Quentin."

I wipe my face with my napkin. "Why would cops snatch him up for dodging the draft? I thought the military arrests deserters."

Daisy smiles. "The cops could arrest us for harboring a draft dodger, a fugitive from the military — then we'd get smacked with a huge fine and jail time, too."

I laugh. "I guess I am a part of this group. I'm dodging my old man. He's running from the military, and, well, what are you running from, Daisy?"

"I'm not running away. I'm running to, honey."

Tobey brushes a strand of hair from his face. The smile has left his lips. "Good news is we're not splitting up."

"We're not some hippie band," I tease.

"We could be — like the Beatles," he counters.

"How about Sly and the Family Stone. They have some white musicians," I say, pleased with myself for thinking of them. "I bet you didn't think I listened to them."

"Nothing you do would surprise me, Frankie." He smiles at me, and damn me, I smile back.

CHAPTER 18
DAISY

Summer 1928
Los Angeles

Daisy didn't respond to Malcolm Barnes right away — she was too busy studying the cracks in the sidewalk.

Had he just asked her to call him by his given name? Should she consider such a thing? He had saved her from being crushed by a stampede at the Apex. But they weren't in the same social circles.

Conversely, her family wasn't a group of vagabonds or beggars, but the Washingtons worked as maids, chauffeurs, and whatnot.

Besides, he was too handsome for her. How would she look on the arm of such a man? Nothing but heartache would await her.

Oh my.

He hadn't asked her for a date; he politely asked if she would call him by his first name.

Lord, if she agreed, should she invite him

to call her Daisy?

"It is completely inappropriate. I have a book on proper hotel staff etiquette and calling you by your first name isn't in it."

"What's the name of the book?"

"I can't remember, but it's in the book." Her voice had climbed to an unpleasantly high pitch.

"Are you going to deny me this request?" he said, sounding so sincere, so earnest.

She looked into his eyes and her skin warmed. "What have I denied you?"

He smiled. "I offered you a drink that night, and you refused. Don't you recall?"

Daisy laughed softly, conceding his point. "All right, then, I'll call you Malcolm, but never in the hotel."

The tension left his shoulders, tension she hadn't noticed until it was gone.

"Thank you."

"My name is Daisy."

"I remember your name," he said quietly.

She grinned. "I meant you should call me Daisy."

"Okay, Daisy." He pulled cigarettes from his pack. "Would you like a cigarette?"

"I told you, I don't smoke."

"That's right. Sorry." He lights his cigarette. "We should move. We're too close to their police wagons for my taste."

"I still don't see Henrietta or Isaiah."

"Perhaps they went home."

Daisy looked worried. "Maybe if we walked around the block."

"Okay."

Daisy looked at the Apex, where the police were still pushing around musicians and anyone who was colored. "You probably don't like coppers because of what happened when you were beaten?"

A frown formed on his brow, and he stopped. "That's not why," he said. "I was someplace where I didn't think anyone cared if I was a Negro."

"You were in a white neighborhood."

"I was raised in a white neighborhood."

"Did your parents work in a mansion?" Daisy's imagination took flight about wealth and fancy meals, but then she thought the worst. "You didn't grow up on a plantation in the South, did you? Some of those white people still believe in slavery, barely paying servants enough money to feed themselves. Were your grandparents slaves? My grandparents came to this country from Jamaica. They were shop owners."

"I was adopted . . . adopted by a white family. Raised in a wealthy white neighborhood."

"Oh my." Daisy blinked hard. Raised by

whites, that explained his speech, almost as if he weren't Negro at all, she thought. And his manner. Somewhat fastidious, even more so than the young men she knew in college. "I didn't know rich white people did that."

"Yeah. They sent me to university, too, and Britain and Europe, London, Paris."

"I'm impressed." She was also jealous, envious, breathless, and hopeful. She'd love to one day casually mention trips to cities and islands on the other side of the Atlantic or the Pacific. She loved the ocean but had never sailed in as much as a rowboat.

"I didn't tell you about my upbringing to impress you. I told you because I want you to understand why I am ashamed of that night. I held myself above other Negroes because of my parents, but life taught me a lesson." He exhaled. "It doesn't matter what you look like — if you're brown or black or anything other than white — whites see you one way. We are beneath them. Colored. Negro. Rich. Poor. Educated, uneducated. Doesn't matter. We are all the same."

"That's why I don't spend any time around whites if I can help it."

He smiled. "I must. They're the ones with the money who can give me what I need to build the buildings I want to build."

"So is that what a draftsman does? Or are you now an architect?"

He grinned like a child, full of joy. "No, not yet. I've been studying for an exam I can't fail. That's why I haven't been around the hotel much."

They passed by nightclubs, betting parlors, speakeasies. The evening had a slight chill, but Daisy had no complaints about a cool breeze. Summer nights in Los Angeles were stifling.

Malcolm had grown silent. An uneasiness seemed to sink into him. But Daisy didn't want their conversation to end. She enjoyed a man of his caliber. Educated, well-groomed, attentive. Although, she might not know how observant he might be. So, perhaps, he was a character in one of the novels she read. Handsome, mysterious. A man who had trusted her and shared his upbringing. That kind of openness intrigued her.

"It was a proper raid, wasn't it?" she said, unable to think of any other subject they might discuss.

They were back across the street from the Apex. The police vans were still parked out front, but two familiar figures caught Daisy's eye.

She stepped forward, feet close to the

curb, hoping her eyes were playing tricks on her. Then she gasped. Henrietta and Isaiah were at the end of a line, holding on to each other as the coppers herded them into a police wagon. "Oh my God."

Daisy grabbed Malcolm by his jacket sleeve and pointed with a trembling finger. "They're being arrested. Lord Jesus. Papa will lose his mind."

Malcolm held her hand. "Miss Washington, let me see what I can do."

"You can help them?"

"I'll look into it. I know some of the cops at the station. I may be able to help, but I'll need to beat the wagons to the jailhouse," he said. He bowed slightly but then lifted her hand to his lips and kissed her palm. "It was a pleasure."

He tipped an imaginary hat. "I'll see you soon, Miss Washington."

Daisy returned to the Hotel Somerville, unable to concentrate. All she could do was hope Malcolm could save Henrietta and Isaiah from a night in jail (or worse). The thought of him failing set the panic in her gut on fire. She rushed into the linen closet, found one of the water buckets, and upchucked.

Wiping her damp forehead (after rinsing

her mouth), she wondered if waiting for news of her sister's fate would be her death.

It had been a couple of hours since she left with her last words to Yvette had been something about returning in a few minutes. She searched for her friend until, in the lobby, she ran into Delilah.

"She left a couple of hours ago," the maid said, sounding obnoxiously cheerful. "But don't worry, I covered for you."

Daisy begrudgingly thanked Delilah, swearing that sometime soon, she'd get to the heart of why the girl bothered her. Meanwhile, she had to stay calm and pray for her sister, Isaiah, and Malcolm.

Around nine o'clock, Henrietta and Isaiah bounded down the hall. Daisy had returned to the fourth-floor pantry.

Relief brought tears to her eyes that she quickly wiped away. "Are you two okay?"

"Jeepers. That was wild." Henrietta said with a shaky voice. "I've never been so scared in my life."

"We were in this god-awful smelling cell." Isaiah paced in a tight circle, going nowhere, gesturing wildly with his hands. "And I swear I saw rats."

As he rambled, Daisy eyed them both from head to toe. "But are you injured? Hurt?"

"It was hideous." Henrietta grabbed Daisy's hand. "When we were in the police wagons, I wasn't sure where we'd end up."

"They took us to the jailhouse," Isaiah said. "Oh, I told you that already." He hugged his guitar case to his body. "Coppers kept yelling at us the entire time. They hit one of the musicians on the head with a nightstick."

"It was the drummer." Henrietta shook a finger at Isaiah, seemed about to collapse with his shirt soaked with sweat.

Daisy inhaled. "But you got out. That's all that matters."

"Malcolm Barnes was the one who saved us," Henrietta added giddily. "He talked to the police captain, and the coppers even returned Isaiah's guitar."

"He knew almost everyone at that jail inside and out," Isaiah said.

"You know Malcolm Barnes?" It was Delilah's voice that made Daisy spin on her heels. She'd forgotten about her hateful habit of showing up unexpectedly.

"Hello," Daisy said, wondering how long she'd been standing there.

"He's that handsome friend of Lincoln Perry's, the one dating that white actress Veronica Fontaine."

"Hello, Miss Washington," Malcolm called

from the end of the hallway.

If his timing was newsworthy, the surprise on Daisy's face was the headline. She hastily fixed her wide-eyed, openmouthed expression.

Malcolm walked right up to her without the slightest hesitation in his step.

"Hello," she said.

He waved at Henrietta and Isaiah. "Am I suddenly a leper? Here I perform this kindness, and you hide from me. Why is that?" He sounded cheerful — and unnerving.

Daisy moved in front of a shocked Delilah.

"Thank you for helping them," Daisy said, raising her eyebrows, hoping he'd sense that the fewer words spoken between them, the better. "There was no need to make a trip back to the hotel at this hour."

He shrugged. "Oh, not to worry."

A valet appeared behind him, loaded down with luggage, and next to him was Lincoln Perry, actor, comic, Stepin Fetchit.

"Malcolm," Fetchit shouted. "Stop flirting with the maids. These girls don't have time for your shenanigans." Lincoln Perry laughed and then propped a boiler cap on his head. "You know we'll have our hands full this weekend. We need to rest."

Malcolm's smile was more of a frown.

"You're the ladies' man, Step." He laughed. "I can introduce you — if you like and if you'll behave yourself."

"Such a pretty group." Step smiled at us, taking an extra second or two to grin at Henrietta. Isaiah stepped to her side almost protectively. He'd made the move with such boldness Daisy had to smile.

Malcolm continued. "This is Miss Daisy Washington, a recent survivor of the raid at Mosby's club."

"Oh, yes. The young lady from the Somerville tour you teased. Good to meet you," said Fetchit. "You remember how stricken you were over that incident, Malcolm worried you'd hurt her feelings, but I'm sure you've apologized by now."

Delilah wiggled into the space between Step and Daisy. "My name is Delilah Jenkins. We didn't think you'd return until tomorrow."

"A change of plans, right, Malcolm?"

Henrietta whispered next to Daisy's ear. "How does he know your name, Daisy?"

"Hush," she warned.

Malcolm and Step entered Fetchit's suite, and the door closed, leaving the maids and Isaiah standing in the hall, holding their breaths. Well, except for Daisy, she exhaled. Her tension was more deeply rooted. "I still have another few hours on my shift," she said. "You two can wait for me or go home."

"We'll walk home together," said Henrietta. "We'll wait for you downstairs."

Daisy folded her arms over her stomach and slowly rocked back and forth. She and Malcolm had had a nice chat. He'd saved her sister from jail and invited her to call him by his first name.

But he was a friend to Stepin Fetchit. Her father hated the man and his friends. Not that anything would happen, but what if she had feelings for Malcolm Barnes. How would she explain them to her father?

"Aren't you the fancy one," Delilah shouted over her shoulder as she strolled ahead toward the staircase. "How'd you meet him? A more handsome Negro man doesn't exist in this state."

She suddenly spun toward Daisy, wiggling her eyebrows. "You know I heard a rumor he's dating a white woman. An actress by the name of Veronica Fontaine. Do you know her? She's been here, at the hotel, was on that tour the other day with the Somervilles."

"I wouldn't know anything about his personal affairs. Just ran into him a couple of times. That's all." I look at her pointedly. "Besides, I'm no gossip."

Delilah shrugged. "No harm, I was just asking."

CHAPTER 19
FRANKIE

Saturday, June 1, 1968
Route 66

After our late breakfast, Daisy wants to drive by the offices of the Oklahoma City Black newspaper, an hour or so away, until I remind her it's Saturday. The offices may be closed. She growls for a few minutes, unhappy that she's lost track of the days, I imagine. But as we pile into the Mustang, her spirits lift. She lights a cigarette and starts telling some jokes by a comedian she saw at Mister Kelly's on Rush Street in Chicago. However, she kept messing up the punch lines.

"What was the comedian's name?" I ask. Interrupting the barrage of lousy joke-telling. "The comedian whose material you are abusing."

"Don't ridicule me. I forget things now and then." The reprimand is lightly given. "His name was Richard Pryor. From my seat, I could see him in the wings and let me tell you — he was shaking like a leaf. But once he reached the microphone, he had a decent set. I must admit, I prefer someone like Pig-meat Markham and 'Here Comes the Judge.' Music and comedy wrapped up in one nice package."

Tobey is focusing on the road, but the scenery is whizzing by. I check the speedometer. We're hauling butt. Sixty miles an hour.

"At this speed, we should arrive in Albuquerque by nightfall."

"Not going that fast, but it's possible. If we don't run into lousy weather or make too many pit stops." He glances at me and grins.

"Don't look at me," I say, pointing at my temple with my middle finger. "I'm not in charge of my bladder or my appetite." I then touch my tummy. Tobey rolls his eyes.

"And I have a fresh carton of smokes," Daisy interjects from the back seat. "I'll make them last until we reach Los Angeles." She sounds proud of herself, as if smoking only ten packs of cigarettes in a couple of days is a triumph.

"Turn up the music, please," Tobey suddenly says.

I hadn't been paying attention to the radio, more interested in the scenery and the conversation. I'm feeling good knowing Jackson won't find me unless he drives to Los Angeles.

A radio station is playing the Billboard Top 40. "Hey Jude" by the Beatles is number one on the charts.

"I love the Beatles." Daisy sounds sleepy. "You know Robert Kennedy is a Beatles fan. He grew his hair long because of them."

"The Democratic primary is happening tomorrow, isn't it?" I had forgotten about politics, protests, voting rights, civil rights, the last twenty-four hours. The world outside the Mustang exists mostly while I'm on the phone with Tamika.

"He grew his hair because he's a politician. Not because of the Beatles." Tobey pushes the speedometer up another five miles an hour.

"I think he's cute." I feel my eyes widen with disbelief and embarrassment. "Did I say that out loud?"

Tobey chuckles.

"The long hair and the open-collared shirt make him human," Daisy adds. "Makes you think he's a white man you can trust." She lies down, curling into a fetal position and using an arm as a head cushion. "He's young and handsome and, hope to God, the next president of the United States."

"If he can win the California primary." Tobey glances in the rearview mirror. "You should get some rest, Daisy. You sound tired."

"Just a little but wake me up if you need a break from driving. Don't forget, now." Her words fade into the wind.

Tobey has better manners than Daisy and keeps the volume on the radio low. And speaking of Daisy, she falls asleep fast in the back seat, resting comfortably.

"I'm glad you decided to stay." The silly grin on his face makes me want to smile, but I won't give him the satisfaction.

"Don't flirt with me. I'm not interested."

"Whoa. Whoa. I'm not flirting. Just talking."

"Unlikely," I say, but perhaps I saw something that wasn't there. The long stretches of road are divided into chunks of music or silence. And since I've decided to avoid taking another Percodan, I can't doze off.

I prop my heel on the dashboard. "When did you meet her? You and Daisy. Such an odd couple."

"Not a couple, as you know. She and my mother used to work together at a hotel in New York City. They were both maids and took care of each other until my mom died. Then Daisy took care of me until my grandmother found me."

"Found you? Were you hiding from her?"

He tilts his head. "Yes, I was. Still am in some ways, but that's another story."

"I can't like you. I thought I'd better tell you, just in case you're getting soft on me."

"Not that I want you to like me, but why can't you? Because I'm white?"

"Yeah, that's it."

He raises both eyebrows, and his eyelashes are brown with red hairs and about as thick as when I put on mascara. "For a pregnant woman running from a stupid husband, you're pretty cocky."

I turn off the radio like we're about to have a long conversation. "You don't have the right to judge me or to call my husband names."

He chews his lower lip and nods. "You're right. I went too far."

"It is what you do."

"I know. We white men are arrogant bastards," he says sarcastically.

"Yep." I decline to add that some Black men can be arrogant, too. "You say Daisy was a maid at this hotel in New York City."

"The Hotel Theresa. Yes, she and my mother started out working as maids. By the time my mom passed in 1955, she was manager of housekeeping, and Daisy managed the bar and hired most of the lounge's entertainment."

"I thought she was a writer for the Associated Negro Press."

"That too. But that hotel was a big deal. There were always distinguished visitors checking in from around the world. And she also liked collecting news on the fly, as she called it. And there was always something going on at the Hotel Theresa."

"Give me some names, please."

"Fidel Castro stayed there." Tobey presses his lips together, thinking. "Malcolm X, Dr. King, lots of important people."

I lean back, as far as possible, which isn't too far, and prop the heel of my foot on the dashboard.

"A few years after my mother died, my grandmother took me in. Daisy and I kept in touch. We always keep in touch."

A question comes to me, and I go for it. "You must know about what happened in 1928 between her and my mom."

He chuckles. "As long as I've known Daisy, she's never mentioned her relationship with her sister." A quick shoulder shrug and he adds, "Though most of our time together, I was a kid, so, pointless to discuss her family's affairs with me."

Tobey is about my age, but he reminds

me of a kid, a dreamer, when he talks about Daisy or when he glances at me shyly out of the corner of his eye. Or am I watching him?

"What do you want to ask me?" Tobey asks, his gaze drifting occasionally from the road to me.

I adjust my arm in the sling. "Give me a minute. I'm thinking." I press my lips together. "Except for your affection for Daisy, I had you pegged as a man who watches rather than does." I shrug the shoulder available to me. "I guess some white men have a conscience, a soul. Are you one of them?"

He doesn't answer.

"When that white man murdered Dr. King," I continue, "you probably felt sad and all, but you didn't hurt the way Blacks in America hurt. So don't think I consider you a nice man just because my aunt likes you."

"Stop berating the boy, Frankie." Daisy rises in the back seat. "He's more like my partner in crime. Once he was old enough to board a train on his own, he'd travel to Harlem from his grandmother's Upper West Side loft, and we had adventures. Didn't we, sugar?"

He nods. "In 'sixty-three at the rally in DC."

293

"We heard Dr. King speak. It was wondrous." Daisy lights a cigarette. "We hadn't seen each other in ten years."

I glance from one to the other in disbelief. "Are you pulling my leg? How did you recognize him after ten years? He had to be a kid the last time you saw him."

"Almost twelve, I think," Daisy says.

"I recognized her. Daisy hadn't changed. She's ageless and loves anything with polka dots."

"His mother used to tell me my fashion sense began and ended in 1950."

Silence descends. Tobey's fingers drum the steering wheel. Something unspoken about his mother remains his and Daisy's secret.

"The next couple of years, we met up at rallies, marches, sit-ins, protests. We had a band of folks working on the cause with us. It was a family," Daisy says.

"Remember the King rally in 'sixty-six at Soldier Field?" Tobey adds.

"That was a humdinger." Daisy pats him on the shoulder.

"Newspapers said forty-five thousand people marched."

Tobey crouches over the steering wheel, blows the bangs off his brow, and smiles at Daisy in the rearview.

"How far are we from Albuquerque?" she asks.

"A few more hours on the road."

"But we're making good time, Tobey. Real good time. We'll be there soon. I'm excited."

"You've been to this town before?" I ask.

"Once upon a time, a long while ago, I lived in Albuquerque."

It's around six o'clock in the evening and we still haven't reached the New Mexico state line. Unfortunately, we made so many pit stops for my bladder, Daisy's sudden craving for sightseeing, and Tobey's demand to stretch his legs every other hour, we won't make it to Albuquerque until nine. We lost four hours; I swear, stretching, peeing, and turning into tourists.

The radio is off, and the silence is refreshing, but not the heat or altitude.

Scampering for a decent breath, I am sticky with sweat and overwhelmed by the lack of breathable air. I don't care for the dry, brittle shrubbery on the side of the highway, either, or the endless vista.

I thought Chicago was the only town where your backside felt like a lit box of matches all summer. Not that Los Angeles doesn't have its scorching days (and chilly nights), but I was a child, and everything was a child's view of heat, wind, and loneliness.

Tobey rolls down his window, wipes his forehead, and glances in the rearview.

I glance, too. Daisy's eyes are closed, and her breathing is steady.

"Don't worry. She's asleep," Tobey says.

"I'm not," I say. "You are worried enough for all of us."

"She does have a heart condition that is very serious," he says softly, attempting a whisper with his baritone. "You'd think she'd be careful, but she's not."

"She's like my mother. She doesn't want to slow down. She insists the doctors have her all wrong. She doesn't need more rest — she needs everyone to stop nagging her about resting."

His smile is brief. "It's not only the slowing-down part with Daisy. She takes too many risks."

"Other than wearing flashy clothes, driving fast cars, getting high, and smoking more cigarettes a day than a military battalion, what risks are you talking about?" I laugh. "I wish my mom would take a few risks, other than finding a new boyfriend every few months.

"My mother has lived in the same house almost her entire life, except for those few years she was married to my father. And I'm telling you, that neighborhood has gone through some changes, too.

"I guess her dating life is her adventure. She's always had a lot of different men friends. She meets them at work, at the grocery store, at bars, but only married one of them. My dad, but he died."

I close my eyes and think about some of the assholes my mother has dated. "My dad was a good man. I wish he hadn't died before I got to know him. Part of the reason I can't get next to you and your Vietnam draft-dodging thing."

"What are you two whispering about?" Daisy's voice is an electric jolt.

The Mustang veers sideways, but Tobey quickly brings the car back to the center of the lane.

"My God, Daisy. You scared us." Tobey visibly tightens his grip on the wheel.

"I figured she was awake," I say, but I had no idea. "How long, Daisy? What parts did you hear and decide not to comment on?"

"I've been awake. Long enough." She sits forward in her seat, and from the brightness in her eyes, she's not fibbing. I'm not sure she ever slept.

"Prove it." I dare her.

She laughs. "Prove I've been up the whole

297

time?" Daisy pulls a box of cigarette wrappers from her purse instead of a pack of cigarettes. "I knew your daddy."

I turn full around in the car seat, and I'm sure my eyes are the size of baseballs. My heart is pounding. "Okay, so tell me. What was he like?"

Dramatically, she takes a deep, long breath and exhales very slowly. Then she straightens her back, sitting as tall as she can in the cramped back seat. A convincing prelude: she's about to reveal a big secret — and I can't breathe.

"No. Don't —" I shake my head and turn back to the windshield. "Don't tell me."

She chuckles. "I wasn't gonna tell you anyway."

"Wait." I do some quick math in my head. "I was born twenty-two years ago. You've been gone for forty — you never met my daddy."

"You may be right, but it's also not my place to tell you. Just like it's not Tobey's place to talk about my heart condition or tell you other stories he shouldn't share."

"Daisy, I wasn't gonna tell her —"

"Sounded pretty much like you were dying to tell her."

"Damn it! What are you talking about now?" My arm starts itching. "Someone tell me something that's not a lie."

"The reason I'm heading back to Los Angeles is in part because of your mother. Not to see her, but years ago, someone I knew in Los Angeles was murdered. A few months ago, well, a newspaper article let me know it was time for me to take care of my business."

I give Tobey a bewildered glance. "What is she talking about?"

Daisy removes a small plastic bag from her purse. "Someone committed murder and went unpunished. I intend to make sure they are punished."

"So you're correcting a wrong? Taking on the man, like on *Mission: Impossible*?" I turn to give her a raised eyebrow of disbelief, but she's concentrating on the joint she's rolling.

"Yes, that's it. *Mission: Impossible,* but not impossible anymore. I know who is guilty and who needs to be punished. And when I finally face him, I'm gonna slit his throat."

A chill drops down my back. "You're joking, aren't you?" I look at Tobey for consensus, but he's staring straight ahead with a ghostly expression on his face. Oh God. *He believes her.*

I scrub my hands over my face. "Are you insane? You shouldn't say shit like that even if you're joking. Someone might take you seriously."

"The world should take me seriously," Daisy says, lighting her newly rolled joint. "I am completely sane. Other than a bad heart, I know what I'm doing and why."

Chapter 20
Daisy

It was late September, and Daisy's workday started the same as the day before, with her in a state of disarray that only grew more confusing as she entered the Hotel Somerville and heard what the front desk clerk had to say.

Cecil Weatherly was gray-haired and round but with the most pleasant demeanor and perfect skin, dark brown with a glow that reminded Daisy of poetry and poets. Cecil was the perfect front desk clerk. A charming man, a bright smile, a rich deep voice that put everyone at ease. He was born to do the job he was given.

The only drawback about him was he didn't seem to like Daisy.

"I have a handwritten note for you from Mr. Perry's suite." Cecil called her over to the front desk as soon as she arrived.

"Why not have one of the bellboys take up his mail?" Daisy strolled toward him, taking her time and thinking hard about why she was the new postman for suite 416. This was not the first time in the past few weeks she'd been summoned to the suite. It seemed Mr. Fetchit himself had taken a liking to her. "Why do they wait for me, Cecil?"

"They should follow the standard policies. It's not good business to make exceptions. Not at all."

Daisy stared at the floor for a moment. She never liked being scolded.

"This is different from the other notes, young lady." Cecil reached for the rack and mail slot 416. "It is addressed to you."

"What?"

"Maybe they left you a tip, but I checked. Held it up to the light and didn't see any dollar bills, and there aren't any coins."

She sighed deeply. He was thorough, too. "Thank you for being so thoughtful."

"You are welcome," he said with a chuckle in appreciation of her sarcasm. "Hurry up and open it. If Mr. Fetchit needs you to do something immediately, I want to make sure I inform Mrs. Keyes."

Although she hadn't had a conversation with Malcolm Barnes, or Malcolm, since the night of the raid, she kept hoping for another chance to have a private conversation. The notes from Mr. Fetchit's suite, the one Malcolm also stayed in when he was around, had given her hope. But that didn't last when she realized that Mr. Perry — Stepin Fetchit himself — had called for her.

"Well, Daisy, what are you waiting for?" Cecil said insistently.

"Mrs. Keyes will have me hogtied if I'm late. I'll open it upstairs and let you know if it's anything you need to be concerned with." She then promptly dashed up to the second-floor landing. Once there and confident she had a few minutes alone, she ripped open the note — and started reading only to almost stop breathing.

Miss Daisy Washington,
This note may surprise you, but since our last meeting, I've thought of you often. I hadn't anticipated being out of the city for such a lengthy time, but now that I've returned, I would like to invite you to join me for dinner. I hope you'll forgive me for my boldness, but I made inquiries and understand you are not scheduled to work this Sunday. If you are inclined to accept my invitation, I would be delighted to have you join me. Mr. Perry is out of town this

week, and I will be residing in his suite. You can leave a message for me there. It would be lovely if the two of us were able to dine and have an opportunity to get to know each other under less harrowing circumstances.

Yours kindly, Malcolm Barnes

Five minutes later Daisy stood in the doorway of Lincoln Perry's suite staring straight at Malcolm Barnes. He seemed uneasy, fidgeting, glancing over his shoulder as if surprised to see her. Entirely unacceptable, she thought, since the reason she was there was at his invitation. Had he changed his mind? Regretted sending the note? Though she planned to decline the invitation, she didn't need to be made to feel foolish.

"Would you like to come in?" he said finally.

She marched by him without speaking, practicing what she planned on saying in her mind. When she reached the middle of the foyer, she faced him. Then she noticed what he was wearing, and his appearance threw her off. He wasn't appropriately dressed.

No jacket, vest, or tie — just trousers and a striped round-collared shirt, unbuttoned at the throat, exposing his neck muscles. He was also in his stocking feet.

What if he hadn't expected her to come to the suite so quickly? She could have replied in a note. Was he alone? "I'm sorry, I can come back later. I didn't mean to catch you at a bad time."

"Stay. It's no problem. It took me longer to get —" He stopped mid-thought and smiled. "It doesn't matter. It's good to see you — without a lobby full of people."

"Thank you for the invitation, but I must decline," she said, wishing she could speak without the annoying lilt to her voice. "As a chambermaid at the hotel, I can't socialize with guests, or . . ."

She blathered on for a few seconds while Malcolm ignored her outstretched hand.

Then he walked by her, and the sweet, spicy scent of aftershave, orange zest, and vanilla trailed behind him, tickling her nose. He must've just taken a bath and shaved.

"Please, please," he said. "Have a seat."

She didn't move other than to lower her hand. "Mr. Barnes, I only came upstairs to explain why —"

"It's Malcolm, and I know we haven't spoken since that night at the Apex."

He hurried from one spot of the suite's parlor to the next, picking up strewn cloth-

305

ing, moving them into their proper place.

How ironic, she thought, he was tidying up for her. A flash of heat burned her cheeks. She looked at the design in the Persian rug and smiled. "I apologize for interrupting you. I should leave."

"No. Please. Will you wait a moment?" He glanced at his feet. "Let me finish dressing. I'll be right back."

Alone in a suite with a half-dressed, barefooted man, Daisy should spin on her heels and march out the door. But he had asked her a question — what was it? "Yes, I can wait."

When Malcolm returned, he was dressed, buttoned-up in his Joe Brooks ensemble. A blue-striped linen suit, vest, white shirt, gold collar bar, and matching cuff links. He also had put on a pair of oxford shoes.

Daisy stood stiffly. "As I was saying, I can't possibly join you for dinner. It would not be proper."

"Because you work here, and I don't, right?"

"Of course, you don't work here," she said with a laugh and then smiled at the humor dancing in his eyes. "I am a chambermaid."

"You said that already." He advanced a step but kept a gentlemanly distance.

"Why are you pursuing me?" Daisy asked,

searching his face for a twitch, a raised brow, a sly smile, something to diminish his effect on her. But his expression gave her nothing. "What do you know about me?"

"I know I like you — and want to know you better."

"Oh, I can tell you everything there is to know about me," she said, eyeing him briefly before barreling ahead.

"I am a twenty-year-old chambermaid and the daughter of a bedridden mother. My father is a hardworking man who loves his wife. And you've met my sister and our boarder. I went to college but had to quit when my mother took ill, after the deaths of my two uncles, her brothers. I want to be a writer one day and hope to have my articles appear in the *Eagle* or magazines like *The Crisis* or *Opportunity*." She paused, waiting for his response, but he only stared at her like she was some novelty in a cage. "Well, that's my life. Is that a woman you see yourself going out to dinner with?"

He folded his arms over his chest, not in anger or defiance, but almost protectively, she thought.

"You kept my secret that night you found me in Step's room," he said. "Shouldn't I want to get to know a beautiful, young woman with that kind of character?"

Her cheeks blazed. He'd called her beautiful. No man had ever said that to her, not even her uncles or her father. Perhaps, he was the person her mother had mentioned? Someone who saw her *for her.*

"It never crossed my mind to break that promise," she said honestly. A lift of her chin and their gazes met, but all she could think about was her secret — she was the Mata Hari of the Hotel Somerville. She'd never betray Malcolm by gathering gossip about him. But looking into his eyes, she felt shame.

"I need to ask you something personal," she began, "and you might find it uncomfortable. But it is important to me."

His head tilted, his shoulders squared in attention. "Go ahead, ask me."

"Is Veronica Fontaine your mistress?"

Sitting on the table next to him was a small gold case with the initials *MWB* etched in cursive on the top. He picked it up and removed a cigarette. "I'd offer you a cigarette, but you don't smoke."

"You remembered." She tried to smile, but she was waiting on his answer. She didn't need to ask the question again. They both knew that.

He lit his cigarette and took a long drag. "She was my mistress, but I broke it off."

She wanted to ask how long — how long they were together, how long ago it ended, why he was with her in the first place. But she was satisfied for now. "How about if we meet for a cup of coffee or tea instead of dinner?"

A triumphant smile spread across his face. "I'll pick you up at four o'clock on Sunday."

"I'll meet you."

"You don't want me to know where you live?"

"I don't care about that," she said quickly. "I'd just rather you didn't have to meet my father right now."

"There's a diner next door to the Lincoln Theatre," he said.

"I'll meet you outside the theater."

"Four o'clock."

"Sunday," she replied.

He opened the door. "I look forward to Sunday."

It was early October and the atmosphere at the Hotel Somerville had changed. The housekeeping staff was no longer flustered by the hotel's rich and famous Negro clientele. It was normal for a renowned colored guest to fill every room, and every evening for the hotel to host lavish parties and special dinners, wedding receptions and

309

anniversaries. Duke Ellington and his orchestra played in the balcony whenever they were in Los Angeles. And with Hollywood producing more film shorts, colored actors, musicians, and activists were in town often.

But mostly, things had become routine at the Somerville. Just like Daisy's life, she liked to think. It was part of the reason she decided to share her news about Malcolm Barnes with Yvette.

"My Lord, Daisy! You never told me you had socialized with the man who humiliated you in front of Vada Somerville." Yvette made a *tsk-tsk* sound. "You do remember spilling the bucket of water on her stockings and shoes?"

Daisy stopped in the hallway so quickly she nearly lost control of the cleaning supplies she was juggling. "Wait one minute. I didn't spill a bucket of water on anyone. It was a splash, a hefty splash, I'll admit, but yes — Malcolm is the same man."

"You've been dating him?"

"No. That's not the right word. I've seen him socially, outside the hotel, only a few times. We've had coffee."

Yvette started walking, heading to one of the dozen or so suites they had to clean. It was early, and the chambermaid chores were plentiful.

Stripping bed linens, opening windows to air the rooms, making beds, organizing closets, hanging up suits, dresses, coats, and trousers, and lining up boots and shoes (and don't forget to replace the trees) — a chambermaid's typical start-of-the-day chores.

Though this morning would include explanations, judging from the deep lines in Yvette's brow.

"So, how often have you two socialized, if that's what we're calling it, and have you had anything more than coffee?"

Daisy twisted her lips to one side, ignoring Yvette's innuendo. "Twice. Okay, three times. First, we had coffee at a small diner on East Washington and Central Avenue. We talked about absolutely nothing and everything. Then, we went to Lincoln Theatre and saw *Within the Law* by Bayard Veiller, performed by the colored Lafayette Players."

Yvette shook her head in disbelief. "How long ago? How long has this been going on?"

"Not long, a couple of weeks."

"In two weeks, it sounds like you've been out three times. How? You haven't missed any hours at work. When are you making time for him? And why didn't you tell me before?"

311

Inside the suite, Daisy placed her supplies in a corner, and the two women tackled making the bed. "Why would I? I never expected to see him after the raid or have a conversation that didn't have to do with changing bed linens, delivering a tray of tea, or restocking the soap and towels."

She left out the part about meeting Malcolm in Perry's suite the night he'd been injured. There was no purpose in mentioning that encounter.

"And now you want to see him again?" Yvette scrunched up her nose. "I don't think you should. You work here, remember, and he's a tenant."

"He doesn't live at the hotel. Just stays here on occasion with his friend Lincoln Perry. That's why we don't see him around that much."

"Everyone who works here notices everything that happens on the fourth floor, particularly the tenants and what they do from what they don't. We aren't supposed to be mixing it up with them, Daisy. I may joke about Lincoln Perry, but I'd never go up to him and start a conversation. Never. If Mrs. Keyes heard about you and Malcolm Barnes, she'd fire you on the spot. And Lord, what about your father? Have you mentioned this to him?"

"Why would I? It's not serious. How could I be serious? We like strong coffee and talking about books and poetry — and reading *The Crisis* and *Opportunity* magazines." He also loved the writings of W. E. B. Du Bois almost as much as Daisy did.

Yvette lifted a warning brow. "From the glow in your eyes, I'd say it might not be serious yet, but it's heading there."

"That's why I waited to tell you — to avoid being judged. But now, I need a favor."

Yvette closed one eye and leered at her. "You are always asking me for favors. What now?"

"He invited me to dinner Sunday night, and I accepted, but it's a fancy restaurant. The Montmartre café, and he's sending a car to pick me up."

"Christ, Daisy, that restaurant is where the Beverly Hills crowd dines. It's not for colored people. They don't even have colored waiters."

"Malcolm has a private dining room." Daisy nodded for Yvette to grab the edges of the fresh sheet on her side of the bed. Together, they gave it a snap and let the sheet float over the mattress.

"Why would a Negro have a private dining room at a fancy Beverly Hills restaurant?

Who is he? I bet the Somervilles don't even have a dining room there."

Daisy just ignored most of what Yvette said. "Can I spend the weekend at your house? Please. Malcolm's driver would pick me up there, and then I won't have to explain Malcolm to my father."

Yvette tucked in her corner of the sheet. "That's the favor, help you hide Malcolm Barnes from your dad?" She huffed. "Sure, but I'm afraid for you. This isn't like you. So, your turn to do me a favor. Don't fall in love with him. Next thing you know, you'll have to get married and change all your plans."

"We're just having dinner."

"Doesn't matter. I was a few months from graduation when I met Sid. I also had an interview for a stenographer job at Golden State Mutual Life Insurance Company." She punched the pillow, fluffing it into shape. "You know what happened. What did I end up doing?"

"You got married and had a baby."

She pointed at Daisy. "Yes, ma'am. But first, I fell in love. That's all I'm trying to say. Falling in love changes things. So, be careful."

"I am not falling in love with Malcolm Barnes."

"And I'm the Queen of Sheba."

They finished the bed, and grabbed clean pillowcases, changing the old and arranging the new ones.

"I don't mean to act like I pay attention to gossip," Yvette began. "But what about the rumor about him and that white actress? Have you considered he may not be the man you should be involved with because of his choices? That is if the rumors are true."

It was the question she'd assumed Yvette would ask, but for some reason, she thought they'd skirt over it for now. Daisy looked Yvette squarely in the eye. "This cannot be repeated. I am trusting you not to tell a soul."

She nodded, her expression earnest. "I promise."

"I asked him if he'd dated her, and he told me she was his mistress, but he broke it off."

Yvette swallowed a visible lump in her throat but then regained her composure. "Okay, then. You believe him. Good. And you two haven't kissed, have you?"

Daisy's eyes widened, trying to figure out what one thing had to do with another. "I'm not answering that question." She returned Yvette's smile. "Will you help me this weekend or not? I want to give him your address."

Yvette leaned sideways. "Yes, you can stay. Besides, when he brings you home, I'll make sure the baby and Sid are down for the night so that you can tell me all about it. Deal?"

Compulsively, Daisy hugged Yvette. "Thank you!"

"Okay. Okay, but I'm not joking. I want to know every detail."

"You'll get it. No problem. Every detail. I promise."

The day of Daisy's dinner and big evening out with Malcolm had finally arrived. After work on Friday she had gone directly to Yvette's house. As far as her father knew, she'd remain there until the two women returned to work Monday morning. The story she told was mostly accurate. She was helping Yvette with her baby while her husband, Sid, worked through the weekend (which was also true; he was working a crew harvesting late-season strawberries outside LA).

Yvette had insisted she borrow one of her dresses to wear, a pale-yellow shift. Daisy pirouetted in front of the vanity in Yvette's tiny bedroom, relishing the swirl of the dress's delicate fringe. But she worried about the depth of the plunging neckline.

"Are you sure this is decent?" In Yvette's full-length vanity, Daisy examined her profile from every angle.

"You aren't endowed enough to have any cleavage," Yvette explained, adjusting her bodice like a doctor examining a sore toe. "And a hint of it is never risqué. I assure you."

"Ample-breasted women always say things like that," Daisy said, still studying her form in the mirror.

"I swear you think of fashion as if we were the turn of the century. It's not indecent — it's a flapper dress. You've heard of flappers, haven't you? They've been around for most of this decade."

"Use a safety pin in the seams in the shoulders — and lift it."

"All right, all right. Stand still." Yvette made the adjustments. "It looked fine before."

Daisy eyed the altered neckline. "Now, it is decent." A sigh of relief filled the small room. "How come you know so much about today's fashions? What do you and your husband do, visit every department store on Central Avenue?"

Yvette laughed. "I wish. Sid is too much of an old fuddy-duddy for such things.

317

Instead of working all the time, I read magazines and newspapers. *Eagle* ads and *Photoplay* magazine give me my fashion tips."

Yvette touched Daisy's shoulder. "Sit. Now, I need to tackle that hair."

Daisy spun onto the stool with a swoosh, tugging at her coarse curls. "Do something special. I want to look pretty."

"You are pretty." Yvette cocked her head.

"This is my first date since the Reverend Beach's son, Jimmy."

Yvette giggled. "Jimmy Beach, the love of your life when you were eleven, and Timothy Jones when you were sixteen. The first boy you ever kissed."

"What is your point?"

"You're not experienced, Daisy, but Malcolm Barnes is."

"I'm not going to give him a test on our first date. Stop worrying."

"I can't help it. What if Mrs. Keyes finds out, and you get fired? What happens then with these new doctors you want to get your mother? When do you have time to write? I may have a baby, but as soon as he gets older and Sid settles into a new job, I'm going to get that job as a stenographer at the Golden State Mutual Life Insurance Company. These were the dreams we had in college. Are you letting go of them for a man like Malcolm Barnes, a lounge lizard?"

"He's not that way. Yes, he had a mistress, but I told you he hadn't lied when I asked him about it. I respect that."

Yvette squeezed her shoulder. "I just worry." She parted Daisy's long hair in the middle. "This mop of yours would be easier to manage if you let me cut it."

"Don't you dare bring a pair of scissors near my head." Daisy said. "Stop trying to spoil tonight for me. After all these months, I need one night, one perfect night. So let me please enjoy this."

Yvette stepped away from Daisy, holding the comb to her head like a weapon. "This hair bun is not for a girl going out to dinner at a Hollywood restaurant."

"I am not cutting my hair."

"Your sister bobbed her hair. And the style would be adorable on you."

"My father slapped Henrietta across the face when he saw her with that bob hairstyle."

"He what?"

Daisy turned her head from side to side, examining her profile. "As I said, I'm not cutting it."

"Fine. Fine." Yvette took a couple more minutes and finally finished her hair, creating a rolled bun with strands of loose curls framing her face. "At least those curls soften the look, and since I can't cut your hair, how about putting on some makeup?"

"I won't go to dinner painted like a whore."

"Come on," Yvette pleaded, kissing Daisy on the cheek. "Please."

"All right, but only a little."

Yvette applied a light dusting of face powder, black eyeliner, mascara, and lipstick.

"That's mighty red."

"It's the cat's pajamas against your skin, so beautifully brown, and with that yellow dress — perfectly divine."

Daisy looked at herself in the mirror, pleased. She wagered Malcolm would like it, too. She hoped. "I do look nice, Yvette."

"Yes, you do." Placing her hands on her hips and looking quite formidable, her friend said sternly, "Don't go anyplace with that man other than the restaurant. And don't you dare kiss him."

CHAPTER 21
FRANKIE

Saturday, June 1, 1968
Route 66 to Albuquerque

The view from my side of the car changes the instant we enter New Mexico. The concrete highway divides the prairie into short grass and scattered prairie shrubs, with the mountain range etched across the horizon. Lazy yellows, tender greens, and a naughty streak of red cover the landscape and remind me of paintings of cowboys and horses and *Wagon Train.* I love a good TV western.

I stare through the glass, nuzzled beneath the jean jacket Tobey tosses over me — after Daisy finally agrees to turn on the air conditioner. I am freezing to death, but I'd rather be cold than burn alive. That's how hot it is in this state.

Did I mention Daisy lit a joint as we crossed state lines? Something about her return to New Mexico must bother her. I could be wrong, but the tension in Tobey's face makes me wonder about the rest of the story.

The smoke from Daisy's joint makes me light-headed. I swear there is such a thing as a contact high. I am not just drowsy; my body, thoughts, and memories tumble about in fits and starts. I am not dreaming. I am reliving a moment from the past. I need to recall a memory and then snap a finger, so it vanishes like the scenery that disappears as we speed by.

My first love since I discovered love was Jackson. The starting quarterback with a toothy grin and a silly laugh. Students, teachers, and parents stop in the corridors of Crenshaw High and shamelessly stare and wonder: How does such joyfulness come from an oversize, football-playing man-child? The way his moods soars from happy, to sad, vanity, to unkindness, never cruel or hateful. The depth of his goodness is visible in how he treats the less popular, the less confident, the lessers in general, and girls like me.

A girl unnoticed by students, parents, and teachers. A painfully shy girl who withers when forced to look you in the eye and trembles when spoken to.

Back then, I was not unaware of my

shortcomings; I nourished them and was uninterested in change. Not because I couldn't but because I could never imagine change.

His energy bounces off the walls and attracts me as much as it frightens me.

Who knew we'd marry one day?

The wedding is the most beautiful day of my life. A man is marrying me, who loves me despite me.

My mother demands we marry in an old hotel on Forty-First and Central Avenue. Not a casual request. She is belligerent about it. As if her life depends upon me waltzing down the circular staircase of the Dunbar Hotel's first-floor balcony.

My mother didn't wear a white dress when she married, so the pressure for me to be adorned in an abundance of white lace and satin and veils is immense. I also must have a long train that spills over the steps, and white roses and ribbon decorating the banisters.

I argue, wanting "My Guy" by Mary Wells played at my wedding, but the traditional wedding march is what I am getting.

Now, imagine that on my wedding day, my anxiety is high not because of the pending marriage (which, in hindsight, should've been the case), but no — I hate long staircases (see my cowardly reaction to the escalator at the Greyhound bus terminal). In my mind, there is no way I will survive a trek down a winding staircase in a long fluffy dress.

Tobey makes a slight noise that sounds like "Hey. You awake?"

"Not asleep, just lost in thought."

"Do you think she's asleep this time?"

I glance at Daisy in the back seat. "Yeah, I see drool on her lips, so guessing the joint knocked her out."

"Cool. Cool. She needs to rest."

"Smoking a pack of cigarettes a day and rolling at least one joint every other hour isn't the best medicine for what ails her, I would think." I adjust my arm and try to put the memories of my wedding day out of my mind. Maybe I will use Tobey's apparent need to chat to discourage my sentimental journey.

I study him out of the corner of my eye, and there's something he wants to talk about. So I should give him my undivided attention and make it easier for him to spill the beans on Daisy.

"I only met her two weeks ago, you know," I say.

"Yeah, I think one of you mentioned that. I hadn't heard her talk about you before.

But that's not unusual. She never discussed her family with me."

"I don't care, you still know her better than me. Other than she's a writer and active in the civil rights movement, I don't know a thing — wasn't she married?"

"She was a correspondent for the Associated Negro Press until they closed their doors in 'sixty-four. She also wrote articles for *Jet, Ebony,* and the *Negro Digest.*"

I am perplexed, frankly; I don't want to call him or Daisy a liar. "That's crazy. I read all those magazines. I would've noticed an article written by Daisy Washington. I may not have met her until recently, but I knew her name."

His knowing smirk irritated the mess out of me. "What?"

"She wrote under a pen name."

"What was it?"

"Ask her when she wakes up."

I sigh. "This isn't as much fun unless you answer all my questions."

"I didn't know we were playing a game," he says, looking and sounding very serious.

I will need to cut back on my sarcasm and snappy wit. "You mentioned she'd been married before. Did you know her husband?"

He shakes his head. "Are you still cold?"

325

Uh-oh. He's annoyed with me. I twist my lips to the side. "You want your jacket back?"

"We could turn off the air."

I scratch my nose and turn to look at Daisy. "She is out like a light. How about if we leave it on and I hang on to your jacket. I think the cool air helps her rest — don't you think?"

He wets his lips and nods again but otherwise isn't talking.

"So, you never met her husband?"

He shrugs.

"Hey, I am desperate. She won't tell me stuff, and I just want to know more about her. Okay?"

I get a side-eye, but also a sigh, and I'm in like Flint.

"The marriages, right?"

"Right."

"I don't know anything about her first husband, but the second one died about seven years ago. She was only married to him for a short time, maybe five years. As soon as he passed, however, she took back her maiden name. I did have dinner with them a couple of times in New York, but Daisy has always been private about her personal life."

"Whatever is going on between the two of

you strikes me as mighty personal." I pick up the box of eight-tracks, thumb through them and hope my questions come off as casual and less prying. But it might be too late.

"What do you mean by *between the two of you*?" Tobey asks with an edge of annoyance in his tone.

"I get that you're close and have shared a lot, but I don't get it. I'm sorry, I don't understand how a guy who is around my age and a woman her age could have such a thing for each other."

"Hey, don't get creepy on me. We don't have a thing for each other. She is my friend. Has always treated me with kindness and respect."

"Okay. Okay. Calm down," I play like I'm teasing, but I know he's not playing.

"I come from a long line of people who don't know the difference between respect and domination." The knuckles of his hand on the steering wheel are bright red. "So, your aunt treated me and my mom like people." He pauses, waiting for another question.

But I've decided to let him talk without prompting and begin looking at cassettes.

"My mother was down-to-earth and came from a poor family but managed to snag a wealthy guy. But when they married, his family cut him off, and he died shortly thereafter in Korea, leaving her eight months pregnant with me."

I remove a cassette by Otis Redding. "I told you my dad died in Korea, too. Why didn't you mention your dad before?"

"I just didn't. But that's something we have in common besides our fondness of Daisy."

"Hey, don't go too far, there. I'm not sure about her yet." I'm smiling when I say this, but I'm not lying. "I think she's hiding something. Maybe we'll find out when we reach Albuquerque."

I settle back into my seat and lift my legs so I can put my bare feet on the dashboard. "My mother has a heart condition, too. How bad is Daisy's?"

He presses his lips together, thoughtfully; strain lines his young face. The way the moonlight is shining through the glass, I notice how much of his blond hair is red and how hard it is for him to answer my question.

"She's that sick?" I whisper.

"She had a heart attack six months ago. She shouldn't travel or be doing any of this —"

"Oh my. She should be in bed." My hand

is to my mouth. Heart attacks were a death sentence. There were no treatments, nothing a doctor could do but prescribe painkillers and bed rest. I bite down on my lip, and glance over my shoulder. "What is she trying to do? Kill herself?"

Tobey's soft chuckle sounds like a sob and makes my heart ache.

"No," he says. "She's trying to live, and for her that means fixing things."

"You know why she's on this trip. Tell me. It can't be about a book she's writing."

"Oh, if she has time, she has a book or two in her." He laughs. "But I guess when you've faced death's door, things look different."

"Sounding mighty wise for a young man, Tobey." I smile, but suddenly, I jab him in the arm and can't close my mouth because I just figured out something. "You liar!"

"What?" He looks at me incredulous as heck.

"How long ago did you get drafted?"

He shakes his head. "I told you my story."

"When did you get drafted? And don't lie."

He turns away from me, keeps one eye on the road, but I know if he looks at me, he'll have to tell me the truth. I think that's the kind of guy he is.

"Go, on. Tell me." I say this like a plea. Not an order. "No judgment. I swear."

"I received my papers six months ago, a week after Daisy had the heart attack."

I nod. "That's the real reason you refuse to go to Vietnam. It's because of Daisy."

He turns off the air-conditioning and nods at the cassette I'm still holding. "Put that one in, okay?"

I do, but I'm still looking at him, studying him, trying to see if there's more to know and if whatever it is will suddenly appear.

He inhales deeply. "Look, here's the deal. She stood by my mom, and then by me. Now, I'm standing by her." He shrugs. "It's just the way it is. That's all."

CHAPTER 22
DAISY

Fall 1928
Los Angeles

Daisy stood shoulder to shoulder with Yvette; their noses pressed to the glass of the living room window as the red-and-black Ford Model A pulled into the parking spot in front of Yvette's house.

Daisy loved the shiny red color and how the automobile looked expensive and flashy, like something that could only belong to Douglas Fairbanks, Jack Johnson, or Stepin Fetchit. Men with plenty of cabbage.

But the young man who had rushed out of the car and jogged up the walkway to Yvette's front door was no chauffeur.

"He looks like Malcolm," Yvette said.

"Kind of, but he's not." The young man was dressed in a tan seersucker suit and carried a straw boater — not the chauffeur outfit Daisy was accustomed to seeing.

"Should I invite him in?" Yvette asked,

her voice pitchy with uncertainty. "Or do you open the door and simply walk out?"

"I'm not sure." Daisy attempted to pull on the pair of lacy white gloves Yvette had loaned her, but that wasn't working, and she flung them on the table. "I'll just leave with him."

The knock on the door made both women jump, but Daisy gathered herself quickly.

"Might as well get on with it," she said to Yvette with a nervous smile.

She opened the door.

"Hello, Miss Washington, I'm Percy. Malcolm sent me."

Daisy snatched her purse from the table and looked at Yvette. "I'll be back in a few hours."

"Good luck," Yvette said solemnly.

Daisy sat in the back seat, nestled against the soft leather cushions, hoping her delight with her surroundings wasn't too noticeable.

They drove by small shops and bungalows, larger houses and larger shops, until the mansions were miles from the road and hidden behind iron gates and high shrubbery. It seemed to Daisy that Beverly Hills was all tall grass, flower gardens, and a rainbow of gold, orange, peach, and rich colors.

They were in the part of town where her

father worked. She had never seen the Alfred Lunt mansion before, but it could be any one of the houses they passed.

The driver pulled into the alley behind the Montmartre café. Not surprisingly, a private room inside the ritzy restaurant didn't mean a colored couple could walk through the front door.

Malcolm was waiting in the alley and stalked toward the car, looking tremendously unhappy.

"Our plans have been scuttled, I'm afraid. We won't be able to dine here tonight."

Daisy detected more than disappointment in his voice. The anger poured from him like water from broken glass.

"What happened?" she asked as he slammed the car door behind him and sat next to her.

"It has nothing to do with the color of our skin, if that's what you're thinking. Another party booked the private room without my family's knowledge. But it's no— Never mind, let's not discuss it."

His entire body tensed. Daisy gladly let the topic drop, but it pained her that it likely meant their dinner date was scuttled, too.

"Of course," she said, staring out the window, waiting for Malcolm to instruct Percy to take her back where he'd picked her up. "You'd tell me if you felt it was war-ranted."

"You are always so blunt, Daisy." A light-ness replaced his dark tone. "I like that about you. Your directness."

"Thank you." The compliment would mean more if she wasn't so sad.

A beautiful evening spoiled, she thought, studying her hands, and wishing she'd put on the lacy white gloves. Something pretty to play with instead of worrying her fingers together.

"Would you like to go on an architectural tour of Los Angeles? Well, not the entire city, but some spots I think you'll enjoy."

"I'm not sure what you mean."

"Architecture is my passion. Indeed, Los Angeles has some of the most amazing buildings in the country," he said wistfully. "I have dreamed of building things, houses, homes, tall buildings since I was a kid. I've even developed my approach to creating or nursing my ideas. For example, I look at the landscape, the trees, the curve of the moun-tain, the slope of a hill. Then I take in the scent and sounds of the earth, the flowers, the trees, the animals that inhabit the area and the birds that fly overhead, how the sunlight will shine into the master bedroom at dawn, midday, and the moonlight at night. What do the rooms in the house look like at sunset?

"Then I take these beautiful colors of the landscape, the sounds and smells, and add living space, a home, an office complex, or a building, places where people work or live."

It sounded like he was describing his version of heaven. The way his eyes sparkled, his voice caressed the words, his body grew tall while seated next to her. How could she say anything but yes? "I'd love you to show me these houses."

"Have you visited any of the homes in Hollywood Hills, Sunset Boulevard, Beverly Hills?"

"No. I've never been," she responded, enjoying his contagious enthusiasm. Still, she was practical. "But is it safe? I mean, colored folks driving around in those wealthy neighborhoods might attract attention."

"Percy, what do you think?" Malcolm asked the driver with a baiting tone. "Will we be safe?"

"Stop scaring her, Malcolm." Percy turned. "We'll be fine. People recognize this car. They know who owns it. So, you two lean back and relax."

"He's right," Malcolm said with a smile.

"Daisy, I should introduce you properly to my stepbrother, Percy Barnes. Serving as my chauffeur for the evening. He lost a round of yo-yo, and tonight, he does my bidding."

Daisy sat forward, her hands on the back of the driver's seat. "I knew it. The moment you stepped out of the car, I told Yvette, you looked nothing like a chauffeur. And she thought you looked like Malcolm."

Percy chuckled. "He's just showing off, miss. He can't afford a chauffeur. So we borrowed our parents' automobile."

She laughed, but something else puzzled her. "What's a yo-yo?"

"It's a toy. Gaining in popularity. The story goes that a Filipino bellhop named Pedro Flores caught guests' attention by playing with the toy during his lunch breaks at a Santa Monica hotel."

"*Yo-yo* means 'come-come' in the Philippine language," Percy added.

"I'll show you how to use it the next time we are together," Malcolm replied. "But now, we'd better get going before dark, or we'll miss the best parts."

Sitting comfortably next to Malcolm in the back seat of the Model A, Daisy watched, listened, and learned as he pointed out home after home, mansion after mansion, building after building. His stories of the great architects of Los Angeles and the inspiration for their designs captivated her. Not that she understood everything he said, but his enthusiasm was like a gift wrapped in satin and silk and scented with peppermint and sugarcane.

"These are the storybook houses," Malcolm said as they passed by a row of oddly shaped homes. "Houses with pointed roofs, winding staircases, and doorways that look like huts instead of entranceways."

"My father built our house, a bungalow, with my late uncles. They bought it in the Sears, Roebuck and Company catalog," she said. "Do you like them?" she asked.

"They are whimsical and old and delightful."

The mansions had impressive iron gates, and they were built at the end of winding roads or on Hollywood hillsides.

"I love these houses. They look like fairy tales," he said glancing at her. "You look surprised."

"I don't know, but I thought you wouldn't have enjoyed fairy-tale houses."

"Oh, like I'm a man who can only be fascinated by mathematics, perpendicular lines, steeples reaching into the sky, and" —

his piercing gaze held hers — "beauty?"

She smiled and looked away. "Maybe?"

The way he breathed the word made her stomach flutter. Daisy glanced at her hands nervously. "My sister would love this. She loves everything having to do with Hollywood, to a fault. And sometimes I think she hates our Sears, Roebuck and Company home, too."

"Most Negroes in Los Angeles have nothing to do with Hollywood and buy their homes from the Sears catalog. No shame in that."

"I'll tell you what's a shame — how a hard-working colored man is denied the chance to do for his family," said Daisy, recalling the struggle of many Negroes. "Even with the money to buy a new home, we are denied a loan due to the color of our skin, unless it's in the 'right' neighborhood. My father, mother, and uncles went through this, too.

"It is a grievous act that the city planners and racist whites work to keep the Blacks, the Mexicans, the Chinese, everyone other than the whites bottled up in the same neighborhoods. It doesn't matter if we make enough money to live anywhere we can afford. The bank lenders support those who want to keep us from ruining their land-scape."

"You are quite the advocate for Negro rights, I see."

"Yes, I am," she said proudly. "Sorry about going on and on, but I don't get to discuss this topic as I used to before my mother took ill. She and I would talk about civil rights all the time. We also volunteered to help civil rights programs whenever we could. But I would think all advocates for the Race believe every Negro feels the same."

The laughter that burst from Percy's mouth surprised her, and from Malcolm's expression, he wasn't pleased.

"Shut up, Percy," he said firmly. "Ignore him, Daisy. His sarcasm is like a case of rabies."

"What did I say that would cause a sarcastic remark?"

"Not all coloreds are about the Race, Daisy," said Percy, speaking over his right shoulder. "There are those who care only about what they have, and nothing else matters."

"You know these kinds of Blacks?" Daisy glanced at Malcolm.

"We know all types," Percy said. "All types."

"Let's move on." Malcolm didn't care for where the conversation had gone. "It is commendable that Daisy is concerned about the Race and what our responsibilities are as men in these times when the big opportunities continue to elude the colored man."

"They don't elude you, my brother." Percy's voice was tinged with more than sarcasm.

"You just won't shut up, will you, Percy?"

"Sorry, my brother, I will refrain from opening my mouth." Percy squeezed the Klaxon car horn as a stray cat ventured into the street.

Daisy wasn't sure what had passed between Malcolm and Percy, and since both had stopped talking, she couldn't force them to explain. So she went back to enjoying the scenery.

They drove through the city for a few hours, but as the sun began to set, Daisy's stomach growled. She hadn't had anything to eat since breakfast.

"Do you think we could find someplace to grab a bite of food?"

"It is getting late, Malcolm," Percy added with a warning tone.

"My apologies. How thoughtless of me. But the best place for a good meal, I believe," Malcolm began, "is our home."

Daisy gulped. "Your home? Maybe I should return to Yvette's house. I've had a fabulous time, but at this hour, it would be inappropriate for me to be in the home of two such fine young men of the Race unchaperoned."

"Don't worry, Daisy," Malcolm said. "There are any number of people in our house. I can guarantee nothing inappropriate will occur." He smiled broadly, adding a shy glance in her direction. Meanwhile, Percy didn't hide his snicker.

Now, what did this mean? Should she not trust Malcolm to be a man of his word? Or should she ignore Percy? Then she caught sight of Percy's expression in the rearview mirror. It held a teasing grin. Perhaps the unease she had witnessed was just two brothers giving each other a playful but hard time like Jedidiah and Marion used to do.

She would have enjoyed a visit to a mansion on Sunset Boulevard, but as much as she wanted to see the Barnes brothers' home, she decided it best to return to Yvette's. "Thank you, but I should head home."

A full week had passed since her evening with Malcolm — and Percy, who hadn't left their side, but she hoped to hear from him soon. She'd had a great time. But with no word from him since their outing, she couldn't stop herself from thinking the worst.

What if he was like a stray cat that had wandered into the road absently and when the *aooga* horn sounded, he hightailed it back to where he belonged? The horn blower was Veronica Fontaine.

It was strange, feeling jealous and not trusting Malcolm. He'd told her he'd broken it off with the actress. He'd also admitted that there'd been something to break off. When he said it, Daisy had believed him. Maybe, that's what she should keep doing — believing him.

It was Sunday afternoon, and Daisy and Henrietta were filling in for some missing waitresses in the dining hall. The Upsilon Chapter of Kappa Alpha Psi was honoring contestants of their Housing Contest and crowning someone queen. So the festivities and the number of special guests and notables were exceedingly high.

Daisy wasn't surprised to see Harry Belmont and Lincoln Perry among the Kappa Alpha Psi guests, but they were seated at separate tables on the opposite side of the room.

"What have you been up to, Daisy?" Harry had dared to follow her into the hallway, leading to the kitchen. Holding an empty tray in her hands, she glanced both ways to see who might be within earshot.

"Harry, have you forgotten the rules?" Her tone was friendly but also held a warning. "This is not the best time or place for a chat."

"I'm in a desperate situation and when I saw you, I just knew you would be the one to help me."

She reared backward a step, not liking the look in his eye or the shakiness of his voice.

"I need something scandalous confirmed, and you're the only one who can help me."

His patented grin was missing.

"Scandalous? What do you mean?"

"I need proof that Step is having an affair with a sixteen-year-old girl by the name of Yvonne Butler. And I know you can get that for me. I'd owe you my life."

Harry was full of dramatics lately, but he sounded serious, extremely so. Something was familiar about the name, other than sharing the same last name as Isaiah's.

"Mr. Fetchit has a lot of lady friends, but an affair with a sixteen-year-old girl?" Daisy swallowed. "Is that legal? He shouldn't be dating anyone under eighteen in California."

"Unless someone's mama is willing to look the other way," Harry said. "And there's more. This Butler girl is Charlie Butler's niece."

"Head of Central Casting's Negro division." Daisy sighed. "This is very touchy, Harry. I want to help, but I don't know if I can."

"You don't want to see your pal Harry pulled out of a ditch with a dozen bullet holes in his chest, now, do you?"

"Harry, what have you gotten yourself into?" A waitress walked by, and Daisy froze. When she spoke again, her voice was a whisper. "I'll do what I can and will drop by the *Eagle* later. But I doubt if I can rustle up more than gossip." She gave him a thin smile, but Harry's eyes were wild.

"What is gossip but slices from a scandal pie?" He leaned forward. "Get this for me, Daisy. I screwed up and owe some bad people some money, and this story will help me pay a debt." He grinned sheepishly. "I know it's a big favor to ask, and you also know I'll pay you for what you get for me. But you're the one to get it. I just know it."

She didn't like how he looked, scared and defeated. "I'll learn what I can, but don't ask me for anything like this again."

He leaned in and kissed her on the cheek.

"You're the best, doll."

Henrietta and Isaiah were in the staff room in the hotel basement when Daisy returned from her break and meeting with Harry. Both seemed to fling themselves at her as she came through the door, stopping shy of knocking her down. Their excitement about whatever was on their minds bordered on hysteria from what Daisy was seeing.

She sighed. "What's happened? Why are you two in such a tizzy?"

"Did you hear about King Vidor?" Henrietta said, practically jumping out of her skin. "He's making a movie with an all-colored cast."

"And it's a talkie," Isaiah blurted, hopping about, unable to contain his excitement.

Daisy decided not to mention that she'd heard rumors about the film during the summer and had passed the information on to Harry. "Where did you read this? In the *Eagle*?" Daisy said. "Are you sure it's not just gossip?"

"Central Casting sent out flyers," Henrietta said, eyes shining. "Isaiah and I want to audition."

Isaiah shook his head. "I mean, if there's a part for a musician. There should be. All the talkies have a colored band playing."

"This could be the first of so many movies with parts for colored actors and actresses. Not just playing servants, slaves, or whatnot."

Daisy felt numb. It was as if her snooping for Harry's column had combined to do what she hadn't considered — give young colored children false hope, in her opinion, about what a career in Hollywood might mean. "Negro-only films are being made, too. Don't make Los Angeles the only place in America where movies are made.

"And to answer your question, no, Henrietta, you can't audition for a talkie. Isaiah, I'm sure your mother would say the same. She should be in touch in a few months anyway. It won't take her forever to get settled up north."

"But Daisy, why not?" Henrietta asked with a sob in her voice. "It's just an audition. We probably wouldn't get picked. Please."

"I said no." Daisy glared at them long and hard, emphasizing her words, she hoped. They could do better than acting in movies, and they'd figure that out with some guidance.

Daisy could use some guidance herself, she thought, still looking at Henrietta and

Isaiah. "I have a question about Yvonne Butler. She's your late father's brother's daughter."

"She is. Henrietta knows her, too. They went to school together," Isaiah said.

"I know." She felt like a racehorse, needing to be ready when the gun went off. "Do either one of you know if she's seeing anyone? Or maybe, Isaiah, you could ask her?"

CHAPTER 23
FRANKIE

Saturday, June 1, 1968
Albuquerque

A little before ten o'clock, Tobey parks across from the Kings Hotel, located on the corner of Central Avenue and a small side street in Albuquerque, and I'm impressed.

I expected sagebrush, horse troughs, and saloons with Miss Kitty and Marshal Dillon, at the bar wetting their whistles on shots of tequila, and gunfire. But it's a city with storefronts, an isolated shopper or two — a cinema, more than one restaurant, and what looks to be a nightclub or tavern next door to the hotel.

If this is where we're spending the night, I don't mind. "Was this hotel in your book, Daisy?" I ask. "It looks nice."

"Just for you, I didn't check," she replies sarcastically.

"We could stay in the car, if you prefer," I reply with the same tone. But I am also admittedly not in a rush to leave the Mustang, and when I glance at Tobey, he might not make it out of the car, either.

He reclines against the seat, his head back, eyes closed as if inches away from taking his last breath. I guess we both need a moment to digest the past few hours.

Meanwhile, Daisy practices her moves with the switchblade, flipping it open, snapping it shut and rattling my nerves with each pop.

"You shouldn't play with that when you're intoxicated."

"I am not intoxicated. I am coming down from a pleasant high. Do not confuse the two."

"Don't do this, Daisy. You're scaring her, and damn it, you're scaring me, too."

"I'm not doing anything."

"Playing with a switchblade after telling us you plan to slit someone's throat isn't a game," Tobey points out.

"He's right. It's scary, Daisy, and you sound crazy — and scary." *And annoying and pissing me off,* I almost add.

I stare at the hotel sign and the nightclub sign next door. It flashes blue and green lights, sparkling in the night like stars in the sky. I also hear a saxophone, its rhythmical breathy chords, a haunting noise. I could listen to this music from where I sit until dawn.

"What did you say, Frankie?" Daisy's elbows drape over the backs of the front seats.

"Who was killed? The murder you are avenging. Who died?"

"A woman I knew a long time ago." She smacks the back of my seat. "I can't get out of the car until one of you do."

Tobey opens his eyes and stares through the windshield while reclining on the head-rest. "The sky is beautiful," he says softly. "Look, every star system, so close, you could hold them in your palm."

Daisy's exasperated sigh is an indication of her interest in astrology. "Oh, Lord, To-bey, you're such a romantic. Like your mother. Now, let me out of the car, damn it. I don't need one of your astrology lec-tures."

"You sure? It might help your state of mind." He reaches for the door handle. "Help you think about something other than opening and closing a switchblade or cutting throats."

Tobey opens the car door and unfolds, standing next to the car, stretching from side to side, touching his toes, and generally looking like Jack LaLanne doing calisthenics.

Meanwhile, Daisy exits the car and shoves her knife back in her purse. "I'm going inside. You two gather our things. I'll get the rooms." And with that, she's off.

"What are we going to do with her?" Tobey is talking to himself, I believe. So I'm not sure I need to respond, but if I did, my answer would be I have no clue.

I wiggle around to open the passenger-side door, but a flutter in my stomach, like a large butterfly flapping its wings, stops me. It's too soon for me to feel the baby, but I believe I do. It's the tiniest ripple in my tummy, reminding me that he's there.

Tobey appears on my side of the car, holding the door open. "You need help?"

I hesitate, weighing the question in my mind, before I reply. "I do." I reach for him. He takes my hand. "Thanks. I appreciate it."

This is a surprise.

Daisy has arranged for us to have separate rooms. She cites my frequent trips to the bathroom, keeping her up half the night, as the reason. I don't object. She is paying the bills, and I appreciate the chance for this unforeseen slice of heaven called privacy.

351

It also makes it easier for me to slip away and find a phone booth.

There are two phone booths nearby, and I opt for the one in the rear of the hotel. A maid tells me that the staff makes personal calls and takes cigarette breaks there without the manager bearing down every second.

I close the doors in the phone booth and start my collect call. The line rings a few times, but no answer. I call back.

Someone picks up. "Hello." I don't recognize the female voice.

"Is Tamika there?"

"Who's calling?"

It bothers me that I'm not sure who I'm talking to and why she sounds upset. "It's Frankie. Her cousin."

"Francine Saunders, married to Jackson Saunders?"

Panic rips through me. "Yes. Is Tamika there? Is she okay? Did something happen?"

"A lot of shit has happened. Hold on. Let me see if she wants to talk."

A thought passes through my mind, and I pray it's scarier than reality. Whatever has happened to Tamika won't be as bad as this woman is making it out to be. I believe she's made things sound worse than expected, and once all the facts are in, they aren't as bad.

Please. Please. Let that thought be real.

"Francine." Tamika's voice is death on the other end of a phone line.

"Jesus Christ. What happened?"

"Jackson. He found me on campus, Francine. On the fucking campus in the lobby of the Pritzker School of Medicine." Her voice broke apart. "I told you he found out about the baby from the hospital."

"God, Tamika. What did he do?"

"Tried to kill me, that's what. Dumb bastard. He lost it. Started screaming at me. I tried to calm him down. I mean, we were in the lobby of the Pritzker goddamned building."

"He hit you?" I thought he only struck me. "Oh my God!"

"He didn't hit me. He pushed me down a flight of stairs."

"Are you okay? Christ. I'm so sorry, Tamika. This is my fault. I'm so sorry."

Another sob catches in her throat. "Actually I fell down three steps. I'm fine but, Francine, he made me mad. So mad, I screwed up. He told me he knew about the baby, and I told him he didn't deserve to be a father."

"You weren't wrong. He doesn't."

"Then I told him that's why you left him. You could handle him hitting you, but you weren't going to allow an innocent child to be his next victim."

"Again, you weren't wrong, Tamika, but how did you screw up?"

"I think what I said to him made him more determined to find you. He said there was only one place for you to go — and he'd wait for you on your mother's doorstep. You did call her, didn't you?"

Damn, I hadn't. "I will but I won't stay with her. He can wait there for the next year. I'll find someplace else where he won't find me. I'll stay with Daisy. She'll help me."

"Good. I'm glad to hear you're getting along."

"It's an interesting trip. I'll tell you all about it once we reach Los Angeles," I said, but my chest tightened with guilt. "Are you sure you're going to be okay?"

"Just bruised. He scared me, though. I can handle his crazy better than his violence. I know you loved him, but Jesus, Francine, how have you managed it all these years. He isn't just angry; he's cruel. Like a mad dog. Since high school, you've been his buffer. The person he can lash out at without consequence. That's not a man. There are plenty of good brothers in the world. Plenty."

"I guess I thought I didn't deserve better." The truth of the words from my mouth surprise me. "Did you call the police on him? Maybe he's sitting in a jail cell and not on his way to LA."

"He ran off after I fell, but I filed a complaint. The cops are looking for him, but he's gone. I just know it. That's why you need to watch out."

"I should go. It's late, and we need to get some food before we crash." I close my eyes, fighting tears. "I'm so sorry about Jackson and what he did to you."

"Stop it. His craziness is not your fault, honey. And I'm okay." She inhales deeply. "And call your mother."

355

CHAPTER 24
DAISY

Fall 1928
Los Angeles

It was quitting time on a Friday evening in November when Daisy picked up the message from Malcolm, inviting her to meet him at the diner near Lincoln Theatre.

Of course, it was Cecil who gave her the note. He always seemed to be working the front desk when suite 416 left her mail. So, she wasn't too shocked by the hairy eyeball he was giving her as he handed her the letter. Suspicion had become a conclusion from the limp smile on his face. Daisy swore she could hear the whispers in the staff room about the chambermaid and suite 416.

Well, she thought, she'd have to live with the gossip until she and Malcolm found another way to communicate. Also, as long as it didn't reach Naomi Avenue or Harry Belmont, she'd be jake. Although, she wondered briefly, which would be worse — her father's anger or Harry's disappointment.

A quick trip home for a change of clothes was met with relief. No one was there other than Mrs. Weaver and her mother (no change in her condition, but Daisy was still confident that her plan would work). Fortunately, Mrs. Weaver wasn't a busybody and didn't ask Daisy where she was going in such a rush. She just smiled and said, have a lovely evening. Daisy promised she'd return soon.

Since the hotel and her home were within minutes of the diner, she arrived before Malcolm and waited near the entrance.

But she wasn't nervous. She'd chosen the path of trust and belief. This was what she'd put in her mind, and she wouldn't waver. A week between dates wasn't a sign of anything other than each of them living their lives.

After all, they weren't a couple. They were friends.

"Daisy, so good to see you." The way he swept into the diner, his arms reaching for her, she thought he would embrace her. As surprising was her body's desire to be embraced.

He relaxed his arms and nodded a greeting. "Thank you for joining me. I know it was last minute, but I've been busy and have much to tell you. I hope you have some time. Shall we sit and have a coffee? Or is it too late for coffee?"

She grinned shyly. He talked so quickly; she wanted to touch his shoulder and encourage him to slow down and breathe. But he was so excited. His eyes sparkled, and his smile was sunlight. There had been so little joy in her life since the dam collapsed; she was uncomfortable this close to happiness. It was painful and frightening.

"Are you sure you want to have coffee? Do you have the time?"

Daisy nodded. "Sorry, I was thinking — oh, never mind. I do want some coffee."

They found a table away from the front door. After all, the diner was in the same neighborhood as the hotel and Daisy's home. Their coffee was served quickly.

"You seem so happy," Daisy said, her fingers wrapped around the warm cup of java.

Malcolm leaned forward, ignoring his coffee. "Could it be that I missed you?"

She tilted her head, watching him closely. "You are very pleased about something. Tell me."

"I passed the California exam! I'm a

licensed architect." His smile was electric.

She covered her mouth with a hand, feeling her smile in response might be too wide to be attractive. "I'm so happy for you. Congratulations."

Next, she reached out to him compulsively and touched his hand, resting on the table. The awkwardness of the gesture nearly sent her into spasms. Then, quickly, she withdrew her hand only to have Malcolm take hers in both of his.

The electricity in his touch was the same as his smile, also strong, warm, and caring.

"I wanted you to be the first to know, other than my family." He laughed. "I've been worried about the exam and feel such relief now. There aren't many Negro architects in the state, but there are some great ones, and I intend to learn. I'm excited."

He released her hand but kept smiling and looking at her in a way that made everything around them small, hard to see, hard to hear.

"Are you free next Sunday? There's a movie at the Colony Theater, *Gang War,* but everyone is talking about a film short, a cartoon, *Steamboat Willie.* It's based on a minstrel song, 'Turkey in a Straw,' I hear. You know that one?"

She didn't but it didn't matter. "I'd love

359

to." Daisy also hoped Yvette would be okay with her visiting on weekends regularly. The way her stomach flipped up, down, and sideways, she and Malcolm would see much more of one another.

By November, everyone who was anyone and Negro in Los Angeles had booked a room at the Somerville, lunched at the Somerville, drank at the hotel bar, swam in the rooftop pool, or hobnobbed with celebrities, dignitaries, and hangers-on in the lobby.

Daisy was in gossip heaven. The extra money flowed from Harry Belmont's pockets into hers. Each week she had a fresh laundry list of news. The week before had been particularly rich:

King Vidor leaves Hollywood to find cast for all-Negro film. He's heading south to hire extras and his leads, too.

Jason Joy of the MPPDA reviews King Vidor's *Hallelujah* script, and the word "nigger" has been struck from the film.

King Vidor finally casts new lead for *Hallelujah,* sixteen-year-old Nina Mae McKinney, Broadway sensation of Eubie Blake's *Shuffle Along.* She replaces Honey Brown.

But it was this past week that had Harry's mouth foaming like a rabid dog because the gossip was all about Harry's favorite subject, Lincoln Perry:

Stepin Fetchit buys cashmere suits from Valentino's estate.

Stepin Fetchit arrested for making "whoopee" on Central Avenue near the Somerville.

Harry had especially liked the last item and used it verbatim in his column.

There was only one catch.

Harry kept stopping by the hotel to chat, ignoring their agreement to meet anyplace but the Somerville. He also was using Isaiah to track her down.

"Harry Belmont is in the courtyard, Daisy." Isaiah found her in the storage room. "He says it's important you two talk. He asked me to find you."

Daisy closed her eyes and breathed. Not only had Harry done what they'd agreed he wouldn't do (and he'd done that more than once), she didn't like involving Isaiah. She'd done that already and felt guilty about it. But she had helped her confirm the rumors. Lincoln Perry and Yvonne Butler's announcement of marriage would run in the

361

newspaper in a few days. The scandal wasn't too much of a scandal.

Daisy entered into the courtyard, fuming. But there was Harry next to the fountain with his patented grin, bright eyes shining, and fedora tilted over his left eye. At least he appeared to be in a better mood than the last time she saw him.

She stalked up to him. "What are you doing here?" she said, omitting the profanity. "We agreed, and I know you haven't forgotten."

His smile vanished as if he had pasted it on only for show. When he spoke, his voice was tight with concern. "I know we agreed, but I had no choice, Daisy."

"Don't they say we always have a choice, Harry?"

When he grabbed and squeezed her arm, pulling her close, she balled her fists, preparing to punch him. He'd never touched her like that before. No man had. "Let go."

"Listen, it's about your sister, Henrietta."

"What about Henrietta?" The worry and panic for her safety seared through Daisy, but it ebbed quickly. She'd just seen her sister, heading for the roof with an armload of towels. Guests were still plentiful at poolside thanks to the balmy fall weather in Los Angeles.

"Go on," she said calmly.

"Did you know she auditioned for the Vidor talkie?"

"No, she didn't. I told her no, she couldn't audition. Besides, she is too busy working and singing with Isaiah."

Her sister, along with Isaiah, had become the toast of Brown Broadway since the raid. They had gigs at nightclubs up and down Central Avenue. Daisy didn't object if the establishment was willing to schedule them earlier in the evening and never on rowdier nights. Though, she hadn't mentioned anything to their father. She'd wait until after their mother was on the mend.

"Oh, yes. I've heard about their act," Harry said. "Probably why she auditioned. Several musicians and band leaders are interested in Isaiah's talents with the guitar, and Henrietta is quite the entertainer."

"That's why she auditioned. She's very good."

"Yes, but you've got it wrong, she didn't audition, so there's no emergency. No reason for you to be here."

Harry kept shaking his head, trying to shut her up, she assumed.

"What?" she said, tired of him eyeballing her.

"She has been cast in *Hallelujah* and is

leaving tonight for Arkansas with the rest of the extras."

Daisy had heard him wrong. "How? That makes no sense. No. I don't believe you."

"I figured as much." Harry removed a sheet of paper from his suit jacket's vest pocket. "Charlie Butler, you remember him, head of Negro casting, dropped this off today, wanting me to run the list in the *Eagle*."

Daisy touched the edges of the paper lightly before taking it from him.

"It should run in the afternoon paper." He pointed like she needed assistance finding her name, which, frankly, she did.

"Henrietta Washington," she read slowly, her breath burning her throat.

What in God's name?

She returned the sheet of paper he'd given her. "Thanks, Harry. I've got to go."

"You're welcome."

She started off to find her sister but she spun back toward Harry. "Can you do me a favor, please?"

"Whatever you need," he said.

"I want you to let Mr. Butler know he'll need to find someone else for her part. Can you do that? Do you understand?"

He half chuckled. "Consider it done, sugar."

Then she hurried off to the roof in hopes that Henrietta was still delivering towels.

"You've got one minute to explain to me what I just overheard."

Daisy had cornered Henrietta on an empty roof, the pool crowd absent for a change. But it worked in Daisy's favor. She had launched into her sister with no preamble.

"And don't give me that pitiful look, like you don't know what I'm talking about. What were you planning to do, just run off? Sneak out of the house tonight without letting anyone know where you went or why or how?"

Daisy grabbed her sister's arm hard and fought the urge to shake her like a rag doll until she got some sense. But Henrietta was too tall, and judging from the stubborn set of her jaw, Daisy's show of temper was having no effect, which only angered her more.

"You're not too old to spank. You know that?" Daisy hissed through gritted teeth.

"So, why don't you slap me in the face instead?" Henrietta glared at Daisy's hand wrapped around her upper arm. "Let me go. You're hurting me."

"I don't care. And I won't let go until you explain what you were thinking."

Henrietta looked around as if searching for some hotel guest lounging at the pool to help her.

"I want to be in the motion pictures. They have talkies now and more roles for coloreds, in particular Negro singers and musicians." She wiped her nose roughly. "I auditioned, and they gave me a part, Daisy. A part in a motion picture. Why can't you be glad for me?"

Since no one was around to force Daisy to curb the scolding she was giving Henrietta, she released her with a shove. "Because you didn't get a part in a picture. You're an extra. A colored girl in a colored crowd. Nothing more."

Henrietta blinked back an onslaught of tears. "That's not what Mr. Butler said."

"That's who hired you? Isaiah's cousin? Did he have something to do with this?"

She shook her head. "He doesn't even know."

"Oh, so you were walking out on Isaiah, too?"

"But he'd understand. He knows how much this means to me."

"What is going on with you? You've never been this way. Why are you so angry? Why won't you talk to me anymore?"

"I said you're hurting me, Daisy."

366

"And I said I don't care."

Daisy began to pace. "Whatever gave you such an idea? With Mother ill and everything topsy-turvy since March, I can't believe you'd leave your family.

"I was helping you and Isaiah, too. Letting you perform at every other night spot on Brown Broadway that invited you. Not mentioning it to Papa, even though I think he knows but has just ignored it for now."

"Why don't you let me explain?"

Daisy looked at her sister in shock. "What explanation?"

"You have dreams; why can't I? I can sing. I can dance. I could be in the moving pictures. I can't just sit around and wait for Mama to get well, and for Papa not to be sad and angry, and for you to stop thinking you can fix everything."

"You're not going," Daisy said slowly. "I will chain you to a bench in the basement of this hotel, I swear. Just forget about it."

Henrietta's eyes filled with tears. "You can't stop me."

"I already have. Harry is contacting Charlie Butler and is removing you from the cast list. You have been fired. So we don't need to discuss this any further."

Daisy feared that one bad thing after another would keep happening on Naomi Avenue.

The feeling she'd had so strongly at the diner had vanished. But then that morning, she'd remembered and smiled. She'd done it and made enough money to put her mother in a hospital where they would help her.

Before her father went to work that evening, she'd fix him his favorite meal and give him the news. He was the one who had to sign the papers to get her admitted.

Mrs. Keyes had agreed to let her off work early on Saturday. Daisy had one stop to make — Yvette's house — before going home to grab some items she'd left.

When the door opened, the expression on her friend's face made Daisy's stomach churn.

"What's the matter? Did something happen to the baby? To Sid?" Daisy asked, taking hold of Yvette's shoulders and squeezing gently.

"No. Nothing like that. It's your father, Daisy. He was here a few minutes ago. Fit to be tied."

"Why?"

"It's Delilah Jenkins's fault. That worthless hussy is a spy for the *California Eagle,* I swear to God. She's been collecting gossip and passing it along to Harry Belmont. I've never been so angry at him. But she must be the one who told Harry about Malcolm Barnes — saying he now has two mistresses. The white actress, Veronica Fontaine, and a colored girl, a chambermaid."

Daisy's breath had lodged itself in her chest, and she wasn't sure how to get it out. She blew air through her mouth and kept repeating the pattern until she believed she could speak. "What does this have to do with my father?"

"It's in the newspaper, honey. In Harry's gossip column. Right there, for every colored man, woman, and child in Los Angeles to read."

Daisy ran her hands down her face. "My God."

Yvette stepped into the living room and picked up a newspaper from the table. "Look."

Daisy stared at the article from the *Eagle* and the byline. Sure enough, it was Harry Belmont's column.

"Oh my God." Daisy stumbled forward and collapsed onto the nearest chair.

"It doesn't mention any names," Yvette said, soothingly. "Besides Veronica Fontaine's, but lots of people will think they know the name of the chambermaid."

"Why would she do this?"

Yvette pursed her lips and rolled her eyes. "The harlot works part-time for Veronica Fontaine. And she even has a part in some film at Fox Hills Studio." Yvette growled. "I think Fontaine put her up to it. Otherwise, how would Delilah know so much about him?"

Daisy held the newspaper in her hands, not needing to read what Harry had written. The harm had been done. "My father saw this?"

"He came here holding it in his hand, looking for you. I didn't know what to do. I didn't know what to say. Then Sid —"

Yvette bit down on her lower lip. Her eyes clouded with despair. "Sid can't keep his mouth shut, and when your father asked man-to-man if you'd ever spent the weekend here to go out on dates, he answered him."

"So, my father put two and two together," she said. "I need to get home."

"Sid will drive you."

"I can run faster than your old car."

Daisy stood at the front door of the house on Naomi Avenue, clutching the sides of her skirt, catching her breath. The run from Yvette's bungalow had her lungs aching and rivers of sweat running down her spine.

But she owed her father an explanation and mustn't forget her good news. She just prayed he would accept it without too much show of his temper.

Courage gathered, she walked into the kitchen where her father was putting groceries into the pantry.

"Hi, Papa." She wondered where to start then decided why not jump right in. "I went by Yvette's, and I know you probably have questions about the *California Eagle* column."

"I don't wish to discuss that article. I just happened upon it. There's something else you need to know."

What was happening? There was no outrage, no sign he was angry or seeking the right moment to grab his leather belt and give her a proper spanking. No, there was nothing but his solemness.

She looked around the kitchen. Why was her father putting away groceries?

She glanced down the hall. The bedroom door was ajar, the door where her mother stayed.

Her heart pounded. "Is she up? Is Mama awake?"

Daisy ran down the hall. "Mama! Mama?" She pushed open the door. "She's not here, Papa." Daisy raced back to where her father

371

stood, staring down at his hands. "Where's Mama?"

"I had her admitted to a state institution this afternoon."

"No, Papa. I have the money. Remember you promised to wait until December. I've been working hard for months to earn enough money to admit her to a place where they want to help her because she's sick. She's not crazy, Papa. She's sick." Daisy gulped.

"I'm sorry you're angry and hope you won't stay angry. But I did what was best for Sophie, for Henrietta, for you and me."

"How dare you say you did what was best for Mama. You gave up on her. The day she fell to the floor, you stopped loving her. I saw it in your face. You just quit. So, don't lie to me. Don't lie. You just stopped loving her."

"You haven't been here, Daisy. You've been working and helping your friends and keeping up with your sister. None of us can handle our lives and your mother's illness. Her mind is sick, Daisy. I know you don't want to see it, but it's true.

"Mrs. Weaver has been a godsend all these months, barely charging us to take care of her while we're all working. But she can't help us anymore.

"I came home and sat with her most every day, and all she's done since March is lie in bed and cry or sleep. She's been wasting away in front of our eyes, and you refused to see it."

There were tears on her father's cheeks, tears he didn't wipe away. "Yes, she had a heart attack and a stroke, but neither one of those awful things killed her. The reason she lies there, doing nothing, saying nothing is because her mind is sick."

Daisy squeezed her eyes shut, wishing she could erase his words.

"I love my wife more than my own life. But I've got you girls —" His voice cracked. "Don't you want to live your life, go back to college, and finish your education? Remember when you had dreams? When your sister had a future?"

Daisy wiped the tears from her face, nose, and lips. "I'll never forgive you."

He slammed his fist on the table. "Do you think I'll ever forgive myself, even if in my heart I know I did what was best for her?"

Daisy covered her face with her hands. The rage inside her threatened to burn her from the inside out. She had to get away from him.

She ran to her bedroom, shoved whatever she could put her hands on and her maid's uniform into a satchel. Seconds later, she stood on the sidewalk in front of the house.

No more words were necessary. Her actions showed she'd made up her mind. If Yvette couldn't take her in, she'd sleep in the pantry on the fourth floor of the Hotel Somerville. But she would never spend another minute in her father's house, not without her mother.

CHAPTER 25
FRANKIE

Saturday, June 1, 1968
Albuquerque

I do not telephone my mother as I told Tamika I would (for the second time). The thought of explaining why I am returning to Los Angeles after two years (I believe it's been that long), without a husband (and pregnant), is something that can wait, wouldn't you think? I mean, honestly, it can wait.

Besides, it's too late — almost midnight. So, instead of a phone call, I return to my room, dress, and meet Daisy in the lobby for a drink. As we enter the tavern, the jukebox is playing Aretha Franklin.

I'm disappointed, not with the song. The inside of the tavern doesn't match the outside. The nightspot looks cool and inviting from the street, but it smells like sour beer, cigarettes, and grease.

Thank goodness for Aretha's "Soul Serenade." It is one of my favorites. Although, the bluesy number does work with the dive's low buzz of quiet conversation.

There are a handful of customers, three at the bar. A few others sit at two of the four-tops. A row of booths lines the rear of the room. So, the joint is basically empty. And that's fine with me. I've had my fill of crowded places.

The bartender is rattling glasses, deliberately trying to draw our attention, I think. A tall man, Negro, gray-haired, goatee, with a well-worn face, dark circles around the eyes, but also deep crevices around his mouth. That means he's spent most of his life with a smile on his face.

"Do you want a drink?" Daisy says. I glance at her and do a double take. Why I hadn't noticed her outfit before, I'll never know. But it's cute, I guess, but daring as hell, too. A slim yellow dress with white lace cutouts — she's dressed for a cocktail party on Aristotle Onassis's yacht not a burger-and-beer joint in New Mexico.

In contrast, I'm wearing pedal pushers and a sleeveless cream-colored shell. Bored with my pleated skirts, ankle socks, and loafers, I borrowed the number from Daisy and was pleasantly pleased when it fit. We sit on stools at the bar.

"Great dress," I say to her.

"Thank you, dear. You look cute, too — in my clothes."

Tobey walks by me just then and sits on the other side of Daisy.

I exaggerate a deep breath. "Did I just get a whiff of aftershave?"

He frowns. "Are you about to give me a hard time about taking a shower and shaving?"

"I didn't think hippies washed." I chuckle. "And you took off the dashiki, too? So, you decided to go for a clean shirt and pants." I glance down at his flare-bottomed jeans. "But a guy can only go so far from his roots."

I expect a chuckle in reply, but the scowl on his face is as wide as Texas. "We should eat and get some shut-eye." He sounds like the principal at my school, handing out report cards.

So this should be interesting: Tobey in a vile mood.

"Can't we just eat and relax for a bit without pulling each other's chains?"

"I haven't done a thing. So don't beg me to behave. Check with your best gal, Daisy." I tilt my head in her direction. "Don't you love her minidress?"

Tobey gives Daisy a side-eyed glance, but

his impatience is showing. "Let's stay focused on tomorrow's drive, or LA and what waits for us there."

"That sounds ominous," I say. "What are you expecting? The Los Angeles boogeyman?"

"Come on, Tobey," Daisy chimes in. "I agree. Chill."

He looks uninterested, and I sense something is up with him, more so than Daisy's outfit and my weirdly cheery mood. "We can make it to Los Angeles tomorrow if we drive straight through for fifteen hours. If we get an early start."

"A shower and a shave seem to have done you more harm than good," I say.

Daisy nods in agreement. "While you're mapping out our trip in your brain, I'm gonna relax and enjoy myself this evening." She suddenly makes a big deal about crossing her legs and tucking the short skirt beneath her hips. Then she pulls a cigarette from her purse. "Let's order some drinks. Maybe that'll loosen up Mr. Sourpuss."

She shoots a glance at Tobey before raising her hand to the bartender. The bartender moves to the spot across from Daisy quickly. His toothy grin is all the toothier looking at the woman in the yellow dress.

"May I get that for you, ma'am." His

lighter is ready before Daisy's cigarette reaches her lips.

I raise a playful eyebrow at Tobey. He practically snarls, still refusing to be pleasant.

"How long have you lived in Albuquerque?" Daisy asks the bartender as she takes the light.

"Been living here most of my life."

"You own this place?"

"Nah. My sister's brother. I just tend bar."

"We'll have tequila," Daisy says. "Three shots, straight up — with a beer chaser."

"I don't think I should." I pat my belly. "Not on an empty stomach."

"Your tummy isn't exactly empty." She nods at the bartender. "Three." Then she says to us, "Why don't you two grab a table. I'll bring the drinks. Plus, I may want to do some flirting." She tilts her head and winks in the direction of the bartender.

"Okay." Tobey stands suddenly, nearly knocking over the stool.

When we reach the table, I plop down in a seat and wait for him to unwrap his limbs and settle.

"What in the hell is wrong with you?"

"That car ride wore me out. That's what's wrong with me."

He sounds surly and looks the same. He

might be clean-shaven, except for the side-burns, but his attitude needs a makeover. He's not helping my chill on the last night before reaching Los Angeles. "If you are grouchy, worrying about Daisy, don't. She seems fine. Just smoking cigarettes and flirt-ing and having some fun."

I nod at Daisy, who is still at the bar, yak-king it up with the bartender, cigarette wav-ing in the air, pushing her bangs off her brow.

"And tomorrow" — I begin — "we'll be in LA, and she'll be fine."

"Have you forgotten about her plans? What she intends to do once she gets there?"

"What? Kill some guy? Do you take her that seriously?"

"Daisy doesn't screw around with a prom-ise." He squeezes his eyes shut, and when he opens them, I see his worry hasn't sub-sided.

"What is it with you and Daisy? Sure, she helped raise you but — are you two so —"

Three full shot glasses descend on top of the table with a firm plop.

"Voilà." Daisy licks drops of liquor from her fingertips. "Am I so what, so beautiful, so charming, so fun. Or insane?"

She drops into the chair between us, throwing back a shot as she does so. "I took the liberty of ordering three dinner specials." She gestures to a blackboard. "Bart says it's the best choice."

"Bart the bartender," Tobey says grimly.

"Burgers and fries?" I add brightly. "And rice and beans."

"Are you going to drink that or not?" Daisy's gaze meets mine.

"I'm fine," I say. "I'm okay with the beer."

Just then, Bart comes to our table with three mugs of foamy beer from the tap. Daisy downs another shot.

Bart rests a pint of beer in front of her. "You know where you're going tomorrow?"

Raising a fist to her mouth, Daisy coughs loudly. "I certainly do — Los Angeles, California."

Bart gives her a curious smile as if her gagging routine confuses him. It confuses me.

"I'll bring your meals right out, then." He hurries off.

I turn to Daisy. "What was that all about?"

"Nothing. Just flirting." She sips her beer.

"Didn't seem like flirting."

Bart returns a moment later with a tray of food, napkins, and utensils. As soon as we are set up, a group of musicians enters, carrying instruments and talking loud.

I eat a french fry. "Why are you so quiet,

Tobey?"

He takes a bite of his hamburger, giving no indication he plans to reply.

I gulp my beer. It's not the way I planned on spending the evening. Yet, unfortunately, I have no idea how to change our course.

"If no one is going to talk, I might as well leave," Daisy says, articulating my feelings.

Still, I wonder if I can add reading minds to her list of talents.

"Come on, Daisy, don't do that," I urge. Sitting alone in my hotel room isn't where I want to be.

"I don't want to sit here half the night and be all tense and irritable. I'll get enough of that when we reach Los Angeles."

Tobey slams down his pint. "Let's go, then."

"Now you're all upset," Daisy remarks. "You didn't seem that bothered when we were on the road. What's putting the burr in your butt now?"

"I know you. That's what, and you're gonna pull some shit."

"What am I gonna do that I haven't already told you about?"

Their voices have hit that octave where the room turns and stares. I'm beside myself. A peaceful meal, music, and dancing aren't gonna happen. "Come on, you two. Don't do this now."

"Why not, Frankie?" Daisy's voice climbs. "I want to slit a man's throat. Don't you want to know why? Aren't you a wee bit interested? Or do you think I'm joking?"

I drop my head into my hand — the one not in a sling. "I don't care if you're joking. I want to eat and relax."

"Relax, huh? Well, I'm gonna tell you something, whether you're interested or not —"

"Daisy," Tobey says in a warning tone. "Don't do this."

"Why the hell not? She should know. She's the one that started this journey we're on. Without her, none of this would be possible."

"Lord." Tobey sighs. "Let's ask for the check and leave."

"No." Daisy leans toward me. "Come on, Frankie. Let's have a conversation about your mother."

"I don't care why you don't get along with her. I don't get along with her, either, but I'm pregnant, and Los Angeles is the only place I can be right now. Until I have this baby."

Tobey reaches for me, and I slap his hand aside. "Don't touch me. If she's going to act all crazy, I'll act crazy, too." I glare at

Daisy. "I have to mend my relationship with my mother because I don't have any place else to go." I cover my mouth as a sob edges into my throat. "I don't want to raise a baby with Jackson, but I can't do it alone. But I'll be damned if I raise a child the way I was raised."

They both stare at me. Mouths clamped shut. I must've frightened them into silence.

Tobey places his hand over mine and gives me a gentle squeeze. I don't slap him away this time.

Daisy stands. "I'm gonna leave you two alone. I've had enough drama for one night."

Tobey stands, too. "I'll get the check."

"No. I already paid — and I said, I'm leaving you two alone." She leans forward. "You finish your meals. Have a few drinks. Enjoy the live music. I'll see you in the morning."

She walks off, leaving us with our mouths open. Or just my mouth, because Tobey waves at the bartender, orders another shot, except this time, he wants whiskey.

"What's wrong with you?" I bark at Tobey because I can't give Daisy a hard time. She's already out the door. "You're the reason she left. All you had to do was lighten up." I take a sip of my drink, and it burns my throat, but I'm okay with that. What I'm not okay with is Tobey's blank stare.

"You don't care what happens to her. I do." The bartender delivers his whiskey, and he gulps it down.

I roll my eyes. "She doesn't need anyone to care about her. What she needs is to entertain. Nothing but show business. Telling us tall tales about what she plans to do in Los Angeles without any rational reason for her actions." I drain my beer. "If she had real problems, then maybe I'd be sympathetic. Instead, I'm the one the real shit's coming down on."

"You left your husband — what's there to worry about? You've made a move. You're free. Nothing is about to bite you in the ass."

"Maybe, but what if he's coming after me?"

"Is he?"

"If you must know. He's on his way to Los Angeles. He'll be waiting for me if I go to my mother's house. So, what do you think I should do? Slit his throat?"

"I don't condone violence."

"Oh, yeah, right. You're a pacifist. A draft dodger. You have no stomach for slit throats or broken bones."

"Wait. Are you serious? He's going to be in Los Angeles. How do you know?"

"I telephoned my cousin in Chicago. The

police are looking for him. He went crazy and attacked her after losing his job — damn it. I didn't want to talk about this. I just wanted to chill. One night."

The band starts making noise, like warming up to play something, a sound check of sorts. I shut my eyes, calming myself.

"Let's have some more drinks. And talk about something pleasant, something other than my husband or Daisy."

"Running away from your problems isn't any good, either."

"Oh, and you should talk? Draft dodger. The name says it all. You're on the run for the rest of your life."

"No, I'm on the run until I get Daisy to Los Angeles, and she gets the medical help she needs."

"Oh, right, and then what, you're going to stop dodging?"

He smiles. "You could say that. I'm turning myself in."

I pause, having not expected him to say something so insane. "Why would you do that? It's not as if the cops are on your trail. You could stay free until the war ends, and the country changes its mind about Vietnam."

"If not this war, then another and another. I will always be on the other side of the fight. Always saying no, I won't go."

"What happened to you to make you such a coward?"

He flinches as if I struck him across the face. The reaction I expected. I am not oblivious to knowing how words can hurt. Between my husband and my mother, I've been trained by experts. I know how to cause as much pain as possible with the fewest words imaginable. Regardless, I am not as satisfied as I thought I might be — dishing on Tobey.

"Excuse me," I stand. He doesn't look up. "I'm going to the bar. Do you want another whiskey?"

The way he turns his head to look at me is measured. Making up his mind about whether he wants to stay with me or not. He blinks. "Yeah. Whiskey would be good."

CHAPTER 26
DAISY

Winter 1928
Los Angeles

Daisy stood in the spare bedroom in Yvette's bungalow, preparing for another date with Malcolm. After four dinners, two long drives, and a walk on the beach, holding hands, Daisy longed for that first kiss. The thought of it made her feel like a schoolgirl. She felt more excited, more exhilarated, and lately, kissing him was all she could think about.

Of course, it was better than dwelling on what her father had done. He had broken a promise which pained Daisy nearly as much as the days after the St. Francis Dam collapsed.

Nothing had changed between her and her father, which made seeing Malcolm regularly a bit easier. She'd also stopped all dealing with Harry Belmont. The only thing she kept track of was her sister. Otherwise, she was free as a bird.

So, Daisy had decided to focus on kissing. The other things were too painful. She also decided there was a difference between desire and kindness. If Malcolm had a mistress, Daisy would learn the truth from that first kiss. It made perfect sense to her.

The clammy palms and fluttering wings of small birds in the pit of her stomach didn't mean she was nervous. Excited, maybe, but she took that as a good sign.

Percy arrived at Yvette's around seven o'clock. She took her seat in the back of the Ford Model A, watching the scenery change from Central Avenue's small bungalows to Sunset Boulevard's mansions.

Different from other nights, they were having dinner at his family's house. His parents weren't home. They spent weekends at a beach house from Friday until Monday. At first, she thought it odd, but after a few visits, it was not a worry she wanted to hang onto.

The kitchen was a huge room, almost the same size as the one at the hotel used to make the meals for guests and diners in the restaurant. The appliances were the most modern she'd seen, too. They had an icebox with two doors, four burners on the stovetop, a double oven, two faucets in the sink that had two sides. The designer had done everything in the room in duplicate.

There was also a checkerboard tile floor, bright curtains, cabinets everywhere, and the most adorable nook, with a bench and table just wide enough for two.

"I am cooking dinner," Malcolm announced.

Daisy laughed softly. "What are you going to cook? Having grown up in a house full of servants, when did you learn how?"

"I am an excellent cook," he bragged.

There was mischief in his gaze, which made her suspicious about his talents in the kitchen, but ruse or not, he was so happy.

As he moved confidently around the kitchen, pulling together the ingredients for their meal, she watched his simple gestures, the smile that stayed on his lips, the way he looked at her.

When they kissed, because they would kiss, what if it was nothing like the kisses they shared in her dreams?

"I make great sandwiches."

She laughed, but he did make great sandwiches. They dined on fresh bread and baked ham and pickles and homemade mustard, and for dessert, strawberries and champagne. And after dinner, Malcolm suggested hot tea and cakes served outside on the veranda.

The evening was going beautifully with the two of them enjoying each other's company. They sat in the cushioned swing side by side, and when a breeze kicked in, Malcolm arranged a blanket over them. So, they snuggled closer, watching the sunset and the coming starlight.

The setting was perfect. All Daisy had to do was gather the courage to kiss him. That would tell her everything she needed to know.

"I have news." Malcolm smoothed the blanket over his lap and faced her.

"And what news is that?" she replied, smiling at his excitement.

"I have my first client. Mr. Alfred Lunt. I'll be the architect for a new building at Fox Hills Studio. He's one of their directors." Suddenly Malcolm rose and tossed the blanket aside.

The next moment was magical — what Daisy had longed for, dreamed about, happened without thought, naturally, out of happiness and need.

The kiss was soft, eager, warm, sweet like champagne, and breathless, and perfect. His mouth possessed her mouth — and his hand touched her cheek lightly as the world stopped.

Malcolm retreated. "Forgive me," he begged. "I didn't mean to be forward, but your lips, your mouth."

She smiled. "I wanted to kiss you, too. And I want to kiss you again."

He did, and she wrapped her arms around his neck and hugged him to her. "Never stop kissing me," she whispered against his lips.

The embrace was passion and fire, fever and chills. Somehow they were back in the swing.

She was in his lap, and his kisses gripped her heart, and her body responded to him, the feel of his chest pressed against her chest. Her hands found the curve of his back, the slope of his spine. She pulled him unbelievably close.

His passion stripped hers. Every bone in her body softened beneath his touch.

He whispered against her ear. "We should stop now." His breath was warm and hard against her cheek.

After the kiss, she felt elated and afraid. How could a man like him want her? "You don't love me, but I don't care."

He drew back, holding on to her shoulders, exploring her with a piercing stare. Indeed, she felt frozen by his gaze.

"Love, Daisy? I care for you deeply, but

love?" He chuckled in that sad way he had when something filled his mind. "Yes, I love you. I've changed my life for you. I'd do anything for you and have done things because of you, but, right now, we can't do more than —"

He smiled shyly, and an embarrassed flush darkened his dark cheeks. "For now, kissing must be enough."

He cleared his throat as his hands stroked her shoulders. "But no more kissing tonight. It's very late. Too late. I'll call Percy to drive you home."

Daisy had no idea what it meant to be in love. There was something about Malcolm that did things to her mind, to her heart, to change her every breath. Unsettling, mesmerizing, unexpected and frightening things, and love was the word that described each moment. The way her heart somersaulted, the way the sound of his voice made her feel like she stood on the edge of a cliff. Her balance was a bizarre merry-go-round. She lay awake all night thinking of him and occasionally wondering if he was replacing all the other lost loves in her heart.

Love was a serpent. It knew where to sting, where to bite, where to chew, where to stay without a thought of leaving. It bothered her, kept her second-guessing her life and her choices.

Maybe she wasn't cut out for love.

Her mother had loved her father. Her father claimed to have loved her mother. Her uncles were great men who, if they hadn't been so busy working all the time, would have indeed fallen in love with some beautiful churchgoing women. Their wives would have given them glorious babies and showed up for their funerals.

"What are you thinking about, Daisy?" Malcolm asked. "You look far away."

They were on the veranda, in the swing, holding each other.

"Nothing," she said, and smiled. "Okay, I lied. I was thinking about you."

They kissed a lot lately, but Malcolm would send her home when the kissing began to overwhelm them. She recognized the signs of too much touching now. Their breathing was labored, hands groped places that felt good but shouldn't be touched.

"You want a smoke?" Malcolm always seemed to need a cigarette when kissing and heat and desire threatened to boil over. He moved away from her.

"Yes, please." She had taken up the habit of smoking around him. It was an option, not the best, to keep from devouring him.

She had grown accustomed to the taste of the tobacco on his tongue.

Daisy took the cigarette Malcolm offered and inhaled deeply. He watched her like she was a bright star in the sky, something he'd wished for and finally could touch. She was not at all confident she could live up to what he expected from her if they ever slept together. But she thought coyly; it would be nice to try.

A week later, Malcolm brought Daisy to a seamstress in Beverly Hills. He said it was time that they started going to Hollywood parties and other social events expected of a young architect and his lady.

Daisy wasn't exactly thrilled with the idea of standing around while a woman with a pincushion and straight pins came at her under the guise of fashion. But when the seamstress had a young woman model some of the ensembles, Daisy stopped complaining. Malcolm's taste in women's attire was as sumptuous as his talent in architectural design. She had seen many of his drawings, sitting in front of the fireplace at his family home while sipping champagne.

It had been a glorious day, and when Malcolm suggested they dine at the Inkwell beach, despite the slight chill, she agreed.

He made a picnic basket of their favorites: baked ham sandwiches, oysters, steak, fried potatoes, strawberries, and champagne. Daisy wanted to say yes but it was too chilly. Malcolm made a call and they were off to a restaurant.

The waiter brought over a bottle and two coupes on a silver tray, but Malcolm did the oddest thing; he removed the coupes and champagne and placed a pink and white winter rose on the table.

"What is this?" Daisy asked, staring at the beautiful flower with its large petals and perfect scent that wafted to her even in the smoky restaurant. "It is gorgeous."

"It is gorgeous — the most beautiful flower for a beautiful Daisy."

She looked down, thankful for the dim lights and dark skin. Blushing embarrassed her more than the reason she blushed.

"I love you," he said, his deep voice vibrated with passion as if she might not believe him unless he spoke that way.

"I love you, too, Malcolm." The declaration was also embarrassing.

"I don't mean to frighten you," Malcolm said, his voice still shaky. "I loved you, I think from that first day; you made a mess of things with Dr. Somerville. But the past few months have been indescribable and the happiest of my life."

The tremble inside her chest took on the effects of tiny earthquakes, shaking the concrete beneath her feet.

Malcolm then added to the wonder of the moment and removed a small box from his vest pocket and flipped it open. "Will you marry me?"

He wanted to marry her. That was what he had said. She tried to answer quickly, tried to say, *Yes. I will marry you.*

She couldn't believe her eyes or the feeling in her chest and heart. She couldn't think of anything but how much she loved him.

Take a chance, Daisy.

"Yes, Malcolm. God yes, I will marry you."

CHAPTER 27
FRANKIE

Sunday, June 2, 1968
Albuquerque

The tavern that smells like spilled beer and a few unmentionables redeems itself after midnight by turning into a noisy nightclub with a loud live rock-and-roll band. The lead singer has a gravelly voice like Janis Joplin, so does that make the band more blues, jazz, or rock? If I'd had a choice, I'd have gone to college like Tamika, away from Los Angeles, some big school like University of Chicago, except I would've studied music, or art history, and earned a degree in English. That would've been a school-teacher or a librarian's assistant. I wished I'd gone to college and majored in music or art appreciation. I could wax on for eons about jazz, blues, rock and roll. I would need Daisy to help me with R&B.

When Tobey orders a third shot of Jameson, I figure I have a decision to make.

Chill, and enjoy the music, and forget my worries or continue to nurse the beer I've been sipping for an hour.

I am listening to music and drinking. Well, mostly, I am watching while Tobey downs shots. He's drunk. I can tell by the way he leans into me, touching his shoulder to mine when he talks.

Oh. He changed seats after Daisy left and the band started to play. Now, he sits next to me on the side of my good arm.

A new waitress asks if we want another drink. She doesn't stare. I pray Tobey says *No, thank you,* but he doesn't.

About this time, the bartender has moved some of the tables to form an open space for dancing. I can still get in some steps if Tobey can stand without falling over. Then I wonder what in the hell I'm thinking. The joint is dark, but everyone will notice Tobey's white skin and blond hair. The clientele is all Negro. But what the hell. Tomorrow is another day, and I might as well enjoy myself tonight.

"Tobey, let's dance."

I am on my feet, and he looks up at me through his haze. He must be in a haze after the number of shots he's downed.

"Okay," he says, grinning. "I love to dance."

Dread falls over me, running down my back and arms and gluing my feet to the floor. Did I make a mistake asking him to dance? I mean, he's already on his feet, excited about the chance to show his moves. Oh God. White men can't dance.

"You know, on second thought, maybe we should skip the dancing."

He takes my hand and gives me a gentle tug. "Come on, Frankie. I won't embarrass you. Daisy taught me how to hand dance when I was ten."

"I learned how to hand dance with the doorknob when I was three."

He smiles. "So, you have a few years on me. I still think I can surprise you."

The band launches into a version of "Shake" by Sam Cooke, except it's half-time and slow enough for Tobey and me to do some hand dancing.

Surprisingly, Tobey hadn't lied about his dancing skills. Whatever he learned from Daisy, he knew well.

A few spins and a twirl, and a two-step, slide-slide spin, and I am in not-worrying-about-a-thing heaven.

I remove my arm from the sling. But, again, it might be the beer. Though I didn't finish my second pint, my arm doesn't hurt as much.

His arm circles my waist, and he holds my hand, and we sway somewhere between a two-step and a slow dance.

Tobey's body pressed against mine feels very different from Jackson's huge bones and broad shoulders. Tobey is not that much wider than I am. Of course, he is taller, even Jackson's height, but Tobey is a lean man with a mop of blond hair that might weigh more than me.

The music slows, and Tobey pulls me close. I don't retreat — at first, and when I feel his hips press against mine, I push him away, but not too far.

We keep dancing through two more numbers until I feel weak in the ankles.

"You okay?"

"I'm fine, but I'd better sit down. I forgot. I'm pregnant."

"Damn. That's right."

He guides me from the small dance floor, pushing anything that might be in our way out of the way.

When we return to the table, his whiskey is on the table.

"That's your last one."

He nods. "Yes, I'm done."

Sitting in the stiff chair, I take the napkin on the table and wipe my face.

Out of the blue sky, I swear, hand to God,

Tobey leans in, and I expect him to whisper some nonsense, but he keeps coming. It doesn't slow down, and his lips appear as if — !

"Tobey, what are you doing? Are you trying to kiss me?" I lean away from him and grab the edge of the table to keep the chair upright.

He rears back. "I wasn't doing anything." His face is about as red as the bottle of ketchup the waitress left on the table.

"You were, weren't you? About to kiss me?"

"I'm drunk."

"No excuse."

He plops his elbows on the table and covers his face with his hands. "I'm sorry." He swears it will never happen again. He promises. "It's Daisy and her antics, all of it. She makes me crazy. God, I swear, I would never kiss you without asking."

"Apologies don't work for me right now. Sure, I'm pregnant by a man I don't love. Probably never loved. Because he's got the ugliest temper of any man I've ever met. But that doesn't make any difference. You should not have done it. I just wanted a nice, easy evening. First, Daisy acts up, and now you."

Tobey places his hands on the table, splaying his fingers. His face sags, and his eyes are moist and sad, and he's definitely had too much to drink.

"You aren't bad-looking, but this isn't the year for me to think about being with a white man."

I return to my room at after one o'clock, after saying good night to Tobey in the lobby. He needed a cup of coffee, and I left him to hunt one down. We didn't speak of the incident again. I sense his regret, buried beneath his intoxicated, clumsy behavior.

We have just one more day of driving before we go our separate ways. Daisy off to mayhem and Tobey off to jail, or both could end up in jail.

And me — I'll be duking it out with my husband on my mother's front lawn.

Alone in my room, I prepare for bed. I take a bath, a hot, soapy bath. I climb from the tub, take off my shower caps (I use two), roll my hair, and cover my pink sponge rollers with a net.

If I don't do all these things, with the dancing and sweating, I'll wake up in the morning with the Afro hairdo Tamika wants me to try — whether I like it or not.

Once ready, I slip under one sheet (it's too hot for anything more), but I check them first. As soon as I think I'm settled I know I won't sleep.

I'll have nightmares.

Nightmares about Jackson, sitting on the steps outside my mother's house on Naomi Avenue, or the baby, the first one, the one I lost.

But the dream isn't the one I expected. It is about an afternoon in Chicago with Tamika.

A cold wind blew over the South Side neighborhood as we left the apartment complex. Wearing wool coats, knit scarfs, and mittens — Tamika and I loved mittens — we huddled together as we marched toward Stony Island.

"What kind of sense does it make for you to come all this way?" I asked as we walked arm in arm.

She smiled. "You know Robbie lives nearby, and I saw him before jetting over here."

Her boyfriend, Robbie, had helped organize a group of mostly undergrad students on campus called the Society for the Promotion of Lobbying in the Interest of Black Students.

"That's a mouthful," I said the first time she mentioned the group to me.

Tamika had rolled her eyes. "We use the acronym SPLIBS."

"What's it about?" I asked.

"Racial pride, Francine. Racial pride. We

404

want more Black professors, coed on-campus housing for Black students, and increased Black student admissions. There are twenty-six hundred students in the freshman class, only seventy Black students. Increase the number of Blacks admitted. Education makes the difference."

"Okay. Okay."

"There's so much going on in the world. Step out of your apartment and look around. You'll see there is a struggle to be found, and we are the generation who will make a difference."

"With all the things you do, you're also worried about me, too?"

"Yes, I am worried about you." She raised an eyebrow. "But I didn't want to lecture you anymore."

She had seen my bruises a month earlier — one of those days when I couldn't hide them.

"You shouldn't be concerned," I said. "It was an accident and won't happen again."

"That boy has been having accidents since high school."

How come I never noticed back then? Why did I ignore the signs? Because my grandfather had died, and Mother didn't know how to care for me?

A month ago, Jackson had been drunk, I explained. It often happened in the past couple of years. He got weepy, a frequent occurrence when he drank and needed consoling, which meant sex.

The smell of liquor on his breath turned me off. But refusing his advances was not acceptable. Roughhousing was next and ended with me nursing a handful of bruises.

Two days later, the one on my cheek, I couldn't hide beneath a scarf or makeup, made Tamika angry — at me.

"We are cousins. We grew up together. I know when you're lying, Francine. And you've been lying about that man for years."

"There is too much happening in the world to worry about Jackson and me," I said. "Far more important matters than my marital woes," I say because I want to believe my troubles are small and will soon fall away.

"The earth is crumbling around us. Things we counted on disappear, and we are helpless to stop the madness from taking over. Look what has happened in Mississippi. The four Black girls killed in a church bombing in Alabama. The Harlem Riots and the Watts Riots nearly destroyed half the city — and always the half that matters to Black people. That's what we should worry about, not a bruise I had a month ago that was caused by nothing more than an accident."

Tamika made a noise with her teeth. "You're

something else, girl. You'll protect that man with your dying breath, which I hope doesn't happen any time soon."

I awake early, sick to my stomach, and am still tired from the late night before and the dream I wish I hadn't had. I am in the bathroom, removing curlers from my hair, preparing for the next long leg of our road trip to Los Angeles, when the front door explodes with the loudest knocking I've ever heard.

A curler falls from my fingers. Tobey is yelling my name as if the entire motel is on fire.

I stomp out of the bathroom, unwilling to be alarmed. There are just too many scary things in the world these days for whatever is wrong with Tobey to be included in the list. I woke up throwing up and will explain to Tobey just how much I don't appreciate him making so much noise, upsetting my baby and me. But he's in the mood to yell because now he's demanding I open the goddamned door. "I'm coming. I'm coming."

He pushes by me, his fingers raking through his hair. "Daisy is missing." Eyes wide, he starts pacing in the tiny amount of space available in the small hotel room.

"What do you mean missing?" I ask. "If

407

she's not in her room, she probably woke up early, dressed, and went for a walk, searching for a convenience store to buy another carton of cigarettes." I return to the bathroom, continuing to remove sponge rollers from my hair until I notice Tobey standing in the archway.

"I tell you she's gone. I went to the front desk and talked to the clerk when she didn't answer her door. He told me she checked out, paid for the rooms, and left."

"That doesn't make sense, Tobey." I drop a handful of rollers into my hair net. I can't believe she'd just run off, and if she did, I'm afraid of where she might be going and what she will do when she gets there. "She wouldn't do such a thing." I hesitate. "She didn't take the car, did she?"

"She just left." He squeezes his eyes shut. "Shit. She wouldn't have walked."

"Calm down, Tobey. Let me finish up in the bathroom, and then let's go and talk to the clerk. Maybe someone saw her leave. If she didn't take the car, she couldn't have gone far."

CHAPTER 28
DAISY

Winter 1929
Los Angeles

On Friday, Daisy needed to find her sister as soon as she arrived at work.

"How have you been?" Daisy asked Henrietta after tracking her down in the flower storage room in the basement. Since she no longer lived in the house on Naomi, she'd seen Henrietta only at the Somerville. With her big news, Daisy didn't want her to hear it from anyone but her.

"Before I told anyone else, I wanted you to know." Daisy remembered to breathe, but she felt the grin spread over her face. "Malcolm has asked me to marry him, and I said yes."

"So, the newspaper column was true?" Henrietta said in the most wicked tone. "You were the chambermaid who was Mr. Barnes's mistress?"

"I am not his mistress. I am his fiancée."

Then Daisy lost her temper. "And why would you say such a thing? Of course it wasn't me. It wasn't anyone. Those are rumors."

"It's all over the hotel. Members of Curtis's band have seen you with him. It's not like you were easy to miss, the dark-skinned colored girl with her a mountain of thick hair and muslin dresses and the handsome Malcolm Barnes. I hear his white girlfriend isn't at all pleased."

"He doesn't have a girlfriend, white or otherwise."

"That's not what she told me." Henrietta cocked her head, looking quite pleased with herself.

For a moment, Daisy felt the chill of a December morning despite the sun blazing down from the sky. She stared at her sister and shivered, seeing something in her eyes she feared. The anger that had plagued Henrietta for months, the unhappiness to be expected from youth, had changed into a dark beast with broken teeth and splintered nails.

"What are you saying, Henrietta?"

"I know Veronica Fontaine. She likes my singing and Isaiah's guitar playing. She says she wants to sponsor us. Help us get seen by the right people."

410

"I'm going to put a stop to your singing if you are associating with people like her."

"Other than being white and having slept with your future husband, what has she done to you?"

Daisy couldn't think of what to say because Henrietta was right. Veronica Fontaine hadn't done anything to her.

Henrietta shrugged. "You know, I thought Harry Belmont was your beau for a while there," she said thoughtfully.

"He wasn't."

She grinned. "You may wish to ask him what he thought."

Daisy closed her eyes and counted to three. "Look, I just wanted to give you my news."

"As soon as I turn eighteen, Isaiah and I will get married, too," she said earnestly.

"Frankly, I believe Isaiah does love you, but a year from now is a long time. But he'll always be there for you."

"He is growing up, isn't he?" Henrietta started playing with her bangs.

"What is it?" Daisy asked with a tinge of exhaustion in her tone. The happy-news conversation had taken some sharp turns.

"Well, this actress, Veronica Fontaine, has come to quite a few of our shows. I don't know if she's there to see Isaiah and me or she likes slumming in the Negro clubs. Of course, there are always some white people in the clubs where we perform. They love jazz and the blues, you know. But she came up to me the other day and asked if I could sing at a party she's throwing for a director friend of hers."

Daisy nearly choked and rubbed a hand over her mouth. "When I say, never in a million years, I mean never, Henrietta."

"She has lots of money being an actress in the movies and all. And she knows directors, too. Isaiah and I could be in a film short or have a small role in a movie."

"I'm sorry. I don't want you around her. You hear me? She's trouble. I feel it in my bones."

Then Henrietta gave Daisy a look she'd become accustomed to — that you can't tell me what to do look.

The following afternoon, Daisy gave her notice to Mrs. Keyes. The soon-to-be young wife of an up-and-coming architect in Hollywood couldn't stroll around dressed as a chambermaid unless it were for a role in a motion picture.

And as luck would have it, she also ran into Harry Belmont. This time she didn't avoid him. She no longer worked at the

Hotel Somerville.

"Hello, Harry."

He tilted his head slightly. "Miss Washington."

"I'm angry at you. How dare you write that story in your column." She hadn't spoken to him since the incident, but now there was no need to hold back.

He removed his fedora and rubbed a hand over his brow. "I didn't know it was you. I had no idea you were seeing Malcolm Barnes. And then you didn't bother to ask me how I got the story now, did you? Just cut me out of your life — after all these years."

"You could've checked with me before printing it. I thought I was your main gal here. I didn't realize you had so many spies on your payroll, Harry."

"There's a lot you don't know, Daisy." He folded his arms over his chest. "Look, would you like to join me for a drink? There are some things you should know about your fiancé."

His words and hard voice caught her off guard, and she may have stumbled backward. "We haven't announced anything yet. How do you know?"

"You have no idea who he is, Daisy. That Joe Brooks exterior masks a legend of flaws,

413

bad choices, and privilege. The boy is just like his pal Step — believes the world revolves around them."

"Thankfully, nothing compels me to believe you, but I'm still curious about how you know about our engagement."

Harry wasn't done throwing barbs. "Isn't he throwing an engagement party for you? Or didn't he bother to mention it?" His lips curled unattractively.

Daisy said with a hitch in her voice, "We aren't having a party."

"Some of his friends, important clients, are hosting it. Your Malcolm Barnes means to show you off. Make sure white folks in Beverly Hills know he's an upstanding Negro, and a darkie who will soon be a happily married Black man."

Daisy's stomach ached. "Don't do that, Harry."

"Why not?" he said, lighting a cigarette. "I'm just asking you to ask yourself, how well do you know him, honestly?"

"This is why I didn't come to you. I had a feeling you'd take this in a bad way."

"You are right, babe. Out of concern for you, I'm not happy seeing you made a fool. Remember, I'm a man who survives on what I know, and I know he asked you to marry him, and you said yes." He paused.

"That and he used to date a white actress who now happens to be Alfred Lunt's new lover."

"And what does that have to do with Malcolm, Harry? That's just gossip for your column."

"This ain't gossip, sugar — one of your future husband's projects has something to do with Fox Hills Studio, and who just tried to buy Fox Hills, none other than Mr. Lunt." He took a long puff of his smoke. "Watch yourself, my dear. Watch yourself."

The wedding plans proceeded in Yvette's capable hands. Daisy found herself spending most of her time being directed and told what to do and when to do it, and where to be. If it weren't for Malcolm's beautiful face, she likely would've called off the wedding. But she didn't. What she did do was something she never wanted to do again.

She had to meet with her father.

She hadn't wanted to return to the house on Naomi Avenue. But, she had to talk to her father and let him know he couldn't ignore Henrietta. He also needed to keep an eye on Isaiah. The two young people were in the house alone. Now that she was getting married he had to pay attention to something or someone other than himself.

He'd deny her feelings about what really caused him to decide to put her mother in a state hospital. But she'd never believe it was anything other than his cowardice and inability to love her mother the way she deserved to be loved.

It was just a coincidence that the Sunday she showed up at her father's home to tell him these things was the day he told her her mother had died. The reason she'd come to his house rushed out of her mind like sand through her fingers. All she could think of, the only words that came to her: she died because of you; she is dead because you let her go.

She turned and walked from the house she grew up in and this time she'd truly never return.

Her mother had died, and Daisy had failed her. The emptiness rested on her shoulders, its roots creeping down her back into her skin and bones and flesh. Loss. The parts of her that were part of her mother ached the most. She missed her touch, smell, smile, and longed for the sound of her voice one more time to keep her company. Like before the dam collapsed, or maybe even further back in time, when Clifford was still alive.

Daisy mourned her mother for two

months while the wedding plans went on around her. Thankfully, Yvette kept up on everything. Also, Malcolm was an angel. He postponed their engagement party; the one Harry knew about before her. But Malcolm understood how deeply she'd loved her mother and how much she'd wanted to fix things in the house on Naomi Avenue. But that would always be her failure.

Malcolm still wanted the engagement party, her spirits were healing. It was a huge affair. She finally met his adopted parents, but they were somewhat distant and reserved, though not unkind. Or perhaps — Daisy having never spent time with white people — she was the one who felt the most uncomfortable.

Malcolm seemed everywhere at once. Greeting strangers like they were old friends, shaking hands, staying aloof when he noticed someone was uncomfortable around him. The invitation wasn't a guarantee that all the guests would take to socializing with coloreds. Or the darkies, as white directors and producers called colored actors and actresses.

Other than the band, only a handful of Negroes at the party weren't servants, chauffeurs, or butlers. One of them, however, was a gorgeous young girl Daisy had

417

seen at another event. She had asked Malcolm if he knew her. He explained she was a protégée of King Vidor. "She's going to be the star. Her name is Nina Mae McKinney."

Malcolm had introduced Daisy to her once before at a party at the Culver Hotel. She was gorgeous. Wide-eyed, beautiful skin, mulatto but not so light she could pass. She was just so young. Daisy would guess she was the same age as Henrietta.

"Do you think they'll make more than this one movie in Hollywood?" Daisy asked Malcolm. "Such a pretty girl, as beautiful as any of these white actresses, should have the same chance at doing what they love."

"Honestly, my dear, unless I get to design the segregated studio lot, I don't know or care." Malcolm quickly hugged Daisy to him. "Darling. I'm joking. I'll admit things are changing. The doors to Hollywood will be open to all of us in time."

"Oh, it's just you wait another fifty years, and we'll see what happens, right?" It was something she'd heard at every party they'd attended all winter long.

Malcolm smiled playfully, but Daisy had learned some things about him in the past few months. First, he believed that to succeed as an architect required parties and hobnobbing. Second, Daisy thought he cared about his career equally as much as he cared for her.

This all came to mind as a beautiful woman cornered Malcolm. They were a few feet away from her. Far enough for her to fade away from the conversation unnoticed. However, Malcolm appeared not only surprised but supremely uncomfortable.

She couldn't blame him. It was Veronica Fontaine, and quickly Malcolm's discomfort risked turning into showing his temper.

She kept grabbing at him, pulling on his sleeve, and he tried to avoid physical contact, but clearly, Veronica had the upper hand. A white woman at a mostly white Los Angeles party. Malcolm had to be wary or he could be beaten again.

Daisy started to turn away and let them have their conversation. But then she remembered, he was her fiancé, and Veronica was old news.

She marched toward them, determined to break up the scene before it became noticeable to everyone.

"So, is this the little woman, Malcolm?" Veronica Fontaine said as Daisy arrived at his side.

"Daisy, I'm fine," he said.

Protecting her wasn't necessary, she'd wanted to say.

Veronica was a petite girl, a white-haired blonde with bright green eyes and skin the color of clouds on a clear, blue-skied day. She bleached her hair, Daisy surmised. Nobody under seventy could have hair that white.

"I asked you a question, doll. Are you the soon-to-be Mrs. Barnes?"

"Yes," Daisy replied.

Veronica touched the fringe hanging from the bodice of Daisy's flapper dress. "You know Malcolm and I were together a year. I thought he'd always be in my life. We enjoyed each other so, didn't we?"

She moved her hand from Daisy's fringe to Malcolm's lapel. And Daisy couldn't rid herself of the feeling of being mauled by a cat in a zoo.

"Oh, darling, don't look so afraid. I don't want him back. Not now, not after he's been with you. I had him for myself, and I don't share. Besides, he was my secret lover. Mr. Lunt, a director of motion pictures, is my new lover. He's buying Fox Hills Studios, you know."

"Veronica, I think you've had too much to drink."

"I can drink as much as I want whenever I want. How are you going to stop me?"

Her tone made clear her meaning. They

might've been lovers once, but here in front of Hollywood's stars and Black society's elite, no matter what might be said, she was a white woman. Her privileges transcended polite behavior.

"Malcolm was just the man of my boudoir. Isn't that right, sugar?"

"Malcolm, would you mind getting me a glass of champagne? Would you like another, too, Veronica?" Daisy asked, tilting her head at Malcolm's openmouthed stare. "Go on, sugar. Let us girls have a minute to chat."

Malcolm bowed slightly and gave Daisy a concerned look before heading off to grab two champagnes.

Veronica laughed. "Aren't you the slick one? Maybe I see why Malcolm chose you."

Daisy harbored a deep desire to grab Veronica's bleached hair or at least shove her face into the jelly mold on the buffet. Instead, she calmly said what she had to say. "I want you to leave Henrietta Washington be. You've been filling her head with Hollywood, and it's not fair. She's colored. You know that, and you know what that means in Hollywood. Nothing. So, if you have a gripe against Malcolm or me, take it out on us, please. She just lost her mother. Please, leave her be."

Daisy walked away then, not bothering to

examine the look on Veronica's face. What was important to Daisy was that she spoke her mind.

She needed some air after her run-in with Veronica and headed for the veranda. But the scenery wasn't any less treacherous there. Henrietta had arrived at the party unannounced. Dressed in a remarkably revealing gown, she was standing way too close to Lincoln Perry. Whatever their conversation was about, Henrietta's face was as bright as the full moon on a clear night.

Daisy intended to put an end to their conversation now.

She stomped toward them, feeling the heat rise from her neck like she was swimming in hot oil, but before she could get close enough to snatch Henrietta out of his grasp, a tall, broad-shouldered man stepped in her way.

"You look like you're about to snap someone's head off, and I don't think that's a good idea at an engagement party." Isaiah had the most authoritative look in his eyes she'd ever seen on him. Daisy was tempted to take a step back and reexamine the young man. Because he definitely had added some weight and something she couldn't quite pin down.

"Okay, Isaiah. I won't go over there and break her in half, but Lord knows she should be smarter than this. He is trouble. Isn't he engaged to your cousin?"

He nodded. "Yes, it was announced last month in the *Eagle,* right after the rumor about their relationship was supposedly confirmed by a source."

Daisy swallowed, not missing the point Isaiah had clearly made. "Of course you knew it was me, giving Harry those tidbits. You were helping me by delivering my notes."

"I also helped you by being a source." He ran his hands down his face, and some of the boyishness she was accustomed to returned. "But don't worry about Henrietta. She likes to flirt, if you didn't know that already. But she'll be heading home with me."

At that moment, Henrietta excused herself from Perry and strolled over to them — or, Daisy noted, to Isaiah — but Daisy couldn't stop from giving her a scolding. "If I see you near him ever again —"

Henrietta laughed. "Why do you do that, Daisy? You have no authority anymore over me."

Daisy looked from Henrietta to Isaiah. "I'm worried about both of you. I can't help that, Henrietta. I may not come at you the right way, but please think about what I am trying to say to you."

The wedding took place at St. Patrick's church. She'd relented and allowed Harry to cover the festivities for his column in the *Eagle.* He brought two photographers, and a stringer.

Percy, Malcolm's stepbrother, gave her away. Henrietta and Isaiah looked fabulous side by side, although there was still enough anger in Henrietta's heart, she didn't attend the reception.

They were well off, too, financially. Daisy wasn't sure how that worked, considering Malcolm had one client she knew of. But he mentioned stocks and money put aside by his parents, still in their name, but a viable source to both him and Percy.

They moved into the Somerville in late April. Within weeks, Malcolm was hired to work on three projects, in addition to the renovation at Fox Hills Studio. Of course he wouldn't be the lead architect; for a Black man to get such an opportunity was unheard of. Except if he were Paul Revere Williams, Malcolm pointed out. He was one of the most well-known Negro architects in the city, perhaps in California.

Malcolm hadn't mentioned him before, and from the nervous drumming of his fingers on the tabletop, Daisy decided not to ask any questions about him now.

The bad dreams started with the sunrise a week after her wedding. She could never remember once she opened her eyes but they always left parting gifts:

a numbing fear . . .

a chilling shot of loneliness . . .

a strange, throbbing pain in her arm.

Daisy turned her head, needing to inhale something other than goose feathers.

She lay on satin sheets uncomfortably close to the edge of the large bed she shared with her husband.

What was she afraid of? She was in love and loved and had learned how to love, too. The incredible need, the desire her body craved when she was with Malcolm, was unimaginable. His touch was gentle and fierce like his kisses, and when they shuddered together, they were sunlight and love.

And that was what she had with her husband.

"Malcolm, you are the best thing that has ever happened to me, and I love you."

"And I love you, and what makes you happy, makes me happy, and what makes you sad . . ."

She stopped him with a finger to his lips. "I think you say things sometimes because you believe they'll make me feel good."

"It is something I always want to do."

She lay naked beneath the sheet, her body spent from their night of making love. Of soft kisses, long rough kisses, his body covered hers with power, strength, tenderness, and kindness.

If her world was perfect, then why was she having the bad dreams, again?

CHAPTER 29
FRANKIE

Sunday, June 2, 1968
Albuquerque

"What time did you last see her?" I ask the front desk clerk, the same young man with a stuffy nose and red-rimmed eyes Tobey spoke with an hour earlier.

"She left around seven o'clock," he says flatly. "Paid her bill, and your bills, too. Then she asked me to call her a cab."

"You didn't mention the cab before," I say to Tobey.

"I didn't know about a damn cab." He glares at the desk clerk.

"Yeah. Yeah. I just remembered." The clerk keeps blinking and searching his desk.

"Do you know the name of the cab company? Or maybe a neighborhood guy you call?" I ask, thinking the worst and starting to panic like we won't find her. "Maybe, they'll have a record of where they took her."

The clerk grabs a sheet of paper from the

427

desk. "She went to the bus station downtown."

"She what?" Tobey shouts.

I touch his arm, trying to get him to chill. "We won't find her any faster if you are hollering at folks."

He huffs and goes back to shooting bullets with his stare at the clerk.

"I had to tell the driver before he'd come out how much of a fare he was looking at."

Tobey's body visibly knotted.

I shake my head. "Thanks. We've got it. No worries." I grab Tobey's arm. "Let's check the car. I want to see if she took her luggage."

"Yes. Yes. You're right."

We search the car — her suitcase is in the trunk.

"She only took her train case." He slams the trunk down. "Do you think she plans on coming back soon? If she had someplace to go, why didn't she tell us she had someplace to go? Or leave us a note?"

Tobey stands stiffly beside me, searching the parking lot and the street as if she'll appear, coming from one of the shops or emerging from an alley.

"We should go to the bus station," I say. "See if anyone there remembers seeing her."

"Sounds like a shot in the dark, Frankie.

She could be anywhere."

I lean against the car, racking my brain. "Let's talk to the cab driver; make sure he took her to the bus station. If he did, we'll go there." I start walking toward the motel. "Let's put our luggage in the car and start looking for her."

Tobey follows me back inside the motel.

"If we don't find her," I say, "we'll wait until the nightclub opens and talk to the bartender — what's his name?"

"Bart," Tobey says. "She and Bart had something going on, didn't they?"

"Maybe that's what she did — spent the night with Bart."

"What if he isn't working tonight?"

"Someone there will have his phone number."

"Yes. Yes." The lines in Tobey's forehead ease up.

I've learned some things about him in the past couple of days. His temper is short when it comes to Daisy's antics, but that's just a mask for his fear. He's always worried about her — and this time, I am, too.

"I'm sure the bartender knows something. He has to."

Tobey raises his head, his eyes are misty, and for an instant, my heart hurts for him. He cares so much for her and knows her better than me.

"Don't worry, Tobey. She'll show up, or we'll find her."

We spent the rest of the afternoon talking to shop owners and other guests at the motel. We visit the bus station, ask different people if they've seen her, including the ticket agents. There are a dozen places where Daisy might've gone and we walk into each one, asking the same question. Tobey even has a Polaroid in his wallet.

We ask the same questions, say the same things. Have you seen this Negro woman? She is in her late fifties but looks thirty-five. She has on pedal pushers and flat shoes or a minidress and heels.

The desk clerk tells us this, and I chuckle. Daisy always makes a memorable impression.

After several hours, we take a coffee break in a diner a couple of blocks from the motel.

Tobey's anxiety hasn't ebbed. He's gulping coffee between tapping the chorus of "Sgt. Pepper's Lonely Hearts Club Band" on the tabletop.

I cover his hand with mine and stop his fingers from moving, but he turns my hand over and squeezes my fingers tightly. He is not in a good place.

"There's something you aren't telling me,

Tobey. What is it?"

"I'm just worried. She's been in a lot of pain, I think, and this detour, well, it's not making sense."

That evening we return to the nightclub, and I swallow my disappointment when I don't see Daisy. I desperately wanted her to be there with Bart, but she isn't. But at least Bart is back behind the bar.

"We're looking for —"

"I know who you two are looking for," he responds before I can finish. "She went to Flagstaff to visit an old friend of hers. A man who used to live in Albuquerque but moved out of town about fifteen years ago."

"What's his name?" Tobey asks, his impatience unchecked.

"An old newspaperman by the name of Harry Belmont," Bart says.

"You sure she went there?" I want to believe him. "How do you know him, and how do you know Daisy?"

Bart shrugs. "Two separate times in life. Belmont used to live here. But as I said, he moved away a long while back. Daisy lived here for a spell about ten years ago, ran one of the Black newspapers in town for a stretch. She asked about Harry back then, too, but nobody had heard from him and didn't know where he went."

431

Tobey steps in front of me. "Do you have his address? Or a phone number?"

"Slow down. The man is in the phone book, and that's what I told Daisy, too."

Tobey turns to me. "Let's go back to the bus station and see if one of those three buses the cab driver mentioned was heading to Flagstaff."

"Thanks, Bart," I say and rush after Tobey, who is already out the door.

I am in a dead run, trying to catch up to Tobey, and I must look ridiculous. My legs are shorter, my arm is in a sling, and my stomach is not doing well.

"How far away is Flagstaff," I shout at his back.

He stops suddenly, probably realizes no way in hell can I keep up.

"Five hours. But Lord help me, I'm going to make it in four."

We reach the Mustang, and Tobey opens the passenger door.

"You're more worried than usual," I say, giving him a grimace of a smile.

"This name Belmont is familiar. I don't know the story about him, but he was someone she knew in Los Angeles, back when she was our age."

"Forty years ago, our age?"

"Yeah. Then let's get going."

He closes the car door and bullets to the driver's side. We're back on Route 66 and hauling ass to Flagstaff.

Chapter 30
Daisy

Spring/Summer 1929
Los Angeles

Cocktail parties had become Daisy's routine since her marriage. Malcolm believed that big business deals occurred over a glass of champagne and a cracker covered in caviar.

Daisy hated caviar, preferring deviled eggs and pigs in the blanket over the too salty taste of the red and black fish eggs. To eat them, she held her breath, exhaling only after the waiters and their gleaming trays vanished to the kitchens.

On the other hand, champagne and cigarettes had become her favorite combination. The cigarettes masked the smell of foods she didn't like while the champagne tickled her nose and dulled her senses.

Malcolm knew she was unhappy, but at every party, every time, he'd promise it would be their last party. Then the ducks lined up and his new architectural business (he'd opened an office at the Hotel Somer-ville) had more than one client.

She believed him, knowing he wasn't tell-ing her a fib. His determination to carve out success outside the Negro community drove him to do things she feared he'd regret one day. But she didn't confront him on the subject. She didn't enjoy the parties, but she found she loved dressing up.

The event on this evening was in celebra-tion of the completion of King Vidor's *Hal-lelujah*. The party was at Vidor's mansion in Beverly Hills, and several cast members, including Nina Mae McKinney and Dan-iel L. Haynes, were among the guests.

Malcolm grabbed an invitation because of his connections with Alfred Lunt and Step Fetchit; Malcolm did manage to be in the right places.

Daisy also didn't like the idea that she had to show up for the party alone. She waited out front for Malcolm, but he'd been hav-ing meetings all hours lately.

When he finally arrived, he seemed ex-hausted and, for once, anxious to return home, to their apartment on the fourth floor of the Hotel Somerville. But even that desire was nullified by the number of people who wanted to meet, talk, schedule this, that, or the other.

The party dragged on and on, and by midnight Daisy was begging to leave. But Malcolm was still on his wining-and-dining high, searching for more clients.

Daisy forced him to hold still after he brought her a third glass of wine. "How come you don't work as hard to do business with the Race? The Somervilles financed several buildings in the Black community," Daisy said, voicing her frustration with Malcolm and the parties. "We have to be different people here than who we are, don't you think?"

He kissed her cheek. "I want to build something other than apartments on Central Avenue. I want the big projects, and that means working with these white men and their money," he said. "But don't worry, my long-range plan is to take what I make and do nothing but build amazing homes for the Race. Give me time. Our stock investments are looking good, and the money my parents are holding for Percy and me is about ready to be invested or we risk losing it. Some relative will come out of the woodwork to make sure the adopted colored kids don't get their inheritance."

Malcolm had explained his plans before, but that hadn't changed her attitude toward the Hollywood party scene. Although, on this night, it was great seeing more Negroes in the room who weren't carrying trays of drinks or finger sandwiches. "I'm still bored, Malcolm."

He looked at her, his eyes softening. "I have been pushing these parties a little hard, more so than I need, is that what you're telling me, my love?"

He had snuggled up next to her, holding her firmly around the waist, pushing his hip against her. "How about one more glass of champagne, and then let's get out of here."

"That sounds lovely," she replied.

He kissed her on the lips. "Okay, let's go."

Before they could move, a group of men gathered near one of the bars, and their loud whispers created quite a stir. More people joined them, and exaggerated gestures and faces compelled Daisy to shoo Malcolm in that direction.

"I can't make out what they're talking about. Please find out what's going on."

"I thought you wanted to leave?"

"Now I'm curious. Find out, and then we can go."

Malcolm wandered toward the group of men who had assembled an ever-growing crowd in front of one of the bars. Daisy casually looked around the room, watching as more and more groups formed.

437

Malcolm returned with an ominous expression on his face. Whatever he'd found out was not good news. He came up to her and said quietly, "We need to go."

The worry in his voice frightened her. "What happened?"

"Veronica Fontaine's body was found in the woods behind her house."

"Oh my God. What happened?"

Malcolm took the champagne coupe from her, guided her toward the door and was moving as fast as he could without appearing to run. Daisy had to move double fast on her rounded heels to keep up with him.

"Malcolm, please tell me what happened to her."

As they exited and moved in the direction of the parked cars, he whispered next to her ear, "She was murdered."

In the days following Veronica Fontaine's death, Daisy spent a lot of time smoking cigarettes and sipping champagne. She lit her first cigarette as soon as she rolled out of bed and drank a coupe of champagne shortly afterward.

It wasn't so much that Fontaine was dead. It was the way the newspapers kept talking about her. The beautiful young starlet was murdered during a night of passion, killed with a vicious blow to the back of her head. Her body was tossed in the flower garden in the back of her beautiful cottage home. It was a front-page story in the *Los Angeles Times*. The *Eagle* wasn't even covering the story except for the occasional mention by Harry Belmont in his gossip column. Daisy couldn't decide why he bothered.

A white woman had been murdered, not a Black woman. There was no connection between Veronica Fontaine's death and Central Avenue. She said this to herself every morning when she lit up her first cigarette of the day.

She and Malcolm were having breakfast together one morning as she read the latest news on the search for Veronica's murderer.

"I wish they'd find the killer already," she said, smearing butter on a piece of toast. "I can't stand knowing that whoever did this to her is free as a bird."

"Daisy, they will find the killer when they find one killer. That's what police detectives do. They search, and ask questions and interview suspects, and make arrests."

"You seem to know a lot about the process, Malcolm. Have you ever known anyone before who was murdered?"

"Remember, I know the police. Friends of mine work in the Police Department, and I didn't mention it, but I was interviewed the other day."

Daisy dropped her fork. The fear she'd been feeling since the night Malcolm told her Veronica had been murdered engulfed her like a plague. "Why? Are you a suspect?"

"No, Daisy, I am not, but I am a Negro man known to be an acquaintance of the dead white woman. I also think that any man who knew Veronica, who spent time with her, is suspect."

"That's an odd thing to say, Malcolm. I mean, anyone who knew her would want to kill her?"

He lit a cigarette before raising his head to look at Daisy. "I didn't mean it to come out that way, but it did. And honestly, I'm not sure I want to take it back." He took a long drag on his smoke. "Why are you so worried about this murder case? You read the paper like it will dissolve in your hands if you don't devour it first with your eyes."

"Something I didn't mention before. It seems that Henrietta and Isaiah knew Veronica. She was like a sponsor to them. I haven't talked to Henrietta about it, but I worry. I'd hate for them to get caught up in any of this."

"Don't, darling. I don't think they have anything to worry about."

■ ■ ■

A week later, Daisy's concern has multiplied, especially after Malcolm told her he had to leave town for a few days.

"Why can't this trip wait? I need you here, Malcolm. I am worried about Henrietta and Isaiah, and with Veronica's murder making all the headlines, it strikes me that it would be best if you were in town."

In the suite at the Somerville, Malcolm hurried from one spot to the next, picking up clothes, toiletries, and books he then tossed into his large leather satchel. "Daisy, it's only for a week, two at the most. This is not an opportunity someone in my position can miss."

"It's a lecture, Malcolm. You won't even be able to meet with this important man socially, will you?"

Malcolm huffed. "For a change of pace, this is not about social connections."

"Aren't you worried about what's happening with Veronica's murder?"

"No. I'm sorry she's dead. And neither one of us have anything to do with her death." He paused. "Isn't that right?"

"No, we didn't, but still. Something about it bothers me."

He grabbed a copy of the newspaper and pointed at the headline. "This is something to worry about. Nobody is buying property. So we have to be prudent and not assume money will always be easy to come by."

"Don't be gone too long, okay?"

"I'll be back before you can miss me properly. Promise."

He kissed her cheek and was gone.

With Malcolm out of town, Daisy's schedule was up in the air. The life of a well-to-do young bride could sometimes be quite dull, she realized.

She had returned to her stenographer classes. Malcolm supported her whatever her interests, including finishing her college education. He even suggested she might wish to pursue something challenging like becoming a doctor or nurse. She just wasn't sure about it. Writing was her first and forever love.

Marriage had made her lazy, however. Or maybe the past year of pain, tears, losing her mother, losing her father, and missing her sister, who she simply didn't get to see often, had taken a toll.

Whatever the case, when Malcolm returned, she'd have to do something about their lives. Find things to do together, explore together, or she could have a child. That seemed a little too much, though.

One thing was certain, she was lonely and moping around the hotel like a lost pup.

At least there was the morning paper, which she had delivered. The Veronica Fontaine murder investigation was still in the news.

It had grabbed the attention of countless people — something about a beautiful Hollywood actress, who hadn't been that famous until she was murdered, spurred obsessiveness.

Daisy chastised herself for being among the obsessed and almost didn't bother to order a copy of the morning edition of the *Eagle.* For the Fontaine story, the only newspaper she needed was the *Los Angeles Times.*

But this morning, guilt, nostalgia, and something buzzing in the back of her mind caused her to order both papers.

When they were delivered to her room, she didn't pay attention to the chambermaid who brought them. She didn't notice the quiver in the young girl's upper lip or that her hands shook. She remembered these things later when they weren't important enough to remember.

Seated at her breakfast table in the grand

suite at the Hotel Somerville, Daisy opened the *California Eagle* before the *Los Angeles Times.* There was something that drew her to do it. After flipping through the pages, she stopped when she saw Harry's column.

Oh my God.

The item in Harry's gossip column read: An arrest has been made in the Veronica Fontaine murder. Suspect behind bars. No other details available.

For Harry to have mentioned the story in the *Eagle* meant one thing to Daisy — whomever they'd arrested was Negro.

Christ.

Panic drove every other sensation from her body. Daisy made phone call after phone call, trying to reach Harry, her sister, Yvette, and Malcolm in Santa Barbara.

But no one answered.

It took most of the day and into the evening before Daisy received a phone call. It was around ten o'clock at night when the phone rang.

When she lived in the house on Naomi Avenue, there wasn't a telephone for a long time. Now that she resided in the Hotel Somerville, she was always reachable. She thought the world would be the same.

She crawled from between the sheets and

444

slipped on a robe before picking up the receiver. It was Cecil, and he didn't sound good.

"Daisy, I mean, Mrs. Barnes, there is someone here who has asked to see you. Is it all right if I send them up?"

Daisy squeezed her eyes shut. Not that she'd been sound asleep, but she'd been close and felt drowsy. Or she was zozzled. The champagne had been flowing with dinner even if she'd dined alone.

"You said, someone. Can you be more specific? A name perhaps?" Daisy leaned forward, rubbing her temples. She hadn't meant to be rude to Cecil. It was the champagne's fault. "I'm sorry, who did you say needs to see me?"

Cecil's voice dropped. She could barely hear him on the other end of the line. "Ma'am, it's a copper from the Police Department. He says he needs to see you. Either way, he says he's a friend of your husband's."

"Tell him I'll leave the door open."

A few minutes later, he was inside her suite, standing in the foyer with his hat in his hand.

"Ma'am, my name is Willie Stone." He bowed slightly.

Daisy was surprised when she opened the

445

door to find a Negro police officer. But he was police — uniform and all.

"How can I help you?"

"I'm a friend of Malcolm Barnes and recalled that a few months back, he helped out a couple of youngsters who'd been involved in a raid."

Daisy felt like she would upchuck all over his clean uniform if the man didn't hurry up and tell her what she feared most in the world. "Please tell me what you came here to tell me this late at night. Please."

"A young man by the name of Isaiah Butler has been arrested for the murder of Veronica Fontaine. A friend of his, your sister, Henrietta, is at the police station, too. She isn't under arrest. But she begged me to let you know. And I didn't want to telephone. And the guys at the precinct won't allow the boy to make a call, either."

Shaking so hard she feared she'd collapse, Daisy nonetheless managed to say, "Thank you for making the trip to tell me. Can I ask a favor? Do you mind taking me to the station? Now?"

"Not at all. I'll wait downstairs."

"Thank you." Daisy closed the door behind him and leaned heavily against the wall but not for long.

She had to dress and get to the jailhouse

as quickly as possible. Isaiah hadn't killed anyone. Daisy had to explain it to them, so they understood.

Isaiah wasn't guilty. They had the wrong man.

CHAPTER 31
FRANKIE

Monday, June 3, 1968
Flagstaff

There are times in life when you step into
the fire without realizing you will burn.
Then there are other times when you watch
from the sidelines, where it's safer, quieter,
less of a breeze, and no flames rising from
the ashes to kick you in the ass.

Sounds silly, but as we motored along
Route 66, driving to Flagstaff, Arizona, I
believe Tobey and I had a feeling about the
kind of hell we'd face once we got to our
destination. It kept us from playing music
or having casual conversation. We were gear-
ing up for battle, putting on our game face
and needed our wits ready and able.

Tobey drove like the wind, and we reached
Flagstaff in less than five hours as he
promised. We'd also ripped a page from the
phone book and got directions to Harry
Belmont's store in downtown Flagstaff.

Surprisingly, we got lucky, too.

"Maybe you should wait in the car," Tobey says as he parks outside Belmont's shop.

I think about agreeing with him, but I want to save Daisy, too. She is my blood relative. But I feel that I know her better now, and the last thing I want is to see her in handcuffs or covered in blood because of something that happened forty years ago.

"No, I'm right beside you, Tobey."

A second before Tobey raises his fist to knock, we hear Daisy's voice, and she's yelling. "Oh, Lord," he mutters.

"We have to get inside. Go on and knock," I say to Tobey.

As soon as he touches the door, it opens, and we step into a bizarre scene from another one of those B movies I watch on Sunday afternoons.

An older man, bald with a gray beard and mustache, as if he hasn't seen the razor in a decade, stands behind the counter. I realize we are inside a card shop but don't have time to look at the things strewn about the store.

Daisy is on the other side of the counter, too, holding her switchblade and pointing it at Harry Belmont, I presume.

"Daisy," Tobey says calmly, as he enters the store.

I am inches behind him, but I don't think I can speak. The sight in front of me is straight out of a police television drama.

The old guy Daisy has cornered doesn't look too healthy and not because my aunt is waving a switchblade at him.

"That's a lie, Daisy," Harry Belmont shouts, leaping to the side, moving much faster than I expect from such a frail old man's body. "Malcolm's career was over the moment he stopped sleeping with Veronica Fontaine. He didn't want to believe it. She got angry, threatened him, and he killed her. Easy. One. Two. Three. He's the one you should be looking for. Your beef is with him, Daisy. I didn't kill her, he did."

"He may have, but you're the one, you and your column of lies, of gossip, and scandals, you are the reason Isaiah was arrested. You are the reason an innocent boy was put away in a cold, dark cell that frightened him horribly. Do you know what happened to him, Harry? He lived to play music. You knew that. But you still wrote that column."

Daisy moves then, jutting forward with the knife, catching the man across the face with the point of her blade. He cries out, grabbing hold of his cheek.

Tobey and I are in the doorway. I can see

Tobey digesting what is in front of him, trying to pick a moment when he can get close to Daisy. Get that knife out of her hand. But she's a madwoman. The switchblade is more than a weapon: it's justice's pendulum swinging back and forth, waiting to yield its verdict. The cut on Harry Belmont's face is a preview of the sentence to come.

Then again, she might have aimed for his throat and missed.

"It doesn't matter if Malcolm killed her. I told you, I'm not here about him," she says in a remarkably calm voice, scarier than the yelling she'd been doing when we first walked into Belmont's shop.

Tobey raises his hands, palms open, trying to get her attention without startling her. He steps toward her. "Daisy, listen to me. We can talk to him about this — you see, he wants to talk. So, give me the knife. You've scared him good, and now, he'll tell you whatever you need to know."

Bravely, I chip in with a much smaller voice. "The knife won't make his tongue any looser than it already is, Aunt Daisy."

She gives me a side-eye, one of the most *Shut your mouth* expressions I've seen. Tobey glances at me, implying with his raised eyebrow that I might offer some better help.

The course of action that will work best

451

for Daisy is if we let this play out a few more minutes and hope she missed his throat on purpose. I gesture for Tobey to chill.

"It's okay," I say. "Let them talk."

"Do you want to hear what he did?" Daisy asks, waving the knife. "He wrote a gossip column, didn't mention names, but he wrote about a murdered white actress and a young colored guitarist who was a suspect in her murder. He wrote he'd been arrested, too." She steps in closer to her target. "He hadn't been arrested yet, Harry. He wasn't in jail when you wrote about him. The police weren't looking for him until your gossip column pointed them in his direction."

She turns to Tobey. "He spent the entire summer digging and digging for whatever he could find. He wanted to hurt people." She spun back toward Belmont. "Why Harry? What happened to you that turned you into such a low-account ass?"

"I don't remember, Daisy," Belmont cries. "It was a long time ago, and I'm an old, sick man."

I see that she's losing it even more. "Daisy, go on, tell us about what he wrote. Remind him. It might help."

She doesn't back away. She moves in closer. "That summer, your column was a

452

scandal sheet. Stories about Lincoln Perry getting sued by Yvonne Butler for breach of promise and marrying someone else. Then he writes about the Barnes newlyweds. Remember the story about me losing a baby? I was never pregnant. You had no right to make up such a thing."

"I was broke and needed money, and the only way I knew how to make money was to write."

"Liar. You were in debt because of your gambling." She looks around the store. "Baseball cards, sports memorabilia, you are still a gambler, aren't you?

"After that article, the cops get a tip, saying how they saw Isaiah Butler at Fontaine's home on several occasions. Folks in the neighborhood say they saw him watching her while she swam in her pool, ogling her as Black men do."

Daisy closes her eyes for the slightest second. "Harry fabricated lie after lie, and kept writing them because why, Harry? It sold newspapers. Put some cash in your pocket. Your excuses aren't good enough."

The man seems to find his spine (and some courage) and pushes away from the counter he'd been leaning against. He points a gnarled finger at Daisy. "You are one to throw stones, Daisy. You forget you were the Mata Hari of the Somerville, isn't that what you called yourself? Like some make-believe character in a novel."

"See how stupid you are," Daisy counters. "She wasn't make-believe. She *was* a spy in Europe during the Great War. If you'd read something other than your sports pages and your gossip column, you might know this."

Her arm is getting tired, I think. She's lowered it, the one with the hand holding the knife so that it's almost dangling at her side.

Harry Belmont scrubs a hand over his mouth. "I know the boy didn't kill her, but Barnes needed someone to save him, and the boy liked Barnes. Didn't Barnes help him avoid jail time once before? Fontaine didn't like losing. When Malcolm called it quits with her, she heard none of it. Malcolm could've saved that boy. Confessed. Or at least spoken up for him. He was an influential Race man in that crowd. Because of his family, folks thought about the color of his skin only on occasion.

"Malcolm Barnes was conveniently out of town in Santa Barbara until after her body was found. He's how she died." Tears falling from his face mingle with the streaks of blood. "I didn't mean for Isaiah to go to jail."

"What was your problem with Malcolm and even Step Fetchit? You had it in for them, especially Fetchit, from the start. Always wanting to write the worst about him."

Harry Belmont's shoulders begin to shake, and the laugh rolls through him like a wave. "You're right, Daisy. That was some hooey. You want the truth?"

She waves the knife at him, and both Tobey and I lunge forward, but she's quick. "That's why I'm here. For the truth."

"I was in love with you. From high school, you were the love of my wretched life. I thought I'd have a chance with you that year until the dam collapse, and the only way to see you was to. . . ."

"Agree to have me spy on guests." She chuckles. "I didn't like you that way, Harry. I just didn't. But you let a child die because you hated my husband?"

The knife is no longer visible from where I stand. But just then, two men, both Negro, walk into the store.

"They trying to kill me."

"Who? This white man? What the hell are you doing in this part of town, anyway? Don't you have enough to do on the other side of the city?"

Tobey raises his hands. "Sorry, man. I'm

455

leaving. Sorry." He gives Daisy and me a glance, like let this happen. We both know that if cops are called, he would have a better chance of avoiding felony charges than Daisy. But that was if these two guys were interested in calling the police.

"You cut an old man?" One of them says, shoving Tobey in the chest. "You muthafucker."

Daisy goes to open her mouth, but Tobey is determined to take this hit for her in more ways than one. "Yeah, that's right," he says shakily. "The old fool tried to cheat me for some baseball cards."

I cringe because Tobey is about to get a butt-whipping. However, it does give me an opening. I grab Daisy and remove her from the scene of the crime.

CHAPTER 32
DAISY

After a week of begging and using every resource she could muster, Daisy was permitted to visit Isaiah.

The police officer opened the cell door and stepped aside. She'd have to remember to thank him later. Colored women weren't allowed to visit a man in jail. But the officer knew Malcolm and, with a broad grin and a deep bow, he unlocked the cell door. She walked along the short corridor to the cell block where Isaiah was being held.

She'd been instructed to remain standing, and the prisoner would be brought to her, but he'd stay behind bars.

Daisy rubbed her hands together as if her fingertips were frozen, but it was her nerves that had chilled the blood in her veins.

After a few long minutes, Isaiah appeared from a dark corner. When he stepped forward on the other side of the bars, she barely recognized him. Isaiah's shoulders were hunched forward, and his head hung low. Something was also wrong with his leg, one or both. He limped, the hitch in his step pronounced. He was in a lot of pain. He also held his hands against his stomach, but they were clenched fists.

"Dear Lord, I am so sorry you are here like this." Daisy wished she could grab him and clean him and feed him. Somehow return him to the boy he'd been only a few days ago. "We will get you out of here. I know you didn't do anything. I know you had nothing to do with her death. When Malcolm returns, we'll be able to fix this, I swear."

"Hi Daisy," he said as if they were in the house on Naomi. Not in a jailhouse.

Tears fell down Daisy's face. "I don't know how this happened or why. God, Isaiah."

He smiled suddenly, his face lighting up, almost back to normal. "I don't need your help, Daisy. Everything is jake. This is the way it should be."

She didn't understand. "No, it's not your fault. This is Harry Belmont's fault. He wrote lies in his column that led the cops to you. I don't even know why he did. I can't

458

find him, but I will."

Isaiah stepped close to the bars, and the dim light struck him differently. Daisy could see his face better, and she gasped. "What have they done to you?"

His face was bruised, he had scratches and cuts, a black eye and swollen cheeks.

Daisy's heart broke, and she couldn't speak.

Isaiah touched his forehead to the bars and closed his eyes. When he spoke, he whispered, "I did kill her, Daisy. That's why everything is as it should be."

He inhaled, and the light changed, shining more on his hands folded against his stomach. It was then Daisy saw the rags wrapped around his hands and fingers and the blood, dried and caked.

"Dear God, Isaiah. Dear God."

He moved his hands away from his body, his twisted, bloody bent fingers. Then he raised his head and looked at her, his eyes full of tears.

"It's the only thing I don't understand, Daisy. Why? Why did they have to break my fingers?"

Henrietta was seated on a bench in the main room of the jailhouse when Daisy spotted her. From the way she looked, she'd been there all night.

Daisy rushed over and, sitting next to her, hugged her around the shoulders. "This is such a disaster. I have no idea what happened but trust me. I am working on fixing it. Don't worry, hon. Malcolm and I will get him out of here. I promise you."

Henrietta glanced up at her, and the look on her face gave Daisy a chill. She wasn't sad or bewildered. She was mad. Her nostrils flared, the veins in her forehead bulged, her eyes were large and wild. Then there were her hands folded into fists pressed beneath her chin. She squeezed them so hard she could've broken her own hands.

"Oh, darling, I know this is horrifying for Isaiah, but it will be okay."

She made a noise in her throat that sounded like a wild animal. "Where's your husband? The mighty Malcolm Barnes. Where is he? He's the one who should be here, not you. You don't have any power. You don't have power anywhere. Always trying to fix things when the truth is there's nothing you can do. Nothing you've ever been able to do." Henrietta abruptly lowered her hands, dropping them into her lap. All the while, she kept dark eyes pinned on Daisy.

"I'm sorry you feel that way, and I know

Malcolm will help. You can count on him."

"You know, all this happened because of you."

Daisy shook her head. "I don't know what you mean?"

"Think about it. See who's right from who's wrong." She pulled fingers through her short, bobbed hair.

Daisy didn't know what to say. "Malcolm will be back in a few days." She didn't mention that she hadn't been able to reach him. But when she did, he'd come back immediately, as soon as news of Isaiah's predicament reached him. He'd come back to help. He'd come back because Daisy needed him.

"Do you want to stay with me at the hotel? We have plenty of room, and if we don't have the space, we'll get another suite." Daisy smiled at her sister, hoping for her features to soften.

Henrietta's expression didn't change, and her words were cold. "I will be home with Papa. Where you should be, too." She stood then, wrapping a shawl around her, lifting her chin as much in defiance as annoyance. "The next time I hear from you is when Malcolm returns and gets Isaiah out of jail."

Then, she left, leaving Daisy rocking back and forth and wondering when her sister

461

had stopped loving her.

Daisy spent the next week visiting Isaiah in jail until he begged her to stop coming. He said it made him sad to see her so unhappy. His words warmed her heart but didn't change how she felt. She was sad, hurt, guilty, and angry. The rage in her was different than any feeling she'd had since her mother passed. Malcolm's betrayal felt as harsh and cruel as her father's. She worried if they would survive this time in their marriage.

He hadn't come back, and Daisy had no excuse to give Isaiah or her sister. So, she gathered some things together and went to the house on Naomi Avenue. At least she could see what she could do for them until Isaiah was released.

She was aware it would be an uncomfortable visit but one she had to make. She'd only walked into the house minutes before a knock on the front door.

A man stood in the doorway who was nondescript, other than his Los Angeles police uniform. The dark blue suit with its brass buttons and the stiff collar and long heavy-sleeved jacket didn't fit with the weather in California. He should've worn a lightweight cotton jacket and never a hat.

And why wasn't he entering the house?

She recognized the scenarios from her studies of the newspaper business and held her breath.

Everything about the officer was rigid and made her want to weep, but her father stood tall, shook his hand, and invited him into the house.

But she knew what was happening. This was how they told you, how the impossible, heartbreaking news took form. They were about to learn the fate of a beautiful young boy who played the guitar and loved Daisy's sister. Who would be remembered up and down Brown Broadway.

His name would have been raised along-side the greats of jazz if he'd lived. Daisy knew Isaiah was dead before the officer said the words.

If he'd never come to live with them, he'd be alive. If he hadn't fallen in love with Henrietta, he'd be alive. If Daisy hadn't used him. If Malcolm had come home when she had asked him, Isaiah would be alive.

The police officer said suicide, but how could Isaiah have hanged himself when they'd already crushed his hands?

Henrietta rocked back and forth, her eyes dead, her face a hollow mask of horror. Daisy desperately wanted to console her, hug her, and hold her tightly, ease her pain. Do something right. But her sister wouldn't look at her, and if she moved toward her, Henrietta folded into herself. Not wanting to be touched, held, or pitied.

Daisy left the house and went to the hotel to wait for her husband to return.

Malcolm should never have come home. Daisy didn't want to see him again, but she didn't run when he called and told her what time to expect him.

She couldn't forget she had asked him to stay, not to leave town. But the trip was about his architecture, his passion, his love, his life, his career. And what she wanted hadn't mattered. That's the way she saw it. Because he could've saved Isaiah, she believed that in her bones.

When he stepped into the suite, she was seated in the parlor, sipping a cup of tea.

She didn't even say hello. The first words out of her mouth were, "He's dead."

Then she took another sip of tea before continuing. "Isaiah died yesterday after-noon. I was at my father's house when the police officer stopped by with the news. They didn't know how to reach his mother, so they told us, the house where he was boarding."

Malcolm stood with the satchel in his hand and an indescribable look on his face. Maybe it was grief and shock, but all Daisy could see were lies and guilt.

"Oh, God. I'm so sorry, Daisy." He walked over to her, his arms reaching for her, reaching to pull her to him in an embrace, but she stiffened, and he knew.

"Do you blame me right now for what happened? I couldn't leave. There was a crisis, and I telephoned, spoke with everyone I know in the police department." He sat down next to her. "But he confessed, Daisy. There was nothing to be done once he did that."

"He confessed to a crime he didn't commit. I don't know why, but that's what he did."

Malcolm shook his head. "It makes no sense." He covered his face with his hands.

His sorrow did not affect her. "I don't give a damn how sad you may seem. He was a talented, brilliant young boy, and now he's dead because you couldn't get back in town in time to save him. You and your white, wealthy family could have made things right."

"My family will no longer be part of the money crowd with what is coming. Everything they have, I have, will crumble on top of our heads like an avalanche."

"You're talking gibberish."

"I guess I am," he said. "I feel like no matter what I say, you won't trust me to tell the truth."

"You're right. I won't." Daisy glared at him. "But why is this suddenly about you and your family? There's nothing different about them. They're still alive and kicking."

"Do you read the newspapers, Daisy? You claim to want to be a reporter, a writer of note one day. But you ignore what's happening in the world. Did you see what's happening in the stock market? Another month of these fluctuations, and my inheritance will vanish."

"And you'll be poor like every other Negro in America," Daisy snarled. "You should've been here, you know these people, you know what they can do from what they can't do, and you were not here."

He gripped her shoulders harder than she would've liked. His eyes burned into her, searching. "You think I know who killed Veronica."

"Let me go."

His face ashen with pain, Malcolm's hands slid down her arms until he held both her hands in his large hands. "You think I did it, don't you? You believe I murdered

Veronica Fontaine?"

"The police said that Isaiah killed himself. That's not true. They murdered him."

"Answer me, Daisy. For the love of God, do you think I killed Veronica?"

She pushed back from the table and stood. Then she moved toward the door and the suitcase she'd packed that morning. "I'm sorry your family may lose its money. I'm sorry you no longer will have an inheritance. On the other hand, though, it might do you some good to work for a living. To see what it's like not to have so many things handed to you on a platter. To be a part of the struggle every Black man and woman in America has to deal with every day. Except for the special ones, like you."

He laughed, and beneath it, she heard the sob, but nothing would sway her. She'd made up her mind.

She had reached the door and could hear his tears even with her back turned to him. "Before I leave, I will answer your question." Now, she turned to look at him. "Yes. I believe you killed her. And damn you to hell for letting that young boy die for you." She opened the door and stepped into the hall.

"Goodbye, Malcolm."

CHAPTER 33
FRANKIE

Monday, June 3, 1968 and Tuesday, June 4, 1968
Flagstaff

Tobey lay in the motel bed, his arms behind his head. "I feel fine, Frankie. You don't have to watch over me."

"This is Daisy's fault. Those men didn't have to react this way."

"We saved her from getting jail time, though. That's a good thing."

Daisy and I had exited Harry Belmont's card shop while, as I predicted, Tobey got an ass-whipping. Now, we all were in one motel room together.

Badly bruised but not broken, Tobey had driven us as fast and as far as he could before begging to lie down and lick his wounds.

"You look far worse than she. We should've saved you," I say, wiping blood from his face and hands. "You could've

468

struck at least one of them in the mouth."

"You might be taking me to the morgue if I'd fought back. Those guys were pissed."

"They thought you were beating up an old man," Daisy says, entering from the bathroom. "Thanks for taking the beating for me. You're a good boy."

He grins and winces at once. "Thank you for not stabbing that man. But did you learn anything today? Like are you going to go back and stab your old friend Harry again?"

She ponders, looking up at the ceiling thoughtfully. "I didn't stab him. I sliced him. And no. I guess not. Other fish in the ocean to be caught and cooked."

"Excellent," Tobey says. "We both learned something today."

I look at him and frown. "What did you learn?"

"I can take three left hooks to the solar plexus without falling."

I laugh out loud.

Daisy grins wildly. "I'd say that's the best lesson of the day."

Tobey joins in the laughter. "I agree."

We are on the road the next morning and it's a beautiful day. The tumbleweed is stark shades of brown and tan. Sunlight burns strips of light into the rocks and mountains.

As the Mustang speeds along the highway, the mountains and the fields of hay and brown grass stand still.

"How long until we reach Los Angeles?" I ask.

Tobey glances at me, his brow wrinkled with concern. "Seven hours."

Daisy nods. "I need some sleep. Wake me up when we're ten miles outside the city."

She curls into a ball like a child, except we know she's not a child. She was hell-bent on killing a man, but she didn't. I fear that she has set her sights on someone new.

We made it. In the allotted time, without a dozen stops on the road, we are in LA. And it looks the same as it did the last time I saw it.

The only problem is Tobey. He's hurting. Seven hours behind the wheel after getting spanked the way he got spanked calls for some profound healing.

"I should call my mother."

"What?" Daisy shows shock first, but Tobey is playfully on her heels.

"What? Are you sure?"

"Why not? Daisy, will you come with me, please?"

She smiles, but a sadness descends, and I can guess what she's going to say. "No. You

470

can take Tobey, but not me."

"Where will you go?" I ask.

"Where I'd planned to go all along."

Tobey shakes his head. "Nope. You are not paying a visit to Malcolm Barnes."

"He still lives in Los Angeles?" I ask.

Tobey rubs his hand over the stubble appearing on his chin. "Daisy, come on. No. You can't. What if he didn't do it? What if you're wrong?"

"Yes, he does live in LA. Found that out a few months ago."

"Well, Tobey needs attention. I don't know who's *what* to respond to, but look at him. We can't spend another night cooped up in the same room." I side-eye Daisy because I still don't trust her not to have another target in mind for her switchblade. So, she still can't be trusted. "And Tobey needs a decent meal. So do I. If I see another potato chip, someone is going to get a beatdown.

"So fine. I'll call my mother. Tell her I'm in town, and we'll go see her tomorrow." I look at Tobey. "You sure you don't want to see a doctor?"

"I'm not dying, just beat up. I'll be cool until tomorrow."

Daisy wanted to splurge on a luxurious hotel. So we ended up checking in to the

471

Shangri-La in Santa Monica. It was an old spot, been around since the late1930s, but Daisy had never stayed there and wanted to check it out. I am learning that she's a real freak about hotels.

After checking in, I make some calls. First Tamika, and she's still worried about Jackson, and I am, too. But I can't live in fear of the man forever.

Next, I call my mother. It has been a while since we talked, and I don't do well with her on the telephone, but she sounds different, but also the same, familiar — if I'm allowed to call anything about her familiar since we haven't been in touch.

"Mom, how are you? Long time no talk," I say, striving for light, but of course, there's always the darkness chasing me.

"Francine, what in the world? Where have you been? We've been waiting on you for hours — some surprise. You are taking your sweet time. That's like you. Always needing to be coddled."

I'm shaking like death is in the phone booth with me. "What do you mean we?"

"Jackson and me. I don't know why you two didn't come in the same car. But you have your reasons, I guess."

I throw back my head and open my mouth in a silent scream. But part of me knew he'd

472

be there, and part of me wants to see him, wants to face him, and end this thing between us because I can do that now. "Put him on the phone."

A few seconds later, his voice comes through. "Where you at, baby girl?"

"Don't call me that. I don't like it."

"You better tell me, I mean, how much longer before you get here? Your mother is promising to cook."

"She can't cook."

"That's why I want my baby girl to fix me a meal."

"I don't need to see you right now."

"I think you'd better. Your mother is looking tired. She should get some rest. Wouldn't want her to fall out making me dinner."

He sounded drunk, high, crazy, or all three. And was he threatening my mother? Had he lost his mind? "What's wrong with you, Jackson? Are you telling me you'll hurt my mother?"

"Tell me where you're at so we can speak face to face, and we won't have to worry about those things."

"Jesus Christ. If you touch her, I swear to God.

"Don't get so excited, Francine. Now, what was that address again," he says, and I can see the smirk.

"Santa Monica. We're staying at the Shangri-La."

474

CHAPTER 34
FRANKIE

Tuesday, June 4, 1968
Los Angeles

Have you ever been in a fight for your life? I mean, the kind of battle where it's all about your heart or your soul?

Well, that's what I'm about to face.

I don't mention anything to Daisy or Tobey. They don't need to be in the middle of my problems — any more than they already have been. After unpacking, I politely excuse myself, saying I have more calls to make and will catch up with them later.

Before I leave, I grab Daisy's hand and squeeze it. I'm not sure why. I just do.

When I reach the parking lot behind the hotel, I am not surprised to find Jackson waiting, where I asked him to meet me.

He steps out of his car, looking no different than when I saw him on Friday. The difference I'm feeling inside me is amazing.

I have no fear. I am not worried about being hurt, physically or emotionally. I'm not concerned about the baby. He'll be fine. My only concern is freedom — my freedom, away from Jackson Saunders.

Okay, I'm thinking big and bold, but the shiver in my knees is too real, as are the sweats that have me soaked to the skin.

"Hi, Jackson."

"Francine. Where's your luggage? I don't want to talk in a parking lot. I'm here to pick you up. We can have a long conversation at your mother's over dinner."

He starts toward me, and I step back, but not a big step. "I told you already. I'm not going anywhere with you."

"No, you didn't."

"Well, I'm not."

"I don't have time for this shit," he says harshly. "I've had a hell of a weekend, and chasing you across the country hasn't helped. Now, get your ass in the car. Let's go."

"Or what, Jackson? Will you hit me? Don't you dare show up here and threaten me. You have no right." I wish my words could put him and his ass back in that old car of his. I'll show him. He can't frighten me.

"I have stopped running. And if you don't like it, go ahead, hit me, criticize me, say or do whatever you want to say, but I swear to

476

God, I'm not going to run from you any-more, and I'm not going to be with you. So, what are we fighting for? Tell me, what?"

"You bitch."

"What's all this noise?" I hear Daisy coming up behind me.

"It's okay. We're having a conversation."

"Oh, I see." Jackson laughs. "That's how you got to Los Angeles. Your crazy aunt."

Daisy laughs real loud and then bites her lower lip. "Damn it, Jackson. You know I don't like name-calling."

Tobey steps forward. "Come on, man. There's nothing here for you. Just go back home. Let her be."

"Who the hell is this white boy, Francine?" Jackson laughs. "I'll kick his ass for fun later."

"I won't let you hurt him," I say.

"Oh, you doing white boys now?"

"Don't talk to her that way." Tobey stands next to me, and I almost wish he hadn't.

"You need to back the fuck up," Jackson says low and slow. "That's my wife and my baby in her stomach."

"You don't have a right to any child," I say. "I'm leaving you because I'm tired of being beaten emotionally and physically. Let's just stop yelling at each other and move on."

Daisy laughs. "Great speech, but Jackson is a lunatic. He doesn't hear what you're saying."

"Shut up, you fucking bitch."

"Oh, Lord," Daisy groans. "I don't like that word at all."

Tobey is still standing at my side. "Look, I don't think we should get too riled up here."

I can see the horns sprouting from Jackson's head.

"Tobey, please go inside. He'll calm down."

"How about if I go right inside those glass doors where I can see what's going on."

I nod okay, and he walks away.

"Send your puppy away, Francine."

"Oh, you must be high."

On the other hand, Daisy isn't leaving. She has a concerned look, but it's tinged with *If you need me, I am there for you.* I believe that she would do whatever she felt necessary, like a mama lion. She was always ready to go in and rumble.

"Jackson, you're gonna stop this right now."

I move toward him. "Everybody's backed off. Can we agree just to stop hurting each other?"

A storm blows across the blue sky and turns it black. Jackson runs at me, and I feel the blow before it lands. So hard I believe my body is broken.

And then I see Daisy out of the corner of my eye, and she has her hand in the purse. Oh, Lord. And there it is, the switchblade —

Now, she's charging him, but he's coming at me again even though I'm lying on the ground.

He punches Daisy. She falls to the ground and the knife slips from her hand. I pick up the blade and struggle to my feet.

I don't know where Tobey is. I hear him but can't see him. I see the knife and pick it up and somehow, I get to my feet. I have to help Daisy.

"I'll cut you. I swear to God, I will cut you if you don't let her go."

He spins at me and is coming and, Jesus God, he isn't stopping. I feel the blow in my gut, and this one is sharp. I do something with my wrist and he slows down. But he has momentum and tosses me against the concrete wall like I'm a pair of old shoes.

With my face in the dirt, he kicks me in the side. And, oh Christ, that doesn't feel good. Oh, Lord, please don't hurt my baby. Now, my memory is wacky, too.

I don't remember where I am or if I am.

CHAPTER 35
DAISY

Tuesday, June 4, 1968

The ambulance arrives, and Daisy directs them to Frankie, who is lying on the ground in a pool of blood. Daisy is hurt, too. But it's no more painful than the kick in the gut at Inkwell beach by the copper in 1928. Or getting tagged with a billy club in Harlem in 1964.

She knew she'd be fine if her simple-minded heart didn't stop.

Tobey was pacing in the waiting room. He is the one who drove off Jackson. But that was after Frankie put Daisy's knife in Jackson's rib cage.

"How is she?" Tobey asked for the tenth time in ten minutes. "Is she okay? Is her baby all right?"

Daisy is afraid to answer. "I don't know anything. She wasn't — God, Tobey, she wasn't moving."

■ ■ ■ ■

Hour after hour, Daisy sits in the waiting room, holding the *Green Book.* The pages are not open, and she stares blankly at the linoleum floor, listening for the sounds she dreads.

The beepers warning doctors and nurses that patients are in need. Cries of mourning from a father or mother, husband or wife or child who have lost a loved one. The involuntary *Oh Jesus Christ.* All she can hope for is none of these words will become an epitaph for Frankie.

Daisy closes her eyes and does her best to recall the prayers from her youth. She wants to say them for her niece's recovery and the child who grows inside her.

She also prays she never sets her eyes on Jackson Saunders again. The next time, her switchblade will not slip from her grasp. It will find its target.

Thank heaven for Frankie. At that moment, she was fearless. Much more courageous than Tobey or Daisy. They'd fought as hard as they could, but Jackson was a beast.

Who knew his life was meaningless as long as he could hurt Frankie? But then Daisy

481

thinks she's not the one who knows how to pray. Years ago, that was her mama's job, keeping the church near and the evil spirits far away.

Those simple things Daisy remembers and misses so deeply she can't catch her breath. But once something is gone, isn't it gone forever?

"Hello, Daisy."

Daisy hadn't seen her sister in forty years, but she recognizes her right away. Still as pretty as when she was sixteen, Henrietta might be a bit haggard around the edges, but she would always be a beauty. And of course she is still wearing something that looked like a bob hairstyle, except a little bit longer. Those freckles and large brown eyes hadn't changed, either.

"Henrietta," she says. "You're looking well."

"No, I'm not, but I appreciate the effort. You look like the Queen of Sheba."

"Slightly bruised and in need of a bath."

"How's my little girl?" Henrietta's eyes wander toward the nurse's station.

Henrietta has had the same anxious look of concern Daisy feels on her face.

"The doctors haven't told me anything. She was unconscious when they brought her in. He hit her pretty hard, goddamned asshole."

"He came by the house, and I figured something was wrong but not this wrong. He had that mad look in his eyes, but I didn't know. Too busy with my own life. Always too busy for Francine." She sighs. "I don't know how she put up with that man all these years. They've been together since high school."

"She told me," Daisy says. "She's gonna be okay. I'm praying for her. She's a tough girl."

"She took after you more than me."

"That's the nicest thing you've said to me in forty years."

"Practically the first thing I've said to you in forty years other than *How's my little girl.*"

They both nodded their heads for a moment, saying the quiet, soft prayer for a daughter and a niece.

Her sister brushed the bangs from her forehead like she always used to do and then sat down next to Daisy.

"Why did you bring her back here?"

Daisy looks off in the distance, down the hospital hallway, unsure what she expects to see. "My heart."

"I hear you. We did inherit some humdingers." Henrietta laughed. "My life hasn't been all that good. Christ, I stayed mad, I think, until maybe, I don't know, yesterday? Nothing ever went the way I thought it would go, and I took it out on that child of mine. The last good thing in my life died in Korea." She gazed into Daisy's eyes. "His name was Baxter. I couldn't get over him. It was like losing Isaiah all over again. I put all that grief on Francine."

Then she eyeballs Daisy.

"How do you look so good? You'll turn sixty any day now."

"I had that heart attack six months ago," Daisy says with a huge grin. "Thought I was a goner for sure but getting that close to the end of it all, I decided to fix some things I'd left undone."

"Did you get it all done?"

"Almost," Daisy says. "Came close to killing Harry Belmont. I blamed his last story about Veronica for Isaiah's time in jail. The way he twisted things just made Isaiah suffer more than he should have."

"He did that because he was mad at you for marrying Malcolm."

"Yeah, I know. He told me. I never knew back then."

"Who else was on your list?"

"Malcolm. I lost some steam going after him, though. He should pay for what he did. I thought he killed her." Daisy looked down.

"You mind if I smoke?"

"Only if you have one for me."

Daisy pulls a pack of Kents from her purse and lights two cigarettes, handing one to her sister. "I blame him for Isaiah. I think he killed her. And that makes me blame myself. I should've said something, but I loved him too damn much. So, I'm more to blame for Isaiah than anyone."

"Be mindful who you blame for killing somebody. It's always something different than you think."

Two doctors enter the waiting room, and both women stand. They know the doctors are looking for them.

The distance between the swinging doors and where they are wasn't more than a few feet, but time played its tricks, and the walk felt like years.

Daisy reaches for her sister's hand, squeezing it tightly as they wait to learn what happened to Henrietta's little girl.

CHAPTER 36
FRANKIE

Friday, June 28, 1968
Los Angeles

A week ago, I was released from the hospital and had spent most of my days and nights lying in bed in this room, healing. Just like the baby in my belly, we're going to be a-okay. I sit up in the bed, rest my back against the headboard, and glance around the room, and smile. My Lady Baltimore luggage rests inside the door (I'll unpack later). Someone — Aunt Daisy — slipped the bags into the room while I slept. She may have a bad heart, but it is kind when she wants it to be.

I like this room, the way the sun pours through the window in the morning. The warmth soothes the hurt, and I face the sun. I'm not in a hurry to rise. I enjoy relaxing, nursing my wounds, and nourishing my child. I can't believe this is the same room I almost died in when I was ten years old,

486

suffering from the poliovirus. As I rest my hand on my belly, I am full of life and no longer afraid of living it.

The baby pushes on my bladder something fierce. I roll out of bed and amble to the bathroom in the hall. The house smells the same as I remember from when I was a kid. The aroma of Grandpa's pipe smoke still lingers, as well as the rubbing alcohol and linseed oil. Smell conjures memories that are wholly formed and vividly affecting. So many years living in this house, and so much I never knew.

On the last day at the hospital, the police came to my room to hear my story about what happened when Jackson caught up with us.

The two men had their notepads and stubby pencils and wore brown suits with thin ties. No uniform. They looked exhausted, I recall, probably dealing with the aftermath of Robert F. Kennedy's assassination and the people in the streets and in their homes wondering how the world went mad.

The two officers asked if I knew how Jackson found us since we didn't take the direct path on Route 66.

I told them I asked him to meet me at the Shangri-La hotel in Santa Monica because

I was afraid he'd hurt my mother. I told them how I'd almost forgotten he was after us. So many other things had stepped in front of any concerns about Jackson Saunders.

I confessed to stabbing him early during the interrogation. But he'd hurt me, and I had to defend myself, didn't I? I told them I was sorry for killing him, and that's when I learned he wasn't dead. It had been a scratch. He was so stunned, he ran.

But they caught him and got the full story from my aunt and my mother and Tobey, who had dragged himself out of bed, ready to fight, except I'd already taken care of things.

The officers weren't interested in arresting me. They just wanted to jot down my side of the story since they'd already arrested Jackson. They also wanted to know if I'd be around to testify. I said, oh yes. For what he did to me, Tobey, and Daisy, let alone the mess he left in Chicago, he needed to spend time behind bars.

I gave them my address in Los Angeles, the house on Naomi, and my mother's phone number. Then they said they'd be in touch and congratulated me on my baby. And I responded with a smile and a *thank you very much*.

After they left, the hard edges of my life floated toward the sky, like a thousand pounds of excuses, leaving me feeling a freedom that's hard to describe. But imagine suddenly growing the wings of a bird.

And knowing with all my heart and soul, I don't have to run anymore.

I can fly.

In the bathroom, I scrub my face and start back to my room, but I hear voices coming from the front of the house.

I'll crawl back into bed in a few minutes, but first, I want to eavesdrop on the conversation.

I am too curious about what two sisters have to say to each other after forty years.

My mother, Henrietta, and her sister, Daisy, are sitting in the sunroom. I slip into a spot in the kitchen and lean around the corner to peer through the dining room. From where I stand, I am pretty sure they can't see me, which is great.

I can't imagine what it might be like, having this conversation, catching up on decades, not just a weekend or two. Tamika and I have talked nearly every day since we learned how to talk. She called the hospital every morning to help me get over the hump.

But these two. When they stack up the years they've lived, you can't expect the book won't be thin. Neither one of them ran from life. They adjusted to it, made choices, good and bad, but neither threw in the towel. Not even with age, illness, death, and despair haunting them, they are still figuring things out.

There are two wicker chairs in the sunroom. My mother sits in one, but Daisy sits on the piano bench.

She is flamboyant this early in the morning, her robe is red with white polka dots, and I can see a touch of makeup on her cheeks and lips. Of course, in a blue robe, my mother wears no makeup; I forget how pretty she is without making a fuss.

They have cups of steamy coffee, and I see small plates with toast and smell bacon and fried eggs. Their meals rest on TV trays, and I am pretty sure my mother cooked. I doubt Daisy has made a meal from scratch since 1928.

I imagine that the last few weeks watching over me has helped them repair their relationship or, if nothing else, reminded them that the world didn't stop those forty years they didn't speak. Life kept raising the stakes, sometimes cutting them a break, other times driving the stake into their hearts, the end breaking off in their bones.

The hum of their voices is peaceful. Easy conversation, the way two sisters speak to one another when they reminisce without anger, blame, or guilt.

It's a blessing, watching forty years of hate unravel.

I stand, listening to their conversation. Knowing I should leave, which I begin to do until I hear Daisy's question.

"Who killed her, Henrietta? What happened on the night Veronica Fontaine died?"

"It wasn't Malcolm Barnes. I guarantee that. He wasn't there." My mother lets out a long sorrow-filled sigh, the kind that fills a room with sadness and heartache. "A lot happened to me that you never knew, Daisy. You thought you knew. You tried to keep up with us, Isaiah and me. But we were on fire.

"He hated closed-in places, he loved the sunlight, the moonlight, and playing his guitar, and he loved me. I've never felt that love since. Not even with Francine's father, a good man, like Papa. He was a good man, too.

"Isaiah and I wanted fame. Life away from parents we couldn't trust to be there for us. He was angry at his mother for unloading him on us. I was mad at Mama, Papa, and you, for not seeing how hurt I was when the uncles died, and Mama couldn't do anything anymore.

"But Isaiah and I fell in love. We sang and played music, worked at the hotel, barely slept, and we made love. All the time, everywhere, every moment we could be together, we were together."

Her voice hitches, stopping on a memory that fills her with pain. She doesn't speak for a long moment. I can't see her face fully, so I can't tell if she's crying.

Daisy reaches for her, offering compassion, but my mother pulls away. She still doesn't like being touched.

"Since I've started this, I might as well finish." She sits up taller in the wicker chair. "Isaiah had a chance to go on tour with Duke Ellington. Everyone wanted him to play. They liked my singing, but a fair-skinned blues singer is a dime a dozen.

"I told you back then that Veronica would come to some of the nightclubs where we performed. The Black and Tans, of course. She was friendly at first. We ended up doing several shows at her house in Beverly Hills. She kept promising to do things for me. Something you wouldn't allow me to do, and then —" She stopped again.

"You don't have to tell me what happened. It's okay."

492

"I got pregnant, Daisy, with Isaiah's baby. I didn't want a baby. I didn't need a child; right when I believed the world was about to change for me, a baby didn't fit. And I didn't know what to do. I knew I didn't want it. And I didn't want to tell you."

Daisy and I both hold a hand over our mouths. My mother's words shock me as much as they do her. And I wager both Daisy and I have an idea of what happened next.

My mother grabs hold of the armrest. "I went to Veronica Fontaine for help. White women had those connections. They had good doctors. I didn't know any. So when I told Isaiah my plans, he asked me to marry him." She laughs. "He was such a romantic.

"Then I find out Isaiah gave up his big chance to travel with Duke Ellington for me. He was going to shine shoes and work the clubs on Brown Broadway so we could get married. That's when I got it — his love had no ego.

"But I wanted to get married and have a baby because of how much I loved him. So, I changed my mind and told Veronica and we tried to keep working the circuit and asked her to sponsor us. You know how wealthy white folks liked to share in the greatness of Negro talent.

493

"So, the night she died, we were outside in her backyard, watching birds fly over our heads and arguing."

"Why? Because you wanted to keep your baby?"

"No, because she found out that I was your sister. You know colored people with the same last name aren't related."

"I told her you were my sister."

My mother's voice turned into a sob. "Isaiah came in and saw us, saw her pushing at me, and he rushed over, but I'm a strong girl. And I pushed her off me harder than him. She hit her head and just like that, she was dead.

"Isaiah watched our worlds die in front of us. There was nothing we could say about her tripping backward, drunk, and falling and hitting her head. We were two colored people who had murdered a white woman. That's what would have happened.

"I wanted to tell the truth, but Isaiah forbade it. Such a strong young man, and there was no sacrifice too big when it came to me." She sniffles. "So, your Malcolm didn't kill Veronica Fontaine. You didn't kill Isaiah. I did.

"It just hurt my heart for years that his sacrifice didn't save anyone but me. You see, the most horrible thing is that baby, Isaiah's sweet baby girl, didn't live but five minutes outside my body."

My mother's voice calms. "Daisy, you should call Malcolm Barnes. He is single. Owns an architectural firm that's doing well. Fine-looking sixty-something Black man, too."

EPILOGUE

I rub my hand over the kitchen tabletop, feeling the rough surface beneath my calloused palm. It is the one piece of furniture I will take with me when we move if I have any say. I would miss the scratches and dents too much to replace them with something shiny, polished, and new.

I don't think I've ever been one to dismiss the past because it has gone out of style. So, the table, along with the wicker chairs, the crystal snifter, and Isaiah's guitar, will come with me to the new place.

"Are you here because you plan to help us prepare for the party this afternoon?" The back screen door slams shut as Maxine bounces into the kitchen. "Or because you want to supervise?"

She is in a livelier mood than she was when she went to bed last night. And now, she's returning from the grocery store. But she hasn't mentioned the letters, the journals, or the newspaper articles in the cedar chest I gave her.

My niece's daughter, Maxine, wages war with a pen. I like her. I love her, too.

Although she never met her great-grandpa Marvin, his letters must've touched her. After I learned the truth so many years ago, I had taken months for it to settle in.

Deep down, I never knew who had killed Veronica Fontaine until my sister told me. I let grief and anger blind me. And there was nothing more to say about that.

"I am supervising the making of my cake."

"We know your preferences, Aunt Daisy. You never neglect an opportunity to tell us know exactly what you want and why."

"It's my duty to be informative. To give as great as I get, don't you think?" I smile. "I love chocolate cake with chocolate on the inside and outside."

I am surprised when Maxine waltzes over to the countertop with a covered container and removes the lid, revealing a carrot cake of all things.

"Don't look at it that way," she says to me in response to my exaggerated frown. "Your cake is coming. Mom is bringing it with her."

"I don't know why you two couldn't have come together. You live in the same part of town."

"Aunt Daisy, we don't live that close, and besides, Tobey wanted to pick her up."

"Oh, has he decided to come after all? That's nice."

"What's so nice about it? He hasn't missed your birthday in twenty years. It would've been a shock if he didn't show."

They were all there, too. My entire family, the ones left breathing. There were not that many of them, but I truly loved each one.

Tobey Garfunkel and his wife, Camille, have two kids. I used to think he'd end up with Frankie. He had such a crush on her for a long while, but she needed to grow up some more before she and her baby girl could be a part of a new family.

Both have been married for years. Frankie, in a fairy-tale romance, married the doctor who saved her life in 1968.

I had told her that falling in love during hard times is the best love — and in many ways, she could've gone either way, because Tobey was with us during hard times, just like her husband, Matt.

No one knows what happened to Jackson. He up and disappeared after he got out of jail for almost killing Frankie and his daughter. I imagine he's dead.

Hard times have continued over the years. Dear Tamika passed away last fall from breast cancer. I've been close to her parents since both of us girls ended up living in Los Angeles. Once I returned in '68, I never left.

Her mother and father are joining us for the party later. They have Tamika's three boys staying with them until Robbie gets back from serving as medical director for a hospital in Iraq.

"I have a surprise for you." I finally decide to share my good news. The reason I'd hung around in the kitchen, waiting for Maxine's return.

"I received the letter from Dunbar senior housing, and we have been approved. We move in next month. Isn't it great that it came on my birthday week? The perfect gift."

"Are you sure you want to move, Aunt Daisy? You've kept this house all these years. Why leave?"

"The neighborhood is too different, and we're too old to keep up with the young people who live around here, and all my old friends have moved or died. No one next door or on the same block anymore knew the Washington clan. Staying at the hotel means we won't be leaving Brown Broadway too far behind."

Maxine tilts her head. "I did read how they used to call Central Avenue Brown Broadway."

I study Maxine's brown eyes, angular features, and the glow of her dark brown skin. I hold back the desire to comb her hair or brush the wild braids from her forehead. She's started her locs with a two-strand twist, and they are apt to do whatever they choose. Like anything brand-new, you've just had to give them time to get in the groove.

"Black women are no different, Aunt Daisy. The struggle of Black people feels timeless, some days. I swear."

"You are a thinker, yourself, aren't you, child? It's hard to remember such a beautiful young lady is no longer an infant."

She rolls her eyes. "Not for twenty-one years, Auntie."

"Where is he? He didn't want any breakfast?" Maxine asks. "Should I bring him some more coffee?"

"No, that man survives on cups of strong black coffee until noon. He's in the sunroom, reading the morning paper."

"I was wondering, did Uncle Malcolm give you the cedar chest?"

"Yes. It was him. He and my father were

friends after a while. Your grandmother never kept up with pieces of paper or such things. So, Papa did. He and my father were friends for years. I didn't know since I wasn't here. Which is funny, since at first, Papa hated Malcolm and his friends."

"Why don't we join Uncle Malcolm in the sunroom?" Maxine says. "I'll fix a tray and bring it to you."

I rise and walk to the room where the piano my uncles used to play still sits. Malcolm is in the wicker chair that matches mine. I sit in the chair next to his, lowering myself slowly. The aches in my bones surprise me more and more each day.

The people we love arrive throughout the afternoon, joining us for the chocolate cake with only one candle. I like to say each year is a fresh start, a new beginning.

Malcolm is making a toast, thanking God that I'd finally grown up and forgiven him for something he would never do. I don't blame him for this little punishment. He likes to remind me I'm not perfect.

He's still giving his speech, but when I find an opening, I say, "How was I to know what you'd do?"

"Trust," he came back quickly. "You should've trusted me. I always trusted you."

"There, that's it. Don't you see? I still

have some growing up to do. You wait until I turn eighty-three."

"Happy birthday, Daisy."

"Happy eighty-second birthday." Everyone shouts.

It's easier to smile about aging when the people you love are in the room.

I look at my husband, the most handsome man I've ever known. His brows are bushier than they were when we met in 1928. His dark, hooded eyes are less dark and grayer, like his hair and parts of his complexion. But we've been together, or back together, since 1972.

Malcolm stands and kisses me on the forehead. "You've done quite nicely, Daisy. Bad ticker or not."

I touch my chest and smile, but something catches my eye out of the tall mullion window.

My God, I can hardly believe it. They have come home. Not just one, but a flock of blackbirds soars and blankets the sky. How beautiful.

AUTHOR'S NOTE

My novel *In the Face of the Sun* is meant to
be a character-driven story focusing on a
multigenerational African American family
and the events and circumstances that
contribute to shaping individual choices,
personalities, and experiences. The novel is
told through a dual storyline and takes place
mainly in 1928 and 1968.

So, what came first: the main characters
or the historical events and/or eras?

My initial inspiration for this novel began
with a trip I made to Los Angeles in 2017. I
attended the Los Angeles Film Festival and
stayed at the Culver Hotel, a 1924 national
landmark in Culver City. As a huge travel
fan, I also love luxury hotels, especially
those with a long history. I cannot always
book a room at these properties — some
are very expensive — but they are fabulous
sources of history and culture.

During my 2017 trip, I discovered the

Hotel Somerville, the first luxury hotel in Los Angeles built exclusively for African Americans.

The Hotel Somerville, located on Central Avenue and Forty-First Street (1920s address), opened in late June 1928. A week later, the NAACP held its nineteenth annual convention, the first on the West Coast, at the Somerville.

The year 1968 was a pivotal one in American history. The dramatic and tragic historical events include Vietnam, the assassinations of Martin Luther King, Jr., and Robert F. Kennedy, the Democratic Convention in Chicago, and so much more.

Most of the characters in my novel are fictional. However, several historical figures are mentioned, such as W. E. B. Du Bois (civil rights activist), Jack Johnson (boxing champion), and Charlotta Bass (*California Eagle,* owner and editor).

Other historical figures have roles in the story's action and include:

- Dr. John Somerville, the first Black graduate of the University of Southern California School of Dentistry, an entrepreneur and civil rights advocate
- Dr. Vada Somerville, the second Black graduate of the University of Southern

California School of Dentistry, entrepreneur, and civil rights advocate

- Beatrice Morrow Cannady, renowned civil rights advocate and editor of the *Advocate* in early twentieth-century Oregon
- Stepin Fetchit, aka Lincoln Perry, American vaudevillian, comedian, and film actor. First Black person to have a successful film career in Hollywood
- King Vidor, legendary filmmaker, produced and directed Hollywood's first all-Negro motion picture, *Hallelujah* (an early talkie)
- Nina Mae McKinney, actress and entertainer, African American star of first Hollywood film with an all-Negro cast (*Hallelujah*)

Malcolm Barnes was loosely inspired by real historical figure Paul Revere Williams, an American architect based in Los Angeles. The latter was the first African American member of the American Institute of Architects in 1923.

Harry Belmont, the fictional sports reporter and gossip columnist for the *California Eagle* in the novel, was inspired by Harry Levette, a multitalented reporter and editor for the *California Eagle*.

Some of the resources used for my research include:

- *Stepin Fetchit: The Life and Times of Lincoln Perry* by Mel Watkins
- *The Negro Trail Blazers of California* by Delilah Beasley
- *Metropolis in the Making: Los Angeles in the 1920s,* edited by Tom Sitton and William Deverell
- *1968: The Year That Rocked The World* by Mark Kurlansky
- *African American Actresses: The Struggle for Visibility, 1900-1960* by Charlene Regester
- *W. E. B. Du Bois, American Prophet* by Edward J. Blum

A few of my Internet Research Sources:

- Newspapers.com
- *California Eagle* Archives
- *Chicago Defender* Archives
- The Library of Congress
- BlackPast.org

The Apex nightclub, located next door to the Hotel Somerville, did not open until late November of that year but was mentioned in the story as being open earlier in October.

ACKNOWLEDGMENTS

Whoever said that writing a novel is a solitary experience, I have some names for you ☺ ! I would never, and I mean, never be able to do the things I do (writing books and such) without the support and understanding of some truly remarkable people. But let me stop gushing over these lovelies and do some name dropping!

I want to begin by thanking Kensington Publishing and my editor, Esi Sogah. Her patience, wisdom, skills, and understanding made this book possible. My second book after my debut has been an intriguing journey, and she's been there to nudge (guide) me forward. In addition, I must mention some of the other stars at Kensington, including Michelle Addo; my publicist, Vida Engstrand; and the entire marketing and sales team. It's always such a pleasure to work with each of you. And next, a special thank-you to my agent, Nalini

Akolekar!

No matter how many texts, phone calls, Zoom calls, or retreats I needed to finish this novel, I could always count on my friends (and cheerleaders) Vanessa Riley, Pintip Dunn, Eliza Knight, Leslye Penelope, Nancy Johnson, Veronica Forand, and Nina Crespo. You ladies are phenomenal and talented and thank you for being such an important part of this journey with me.

Additionally, I must extend another huge thank-you to Nadine Monaco and Eliza for being my fantastic beta readers!

I want to send a special shout-out to my dear friend Sharon Shackleford Campbell. Your friendship and support have helped me for many years, including this past crazy-pants year. Hugs and kisses. Also a special thank-you to Krista Stroever — your idea worked!

I also must credit some of the women in my family who helped shape the fictional characters in the book. Kudos to my aunt Hazel and my late aunt Maxine — you will always inspire my writing.

∎ ∎ ∎ ∎

A Reading Group Guide:
In the Face
of the Sun

∎ ∎ ∎ ∎

About This Guide
The suggested questions are included to
enhance your group's reading of
Denny S. Bryce's *In the Face of the Sun*.

DISCUSSION QUESTIONS

1. What similarities do you feel exist between 1920s Hollywood and Hollywood today?

2. Black newspapers and magazines were a critical source of information about events, people, and actions taken by people of the Race on behalf of the rights of Black people during the 1920s and beyond. Can you name a major Black newspaper or magazine that had national awareness in the Black community?

3. During the 1960s the escalation of the war in Vietnam impacted young men eligible for the draft in varying ways throughout the country. During 1968, what were some of the tragic events that impacted the nation, and, in particular, the African American community?

4. The main characters in the novel *In the*

Face of the Sun are women experiencing various stages of grief, discovery, love, and forgiveness. In what ways does the Hotel Somerville serve as a metaphor for these themes?

5. In 1968, one of the passengers in the cherry-apple red Mustang has an unlikely relationship with Daisy Washington. How does this character add to the conflict between Daisy and her niece, Frankie Saunders?

6. The Hotel Somerville eventually became the Dunbar Hotel, the cornerstone of the Los Angeles jazz scene from the 1920s through the 1940s. What is the role of music in the novel's 1928 storyline versus the 1968 storyline?

7. Several of the characters in this novel face various forms of abuse: physical, emotional, and racial, for example. How would you describe the long-term affects of abuse on an individual, male or female, versus its impact on a culture, gender, or ethnic group?

8. What do you see as the role of the Black press in historical novels such as *In the*

Face of the Sun?

9. What role does music play in the 1968 storyline?

10. In what ways did the road trip bring its passengers closer together?

ABOUT THE AUTHOR

Denny S. Bryce is an award-winning author and three-time Golden Heart® finalist, including twice for *Wild Women and the Blues*. A book reviewer for NPR Books who's written for *FROLIC Media, USA Today,* and *Harper's Bazaar,* the former professional dancer also worked for more than two decades in public relations. A member of the Historical Novel Society (HNS), Women's Fiction Writers Association (WFWA), and The Tall Poppies, Denny is originally from Chicago but currently resides in Savannah, Georgia. Visit her online at DennySBryce.com.